A SURRENDER TO PASSION

MOIRA TURNED HER HEAD to find Addis looking at her. Despite the dim moonlight, she read, nay she felt, his expression and her heart turned over with an alarming jolt.

His lips took hers before she could marshal any resistance. Gentle but firm, that first kiss spoke a determination that said nothing less than a pummeling struggle would stop him. Weak objections briefly drifted through her mind before she succumbed to the sweet beauty of it. That invisible cloak wrapped them both now, so comforting in its warmth and protection. The delicious connection overwhelmed her, and the careful explanations just articulated disappeared along with all her thoughts, carried away by the night breeze.

He ended the kiss and caressed her face, his fingers drifting behind her ears to the pins holding her wimple. He slid the cloth off and pressed his mouth to her neck before carefully going to work on her veil.

"You asked what I want with you, Moira," he said while he kissed and bit and licked her ear in ways that made her shake.

"I want everything."

ALSO BY MADELINE HUNTER

By Arrangement

and coming in early 2001

By Design

BY POSSESSION

MADELINE HUNTER

Bantam Books
New York Toronto London
Sydney Auckland

BY POSSESSION

A Bantam Book / September 2000 by Alan Ayers
Insert art copyright © 2000 by Franco Accornero

All rights reserved.
Copyright © 2000 by Madeline Hunter
Cover art copyright © 2000 by Alan Ayers
Insert Art copyright © 2000 by Franco Accornero

ISBN 0-553-58221-6

Published simultaneously in the United States and Canada

Bantam Books are published by Bantam Books, a division of Ran-
dom House, Inc. Its trademark, consisting of the words "Bantam
Books" and the portrayal of a rooster, is Registered in U.S. Patent
and Trademark Office and in other countries. Marca Registrada.
Bantam Books, 1540 Broadway, New York, New York 10036.

PRINTED IN THE UNITED STATES OF AMERICA

OPM   10 9 8 7 6 5 4 3 2 1

FOR JEAN,
MY DEAR FRIEND AND MY FIRST READER

BY POSSESSION

PROLOGUE

+ 1324 +

ADDIS WAS SURPRISED BY the witch woman's summons. She normally only called him to service her on nights when the full moon rose. All the same he obeyed and left the corral where he tended her father's horses and walked to her house near the forest's edge. He would be killed if her father ever discovered their furtive coupling amidst the pine trees while the white disk hovered in the heavens, but still he went. He had learned to take the rare opportunities for human warmth no matter how strangely they came to him.

He found her outside, holding the reins of a horse. That surprised him more than the summons. The normal ritual was for her to make an excuse for his presence by giving him work to fill the evening hours of light.

During the first year of his enslavement she had called for him frequently, and sat by the door watching him while he fixed her house and dug her paths. She had taught him her language and demanded to learn his until they could communicate in a rough, blunt way. And in that rough, blunt way she had finally told him that she suspected he was a knight and not a groom, and that to fulfill her calling as priestess she had a special need of him. He had fully expected to be sacrificed amidst those trees, which was the occasional fate of Christian knights captured by these pagan barbarians, not stripped naked and joined with the witch woman while she chanted incantations to her moon god above.

Her face bore a hard expression which did not soften when he approached. The late afternoon light showed faint lines etching her skin near her eyes and mouth. Not a young woman, and thin in a gaunt way that spoke of the fasting and other self-denials that were a part of her magic.

"I did not expect this," he said in her Baltic tongue. The formalities between them had eased a little over the years. He might be a slave and she the daughter of a *kunigas*, a priest, but two people cannot make love repeatedly and remain strangers.

"I need some plants that grow only near the river. You will help me." Another surprise. She retrieved a large basket near the door and handed it to him. A cloth covered its top, but it was not empty.

Curious now, he lifted her into the saddle, then took the reins and led her toward the forest path that snaked to the river. She did not speak the whole way, and he wondered if anyone in the big house or in the scattering of huts had seen them leave and would follow. She had never been this careless with his life before.

They emerged by the river's edge, where the trees fell away and the boggy banks shot high with reeds and growth. He helped her down and tied the reins to a spindly sapling.

"Our king will refuse baptism," she said abruptly. "We heard this morning. He will wait until the papal legates come in the fall to say so, but he has chosen."

His chest suddenly felt hollow. He knew that her king had been negotiating with the Pope. It was to be a political bargain to ensure that the Pope stop the Baltic crusade led by the Teutonic Knights. It required that the king accept the Christian faith of Rome, and with him his people.

He had refused to hope, had dug out the seedlings of frantic hunger in his heart that yearned to grow toward the light of freedom, but all the same a few had flowered and spread, much like the wildflowers peeking through the late summer greenery at his feet. Conversion might have released him. Fingers in his soul grabbed the disappointment and dragged it into the shadows where he had learned to bury and hide every emotion.

"There will be much fighting again, worse than this last year," she said. "The knights will come once more on their crusade. And there will be other repercussions. Many are angry that our king considered such a thing. They will want to appease the gods who have been insulted, and the *bajorai* will not stop it now."

He heard a note in her low voice, a caution, a warning. "Does your father know?"

"About us, no. About you . . . maybe. He has said things sometimes. I mock the suggestion, and he does not pursue it, and he admires your skill with horses, but the skill itself, when you ride . . . he has wondered. And you do not look like a groom. Too big. I remind him that your people are larger, but . . ."

But his danger was real, more real than it had been since that day they found him six years ago amidst the dead killed in that *reise*. He had been conscious and seen them searching and managed to pull off his heraldic surcotte and most of his armor. If they had wondered they had put it aside because they had found another knight, unmarked and unscarred, to burn to their gods that night. Over the years his skill with the horses had gained him favor and safety. These people considered them sacred animals.

The witch woman named Eufemia walked away, her body a little stiff, her bony arms pressed to her sides. "Wait here. I will gather the plants and be back soon." Her voice sounded low and harsh. The growth of the high plants began absorbing her form. He looked down and realized she had not brought the basket. Lifting it, he called to her.

She turned, only her head and breast visible. Behind her the river roared, almost swallowing his voice, its force throwing up the fresh smell of water and earth. She looked at him, dark eyes glinting, and her gaze slowly drifted down his length. Ignoring the basket with which he gestured, she turned away, leaving him standing there alone.

Alone. Suddenly the sounds of the forest and river became deafening. The horse refooted itself, jostling his shoulder. The basket weighed heavy in his hands. She wouldn't . . .

His mouth dried with fear and hope. He looked at the horse, and then the path winding beside the river, and then at the spot where her black hair had disappeared. The blood of excitement beat in his head, a painful sensation which he hadn't felt in years. Grabbing at the cloth, he uncovered the basket.

Two daggers, some bread, and some salt pork lay within. Something glittered below the food and he rummaged and pulled it out. Two gold armlets that Eufemia wore during ceremonies slid down his fingers.

He looked for her again. Would she pay for this? She was a daughter of a *kunigas*, and a priestess of rites older than the moon god and the sky god. Perhaps they dared not disbelieve whatever story she gave.

He wished she had said something. He had never let himself care for her or anyone all these years because it would be a form of surrender, but she had been the closest thing to a friend and in this instant he experienced a nostalgic pain and gratitude.

She might be risking much for him. The final surprise, since she had made very clear that he wasn't really with her under those moons, that he only provided a body that the god Menulius used. Well, for whatever reason, she had decided to give him a chance for freedom, and he would take it.

The hope long suppressed scorched, moving him to action. He swung up on the horse, noting that it was one of her father's finest. He quickly tied the basket to the saddle, noticing some garments stuffed into a leather bag on the other side. Eufemia had provided well for him.

He paused, looking once more to the river. From his height he could see the top of her black head bending toward the water. Mouthing silent words of farewell, he dug his heels into the horse's flanks.

CHAPTER 1

🖋

Wiltshire, England ✦ 1326

MOIRA FELT THE DANGER BEFORE she heard it. It rumbled from the ground up her legs and through her back while she bent over the hearth setting some water to heat. She froze as a distant thunder began shaking the cool dawn air entering through her open door. She darted to the threshold as the sound grew stronger. Stepping outside she saw the men approach through the morning haze.

They poured down the hill from the manor house of Darwendon, aiming for the village, four dark shapes flying on fast steeds with short cloaks waving behind them. They looked like legged falcons soaring through the silver mist.

Rushing over to a pallet in the corner, she crouched and shook the small body lying there. "Brian, up now! Quickly."

Sun-bronzed arms and legs jerked and stretched and she yanked at one wrist while she rose. "Now, at once, child! And silence, like I told you."

Blue eyes blinked alert with alarm and he scurried behind her to a back window. She could hear the riders galloping toward the cottages now. Brian paused on the sill, his blond head out and his rump still in, and twisted with apprehension toward her.

"Where I showed you, and cover yourself well. Do not come out, no matter what you hear," she ordered, giving him a firm push. *Even if you hear my screams.*

She watched until he disappeared behind the shed in which she stored her baskets, then she closed the shutters and sat on the narrow bed. With quick movements she tied her disheveled hair behind her neck with a rag, smoothed her stained homespun gown, and stretched to move her darning basket near her feet. Lifting a torn veil, she pretended to sew.

She tried to remain calm while the horses clamored toward her with a violent noise. They were not stopping in the village. They were coming here, to this house. The sour bile of fear rose to her mouth and she sucked in her cheeks and forced it down.

Two horses pulled up outside in a mélange of hooves and legs and pivoting turns. Two men swung off and strode toward her. They barged in and peered around the darkened chamber.

"Where is the boy?" one of them asked.

"What boy? There is no boy here."

The man strode to the large chest against the wall, opened it, and began rummaging through the garments inside. She did not protest. Brian's things were not in there, or anywhere they would easily find them. She had prepared for this day, although the passing years had led her to believe him safe and forgotten.

The other man grabbed her arm and pulled her up from the bed. "Tell us where he is or it will go badly for you."

"I have no boy. No son. I do not know who you mean."

"Of course you know," a new voice said.

She twisted around to the doorway and the tall, thin man standing there. His long blond hair looked white in the dawn's glow.

"Raymond!"

Brian's uncle, Raymond Orrick, smiled smoothly and stepped inside, his knight's spurs glinting. He gestured lazily and the gouging grip released her arm. "Forgive them, Moira. It was not my intention to frighten you. We got distracted in the village and they moved on ahead. They thought . . ."

"They thought I was a peasant and undeserving of any courtesy."

He sauntered over to the hearth, glancing around the simple chamber, taking in her two chests and bed and table and stools. His eyes finally came to rest on the pallet. "He is safe?"

She moved up close to him, shooting cautious looks at the two others. Even if they were his liege men he should not speak of this in front of them. "Aye, he is safe."

Raymond smiled in the familiar way he had used too often since her fifteenth year. It was the smile that a magnanimous lord might bestow on a favored servant. But she did not serve him, least of all in the way he would most like.

"You have done well for us, but we have come for him," he said.

"Come for him?"

"It is time."

A sickening strumming began in her chest. She wished suddenly that she had claimed that Brian had perished in this summer's fever. Behind her she felt the presence of a fourth man enter.

"He is safer here," she said.

"It is time," Raymond said more firmly.

"Nay. It is unwise and you know it. Your sister, Claire, asked me to care for her son before she died. You agreed because you knew Brian could be hidden here. If you take him back to your home at Hawkesford now, the men who wish him harm will learn of it and take him from you. You cannot withstand those who invoke the king's name as they commit their crimes."

The latest man to arrive moved. He came around her, taking a place in Raymond's shadow near the hearth. "Where is the boy?" he asked in a commanding voice that expected a response.

She pivoted and peered at him. He stood taller than Raymond, and broader too, and she could make out similar long hair, but dark, not fair. He wore a peculiar garment on his legs, and no armor or sword. She could not see his face well in the shadow, but he did not appear friendly.

Raymond looked over at the man and seemed to shrink a little, as if in natural deference. That was not like Raymond at all. He counted his own worth very high.

"The boy," the man demanded.

Raymond caught her eye meaningfully. He stepped toward her, whether to signal that he relinquished responsibility for what occurred, or to protect her, she couldn't say. With his movement, the hearth glow suddenly illuminated the stranger.

She gasped. *Surely not. It was impossible!*

A handsome face composed of sharp planes emerged from the retreating shadows. Deep-set dark eyes met her gaping stare, the low fire highlighting golden sparks that brightened while he considered her. He turned slightly and she gasped again when she saw the pale scar slicing down the left side of his face from forehead to jaw, contrasting starkly with his sun-browned skin.

Impossible!

"You know who I am?"

She knew who he appeared to be, who the scar and eyes and dark hair said he should be. But that was all that reminded her of him. Certainly not the suspicion and danger quavering out of him and giving that face a harsh, vigilant expression. Especially not the crude garments that made him appear like some marauding barbarian. In the hearth light she could see that they were made of buckskin, not woven cloth. The hip-length sleeveless tunic displayed the sinewy strength of his arms. More leather clad his legs to the ground in two narrow tubes. The tunic was decorated with orange beads that picked up the fire.

"You spoke boldly enough before, woman. Do you doubt your own eyes?"

"I doubt them, since the man you appear to be is dead eight years now."

"Well, I am not dead, nor a ghost."

"If you are who you appear to be, you should know me as well."

The eyebrow bisected by the scar rose. "Come here."

She stepped closer and he scrutinized her face. She managed not to flinch as his gaze pierced hers, invading and probing with a naked contemplation. Still, he didn't look quite so fearsome up near, and her own examination revealed something of the handsome, blessed boy she remembered. Leaner and harder, but the same high cheekbones and strong jaw defined the face.

"In the last few years that I served Raymond's father, Bernard Orrick, as a squire, Bernard kept a serf woman named Edith as his lehman," he said. "You are Edith's daughter, but you are well grown these eight years, and not the plump child you were when I left." His intense gaze drifted down and then returned to her face until their eyes met in a frank connection of familiarity. She saw recognition and maybe something else in his expression. Her nape prickled.

Another count against him and she doubted anew. The man he claimed to be had never looked at her like that, and never would.

"Raymond no doubt told you who I am," she said.

"So you do not trust Raymond either? No wonder you have kept the boy safe. In these times you are smart to suspect everyone. But Raymond would not know the name I called you when you were underfoot and in the way, would he?"

Nay, Raymond would not know that name that spoke volumes about her youth, her appearance, her status in the Orrick household. Her insignificance.

He reached out and touched the tip of her nose as he had done on occasion when she was a child. "You are little Moira, Claire's Shadow."

A stunned acceptance swept her, splashed with relief and joy and heartbreak. Brian's father, thought dead these last eight years, had come for his son.

"Now, where is the boy?"

The heartbreak submerged the other emotions. She turned away, castigating herself. She had been keeping Brian safe for a reason, hadn't she? He was not really hers and did not belong here. This man above all others would ensure that he someday sat in his rightful place and lived the life he was born to live.

She should be happy, not devastated, but her spirit began a silent, grieving moan as she realized that she would lose Brian forever. "I will show you. Tell the others to stay here. They may frighten him."

Raymond and his men remained in the cottage while she led the way around to the shed in back. She called Brian's name when they approached the stacks of reeds drying for her baskets. The bundles shifted and a blond head stuck up. Young blue eyes examined the stranger cautiously.

"It is all right. Come out now."

He scrambled up and came over to her. Moira stepped away. Man and boy examined each other. She was glad that Brian had the good sense not to comment on the scar or garments, even though both obviously fascinated him. He looked so small and brave there, struggling not to shrink from the hard countenance above him. Her heart swelled at the image of them taking their mutual measurements.

She slipped back beside him and knelt, placing her hands on his shoulders, closing her eyes, and savoring the feel of his small frame under her palms. *Probably never again.* She wished she had known that it would be today. She would have taken him to the stream to play yesterday, and cooked him a special meal. Tears puddled in her eyes and she looked away, biting her lip for composure. Then she pressed his shoulders and smiled at his questioning face.

"This is Addis de Valence, Brian. This is your father."

"My father is dead. He died on the Baltic crusade."

"Nay."

He frowned up. Realization began dawning. Fear and panic masked his face and he lunged into her arms, burying his face in her breast. She embraced and rocked him and silently pleaded with her eyes for Addis to be patient.

The scarred face turned toward the house and she twisted and saw that Raymond and the others had followed. Perhaps they thought Addis de Valence needed help subduing one seven-year-old boy. She tried to disentangle Brian but he burrowed in deeper. Perhaps they were right.

Addis reached down and pried the boy loose. Brian squirmed in resistance but Addis lifted him and gave a sharp look that quelled the rebellion. He began walking away with little Brian's distraught eyes locked back on her. She reached out a reassuring hand to the boy who had been her son for four years.

Addis walked as if indifferent to the boy's tears. When he passed Raymond, he glanced back. "Bring the woman."

The solar of Addis's manor house at Darwendon rose above the eastern half of the hall. He stood on the stair landing in front of its door, looking down on the activity below. This property had been his wife's dowry when he and Claire had married. Its value lay in the surrounding farms, not the old house protected on its hill only by two circles of wooden palisades.

The boy had stayed close to Moira, but now some servant children whom he knew approached and he ran off with them. Moira's presence should reassure the child for a while, but Brian could not stay here, nor in that house outside the village. Addis would have to arrange for his safekeeping, and very soon.

"He looks like Claire," he said to his brother-in-law, Raymond, who stood beside him. Addis had not even known that Brian existed until several hours ago. The boy's similarity to Claire disturbed him. Seeing the boy evoked old memories, many of them bitter.

Raymond nodded. "He does at that," he said quietly.

Addis looked back at Raymond's nostalgic expression. They had known each other since childhood, both the eldest boys of two old friends who traded sons for fostering and training. He had served Bernard as squire and Raymond had served his own father, Patrick. His marriage to Raymond's sister, Claire, had been foreordained since the day she was born. A perfect match, everyone had said, and he and Claire had agreed. A beautiful girl and handsome boy fated to live out a romantic poem.

He would not think about Claire now, although he had contemplated her often during the two years since Eufemia had freed him. Had it been thoughts of Claire that delayed his return and led him to take passage up to Norway and sit out first one and then two long winters? Finally he had forced himself to come back, only to find that the problem that had sent him away had been solved by God, and that far bigger ones loomed. Maybe it had not been Claire at all. Eufemia would have said that his soul had foreseen what awaited.

Addis gestured to Moira. She had presumptuously sat in the lord's chair near the hearth, but then there were no stools or benches about. Still . . . "How did Brian come to be with her?"

"When your father died, Claire had the good sense to leave your family's home at Barrowburgh. She came back to us at Hawkesford. Moira attended her as in the old days, and when Claire took ill she asked Moira to care for your son. When your stepbrother, Simon, usurped your father's lands, we all knew that Brian represented a threat to Simon's hold on the estate, and that he might be in danger. Moira brought Brian here when Claire died. Your stepbrother would not have known Moira well, and never guessed Brian might be with her."

Servants hustled around quickly, occasionally glancing up at their watching lord. When he had approached the gate during the previous night they had almost refused him entry. They had secretly sent a messenger to Raymond, and Claire's brother had arrived just before dawn determined to throw the impostor out.

He looked down on Moira. She rested her head on the back of the chair and closed her eyes. She had changed much in eight years, and he almost had not recognized her. Raymond had not told him who had been caring for the boy, but she had looked vaguely familiar as soon as he entered that dimly lit cottage.

Her old green gown hung loosely from the shoulders, but the flowing fabric could not hide her thrusting breasts. If anything the drapery emphasized them. She wore no wimple or veil, and mussed chestnut hair fell over her shoulders, looking like the mane of a woman who had just been well bedded. Her skin wore a light golden bronze from the sun. While she had gaped at him near the hearth he had noticed the incredible clarity of her light blue eyes and their bright, intelligent sparkle. He imagined that if he smelled her hair it would be full of the scents of hay and clover. Her whole appearance spoke of sensuality and warmth and comfort. He didn't wonder that Brian had not wanted to leave the security of her breast.

Moira Falkner. Claire's Shadow. The quiet daughter of Edith, Bernard Orrick's whore. Moira's father had been an Irish falconer who had silently accepted the arrangement until the day he walked away from the estate forever. Moira . . . the easily ignored and forgotten playmate and confidante of perfect, radiant Claire.

Addis could barely remember anything specific about Moira. He had rarely even spoken to her during those years at Hawkesford while he served Bernard as a squire. But for some reason the buried memories that would not take form floated in their insubstantial way on a peaceful breeze through his spirit. She was the only person besides Raymond whom he had seen since he returned who belonged to the contented past of his youth.

Aye, she had been no more than a shadow to the pale brilliance of Claire. If lovely, lithesome Claire entered the hall right now, Moira would dissolve into a dark blur beside her. It had always been thus with his wife, and he had been as susceptible as the others. But right now, resting in the chair that he should whip her for touching, Moira looked very womanly and not at all insubstantial.

"She is still a bondwoman?"

"That house and a field are hers. You remember, when my father gave Darwendon to you as Claire's dowry, he noted the farms owned by freeholders. That was one, given to Edith, her mother. When Edith died, it passed to Moira."

"But the mother was a bondwoman, so she is also, property owner or not."

"She claims my father freed Edith and her descendants on his deathbed. I was not there, and the priest is gone." Raymond's lids lowered in a predatory way. Addis followed the calculating gaze down to its destination. Well, well. So the son of Bernard had sought to continue what his father began, but with the daughter. He had tried to lure her to his bed, but she had refused him. It explained the lack of comfort in that cottage. Raymond had withdrawn the Orrick largesse until she came to him.

"Unless she can provide proof, she is still a bondwoman and attached to this manor," Addis said. "With the little left to me, I do not intend to lose any more."

"There is still Barrowburgh, but you will have to fight for it."

Aye, he would have to fight for it, and against men favored by the king. A desperate quest, and unlikely of success. According to Raymond, Addis's stepbrother, Simon, was firmly in the camp of the Despensers, the family who controlled the king, and with their aid had managed to take Barrowburgh and its lands upon Patrick de Valence's death. He would not relinquish one hectare easily.

His spirit heaved with exhaustion. He had learned nothing but bad news since he stepped off that ship at Bristol. He returned to a realm torn apart, baron pitted against baron, laws ignored with impunity by the mighty, the people oppressed by unchecked brigandry. King Edward was continuing his reign the way he had begun it, ineffectually, a weak monarch who was wet clay in the hands of ambitious men who flattered and manipulated him.

An outright rebellion had occurred in his absence, led by his father's friend Thomas of Lancaster. Four years ago Thomas had been defeated and executed, and the taint of treason had smeared Patrick de Valence's name too, making Simon's grab that much easier when Patrick suddenly died.

His jaw clenched. They had all died during his absence. His father. Claire. Bernard. Edith. Even cousin Aymer, the Earl of Pembroke, had been murdered two years ago by men in league with the Despenser family. Only Raymond remained, resisting Simon's claim on Darwendon by arguing it had not been Patrick's land but Addis's, and before that Bernard Orrick's. He had insisted that with Addis dead it should be held by the Orricks for Brian.

His shifting gaze came to rest on the woman below. Nay, not only Raymond had survived.

"She sings, as I remember." The clouded image of a plump girl filling a hall with a sweet voice took form in his mind.

"Aye, but not for me," Raymond muttered. Addis raised one eyebrow and almost laughed. A strange sensation, wanting to laugh. "She makes baskets," Raymond continued. "It is said they are exceptional." He shrugged to indicate he wouldn't know himself. "She will probably want to leave now that you have returned and taken the boy. She spoke once of selling the house and land and using it for a dowry."

"She is unmarried yet?"

"Married twice. My father arranged the first. An old man. Gentry, actually. He died right after the wedding banquet. The second was not so old and lived a month." A leer contorted his features. "She is called the virgin widow. After two such deaths, none has asked for her that I know of."

"They think she killed them?"

"Nay. They think the sight of her naked body stopped their hearts. She is very . . ." He made a curving gesture.

Addis looked at the swells beneath the gown's drapes. Aye, she was "very." She had been, what, five and ten when he left? He couldn't remember noticing before.

She shifted and opened her eyes and looked around peevishly. Rising, she paced in front of the hearth with her arms crossed over her chest. The swaying fabric hinted at a narrow waist and curving hips and long striding legs. He had kept her waiting a long time while he spoke with Raymond and learned the worst of what he faced. She threw up her arms in annoyance and retook the chair.

"I will send word to the villeins and tenants that I will hold a court under the old tree tomorrow," he said, turning to the stairs. "How many men can you leave with me for now?"

"The six I brought, and I will send six more, but if Simon learns you are here and moves against you, it will not be enough. And I will send some proper garments so you do not look like a barbarian when you meet with your people."

His people. The few hundred who still served him on this patch of land that was all that remained of the great holdings that were his by birthright.

He knew what he was expected to do, what his family honor demanded, what his stepbrother, Simon, would anticipate and try to thwart. But he found that he had no taste for it. He felt unbelievably weary, and bitter that his old world had not been awaiting his return. He had expected to simply step through the gate of his family's castle at Barrowburgh and have those years in the Baltic lands disappear. It would take all of the will he could summon just to hold on to what was left, let alone fight for what had been lost.

He walked toward Moira, feeling sour about the course forced on him. She saw him approach and did not rise. Perhaps she meant no insult, but it annoyed him nonetheless. Her mother's place in Bernard's household and her own place behind Claire may have given her a lady's manner, but she was a bondwoman and should never forget her true place, which, at the moment, was certainly not in his chair.

The temptation to grab those brown locks and force her to kneel almost overwhelmed him. Only the memory of once being compelled to kneel himself stopped his hand. He forced down the rancor and his inner voice chastised that it had not arisen in reaction to her at all, but because of all the other insults and indignities to his person and status.

She met his eyes and he noticed that she did not look away from his face as most women did. Even in the cottage her gasps had come from the shock of recognition and not repulsion. He had grown used to the polite eyes that looked above or below his head or over his shoulder, had come to anticipate the extra coin demanded by the whores. And so her unwavering gaze had been a little unsettling in the cottage but right now, in his present mood, it struck him as insolent.

He looked pointedly at the chair. She flustered and rose. "You bid me wait here for you when we arrived," she explained. "It has been some hours, and the rushes on the floor are filthy."

They *were* filthy. The servants had grown slovenly with no lord or lady watching them. His first order had been that the entire manor be scrubbed and they hustled around now doing it.

He eased into the chair and she stood in front of him, her arms again crossed over her chest as if she sought to hide it.

"You will stay here a few days until the boy grows accustomed to me," he said.

Her cheeks hollowed as she bit their insides. She had not liked his tone. At the moment, with Raymond's tales still weighing on him, he didn't give a damn.

"If it will help Brian, I suppose that I could do so but my house is not far away."

"You will stay here."

"I will agree to it, but only for a few days."

Raymond had been right about her claims of freedom. He might be indebted to her for protecting Brian, but it was best to have it out now. "Your agreement is not required. You will do it because I bid it, and you will do it as long as I say. When I have no more need of you here, you can return to your house."

Her color rose. "You have been gone many years and can be excused for misunderstanding how it is with me now. I am a freeholder of that house and property."

"You may hold that property, but you are not freeborn. Your mother was a bondwoman of these lands. When Bernard gave them to me, he gave you as well."

She visibly struggled to control her anger. Not a beautiful woman, but clearly spirited, and her bright eyes made up for any deficiencies in her other features. As a youth he had never noticed the Shadow's eyes and spirit, but then his own eyes had lingered only on Claire.

"Sir Bernard freed my mother after you left. I was present and heard his words and he included me."

"Raymond told me you claim this. Are there any witnesses?"

"The priest. The woman Alice who served Claire. *Me.*"

"Raymond says the priest is gone. Where is Alice?"

"She left . . . London, I think . . . after Claire died. There were documents. I remember Bernard signing them. But if the priest took them, they would have been lost when the manor chapel burned a few years ago. . . ." She spoke disjointedly, verbalizing scattered thoughts and memories. "Perhaps Raymond has them."

"He did not speak as if he did."

She still looked angry, but also distraught. It would be an easy thing to accept her claim. After all, she had served him well even when she believed she had no obligation to do so. But something rebelled at the notion of releasing her, and not just his resolve to hold on to what little was still his. Raymond had said she planned to leave the estate. She was of his old world, and he would not permit yet another part of it to disappear.

Her arms unfolded and her fists clenched at her sides. "Ask in the village what I am, who I am. Everyone knows."

"Everyone knows your mother lived in Bernard's keep and slept in Bernard's bed. Everyone knows that she lived like a lady and that her daughter was treated like Bernard's own. But that is not the same thing as having the bonds of one's birth broken."

"You are calling me a liar."

"Nay, I am calling you my bondwoman. Even if Bernard spoke thus while he died, it is not legal without witnesses and documents."

Her eyes glinted magnificently. "Is this the thanks I get?"

"You have my gratitude, although you did not give

Brian care for my sake. For Claire's perhaps, or maybe for your own, but not for mine. I was dead. Remember?"

"I find myself wishing you had remained so!"

"Oddly enough, so do I. Now go and find the boy, and tell the women to prepare a chamber for you both. A man will take you back to the cottage later so you can get whatever you need for yourself and him."

She began walking away, stiff-backed and furious. He remembered Raymond's predatory look. Raymond was an old friend, but he knew the man's way of handling women, and he guessed that this one had been resisting his coercions for years. Perhaps that was why she sought to leave.

"Raymond will be staying for the midday meal," he said to her retreating form. "You will sing for him."

She froze in mid-stride, and turned her head slightly so he could see her profile. "Even bondwomen have rights," she said sharply, her visible eye sparkling like clear water reflecting sunlight. "In this I am not my mother's daughter. Do not expect me to whore for your brother, or for any other lord or knight."

The message was unmistakable. *Do not expect me to whore for you.* No doubt this attractive, voluptuous woman of uncertain status had fought off her share of men of every degree, so it was not really a presumptuous assumption.

As it happened it was also an accurate one, but he knew that he had given no indication of it. A slave learns to hide his desires as surely as he learns to bury his hopes. She could not know that images of having her in bed had been forming since he walked into her humble cottage.

"Bondwomen have rights, but they also have obligations for which they are paid with protection. You will sing for him, but at my command, and he will understand what it means. After today he will not bother you again."

She turned and faced him squarely, as she had in the cottage and when he approached her a few minutes ago in this hall.

Her gaze did not appear shocked or insolent now, but familiar and knowing, as if she were accustomed to seeing the scarred barbarian every day and knew him far too well to find him at all remarkable or frightening.

And, during that moment while their eyes met, Addis did not feel like a stranger in his own homeland for the first time since setting foot back in England.

CHAPTER 2

FOOTSTEPS SOUNDED BEHIND HER *in the twilight
as long strides brought the youths closer. She tucked her chin
down and hunched her shoulders, trying to become invisible, and
walked a little faster toward the village. They laughed and jostled the way boys do, full of the horseplay that signaled squires
freed for a while from their duties and out looking for trouble.
She prayed that they would simply pass by.*

*They closed in behind her, their presence prickling her spine.
Silence fell, broken only by whispers and snickers. Boots and long
legs stretched into step alongside.*

"What do you have there, girl?"

*She hunched further and ignored him, clutching the basket
that held the bits of old ribbon Claire had given her.*

"I'm talking to you, girl. What have you got there? Something you stole?"

"It's the daughter of the falconer. You have a gift for the
husband of Bernard's whore in that basket? Payment from the
lord? Some wine or meat?"

"If it's wine, let's have it. Will save us the cost of ale."

They had surrounded her and she was unable to walk forward. Despite the fear trembling like a plucked harp string, she dug in her heels and glared at them, "My mother is not a whore!"

"Ooo! Spirit. Too much for your place, girl. And your mother doesn't visit Bernard to read him the Hours. Maybe he'll share her with all of us. Make her a gift to us when we earn our spurs."

"Why wait for the mother when the daughter is right here?"

"Aye. She looks like a dumpling, but maybe there's more curves under that robe than it appears."

They all stepped toward her, enough to close the circle and intimidate her with their size and strength. A hand reached out and twitched the fabric of her garment with an insinuating taunt. Bright eyes and twisted smiles peered down at her, still just teasing, but approaching a dangerous line. "Leave me alone!"

One, bolder than the others, the first who spoke to her, gladly crossed that line in a way that showed in his eyes. "I don't like the way you talk to us, girl. Perhaps you need a lesson in what you are."

"Leave her alone, John," another voice said from behind. She twisted and saw him stride toward them, a little winded from running to catch up with the others, tall and beautiful with raven hair falling around his face. Some said he was the image of Adonis, whoever that was. Her heart made a little flip of relief and then rose to her throat.

"It's just a serf girl, Addis. Not a damsel in distress."

"She's a child. Leave her alone. What do you think Bernard will do if he finds out you molest Edith's daughter?"

On the warning of their lord's disfavor, all but John eased back. They stepped just enough to open the circle, suddenly looking bored and impatient to be off. She faced John defiantly, feeling much braver and almost indignant now that she had

*him one-on-one with Addis de Valence to back her up. "My
mother is not a whore," she hissed.*

*John sneered a laugh and turned on his heel. The others
walked off with him, leaving her to glare at their backs. Addis
made to follow, then paused and looked directly at her. It was
the first time, she was very positive, that he had ever done so.
"Get on home to your father, girl. It is almost dark and you
shouldn't be here."*

She awoke from the dreamy memory that had materialized while she awaited the dawn, annoyed that it had
surfaced to remind her of that childhood awe and infatuation. Other memories, of watching for any sign of his recognition during the next weeks, of elaborating on his
rescue in her imagination until she was in fact a beautiful
damsel in distress, tried to take form but she banished
them to the shadows of time. She turned on her bed, embarrassed by the recollections. Oh well, if a twelve-year-
old girl can't be foolish, who can?

Perhaps the supper yesterday had provoked the memory. He had made her sit at the high table, two places
down with Brian between them, so that she could care for
the boy. Raymond had sat on his other side, and she and
Brian had been ignored until the meal ended, when Addis
had turned and courteously asked her to sing.

She had risen and sung an old religious melody and had
seen Raymond's bright attention as he leaned forward to
watch. It was the first time that she had sung publicly in
years, and a full silence descended in the hall while she
continued. Out of the corner of her eye she noticed Addis
say a few words to Raymond that provoked a sharp expression and then a suddenly much duller contemplation
of her.

Perhaps he had given Raymond the message he intended. When Raymond left after the meal she had been

spared the usual insinuations with which he habitually took his leave of her. In fact, he hadn't taken his leave of her at all this time, but then a knight does not concern himself with courtesies toward a serf.

The first light leaked through the window slit and she sat and reached for her shift. If Addis thought that his gesture of protection was going to make her content, he was much mistaken. She had lived as a serf long enough to learn their few rights under the customs of the land. She did not need his help with Raymond. She had been handling that man almost as long as Addis had been gone.

She woke Brian and made him dress like a lord's son in tunic and hose. No sooner had he washed and dressed than he darted out of their chamber in search of friends.

The hall was already buzzing with activity when she entered. She spied Leonard the bailiff and walked over to him. Leonard had been Bernard's man, and the only authority on the manor during the last years. He collected the rents and saw to the villeins' service, but he was old, with filmy eyes that didn't see well anymore, and no steward or lord had been coming for visits to support his voice as was customary.

"Why are you wearing your best garments, Leonard? Those green velvets are too warm for a summer day."

"There's to be a hallmote. Word was sent out yesterday."

"So soon? Addis does not waste time."

"Long overdue. Haven't held one in years. Most of the cases are so old, it will be a wonder if anyone remembers the facts. Still, I've my records, all written down. Them that thought they'd never be called to a reckoning are in for a surprise." He smiled contentedly, proud to have done his duty despite the ambiguous ownership of the manor. "I spent several hours with him last night, showing him the accounts. In good order, he said. The fines should bring in some nice income today, but me thinks he needs more since the word has spread that he is willing to sell the freedom to any with the price."

That surprised her. It had become common for lords to sell their villeins their freedom, but his treatment of her yesterday had suggested that he preferred the old ways. Still, if he needed coin, it made sense. Even freed, those peasants would still work the land and accrue income for him, paying tenants' rents instead of bondmens' fees, and so their manumission meant extra funds in the short term and no real loss in the long.

His insistence on her bonded status suddenly made sense too. It would annoy her to pay for what she already owned, but if it would make short work of this misunderstanding it might be the smartest choice. If Addis just wanted a lord's fee, he should have simply named his price.

"What do you think the fee will be?"

Leonard shrugged. "Depends on the man and his worth. He won't set them too high. No one could pay then, could they? Wouldn't be any point to it."

Relief replaced the indignant anger that had been weighting her mood. The issue of her status was a small thing, some might say. There were villeins in the village who were wealthier and more respected than most freemen. But, for all of the changes, a bondman still belonged to the lord, and if that lord proved cruel even the rights accrued by time and custom would avail him little. Freedom had been one of Bernard's three important gifts to Edith, and the greatest by far.

The hallmote was held under the old oak tree just outside the village. The manor-house folk streamed there at midday to join the villeins and freeholders who had traveled from the other parts of the estate. Perhaps two hundred gathered around the benches set out for the twelve jurors. The lord's chair stood to one side.

Addis arrived last, impressive and frightening with his height and strength and scar. He appeared very much the lord in the long blue cotte that Raymond had sent in the morning. Moira sat in the grass with some women.

A stream of petty offenses filled the next few hours. Villeins shirking their day work and freeholders refusing to contribute to the harvest. Women accused of brewing weak ale, unmarried girls caught coupling, and a few cases of petty theft. The jurors assessed the fines with which most lords had long ago replaced physical punishments.

Leonard spoke for the lord's rights and Addis sat silently, only asking questions on occasion when explanations conflicted. The sun hung low in the sky when the legal debris of the years was finally swept away. Then it was time for petitions directly to the lord. The farmers and herders and craftsmen approached who sought to purchase their freedom.

She moved closer while Addis determined the worth of each man to the land and then set the fee. Most fell between three and ten pounds, but that would be a year's income or more for these people. Everyone thought him fair enough. She waited until all the rest finished and then approached herself.

She knelt as was customary, since she could hardly ask to buy a freedom that her actions implied was not his to sell. It hurt her pride to do so. She heard some gasps, for no one considered her a serf any longer. Looking to the ground she waited for his acknowledgment. It was a long time coming.

"You want to beg a favor or judgment, Moira?"

She looked up and saw that he was not pleased. A dangerous humor sparked in his eyes. "Aye, my lord. I too ask to buy my freedom."

"So you acknowledge publicly that you are indeed a bondwoman?" She did not answer and his eyes locked on hers. "You think that you have enough coin?"

"I think so. A woman's fee must be lower than a man's, and my value to you is negligible."

"You are wrong there, Moira. Your value to me is very high."

A low buzz scurried through the crowd. "Name the fee and I will pay it," she said tightly, thinking that she would like to strangle him for that unwarranted insinuation. He regarded her with a warm intensity that unsettled her further. A bit like Raymond, but more shielded and dangerous. He wanted to embarrass her as a punishment for daring this. Addis de Valence would never really have an interest in her like that. But the twelve-year-old girl inside her flushed from his attention and she cursed at that foolish, inner child.

"The fee for you is two hundred pounds."

Two hundred pounds! She almost upbraided him with scathing words that could earn her a public whipping. "Then I ask the amount of the merchet for a woman who marries."

"On the manor or off?"

"Off."

"Who is the man?"

"I will find one."

"Not from what I hear."

Laughter waved through the crowd. Her face burned. Dear God, he had already heard about that. Probably from Raymond.

"Not all men are superstitious."

"Indeed not. I, for one, am not superstitious at all."
Some women clucked their tongues at this more blatant
suggestion. "If you find another, on the estate or off, I
hope that he is rich and extremely enthralled, Moira. The
merchet for you is one hundred pounds."

Fury almost strangled her voice. "That is not within
the customs of the manor."

"Do not presume to instruct me, woman. If you marry
off the estate, it is the same as losing your services through
freedom. The price should be two hundred then, but since
you will pay a yearly fee while absent I have decided to be
generous. In the old days I could have refused permission
for you to marry at all, but the Church has interfered with
that. Still, it is my right to set the amount."

More for the crowd to chew on. The rumbling comments grew into a low roar. She rose with humiliated
exasperation and turned to the jurors. "I ask a judgment
then. My mother and I were freed upon the last lord's
death. You all know this."

The twelve men squirmed. Addis stood. "The woman
claims this, but even if it is so, it does not apply. Her
mother was bonded to Darwendon and even though Edith
moved to Hawkesford when she married the falconer, her
tie was to this land. And this land was given to me before
Sir Bernard died. This freedom, even if the woman speaks
the truth, is invalid."

Her jaw clenched and she faced Addis down. "My
mother was born here, but I was not. Bernard's freedom
may have been invalid for her, but not for me."

"At best your situation is ambiguous and you owe obligations to both Hawkesford and Darwendon. As to
Bernard's freedom, is there anyone here who will pledge
for you, Moira? Anyone who will swear that they know
you speak the truth?"

Even if there were, they would hardly come forward

with that hard countenance challenging them. "I will find a pledge. I ask time until the next hallmote to do so."

The jurors began agreeing with relief, glad for the delay. She waited tensely until Addis nodded. "It will be so, but until then, you will serve me any way that I order." Suggestive coos emerged from women at that. He stepped closer and spoke to her ears alone. "Until you find the proof or the pledge, do not challenge me again."

She made sure only he could hear her reply. "I will challenge you every way that I can about this, *my lord*, until I break these bonds that you have illegally placed on me."

"I am within the law and my rights and you know it," he said sharply. "You should be glad for my protection. Freedom has its perils for a woman alone."

"I managed well enough, and have no need or interest in whatever protection you imagine you can give. Until I can undo this outrage, I will serve you according to a villein's customary obligations, but do not interpret my doing so as acceptance. And if you ever think that I challenge your rights and power, then do your worst."

The words poured out in a seething whisper and when she had finished she glared at him. He looked at her long enough that her defiant stance began to feel a little ridiculous. Then his lids lowered over lights of surprising warmth. He found her dare amusing!

"I am pleased to find you so willing to submit. You will continue caring for the boy, and you will help Leonard by supervising the women in the manor house."

Submit! "I will gladly care for Brian. As to the rest, that is your lady's duty."

"I have no lady, so you will do it, and the women will obey you because I say so. I'm sure that you know how it is done. Your years at Hawkesford as Claire's Shadow should have taught you."

He was reducing her to a manor servant! It was the

final insult. She turned on her heel without waiting for his dismissal.

She halted with the first step, startled by the silence and rapt expressions surrounding her. A field of eyes had been watching their private confrontation with fascination.

He had claimed that he wanted her to care for Brian, but that became irrelevant when three mornings later he instructed her to pack the boy's garments. She listened to his abrupt order and her heart split.

"You are taking him away?"

"He is not safe here."

"Where is he going?"

"Only I will know where."

"When do you leave?"

"At once."

He stood at the threshold of the house, looking out over the yard, his unscarred profile facing her. A sickening anticipation of loss hollowed out her insides. She resented that this man did not feel the same thing. Easy for him to send Brian away. He had barely paid the boy any attention at all since he found him. She examined the unwavering expression that said he privately contemplated many things, but not his son or her grief.

He had changed more than time could explain. The smiling, happy youth had become encased in impenetrable layers, much like the insects captured in a few of the amber crystals that decorated his primitive tunic.

And yet she could see that boy in him still and could picture the fuller face before it had matured, could remember the generous mouth when it was mobile and quick to laugh and not an uncompromising line more frightening than the scar. And the eyes—how their golden lights had danced when he was young! Now they glinted with danger and caution, full of tiny bonfires no one could see behind.

They were all afraid of him. The servants, the peasants, even Raymond. The piercing regard could reduce them to puddles of obedience. The severe expression brooked no defiance. The lean strength of his body and the pale slashing scar eloquently announced that he had survived far worse than any of them could offer. He still wore the buckskin garments sometimes, but even when he donned woven cottes and tunics his aura remained slightly foreign and mysterious, as if the barbarian ways had seeped into him in ways he could not shed so easily as clothing.

They were terrified of him, but she was not. At least not in the ways that the others were. That, more than his orders, had established her authority with the women. It surprised them. Sometimes, when he spoke to her and she did not fluster and tremble, she wondered if it surprised him too. But she could never be afraid of a man after she had held his grief and despair in her arms, even if he did not remember that she had done so.

He turned suddenly. "You think that I should have told you sooner. The pain would have been no lighter if you had known."

Nay, no lighter, and certainly longer. Perhaps it had been a mercy that he hadn't warned her. She had been able to enjoy the few days' reprieve.

"When he is gone, I assume that this will be over?"

"Over?"

"My imprisonment and slavery here."

He looked at her much as he had at the hallmote, with a combination of anger and amusement and curiosity. Her throat dried. Nay, he did not terrify her the way he did everyone else, but this intense attention badly unsettled her and she worked not to show it.

His silent appraisal drew out and turned invasive, as if

he sought to learn something about her that his eyes could not quite see. She resented this inspection, but she could not turn away from it and sever the peculiar connection it created between them.

"You do not know what you speak of, Moira. Perhaps I should tell you what happens to women who are truly imprisoned and enslaved." He reached out and fingered a strand of her hair escaping the front of her veil. "Be glad I do not show you."

For a moment they stood there, his fingertips barely grazing the feathery hair, his arm spanning the space separating them. A frightening, thrilling tension throbbed through that instant. Then he stepped forward abruptly, away from her, so that she barely saw his face. Only then did she realize that she had frozen into breathless immobility.

"It is over when I say it is over. Now prepare the boy. It is time for him to leave here."

It is time. Raymond had said that in her cottage. Well, now it was truly time.

She packed Brian's things. His young eyes solemnly watched her while he comforted them both in his childish way, reassuring her bravely that his father had promised he would see her again.

Addis awaited with two horses. The privilege of being permitted to ride his own mount obliterated Brian's sadness. He joyfully let his father lift him up and became absorbed with the saddle, barely looking at her until their farewell kiss.

She watched them ride out with a breaking heart and stood at the gate almost an hour until their specks disappeared over the southern horizon.

And then Brian was gone, and with him her purpose in life.

She stayed there for a while longer, absorbing the numbing grief of what had just occurred so quickly. Then, since no one seemed inclined to stop her, she walked down the road to the village.

Cottages and longhouses angled this way and that off the lane, each with its small toft in front surrounded by a ditch or fence and filled with pecking poultry. Men were returning from the fields for dinner and their women appeared in the doorways to greet them. She pretended not to notice the unusual amount of attention that her presence raised.

Paul the cooper fell into step beside her as she passed the alewoman's house. A handsome young man with a lanky strength, Paul had been the one to coin the title "the virgin widow." One night some men had dared him to test the superstition he had helped create and he had come to her house in a drunken stupor, determined to prove his fearlessness. She had been forced to knock him unconscious with an iron pan.

"So you've the lord's favor now, have you?"

"Nay. Do not start on that, Paul."

"Two hundred pounds he put on you. Makes a man wonder what a woman could offer that's worth that much. No wonder those old husbands died."

"We barely speak. He has no interest in me in that way, nor I him. There is nothing like that between us."

She spoke with more conviction than she felt. To be sure, Addis had done nothing specific to raise her concerns. Unlike Raymond's, his eyes did not undress her and he did not find excuses to sidle too close. And yet, sometimes she would turn and find him there, looking at her with that intensity he had shown again today, contemplating her as if his mind followed some debate toward a judgment. A peculiar pull would tug between them that unnerved her more than any leer from Raymond ever could.

Her woman's instincts had grown alert even while her mind kept rejecting the possibility. This was Addis de Valence, after all, and she was Claire's Shadow. But all these subtle attentions had made her feel wary when he was present, and not nearly so fearless as she appeared, but for reasons that had nothing to do with his power as the lord and everything to do with those old feelings that kept wanting to surface.

"We all heard him under the oak tree. All saw him and you and how cozy things were," Paul said, leering.

"You are drunk again."

"Word is that he has you sit at the table with him and run his household. Quite the mistress of the manor, from what is said."

"I take care of Brian. I . . ."

"We men in the village aren't good enough for a fine lady like you, eh? First a gentry knight and then a townsman and then the image of virtue for four years, but in a blink you go whore up the hill."

That, of course, was the crux of it and the reason for the looks and whispers that had followed her progress down the lane. The villagers took such things in stride if it was among themselves. A woman who coupled out of wedlock with a man of her own degree did so for love or pleasure, but if she went to the bed of a lord or knight it was probably for gain, and she was a whore.

That had been the assumption about Edith despite the affection she and Bernard had shared, and it looked as if it was becoming the judgment about her. If she ever returned to her cottage the men would probably start lining up in her garden, jingling the coin in their purses.

Well, she had already decided she would not return,

nor would she remain in the manor house. The reason for staying had just ridden through the gate. It was time to get on with her life, and not the life Addis de Valence had decreed with his insistence that she belonged to him.

She would simply leave. Others had done so. Her father, and Claire's servant Alice. Rare was the lord who pursued.

She shook off Paul's company, and strode past the last of the village and on to the cottage inherited from her mother. It was another of Bernard's three gifts. No time now to sell it or the field, but land made as good a dowry as coin, so that shouldn't matter.

Aye, she would leave, and she would go far away. Far from the stupid rumors about her husbands' deaths, far from the memories of Brian that tore at her composure, and very far from Addis de Valence, who wanted to own her for reasons she couldn't fathom.

Years ago I would have accepted shackles of iron, Addis. But I am not that awestruck girl and you are not the boy whom I admired.

She would speak with Tom Reeve tonight, and trade him the use of her own virgate and this house in return for his extra donkey and cart. She would leave tomorrow. Addis expected to be gone at least a week, but she wanted to be far away before he returned.

She bent to the hearth and probed at some rocks near its base. One shifted and she clawed it away. Feeling into the recess, her hand closed around a little leather sack. She pulled it out, then sat on the bed and emptied it.

A heap of coins fell into the fabric between her thighs. She didn't need to count them to know they amounted to eight pounds, five shillings, and ten pence, the profits from planting her virgate and selling her baskets and living very frugally for four years.

She sifted the coins away from what lay beneath them. She lifted the small object and a light beam from the window fractured its red watery planes into a display of brilliance.

A ruby. Bernard's third gift, easily worth two hundred pounds. The temptation after the hallmote to march to this cottage and retrieve this jewel and throw it into Addis de Valence's face had been intense. Two hundred pounds was too high a price for smug satisfaction, however, especially when she could easily escape for nothing. She had been saving this jewel for a purpose, but that purpose had just been severed from her life, and so now she would use it to find a new one.

She scooped the coins back into their sack, but held the ruby while she pulled over her sewing basket. It glittered warmly in her hand. She smiled. If Edith had been nothing but a whore to Bernard, she had been the most expensive whore in Christendom.

CHAPTER 3

SHE SLIPPED THROUGH the croft toward the stream, delighting in the faint sounds of crickets and animals and scraping branches. It was a perfect night, cool and breezy after a hot day, so clear that stars specked the sky as far as one could see. She followed the line of the gurgling stream, aiming for her favorite spot, the big flat rock where she could lie in total privacy and dream. On a night like this a girl could be anyone and anyplace on that rock.

She approached the small clearing in the growth where the stream widened and the rock jutted out. Something moved and she paused. A dark form hunching on her rock took shape in the shadows. She stepped forward curiously.

"Who goes there?"

She recognized the voice and it took her a moment to find her own. She should probably run away, but it was her rock after all. "Just a village girl."

"Your father will beat you if he learns you are out this late." The voice, normally low and melodic, sounded tight and strangled.

*Her father would do no such thing, since he had been gone
three days now. It had finally occurred to her that he might not
return, but she had not told anyone yet, not even her mother,
who had not come down from the castle for over a week this
time. She moved in closer. He sat with his legs drawn up, his
arms resting on his knees.*

*"You should not be out this late either," she said, knowing a
thing or two about the rules for the squires.*

*"They will not miss me. They still celebrate Claire's birth-
day."*

*An odd thing to say. Claire at least should miss him. She
herself had been to the feast at midday, but had not been invited
to the evening meal.*

*She thought about his expression at that earlier celebration,
and his sober withdrawal amidst the revelry, and Claire's pique
that he hadn't been as much fun as usual. Thoughtless Claire.*

*"I'm sorry about your mother," she whispered, wanting him
to know that she understood why he was here. In a way it was
why she had come too. Her own heart was heavy with the realization that her father had left for good and might as well
have died.*

*He turned to her, the shadows barely showing his features
except the lights in his eyes which burned like an animal's in the
night. His silent regard lasted a long time, and she wondered if
she had angered him. "Will you be going home?" she asked.*

*"Nay. She would be buried before I got there." He looked
away and spoke bitterly. "It is a small thing to them. They
hardly knew her, except Bernard, but even he . . . a person passes and life goes on. The day has been so damn
normal. . . ."*

*"It is astonishing, isn't it? I remember when my little
brother died. I felt the earth, the air, every plant had changed.
After we buried him my mother came home and began cooking
and cleaning like she did every day. I was furious with her. A
momentous event had occurred, to my mind, one that changed*

everything. But almost immediately the hole he had left just began filling in."

"At least you were among people who acknowledged his small significance. At least, for a few hours or days . . . Bernard has said the mass tomorrow will be for her, but I do not know how I can attend. People will chatter through it like a normal daily mass, and I will want to kill them."

She hopped up on the stone next to him. His words broke into odd groupings, as if his thoughts ran ahead of his tongue. His sadness subtly quaked the air around him and tore at her heart. He had come here to be alone with it, but he had not insisted that she go. "What was she like?"

At first she thought he would not respond, or do so angrily and indeed tell her to leave. Instead he stretched out one leg and rested his cheek against the knee of the other and spoke of her. He described scattered images and memories such as a child has of his mother, of small kindnesses and comforts and securities. He talked a long time. At first the words came haltingly, then more smoothly, but finally with a rough, throaty tone that said his composure was breaking. Without thinking she placed a hand on his shoulder.

She did not remember how they ended up lying on that warm rock with her arms around his large frame, cradling him the way her mother had comforted her when her brother died, his face against her breast. If he cried it had been silent, more soulful than physical. Her own sadness about her father was relieved by absorbing this higher grief.

They lay there a long while after it had passed with the sweet mood of exposed emotions binding them. She looked to the beautiful sky and savored the sound of the stream, thinking it was delicious to be close to someone like this, even if he was practically a stranger and if in the dark he didn't even know who she was.

In the oddest way the mood slowly changed and became imbued with something tense that she didn't understand. He rose up on his arm and gazed down at her. "How old are you, girl?"

"Thirteen."

He looked away into the night. "Too young."

"Too young for what?"

He laughed and her heart skipped with joy that he didn't sound so sad anymore. "Definitely too young." He rolled away and slid off the rock. "Run home now. If your parents find you gone they will raise the hue and cry."

She emerged from her reverie as she had entered it, watching the mesmerizing rhythm of the donkey's flanks as it pulled her cart down the road. She glanced back to check how far she had sightlessly traveled. Her pace must have slowed, because the wine merchant's wagon that she had followed most of the morning had disappeared ahead.

It was all coming back to her in memories like this, little pageants from her childhood that had become buried by time and blocked by grief. People die and life goes on and the memories of them are best put away since the grief never really dims otherwise. Still, details ignored are not details forgotten. If she let herself think of Claire or Edith she could still feel the anguish of losing them as if it had been yesterday.

And so it had been with Addis, except that now he had returned from the dead. These thoughts kept insinuating themselves into her mind, sometimes taking it over completely until they ran their course, forcing the old feelings to emerge even if he was no longer the youth on whom they had dwelled.

She looked back at the cart stuffed with trunks and baskets and reeds and stools. The coins were tied in their sack below its planks. The ruby was stitched into the lining of her sewing basket. The emotions of her recollections weighed on her.

A good thing that she had left. If this kept up, she

would have been unable to deny him anything, even seeing now what Claire had done to him and knowing full well the revenge he had taken on her.

She vaguely remembered passing the road south to Salisbury while she daydreamed. In her old plan, that city had been her destination when she finally left. Now it was too close and too small. She headed farther away than that.

The road had been active with travelers all morning, but it had become deserted. She switched her willow at the donkey's flank, thinking it would be wise to catch up with that wine merchant again.

She rounded a bend and, as if summoned by her vague foreboding, three men materialized on the side of the road ahead. Light reflected off their spurs, but then their postures alone bore the arrogance of knights. One crossed the road and they waited for her approach. She urged the donkey to a faster gait and looked straight ahead, hoping they would let her pass.

The two on the left seemed inclined to do so, but the one on the right stepped out and grabbed the donkey's bridle. Instinct alerted her caution.

"Where do you hail from, woman?" he asked. The heavy stubble of a dark beard shadowed his face and his cotte looked soiled by dirt and food.

"My home is far from here. I have just been to the markets in some towns back a ways."

"Did you stop at Darwendon?" another asked while he lifted one of her best baskets from the cart. She wondered if he could assess its value and hence his question. A basket like that, with its several colors and intricate weaving, was not the sort one sold at a town market but rather to the mistress of a manor.

"Nay. If you like that you may take it for your lady," she offered, hoping she could buy them off.

"Still, you must have heard talk at the towns. About Darwendon."

"I seem to recall some comments, but I was just passing through and paid little attention."

"What sort of comments?"

"This and that. The condition of the crops, the number of young sheep . . ."

"Nothing else? About the lord, perhaps?"

A pluck of apprehension scurried up her spine. These knights wore no livery that proclaimed their lord's retinue. Either they were without a liege lord, and possibly brigands living off the theft of travelers, or they sought to hide their identity. In either case they were dangerous. "The lord? Oh, you mean the one who returned recently. Aye, there was some talk of him. A hard man, they say."

"Is he there now? At Darwendon?" The knight holding the donkey peered at her. His eyes reminded her of a fox.

Which would be the better answer? If they knew he was gone, perhaps they would go and lie in wait for him. "Aye, he is there."

The fox released the bridle with a thin smile that said she had chosen wrongly. Hands on hips, with a swaggering authority that made her stomach churn, he paced around the cart eyeing its contents. "Others who passed said he left yesterday. You are lying. I wonder why."

"I do not lie. As I said, I did not pay attention. What do I care about the doings at Darwendon?"

He returned and gave her a look that suggested her truthfulness didn't really matter, that he had moved on to other considerations. The fox eyes glowed and drifted down her body. "Does a basket maker visiting markets always bring her chests and stools? Perhaps you came from there. Perhaps while the hard lord is gone you seek to escape him."

"Perhaps I do, or perhaps I come from one of the other manors or towns nearby. What difference does it make?"

He grinned at his friends. "None."

She flicked the willow switch and the donkey stepped forward. "Then I bid you good day."

Her dismissive tone usually did the trick with men. Certainly it always checked Raymond, but then Raymond at his core was an honorable knight. These three were not. A hand shot out and clutched the bridle again. She watched those fingers close on the leather and knew for certain that she was in horrible trouble. Raw fear gripped her.

"Where is your man?" the fox asked, looking up and down the road, toying with her, emphasizing their isolation.

She battled the panic that wanted to shriek. "Back a short ways. Just behind the bend. A wheel came loose on the other cart. He will be here shortly."

He smiled, charmed that she would even try such a ruse. "The road has grown very quiet," he said to the others. "It must be mealtime."

They laughed and stared at her like so many wolves cornering a chicken. Her stomach heaved. Blind desperation broke. She swung the switch around, slashing all of their faces, then brought it down hard on the donkey.

He lurched forward into an awkward gallop but a donkey leading a cart could hardly outrun them. Still she whipped and whipped, praying they would give up their game. Instead boots pounded up behind her and hands pulled at the cart's walls. The fox leapt up beside her and grabbed the reins with one hand while he twisted her veil and hair with the other.

"Bitch!" he growled, wiping the thin line of blood on his cheek with his arm. He shoved her out of the cart into the arms stretching up to grab her.

She fought like an animal, terror and fury giving her strength. She pummeled and twisted and kicked and bit in a blur of movement. An arcing hand landed hard against her face, snapping it back, but she still resisted. A fist swung into her stomach and the pain quaked through her whole body.

Resignation nearly defeated her then, but while they carried her into the trees the panic returned and she scratched at the eyes of the man who held her shoulders. Her rebellion slowed them and it took a long while to pull her into a clearing.

They hauled her over to a fallen tree trunk and threw her facedown over it. The hard bark pressed into her sore stomach.

"Hold her down. Christ, she's a hellcat."

"Aye, better that way though."

"Hold her still, damn it!"

One stepped over the tree and knelt facing her, pressing his weight onto her back with his hands. Other hands began pushing up her skirt. Senseless with terror, she twisted her head and bit an arm above her and the hold released.

"Damn bitch!"

Leveraging up she kicked blindly behind and her heel connected with a crotch. A guttural cry filled the clearing.

"Looks like you'll be last," the fox laughed. The hands pressed her to the log again and then the man bent over her, his whole chest immobilizing her torso and shoulders.

"Get her skirt up. I'll soften her up some so she's not so much trouble," the fox said.

She couldn't move. Her head was crushed into the stomach of the man holding her and she could barely breathe. What gasps she managed were full of the reek of him. He grabbed up her skirt, exposing her buttocks. She still struggled, but futilely.

The man she had kicked laughed. "God, now that's a sight. Give it to her good so's she learns her lesson."

The sharp sting of a strap landed on her buttocks. She clenched her teeth and her mind went black with rage. She tried to heave up the chest pressing into her back. They all laughed. The tip of the strap tickled at her skin, taunting her, then seconds later it struck again.

"Hell, it's making me hard as rock just watching," her captor groaned. "More."

She braced herself. She would kill them, *kill them*, even if it took her whole life to do it.

Suddenly he groaned again. More a garbled cry, actually. Weight collapsed on her back. Yelling and shouts and furious activity crashed all around her. She pushed up against his stomach and chest. When that didn't work she rolled her body until he slid off.

A chaos of violence assaulted her. Swords flashed and rang and pain-curdled cries echoed. At first it appeared that ten men fought in the clearing, but her befuddled mind slowly realized it was only three and then only two. She glanced down at the head lolling over the tree trunk. Blood dripped from its neck into a puddle in which she sat.

Abruptly a horrible silence fell. She stared wide-eyed at the carnage filling the clearing, unable to absorb it coherently. Blood everywhere, bright and garish, like gaping wounds on nature's bounty, flashed into her senses. With the danger past she succumbed to the terror and began shaking from a cold that arose from her core.

Strong arms lifted her up, crushing her face against a broad chest while the trees sped by. Then she was cradled on hard thighs near the ground, encased in human warmth and flooded with sunlight that began to banish the cold and calm her trembling.

Her senses slowly righted themselves and she found herself staring at a little amber crystal with a bug trapped

inside. She lifted her head to a stony profile with a pale
scar slicing from hairline to jaw. "What took you so
long?" she mumbled.

He turned his eyes on her. Small quakes still shook her,
but her gaze seemed to be clearing. Blood streaked her
gown but he could not tell if it came from her. Her veil
and wimple hung limply from behind one ear and her hair
was half-unbound. "I decided to let them whip you to save
myself the trouble later."

She pursed her lips. He had hoped for a more spirited
reaction that might indicate whipping was all they had
done.

"How did you . . . ?"

"I saw the cart left on the road and became curious."

"But the road was empty all the way east."

"I came from the west, around the bend."

Her brow puckered. "Not heading to Darwendon, but
away from it?"

She still looked dazed and shocked. He rested his palm
against her cheek. Still too cool, but warmth was flowing
back. She seemed oblivious to the gesture, so he let it lie
there a bit longer than necessary. "I must go elsewhere
before I return to Darwendon."

He had almost ridden past that cart until the household
goods had caught his eye. And then the baskets. *Exceptional* baskets, as Raymond had described hers. Not really
believing she would be either so stupid or so bold as to run
away by herself as soon as his back was turned, he had let
curiosity lead him to the sounds in the trees.

He had known it was she even though he could see
nothing but creamy buttocks and naked legs. Had just
known it, and gone berserk. He had let them whip her
again while he moved to a better position for first killing
the one who held her. He remembered little of the rest.
The rage still boiled in his head and in truth he hadn't

been in much better shape than she when he carried her away.

She suddenly realized that she sat in his arms and pushed herself onto the ground. She grimaced when her bottom landed, and then rocked forward with an arm over her stomach.

"They asked about you," she muttered. "Maybe they were waiting for you." With disjointed words she told him about the questions.

"Wait here. Do not move. I will be back very soon." He gave her a glance of concern before walking back to the clearing.

He couldn't remember doing half of the damage waiting there. Not like him to lose his head like that, but since it had been three against one it was just as well that he had. He paced over to what was left of the man who had dared abuse her with that strap. He knew him. A youth back then, full of lewd talk when he visited Simon at Barrowburgh.

He doubted they had been lying in wait. Most likely, from their questions, they were just collecting information. But if he had turned that bend unawares he didn't doubt that they would have availed themselves of the opportunity to win Simon's further favor. They would have recognized him more quickly than he did them too. The scar was like a banner announcing his identity.

He returned to Moira. She rested on her hands and knees, getting sick under a bush. Her abuse had probably saved his life. How long had they had her? He couldn't tell from her behavior. He had seen enough slave women after their rapes to know that different ones dealt with it in different ways. She was tough-willed and might act as if nothing had happened and so her calm expression when she struggled to her feet didn't reassure him much.

He took her arm and guided her to the road where his

palfrey was tied to the back of the cart. He handed her a water bladder and she washed out her mouth.

"You are limping," she observed while she pulled the dragging veil and wimple from her head. "You haven't done so before. I thought your hip was fully healed and whole."

"Normally it does not trouble me, but it caught the broadside of a sword back there." He lifted her into the cart and climbed up alongside.

"We expected worse, of course. With the hip. When they brought you to Hawkesford it was corrupted and it looked like you might die or never walk again. Of course, you don't remember any of that. You were out of your head from the fever."

If speaking of ordinary things would help, he'd let her do it, although he would prefer any topic to this one. "Nay, I remember very little. I remember riding off to war newly knighted and newly betrothed, determined to win glory for my lady. I remember the glint of the sun flashing off the falling sword. And I remember healing at Barrowburgh." Actually he remembered much more.

"They brought you to Hawkesford first. It was closer."

He remembered that more than he'd like, even if they were fragmented recollections lost in black despairing fog. "You were there?"

"Where else would I be? Edith and I lived there then. She tended you. Reopened your hip so it could be cleansed. She sewed your face."

"I am indebted to her then. I have been told that I should have lost the eye and most of the movement on that side if it had been done less well."

She peered at the scar curiously. Reaching out, she ran her finger pads down its length, examining it as if it were a new basket weave. He almost recoiled from the gesture.

He couldn't remember any woman welcoming its sight let alone its touch.

"A clean line, not deforming at all. But it wasn't too deep. Edith said that made all the difference. You were lucky."

"Aye, I was very lucky. It only cut my face in half."

His sharp tone flustered her and she snatched her hand away. She looked around, suddenly aware that he sat in the cart too and planned to drive the donkey. "You need not take me back. I will promise to return to the manor."

"You will not travel alone."

"I can take care of myself."

"No doubt you think so. That is probably why I found you bent over that tree with your bare ass to the sky less than a day after you left the manor."

A blush showed beneath her tan. "Then continue on your way. When we pass the first wagon heading west, I will join them."

He'd had no intention of turning back, and he switched the donkey. "Where were you going?"

"To a town."

"A free town? Far away? Where I could not find you for the year and a day it takes to break the bonds?" He could not keep the annoyance from his voice.

She turned her head primly to the passing trees. Her hands rested on her bloodstained dress. Lovely hands, long-fingered and with delicate planes shaping the back of the palms. He could still feel their warm tips tracing the scar on his face.

"What did you plan to do in this free town? Find a husband?"

"Aye." Her blue eyes glinted and the return of their bright clarity heartened him.

"A particular man?"

She shook her head.

"What are your requirements? A proud woman like you probably has a whole list of them. Perhaps I will meet a man who fits your demands. I can reserve him for you. Assuming, of course, that he has one hundred pounds to spare."

She cocked her head. "A freemason, I've decided. Well established and highly skilled. Preferably on his way to becoming a master builder."

"Why a freemason?"

"The ones I have met are intelligent. They make good wages, are respected, belong to major craftsmen companies, and are almost always employed."

"When employed they are away from home most of the year."

"Aye, there is that benefit too."

Well, well. So the virgin widow was not a virgin but had decided she didn't like bedding much. Her choice of a mason made excellent sense.

She seemed back to normal. He had to know. "Back there, did they hurt you more than I saw, before I came?"

"Nay."

The firm response relieved him more than he expected. He didn't know what he would have done if the answer had been otherwise. He'd already killed them, so he could hardly track them down and kill them again.

They rode silently for some time. Moira twisted and grabbed a sack with some bread and cheese and offered him some. She forced herself to nibble, but had no appetite. Her stomach hurt and her buttocks still stung and the day's experiences had cast a pall over everything.

Those men had sapped her courage. Soon she would be headed back to Darwendon. It might be a long while before she found a way to leave that didn't include this kind of danger.

Maybe she would never find the heart to leave again at all. She certainly didn't feel strong enough to consider it now. In fact, the idea of living out her days at Darwendon, within shouting distance of Addis's sword, appealed to her. The size and strength of the man sitting close beside her offered a seductive comfort and his rescue and their shared danger had produced a raw intimacy.

She looked to the bloodstains on her garment. They would never wash out. It didn't matter because she would never wear it again anyway. It smelled of that man. *She* smelled of him.

"Were they from Simon?" she asked.

"Aye. I recognized one. He must have sent them when he heard, to see what they could learn. Simon is shrewd. He will take his time to decide what to do."

"How would he know?"

"Someone must have gone and told him. Many have seen me since I landed in Bristol. With this face, I cannot hide who I am."

His casual attitude toward his danger irked her. "He will try to kill you."

"Not necessarily. If he is secure in the king's favor, he may decide that I am a nuisance that can be ignored."

"He must know that you will move against him, king's favor or not."

"Why must he know that? I do not even know it myself."

"You cannot intend to accept this! Simon has taken what belongs to you, to your son. It would be a fine thing if I spent four years teaching Brian about the duty for which he must prepare only to have his father turn his back on their honor."

"Is that what you were doing? Raising the boy to be strong and true so that he could fight Simon when he was grown?"

His tone fell somewhere between fascination and sarcasm. It did sound foolish when he put it like that. "He had a right to know who he was, what rightfully belongs to him. You find that amusing?"

His mouth softened into a smile. It was the first one she had seen in all these days. "Not amusing. I find it ironic."

She noticed distant movement on the road ahead. A large wagon drawn by horses lumbered toward them, with a man and woman in front. They looked safe enough, and she could follow them most of the way back home. She raised her hand to hail them.

"Nay," Addis said. "If I send you back, you will just run away again."

"I would say that I have learned my lesson."

"For a day or two, no more. You are a stubborn, willful woman. Soon you will convince yourself it would not happen again. I may be gone for several weeks, and if you go back one less villein will be there when I return. I have decided that you will come with me."

"*You* are a very stubborn *man* if you saddle yourself with the inconvenience of a woman. . . ."

"It will be very convenient. Finding you has proven fortuitous. You want to go to a free town? I will take you to one. London. My mother had a house there, and it occurs to me that it will have been vacant for some years. It will need attention, and I doubt that any servants remain. While you serve me there you can look for your freemason."

"You go to London?" She tried to keep the excitement out of her voice. London, the biggest town of them all. London, with its royal charter of freedoms, beholden to no lord. London, with so many people and lanes that a woman could easily dodge anyone searching for her, for a year and a day if necessary. Claire's servant Alice had gone to London, and it was to London that she had been heading when those men assaulted her.

Her spirits renewed immediately and all thoughts of cowering at Darwendon disappeared. She smiled inwardly, and glanced at the man who claimed to be her lord. She would let Addis de Valence escort her to London, but once they got there she would not serve him.

"Aye, we go to London," he said. "But first we go to Barrowburgh."

CHAPTER 4

PEACE. THAT WAS WHAT he felt in her presence. He could not account for it. She did not have to speak, she did not even have to know he was there for the comfort to flow like warm water. He had experienced a peculiar strangeness since returning, as if he walked foreign ground during a distant time. Only when she was near did he feel properly centered inside his own body and existing in the world in the normal way.

He had almost turned back to Darwendon because of her. He had stopped where the road from Salisbury met this one and debated it. The peace waiting in one direction held much more appeal than the conflict promised in the other. She would not welcome his return or his demands for her presence, but the peace would still be his while she moved through the manor and sat aside at the table. He doubted that he could flatter or bribe her into more than that. She resented his claims, and the deformed Addis de Valence would hardly succeed where the handsome Raymond Orrick had failed.

He drove the cart until twilight began falling even though his hip pained him and Moira grew weary and uncomfortable. She was not an inconvenience, but the cart and donkey were. It would take much longer to make this journey now. But he also pushed on because he wanted them both exhausted before he made camp for the night. She would sleep then despite what had happened this day, and he would sleep too, despite the temptation of ultimate peace lying a few paces away.

It did not work that way. Sleep did not come quickly at all. He lay by the fire listening to her soft breaths carried to him on the night from the place he had made for her in the cart. He imagined that breath in his ear and on his body and felt himself sinking into her softness and warmth. He rose and walked into the trees, away from her, and forced himself to reconsider the decisions he had taken regarding Simon.

The man would not move against him publicly. He would not risk the king's disfavor by committing an open murder that might inflame the opposing barons. If the quiet opportunity came his way, that was different, but in that perhaps nothing had changed. The truth regarding that suspicion should be clear soon enough, but barring such a chance Simon would bide his time.

So the immediate future depended upon the king and the law and the customs of the realm. If those failed him then the choice would be faced squarely, but he suspected it would be a bigger choice than Raymond or Moira saw. At least he would face it in London, where he might better learn the odds and risks. He would face it while Moira's peace would help him to think more clearly. And Simon's quiet opportunity would be harder to find or arrange in London.

Contemplation of what awaited unsettled him, and he paced back to the fire. He paused at the cart and looked in.

She rested on her side, one hand in a loose fist by her face as a child might sleep, her dark hair making a nest for her head.

He had planned to make this a fast journey, but that would not be necessary now. He could stay in London for as long as it took, because the reason beckoning him back to Darwendon would be with him.

He should let her go when they arrived in the city, release her to the life she claimed as her right, but he could not. If she found her stonemason he should allow her to wed, but he would not. A man who had been enslaved should be sympathetic to her quest, and he was, even though her status was not that of a slave and he knew the difference all too well. For one thing, if she were a slave she would have been in his bed from that first night, and he would not be peering over a cart wall at her, battling his desire.

He might be sympathetic, but that weighed little against that desire, or the peace, or the inexplicable possessiveness that had made him kill three men for trying to defile her.

He roused her at dawn and got them back on the road in quick order. Moira found some dried grasses among the trees with which to make a cushion on which to sit. She looked like some harvest goddess perched on a bed of hay beside him, reminding him of ceremonies that he had seen in the Baltic lands. It was at planting and harvest that the oldest rituals were performed by Eufemia's people, rites that alluded to an ancient time when their supreme deity had been a woman and not a man, when the physical vitality of the earth had possessed more importance than the vast abstractness of the sky.

They rode past more woods, and he thought about those years among the Baltic people. The experiences seemed more familiar to him now than the memories of his own family and land. They believed that every shrub and plant, every stream and pool, even every rock, was a home to a spirit. After a few years he had come to understand. After he had lain with Eufemia he could sometimes sense the spirits quivering in the growth around him, speaking a primitive language to his soul.

The trees now flanking the road contained none of that. If there had ever been spirits in the land of England, they had long ago left or been silenced. Here the rocks were for moving or chiseling, the streams for washing and drinking, the trees for cutting and burning. Eufemia's people performed their ceremonies in the open air, surrounded by the spirits. The Christian God was worshiped in buildings constructed by clever, intelligent masons who deformed the stones with tools and logic.

He glanced at the woman who had concluded she should marry such a man. Her head was bent and she sniffed herself, making a little grimace. Long fingers plucked at the cloth over her breast, pumping it slightly to let air flow. He had driven the cart off the road at sundown yesterday, not worrying whether there was water nearby, but he knew it was not the day's sweat that she smelled so distastefully.

She noticed him looking at the swells appearing and disappearing beneath the puffing cloth and straightened in her ladylike way.

"Were you imprisoned all those years?" she asked to divert his attention.

"Nay." She had been the first person to ask outright. Not even Raymond had sought the details. Everyone assumed he had endured horrible, heathen tortures that were unfit for discussion.

"Then why didn't you come home or send word? Everyone thought you were dead and look at the problems it created. God's crusade or not, you had duties and obligations here."

"For a woman determined to escape her duties and obligations to me, you are sharp-tongued enough in reminding me of mine to everyone else."

"Do not be ridiculous. You were born to your responsibilities."

"As you were born to yours. Tell me, how was it learned that I was dead?"

"When the others returned to Barrowburgh. The knights who had joined you. They came back with the tale that you had fallen during one of the campaigns, during one of the r . . . r . . ."

Lost in that swamp, the French fool leading them having no idea where to go. "During a *reise*. It is a German word. The Teutonic Knights who led the Baltic crusade are mostly German."

"They said that you had been cut down. One saw you fall."

Horses pouring at them from every direction. The enemy whom they had been running down for days suddenly materializing en masse, swords and spears ready, possessing a determination the haphazard collection of crusaders could never match.

"But they could not be sure I was dead." *Which one had seen him fall? Who had been with him that day?*

"Only a few escaped that attack. They said that even if you had only been wounded the pagans would kill you as they always did the fallen crusaders."

"It is the Teutonic Knights who kill all the defeated. Women and children too. Not the pagans." *Not one of our spears, Eufemia had said. The wound is the wrong shape.*

"If they would just convert, this would end," Moira said, articulating the logic of all of Christendom.

"If they convert, they do not lose only their gods. That crusade is not just about Christianity, but about land. The Teutonic Knights have a kingdom stretching for hundreds of miles out from their city of Marienburg, all of it taken when they defeated tribe after tribe, and they seek more. They give the land to crusaders who fight for them. They even gave me some, to compensate me for my ordeal. But now they have met a people who will not be easily conquered, and a king as shrewd as any Teutonic Knight or Roman pope."

It just poured out, unexpected, thoughts never before articulated since, freed by Eufemia, he had suddenly seen that crusade in a different way. In Eufemia's way. Back with the Knights, no longer needing the illusions that had sustained him for six years, the scales had fallen from his eyes during his final *reise* into the Wildnis. It had been a campaign of personal revenge when he embarked, but riding his horse through the carnage of bodies in that first defenseless village, he had known that he could never do it again.

He expected Moira to look more shocked. They were pagans, and one did not defend them. Instead curiosity lit her eyes. "What ordeal? They gave you land, you said, to compensate you for your ordeal. If you were not imprisoned, not captured . . ."

"They are a slaveholding people. They trade in them, sending most of them east into Rus'ia or south as far as the Saracens. They make slave raids into neighboring lands. I was captured, but not imprisoned the way you think. For six years, I was a slave. I was not traded, but kept by one of their priests." He had sworn to tell no one in England about that degradation. Perhaps this peace had its dangerous side.

Her blue eyes sparked. "You lived as a slave, you know what it means, and the first thing that you do upon returning is force me back into bondage!"

"It is not the same thing. I was not born to it, and you

are not a slave. A slave does not ride in the cart, but pulls it. A slave does not own property, but is property. A slave does not speak to her master as you do to me without being punished."

He had not meant it as a threat but she retreated as if he had, as well she might. A serf did not speak to her lord the way he allowed her to address him either.

"Still, one would think . . ."

"One would think that upon his release a man once enslaved would want to free the world? It does not work that way. A man brought low wants to raise himself up, and make clear the distinction between the past and the present."

"So you use me to remind yourself that you are no longer as I am. I enhance your self-worth, much as Darwendon does. I trust that when you get Barrowburgh back and are drowning in status and property and serfs that you will no longer need me to feed your pride and remind you of who you were born to be!"

He doubted that it would turn out that way because he did not keep her for those reasons. Her explanation made much more sense than his, however, so he did not correct her.

She turned her body away and did not speak for hours. Her annoyance could not affect the peace, and he was not much given to talk anyway. Angled this way he could look at her without her seeing it, so he did not disturb whatever thoughts occupied her. On occasion he saw her repeat that private sniffing.

He should have thought about that yesterday. Almost all those slave women reacted the same way about that part of it. After being used they would want to wash. He kept a lookout for a stream or pond.

"Did you have a family there? Is it permitted with their

slaves?" she asked suddenly, as if hours had not interrupted their conversation.

"It is permitted, but not freely chosen, and of course there is no Christian marriage. Another way in which slaves are different than villeins."

"As you said at the hallmote, only because the Church has interfered."

The sun had peaked and begun to fall when he left the woods behind and scanned the countryside. He spotted the glitter of water not far ahead and drove the cart toward it, angling off the road and down a low hill toward the small lake.

Moira climbed off the cart, stretching and sighing with exaggeration to let him know that he had waited too long to stop.

"The lake looks shallow. Go and wash if you want. I will stay here with your cart," he said.

She looked at him with surprise and then suspicion. He stretched himself out on the hill behind the cart where he could observe the road. She must have realized that he could not watch her from that position, because she rummaged in a basket, then walked down to the lake.

He stripped off his buckskin tunic. The thin leather was cooler than wool but still too warm for the summer sun. Lying back in the grasses, he closed his eyes and tried not to imagine the lush body being uncovered thirty paces away.

That proved impossible, since all morning a part of his mind had been divining the various parts until it had constructed a fairly complete image. Full breasts, high and firm, enough to fill his hands, probably with velvety brown tips. The rest creamy in color, like the round buttocks he had seen, much lighter than the tan of her face. Elegant curving lines where torso tapered to waist and then flared to those womanly hips. Long legs, with thighs . . . Having her in London was going to be very uncomfortable if the condition of his body right now was any indication. Her presence might bring peace to his soul, but the price would be torture of a different sort.

Slapping water joined the sounds of birds and wildlife. Moira could find no place in the little lake that would be invisible from the road, so she refrained from stripping as she wanted to do. Instead she bunched her skirts up around her thighs and, turning her back to the cart, scrubbed her legs.

Untying the lacing across the top of her bodice, she slipped the gown off her arms and shoulders. The smell of those men had wafted to her nose for over a day now, reminding her of the experience. This stop would delay them a good hour, but she was grateful that Addis had made it. He still limped and presumably needed to rest his hip, but she suspected that he had guessed that she wanted to wash. In small ways like this she had seen a few cracks in the hard facade.

It would be nice to believe that one day the whole shell would crumble away and the old Addis would emerge, but she doubted that could ever happen. She wasn't even sure she would want it to. He may have grown hard, but also thoughtful and sharp, and that might serve him well in the months ahead. Her own maturity had also given her the wisdom to admit that the youthful Addis had not been without flaws. The girl in her might wish the young squire would return, but the woman rather preferred the man.

She splashed water on her arms and neck. Glancing over her shoulder she could not see him, and so she lowered the gown and washed her breasts. Aye, she rather liked the man, but she could do without his silent self-possession. It had not been just his years in the Baltic that had done that to him. His life as a slave may have forged the hard privacy that armored his person, but the internal changes had begun before he left. Probably they were why he had left, and Claire lay at the root of it all.

Beautiful Claire. Elegant, charming, radiant Claire. Frivolous, spoiled, vain Claire. She had loved Claire with acceptance the way a sister might, but had always known what she had in her and had marveled that no one else ever noticed how little of substance lay beneath the light. Certainly not the men. Definitely not Addis, but then he had been spoiled and vain too. They had been born for each other, two perfect, self-centered children who assumed the world had been created as a setting for their idyllic love.

She remembered them at their betrothal, looking like figures who had stepped out of a tapestry. She had been awed like everyone else. Who could not be? Addis stood so tall and strong, the perfect knight, his dark, deep-set eyes ablaze. Claire appeared ethereal, floating in silk and virtue, secure in the belief that in Addis she had gotten what she obviously deserved.

Then the dream had ended, the idyll had shattered, and the world had intruded with its harsh truths. And Claire had been unable to even look at the resulting wreckage, let alone touch it. Moira knew more about Claire and Addis than anyone else. Much more than Addis suspected. Far more than she would like.

A flurry of activity on the lake crashed through her reverie. Birds and waterfowl suddenly took to noisy flight. She turned to see Addis striding through the shallow water, naked to his waist, creating violent eddies and splashes, coming right toward her with a dangerous expression.

Woman's instinct screamed a warning. She looked down

and saw naked legs and thighs and a wet garment clutched to breasts, barely covering them. Frantic about her vulnerability, and not liking the determination with which he hurried toward her, she turned and tried to run, her thoughts scrambled by her alarm.

Why now? If he planned to force her he could have done so anytime. Last night, even yesterday.

"Do not run away." He did not shout but the command carried clearly over the water. His lordly tone did not reassure her at all. Holding the gown made movement awkward and she let the skirt fall. A mistake, that. The fabric served like a wick and immediately she was dragging heavy sodden drapery.

He was upon her in an instant, grabbing her around the waist. She twisted and squirmed and pushed with the arm not clasping the gown to her body. She opened her mouth to scream but a rough palm gagged her. "Cry out and I will hit you," he growled.

He began dragging her toward the bank, saying something she didn't hear while she blindly struggled. How could she have been so stupid! Of course he wanted his bondwoman with him. More convenient than seeking out whores.

She leveraged an elbow sharply into his stomach and he spit a curse. The lake and bank blurred past while he turned her around, lifted her, and slung her over his shoulder.

She poured desperate arguments onto his back. "Release me! Do not do this! You are an honorable and chivalrous knight—"

"Be silent!"

"I won't! Think of your soul. My God, you went on a crusade. You are probably guaranteed salvation. Would you risk that for a few moments—"

"Hell's teeth, woman, I just told you . . ." He climbed up the bank and dumped her down beneath a tall bush. She rolled and scrambled to crawl away, still clutching the wet gown to her chest. Firm hands grabbed her hips and dragged her back, then flipped her. She watched in horror as he descended on her, immobilizing her with his body.

"Spread your legs."

She beat at his shoulders and face with her free hand. "You had better kill me, you animal, because if I live I will not be silent. I will go to the royal courts! I will see you burned or castrated!"

"Spread them!" He pressed her flailing arm up over her head with one hand and yanked her legs wide with the other and pushed the wet skirt up to her thighs.

Oh saints! How could she have been so wrong? How could she have been so foolish as to ignore what he was capable of?

He grasped her hair, forcing her face to meet his. "I said I am not going to hurt you! Listen!" His tone and eyes brought her panic up short. He glanced over his shoulder, across the lake. "Listen."

Gasping shallow breaths, she turned her attention in the direction of his gesture. Sounds of horses and talk rumbled across the water. A different alarm replaced her fear.

"How many?"

"Between twenty and thirty."

"Colors?"

"White and scarlet."

"Simon . . ."

"Perhaps not. No doubt you think I should have stood in the road and hailed them to be sure first."

"We are a long ways from Barrowburgh though."

"But we are close enough."

She could see the road over his shoulder. The first riders appeared in view. What would they see if they looked down to the lake? A basket maker's cart and donkey, and a man and woman coupling under a bush. Better than a half-naked woman bathing and Addis de Valence sleeping on the hill, especially if they came from Barrowburgh. Or an unattended cart which might tempt the overbold. A cart *with her ruby in it*.

"Can you see a banner or standard?" Addis asked quietly into the crook of her neck. Despite her attention on the road, his warmth and breath unsettled her.

"Aye. One passes now. A banner. Scarlet, then white. A gold falcon crosses the colors."

"Simon's."

"Do you think that they head to Darwendon?"

"No way to tell. Would you have me go and ask?"

"The horse . . ."

"He grazes nearby, below a rise. They may not see him and if they do there is nothing to say he is mine. The sword is not even a knight's weapon."

She embraced his shoulders with her free arm. She doubted much more was visible than the entangled forms of two people and a woman's naked legs, but if they looked this way let them assume a craftsman and his wife had paused to dally.

They were noticed. She saw a hand point and heard low laughter and a few ribald comments. "A few are stopping."

"Then forgive me, madam." He leveraged his weight slightly and pressed his hips forward. She closed her eyes in humiliation at the evidence that their ruse was not entirely a fabrication. Well, if he didn't react to being held between a woman's thighs there would be something wrong with him.

"They are moving on." She kept her eyes peeled until the sounds began to grow faint and the last man passed. "They are gone," she said, smiling up with relief.

The face looking down mere inches from hers caused her to go very still. His expression looked severe and intent and devoid of any concern for passing soldiers. Their physical connection abruptly shouted for attention.

She grew acutely aware of her arm embracing the straight shoulders hovering above her and the feel of his warm skin beneath her hand. Stripped of the fear she saw him anew striding through the water, the slabbed muscles in his chest glistening in the sun, the buckskin soaked against his hips and thighs, his dark hair flying behind him. The images carried a perilous appeal.

The silence became heavy. She tried to ignore the erotic nature of their positions, but instead she was stunningly conscious of every inch of him and the expression in his eyes spoke his awareness too. He slowly looked at her brow, her nose, her jaw, and then tilted his head to examine the shoulders and chest all too visible above the hand still holding the garment to her breast. Her skin flushed beneath his meandering gaze, making it impossible to pretend she was indifferent.

"You would go to the royal courts, Moira? To have me burned or castrated? You are a vicious woman." He smiled. The second one that she had seen. "And here I thought that you at least were not afraid of me."

Not like the others are, but I am afraid. Expectant apprehension scampered through her with a vengeance now, strangely delicious and full of a stimulating quality. It filled her belly with a curious weightiness and made all her senses unnaturally alert. *Nothing but trouble, nothing but shame,* her conscience warned, but even as it did her body began relaxing beneath his of its own accord, molding to his strength, welcoming his pressure. Could he tell? Did he feel the warmth tingling her? A power poured off of him that said that he did.

"I have this ridiculous tendency to get hysterical whenever a man throws himself on me and orders me to spread my legs," she said dryly, hoping to push them both back from the chasm they seemed to be hurtling toward.

He shifted his lower body off of her, releasing her legs, but he didn't move away. His eyes examined hers thoughtfully in that invasive way, demanding an invisible connection. "If you had stopped fighting for a moment you would have heard me explain."

She could get away now. She had only to push at those shoulders and it would be over. She would never be able to pretend it had been otherwise. But his maleness intoxicated her and his power and mystery compelled her, and her whole body felt anxious and waiting in a way she had never experienced before.

It took him forever. Time pulsed in silence with their heads a hand span apart, their eyes locked in a mutually naked gaze. Long after her breath had quickened and her confused heart had accepted it, he waited. They both knew she would not stop him before he lowered his mouth to hers.

Who would have thought that hard mouth could kiss so softly? His lips pressed and moved and bit in a slow, luring dance, as if he tested her taste and checked her compliance. From what Claire had described she had expected a burst of violent passion, not this courtly, almost boyish restraint. Those delicious, searching kisses summoned the remembered heartache of a girl watching from the shadows and the breathless desire of a woman too long without a man, and her complex, poignant response to the joining stunned her. Was it the girl or the woman who impulsively embraced his shoulders, pulling him closer?

His arms circled her body and arched her up to him and the next kiss wasn't nearly so careful. It consumed with possessiveness that grew primitive. His tongue seduced an opening and then explored with a gentle intimacy that rapidly transformed into demand. The warmth of his chest burned through the cool dampness of the gown barely covering her breasts, teasing her skin with the contrast. Memories and emotions and thrilling sensations merged into helpless acceptance. She stretched her hand into his hair and joined him in an ascending passion that blotted out everything but the astonishing urge to give and take.

He ended it, not her. The tension of control slid through him like an eddy of water. He eased the embrace and, separating slightly, trailed his mouth over her neck and shoulders, making little patterns of heat on her water-cooled skin that seemed to sink into her blood. A groan of affirmation almost escaped her when he began exploring her body, learning its shape with a firm hand that wandered over hips and belly and found the thighs buried under the sodden drapery.

She had learned something of lovemaking with her second husband but she had never wanted like this, had never trembled from small touches or waited with such concentrated anticipation for that possessive hand to move on. And that townsman had never taken this long just to kiss and caress, and had never made her body experience such delicious, trickling desire.

He peeled down the cloth plastered against her chest, exposing her breasts to the dappled sunlight. He caressed them and she gritted her teeth at the breathless craving his touch and gaze created. When a thumb curved up and grazed a tight nipple, her whole body reacted with an instinctive stretch of offering. He stroked her softness with his face and then rose up on one straight arm.

"Not here," he said. He covered her breast totally with his hand, the palm pressing the hard nipple and the fingers spreading down its sides. He watched his hand move down her body, curving around waist and hip, splaying over belly, lining down and up thighs. He finally cupped her woman's mound with a subtle pressure that caused hungry thrills of sensation. The long, studied caress pronounced possession claimed but delayed. "Not now."

He kissed her, a mere brushing of lips, and turned to rise. The muscles in his back stretched and corded while he leveraged to his feet, leaving her arms empty and her body tight with discomfort.

Conflicting emotions assaulted her. A vague gratitude that he had shown restraint but strong disappointment that he had gone no further. A prickling resentment that he had denied her the one time she had wanted this thing.

She glanced to the water and the road and reality slashed into her dazed perceptions. She realized with a shock how exposed they had been.

He reached down a hand and she looked up the length of his arm. She suddenly saw them as others would, a half-naked bondwoman lying at the feet of her lord. In fact, that was undoubtedly how *he* saw them. The assumptions implicit in his last words echoed. A devastating knowledge that she had just made a horrible mistake closed in on her.

She reached through the echoes of yearning and found her common sense. Not now? Not ever. She pulled her gown up and struggled to her feet. She turned away from him with embarrassment.

"Do you have other garments?" he asked.

"On the bank . . . near where I was standing . . ."

He left and fetched them and brought them to her. He strode off into the water and she nipped into the trees to change, listening to the splashes of his washing. She slipped on the blue gown thinking that in the future she would also wear a shift despite the heat. She set a veil low over her hair and pinned the wimple around her neck even though the headdress would be uncomfortable while they traveled.

Encased from head to toe in cloth, she ambled around the edge of the lake until she joined him near the cart. Water sparkled off his hair and tanned chest and soaked his lower garment against his hard legs. His dark eyes carried the intensity that had unsettled her from the start. Their message seemed very obvious now, and she wondered how she could have been so ignorant.

He hadn't played fair. Why couldn't he have leered and groped like other men so it *would* have been clear? Why couldn't he have been a total stranger and not someone who old memories insisted was incapable of seeing her this way? She would have insisted on returning with that wagon that passed instead of staying with him. Now they were traveling to London together, and this other thing would stand between them the whole time creating saints knew what problems. He had probably intended for her to serve as his lehman while there and now he assumed that she had agreed to it. It was going to be very awkward, very difficult, and maybe very dangerous.

She began climbing the hill. The sounds of the cart followed her. The danger, she admitted with chagrin, came from herself as well as him. The offer of childish dreams fulfilled pulled the reins behind her. The promise of passion and warmth walked nearby, beautiful in form, slicked by water, glistening in the sun. The suggestion that maybe it would be worth the shame and ruination stuck one finger into her mind, horrifying her.

Dear saints, what had she done? She knew the answer with groaning certainty. She had jeopardized everything, her chance for a decent future, her plans for a marriage and family, her right to respect, even her own resolve, for an intemperate flurry of kisses and caresses.

"I will walk a while," she said over her shoulder when they reached the road. The cart followed. She glanced back and saw that he rode in it. She looked again some time later and noticed he had put on the tunic, which helped some, but that the sun lit beautifully on his face, which didn't help at all. In this light his tanned visage was all sculpted planes and ridges and angles, and the deepest shadows held eyes that studied her.

Nothing but trouble. She sighed. She had been carrying a bowl very full of emotional oil the last few days and now some had spilled out and she didn't know how to mop it up.

She must have walked an hour before the cart pulled closer and the donkey's breath warmed her shoulder. "Get in now," Addis said. "You are slowing us down too much."

She just plodded forward. The cart stopped. A few moments later arms lifted her up. He carried her past the animal and dumped her on the seat, then climbed up and took the reins. "Do not be a child. I am not going to devour you."

She perched as far from him as possible and settled her draping gown in billowing, abstract mounds. Addis watched the preparations with both annoyance and amusement. Did she really think that shrouding herself would make a difference? He had only to look at her and his memory replaced her wary expression with the sparkling passion he had seen a short while ago. His mind easily stripped away the blue garment and examined again the strong body and full, begging breasts. Her strict, unmoving posture now could hardly obliterate the feel of her languid stretches and trembles of pleasure.

Her serious mouth only reminded him of her warm, bonding kisses.

Wonderful kisses. He had forgotten how long it had been since he had just enjoyed kissing a woman. Years. Since his youth, now that he wondered about it. There had been little kissing with Eufemia and none with the whores before her. Kissing was something he had done as a squire, little milestones on the way to goals often unattained with those servants and village girls who substituted for the virtuous Claire. If they hadn't been in full view of the road he might have lain there for hours just kissing Moira's lips and body.

She regretted it. She would have walked all the way to London if he hadn't let her know that she had made her point. His annoyance said he should have given her more to feel so guilty about. Just claimed her there in the dirt by the lake, instead of worrying that she would feel degraded by a quick coupling in full view of the road. She was a bondwoman, *his bondwoman*, and he had retreated as if she were some lady virgin needing feather mattresses and velvet bed-hangings. From the look of things, getting her willing again would not be easy.

He glanced at the water-blue eyes fixed resolutely on the road ahead. Not easy, but compelling. He would have to seduce her though. Something else he hadn't attempted since he had been a squire. Could he even remember how it was done?

He would wait until after Barrowburgh. His restraint should reassure her, and success would be unlikely with her skittish like this. It would also be very unchivalrous to seduce her and then immediately get himself killed.

She caught him contemplating her. Her look darted away and she flushed as if she had read his calculations. He smiled a smile that she didn't see.

You fear that you have made a strategic mistake, little Shadow, and you are right. I would have assumed that you did not want me and settled for the comfort of your presence, but desire thus encouraged can never really be denied again. Now this ends only one way. Sooner or later, you are completely mine.

CHAPTER 5

❧

"CUT IT."

Addis held out the well-honed knife. Moira regretfully examined the raven locks cascading thickly over his naked shoulders and back, waving slightly, more beautiful than most women's. They were the first words he had spoken all morning while they broke their fast and prepared to decamp. He had barely acknowledged her, as if all his sight had turned inward. Darkness tinged his mood.

"Do you really need to?"

"No knights in England wear it thus."

"Raymond does."

"Raymond was always more vain than even Claire about his hair. Do it. I will not ride into Barrowburgh looking like a barbarian."

Her hand snatched away from the blade. "Ride into . . . you cannot intend . . ."

"Do you think I came just to gaze fondly upon the walls of my home?"

"You are mad! He will kill you!"

"You should hope so. You will be free then. Brian will hardly insist upon your bondship." He took her hand and smacked the knife's hilt into it. "Now, cut."

She lifted a thick section and the blade slid through it as if it were silk. Beautiful hair. Just like God to waste it on a man. The waves grew more pronounced while the heavy strands fell to the ground. When she finished Addis ran his fingers back from his forehead. Without a word he went to his saddle, removed garments from a bag, and disappeared into the trees.

She set about replacing the stools and baskets into the cart from where Addis had removed them so that she could sleep. After what had happened by the lake two days ago she had worried about the nights, but he had acted as if nothing had changed when they finally camped that day. And so she had been spared having to bombard him with the denials that she had practiced all afternoon.

In fact, he had been exceedingly courteous these last two days, talking more than normal, behaving with a rather indifferent politeness and acting, if the truth be told, a bit more like the old Addis. It was clear that he also recognized that their intemperance had merely been an imprudent response to the embrace forced on them by danger. Yesterday she had slowly grown less wary. When they had traded some reminisces about two comical guards from Hawkesford she had finally laughed herself into relaxation and accepted that her transgression hadn't created the problem she had feared.

Their brief talk about Hawkesford had produced a new intimacy, born of the acknowledgment that years ago they had lived lives connected by that household. The ease with which he spoke of it startled her since he had never mentioned such memories before. She had waited within that warm connection for him to ask the questions that surely he must have about Claire and Brian and all the rest.

Instead he had lapsed into his stony silence, burning the little bridge they had built. He might jest about a bow-legged guard but would not discuss the important things. If he hadn't just mentioned Claire before she cut his hair, one might easily wonder if he had forgotten that she ever existed. Had her name surfaced now because they were a mile from Barrowburgh, and that was where the worst of it had occurred?

She should not judge him. Claire's story had never rung completely true and even if it had been as she said, Claire had not been blameless. What had she expected? Moira knew the answer to that. Claire had expected her own way. She had always gotten it before.

He emerged from the trees. Her heart made a flipping little thud at the transformation. He no longer looked like the displaced barbarian, but very much the son of Patrick de Valence. Hair fell back from his face in thick waves the way it had in his youth. The face itself suddenly looked distressingly familiar, only weathered and seasoned and forever marked by experience. He wore black leather hose and a short blue cotte bound by a knight's belt, and golden spurs flashed at his boot heels. She had seen neither symbol of his status before, and guessed that he had procured them on his trip with Brian. The only other signs of wealth were two gold bands circling his forearms, but every inch of him proclaimed the birth and blood that decreed his right to Barrowburgh.

He began readying his horse. She watched, feeling oddly disconnected from him, as if their small friendship had evaporated with the morning mist while he dressed. She sensed determination in him, but also still that unsettling something else.

"The sword is here in the cart," she said, starting to lift it out.

"I will not take it."

"You go without arms?"

"I will not need them."

"You are a fool."

He swung up onto the horse, shooting her a warning glance that made her shrink. Much harder to speak boldly to this Addis than to the man who had sat beside her in the cart. "I have no armor, and that sword is not the blade of a knight. Weapons and plate will avail me little if Simon chooses to kill me. Let everyone see that I ride in with no sword then, so my death will be known as murder." He looked to the treetops. "Come here."

She moved close to his leg. He bent until his head was near hers and pointed up. "Wait until the sun moves just behind those high branches there. If I have not returned, take the cart and go back up to the Roman road and head east. You should make Waverly by nightfall."

"For a man so sure that he is not in danger, you certainly cover the eventuality of your death with prudence."

He straightened. "One never knows."

"Indeed. Then let us be thorough. If you do not return, I will head west, not east, to fetch Brian. Where is he?"

"He is safe, and no longer your concern."

"Nay? Then whose concern will he be? Do those who care for him know what to do if you die? Will they understand that Simon must never—"

"If I die no one will ever find him."

"He will be frightened and think he has been abandoned by everyone. Tell me and I will let Raymond know and we will get him and keep him safe. I will go live at Hawkesford and care for him."

"Would you go to Raymond's bed for Brian's sake? You

must know that is the only way that you can ever return to Hawkesford."

Would she? Raymond had never used her love of the boy against her, but if that became a condition of having him back, would she accept it?

"If I am dead again, things are no different than they were a month ago. He would not be safe at Hawkesford, and Simon will search at Darwendon as well now. Better that he grow up where he is." He turned the horse, and headed toward the path that would connect with the road to his home. At the woods' edge he paused and looked back at her. "Come here," he ordered again.

She walked over. He looked magnificent on that horse. No banners or retinue would announce his honor, but his presence commanded attention and managed to exude authority anyway.

"Do not think to run away, Moira. I will find you if you do, and will be displeased about the time it takes."

"Saints, we certainly would not want you displeased, my lord." She spoke flippantly to hide her worry about his safety and her annoyance about Brian. And her dismay that she hadn't even considered the chance for escape that his absence would create.

The Lord of Barrowburgh did not find his bond-woman's sarcasm amusing. Rough fingers cupped her chin and tilted her head up. "Nay, you would not. I indulge you much, but do not misthink my will on this. A part of your lord's soul no longer lives by Christian chivalry or embraces the customs of this realm. He knows full well how to enforce obedience if it is necessary. You are smart enough to know that this day of all days is not the time to challenge me. Pray that he kills me if you want, but be waiting here if he does not."

He kicked the palfrey and disappeared into the woods.

She watched the forest swallow him. With a horrible intensity she experienced anew that severing certainty of loss that she had felt when he and Brian rode away from Darwendon. Was it talk of the boy that did this to her?

She busied herself packing the remaining items on the cart, seeking distraction from the strange mood. She *should* pray that he died. Hadn't she left Darwendon deliberately intending to end one life and begin another? One sign from Simon during the next few hours and she would be free.

She suddenly pictured it happening with an eerie clarity. She saw in her mind Simon greeting Addis like a brother, offering him wine, subtly making the signal that brought a sword down. A silent, visceral scream shook her while the weapon fell. She saw his eyes, placid and accepting, and something like relief pass in them while the lights were extinguished.

She blinked away the image and whirled to stare at the spot where he had disappeared.

Suddenly she recognized the emotion darkly edging his aura all morning. A small part of him hoped it would happen that way. She just knew it, even if he did not. She had felt it in him once before, like a force urging him toward a despair that made the abyss alluring. It might gain succor from what he would find at his home, and spread until it weakened his vigilance and dulled his instincts. She should have known it sooner for what it was, and said or done something to thwart its insidious power.

Cursing her stupidity, she fished for a knife in one of her baskets. Kneeling, she cut the thongs tying her coin purse beneath the cart's planks. Then she pulled out her sewing basket, stuck the little sack inside, and walked into the trees. Finding a thick patch of undergrowth, she buried it.

He had ordered her to remain here and threatened

punishment if she did not, but she could not sit and watch the sun move until time's passage announced the worst. She had to be there. She could not help him if something went wrong, but she could bear witness. Let at least one person in Barrowburgh be willing to speak the truth.

She quickly plucked a variety of baskets from her cart, stacking them inside others with handles that she slung over her arm. She looked down at her blue gown, suitably frayed and a bit dirty from the last two days. Anonymous in her craftswoman identity, she hurried down the path after him.

The town gatekeeper stepped aside without a word of challenge, mouth agape with astonishment. No one raised a cry, no runners preceded him, but almost immediately people began edging the main lane to ogle while he passed. Simon might already know that he still lived, but the townspeople of Barrowburgh gawked at the resurrected Addis de Valence.

He took his time, knowing that word would reach the castle long before him. He wanted to give Simon time to decide what to do. The lane grew thick with onlookers as the houses and shops emptied. Some in the crowd began to follow. By the time he passed the manor's ovens and dovecote, a large retinue of townspeople had joined him.

The castle gate stood open. Carts jammed its outer yard, where merchants and craftsmen sold their wares. Scarlet and white flew from the battlements and colored the livery of the guards and knights mingling with the sellers. The din of bargaining lowered while he pushed through to the inner wall.

This gate remained closed. He brought his horse up close and waited. A guard scanned his animal and body for weapons, and then gave the signal to permit his entry.

The townspeople had followed behind him and they choked the yard. When the gate rose and he passed beneath, they surged along, making it impossible for the portcullis to be lowered again.

He rode to the keep's stairs. His eyes immediately lit upon the burly dark-haired man waiting at their summit in a rich red robe decorated with gold thread and yellow jewels. Beside him stood a pinch-faced woman of middle years and a handsome red-haired young knight.

Simon's florid, bearded face broke into a broad smile when Addis neared. Lifting his arms in greeting, he descended the stairs. "A great day, brother, and one blessed by God! I wept with hope at the rumor that you still lived, but now that I see the evidence of its truth, I am overcome with joy!"

So that was how it would be. Addis dismounted and accepted his stepbrother's embrace. "It is good to walk English soil and breathe English air again," he said, picking up the pretense.

"By the saints, you look well! Thinner, but none the worse for your ordeal."

"As do you, brother. Thicker, but content and happy. It brings me great pleasure to find you thus."

"Aye, a tad too thick, I fear." Simon laughed, smacking his barrel chest. "But come, come." He gestured to the stairs. "Our mother has been anxious for news and nagging me for days now. See, she grows impatient."

Addis looked up at the forced smile on the woman swathed in rose silk. His heart held nothing but distaste for Lady Mary, the manipulative widow who had played on Patrick de Valence's grief after the death of Addis's mother. By the time Patrick had emerged from mourning, Mary had already established herself and her son at Barrowburgh. Within a year Patrick had comprehended the error which could not be undone. Lady Mary must have grown too old for effective dissembling, because her own stiff greeting carried none of Simon's effusiveness.

"And you remember Owen," Simon added, presenting the red-haired man. "He was Sir Theo's squire back then."

Addis studied the young knight. Sir Theo's squire back then, and Simon's favorite now. Sir Theo had been one of the other knights on the Baltic crusade.

Simon draped an arm around Addis's shoulders, turning him toward the doorway. "We have much to speak of, brother. Some of it very sad, I'm afraid, and I am sure that you have many questions. Our mother has given instructions for a feast fitting to celebrate your return, but let us go up to the solar, where we can talk freely."

Addis allowed himself to be guided into the large hall, a space that he knew so well that he could walk from one end to the other blindfolded and not trip over a stool or loose stone. Its lighting and cool scent assaulted him like a suddenly remembered dream full of ghosts and nuanced emotions. Snippets of memories flashed while he moved through it, obscuring the flow of pleasantries poured into his ear by the man beside him.

The sensation grew stronger in the solar. He gazed around the chamber that had been his father's. Finally standing here again contained the eerie quality of being both unreal and acutely real at the same time. Only when Simon sat in the lord's chair did his perceptions partly right themselves.

Owen settled himself against the hearth wall opposite Simon, behind an empty chair. Addis noted the vulnerability of the position being allotted to him. He glanced at his stepbrother lounging comfortably, smiling peaceably, calling for wine. *He is well content sitting in my father's chair. In my chair.*

He calmly took the one facing and proceeded to ignore

Owen's presence. "I did not see your wife. How fares Lady Blanche?"

"Died last year in birth. A mercy perhaps. She had been a sickly girl, and too weak to carry a child to term. Lost four babes over the years. Well, such is the will of God. I am negotiating a new marriage contract right now. A kinswoman of Hugh Despenser. You must attend the betrothal."

Addis nodded as if Simon had not just inserted an unsubtle reminder of the power behind his hold on Barrowburgh. Raymond had not known of this convenient death of Lady Blanche.

"Tell me of my father's passing."

Simon had the decency to look mournful this time. "There was a bad fever in the land that year. It carried away many. He did not suffer overmuch, and your wife tended him, but I fear, in the end, her long hours weakened her and may have led to her own sickness after she left. My heart broke when he died, but I must be honest with you, Addis, and say that perhaps that was a mercy too."

So many merciful deaths. God was very compassionate while he cleared Simon's paths for him. "How so?"

Simon's lips folded in thoughtfully. He became the image of a man uncomfortable with discussing unpleasant truths. "Do not be angry when I tell you this, and know that I do not say it to dishonor that good man. But Lancaster's rebellion was the devil's doing, and when our king suppressed it he knew no mercy. There was hardly a crossroad in the realm without a body hanging on its gibbet. Your father had been too generous toward the traitors in his advice on how to deal with the uprising, and suspicion fell on him. If Patrick had lived . . . As it was, the king spoke of confiscating the lands because of treason. It was only because of my friendship with some of his councillors that I was able to keep it in the family."

"But you are not de Valence, Simon, nor Patrick's son. But for your mother's marriage, you are in no way family."

"Which is why the king was amenable. If it had not been me, it would have been some distant baron of no relation, to whom he owed a favor. At least this way his wife has been cared for, and his retainers maintained. The lands remain whole, and not broken apart and dispersed."

"What was the evidence against my father?"

"His friendship with Lancaster. Some meetings during the year before the rebellion broke. I heard there was more, but since no trial was held . . ."

"I have heard that no trials were held for any of them. That men close to the king used it as an excuse to rid themselves of enemies and grab rich estates."

"The king's councillors are honorable men, who offer him much-needed guidance," Simon said testily. "You know how it is with Edward. He needs strong men beside him. He has little interest in matters of governance."

"All kings need strong men beside them, and good council. But I have heard that Hugh Despenser is more than that, and that his influence over the king is of a more personal nature. It is said that he is another Piers Gaveston."

Simon's face flushed at the mention of the young Gascon knight reported to have been Edward's lover when the king was a young man. "Those are scurrilous lies, and always have been."

"If you say so. I only met Edward once and wouldn't know. Are you saying that Barrowburgh was given to you without any formalities? A family is not disseised of its rights so easily."

For the first time Simon looked less than wholly confident. "The realm was in an uproar. You were dead. . . ."

"I was on crusade, and a knight's rights and property are protected while he fights for God."

"You were seen cut down. There was no reason to believe . . ."

"And the boy? What of the boy?"

Simon's expression froze. "What of the boy?"

"Without my body, who could be sure that I died? Under the circumstances, until fact or time proved my death, I would think that the lands would have been held for Brian. You might have been named guardian until he came of age, but it is peculiar that the son of a crusader was so easily disinherited. Do the customs of the realm mean nothing to our king?"

Simon had never been a stupid man, and he knew that Addis was laying out the ambiguities that threatened his hold on Barrowburgh. "Our king faces treason at every turn, and his rights supersede all custom. As for the boy, I looked for Brian, to give him a home and care."

Addis smiled. "That was very generous of you. But my wife's brother saw to his care. You will be relieved to know that he is safe and well, hidden where only I know, and secure from any strife that may develop."

He let his words hang there, and watched Simon absorb their implication. A sharp, speculative stare met his and a palpable tension flowed in the air between their chairs. The silence stretched with Simon examining him, taking his measure. The silent presence of Owen suddenly loomed large, alert and waiting.

Just how confident are you of the king's favor, Simon? Enough to have me slain here in your solar? Addis felt the dangerous contemplation of the man facing him and the tense preparation of the one behind. He glanced around the chamber, at the table and bed and tapestry, each in the place it had held for generations. The sense of unreality swelled again, and with it a numbing indifference for the peril surrounding him.

"Where is the Barrowburgh sword?" he asked, noting the empty wall where the heavy weapon used to hang. When the last king had insisted that all his tenants in chief document their charters to their lands back to the time of King William, Addis's grandfather had pulled that ancient sword from the wall and presented it as his evidence.

"Lost. Stolen."

Interesting. How does one lose a sword? He still felt Owen behind him like a hovering angel of death. Prudence dictated that he appease Simon's suspicions for the time being as he had planned, but he suddenly didn't care much about such things. Instead he felt a profound urge to provoke him.

"You must know that I cannot accept this."

Simon's eyes flickered with surprise that the pretense would be so boldly dropped. Then they narrowed in the shrewd, cold way Addis knew well from their youth. "You will gain naught unless you do."

"I will gain naught *if* I do. Or is it your intention to step aside now that you see I am alive?"

"When the king gave me these lands, the issue of your death was barely considered. The fact of your life will not matter either. Your father's treason lost Barrowburgh."

No longer "that good man," but a traitor now. "My father's convenient and merciful death lost Barrowburgh. With my absence there was no one to speak on behalf of our family, but what has occurred can be undone." He rose. "Now I must take my leave. Apologize to Lady Mary that I could not attend the festivities that she planned in my honor."

Simon stood, no longer the affable brother but an adversary who had just been given fair warning. Addis turned to Owen. "You were with Sir Theo on the *reise* where I fell. Did Theo survive?"

Owen shook his head.

"But you did. How fortunate for you."

Owen colored at the insinuation that cowardice had saved his life in a battle where most had died.

"Do you return to Darwendon?" Simon asked while they descended to the hall. Addis perversely arranged it so Owen walked behind them. That dreamlike sensation had expanded, surrounding him with an entrancing mist. A small part of him dared Simon to give the signal to his henchman, because it really wouldn't matter. He could hardly be killed if none of them truly existed in this time and place.

"Nay. I do not think I will be at Darwendon for some months hence."

He floated through the hall being prepared for a feast that he would not attend. Late morning sunlight blinded him for a moment when they emerged from the keep. He stood looking down on the townspeople and merchants milling in the yard. The colors of their garments appeared too bright. The details of the walls and battlements looked too sharp. Something jostled his elbow and he glanced to see Simon turning slightly, communicating silently with the red-haired man whose presence warmed his back. He knew his danger with a calm certainty, but also experienced an odd irritation with Simon's reticence. *Do it*, a corner of his mind whispered. *Think of the trouble it will save us both.*

He stood at the top of the stairs longer than he ought, immobilized by that small voice while waves of nostalgia and weariness and resignation inundated him. The formidable strength of the fortifications loomed all around, the walls of the home he would have to destroy to regain. Fearful, shielded glances from guards and townspeople met his gaze. He felt Owen move, and sensed the hand easing up to the belt where the dagger hung. He did not react, tempting them still, blindly scanning the crowd below.

And then, like sun breaking through fog, he found himself alert and aware again in an instant. His gaze swung back to where it had just passed, to a woman near the gate peering up at him over the shoulder of a merchant to whom she showed her baskets.

The danger howled. The dreamy lethargy vanished. Stepping abruptly, he placed Simon between Owen and himself.

"Fare thee well, Simon."

He turned and walked down to his horse.

CHAPTER 6

HE JUST STOOD THERE, a nod or a wink away from death. Moira watched while she showed the merchant her best baskets. She wished that she could fly. She would wing up those steps and give him a good shake and wake him up to the danger increasing with every moment of delay.

You could feel death in the air, as if the tension growing among the three men had settled over the whole yard, stilling the breeze and slowing time. Even her oblivious merchant had been affected. He kept peering about himself curiously, as if his spirit knew something was not quite right.

Addis looked magnificent. Simon, for all of his jewels and gold, could not compete and appeared a vain and pompous man who neither liked nor comprehended the commanding nobility beside him that garnered so much attention. Her heart swelled with both pride and sorrow at the image Addis presented. So right. So inevitable.

Her own rightful place among the lake of commoners
flowing below him also struck her with force. She did not
resent the reality of it. One might as well resent the movement of the sun or the change of the seasons. She watched
him survey the walls and crowd, oddly at ease despite his
danger, comfortable in the place he would one day stand
again by force of his own will. When that day came Moira
the basket maker would be a shadow again, a dim memory
of a bondwoman who had served him while he decided his
course.

Her eyes never left him and she answered the merchant's questions without really hearing them. She
thought that her head would split from the suspense. She
observed with trepidation the silent conversation between
Simon and the red-haired knight, noted Simon's wavering
hesitation, watched the knight's stance of preparation. If
he used a dagger he could drag Addis back into the hall
before anyone knew what had occurred.

You push too far, Addis. He is going to do it. Move now!

As if hearing her silent urging, his dark gaze slid past
her, halted, and snapped back. For an instant they looked
directly at each other. Just as Simon made the vaguest
gesture to the knight, Addis moved to his brother's other
side.

"Thank God," Moira cried softly, exhaling the breath
she had been holding.

Not too softly, because a knight in scarlet livery turned.
She had not noticed him take his place nearby. He stepped
closer, angling his bald head to peer at her. Moira tried to
ignore him by giving the merchant more of her attention,
but she kept one eye on Addis's progress to his horse.

"I know you," the knight said.

"Nay, surely not. I am not from these parts."

"At Hawkesford. I saw you there." His dark eyes

squinted over sharp cheekbones while he searched his memory. The merchant had decided to take all the baskets and she clasped his coins in her hand while she walked away.

A heavy hand came down on her shoulder. "Now I remember. Lady Claire's little friend. 'Tis your eyes, and they don't change. Can always remember a person by the eyes."

"You are mistaken." Addis was on his horse now, aiming for the gate. The knight grabbed her arm and pulled her into the shadows of the wall. While she resisted his grip she glanced to the stairs. Simon still stood there watching Addis with a dark expression, but the red-haired knight had disappeared.

The man pressed her against the stones, hovering his body so she became invisible to anyone in the yard. Not a young man, but the years did not appear to have blunted his strength. "Are you with him?" he asked.

"Who?"

"Do not play the fool with me, girl. Did you come with the lord? I saw you look at each other just now."

"You saw wrong."

He gave her arm a firm shake that jerked her whole body. "Listen you now, and listen well. If you are with him, tell him Sir Richard advises he go to the village of Whitly, near the abbey of St. Dominic. Our reeve there, a man named Lucas, will give him shelter this night, and I will come in the morning."

Addis was passing not fifteen feet away. He looked for her, but could not see her against the wall with Sir Richard blocking her from view. "Tell him yourself."

"And have that wolf watching from the stairs see me do it? Nay, girl, those loyal to him are no use if they are dead."

Simon did watch. His eyes might have bored holes into Addis the way he watched. Moira nodded, and pushed Richard away. Where was the red-haired knight?

She glanced to the gate through which Addis had just passed. The crowd in the outer yard separated, creating a lane for him. Simon remained on the stairs, as if waiting for something to happen.

She scanned the people, looking for that red hair. Impossible to see much in this crowd, but then he could do nothing down here. She peered up at the battlements, pushing into the yard's center for a better view.

A red head moved along the wall walk, heading back to the keep. She turned in the direction from which it had come. A guard bent in the shadow where the wall met a tower. Panic split through her. She stared at him sighting his crossbow, and then pivoted to see Addis approaching the outer gate, a slow-moving target.

She did not hesitate. "Look!" she cried, pointing to the bowman. "Up there! Look!" She yelled this time, using all of the force of a voice that had sung in large halls when she was a girl.

Bodies and faces turned. She kept pointing and yelling, and other hands and voices joined her. Excitement and confusion rippled through the yard. Dozens of fingers led hundreds of eyes to the guard preparing his shot.

The noise distracted him. The bolt flew and Moira heard its high whistle despite the din. Addis's horse reared while he twisted and looked back to the battlements. The bolt missed its target but everyone had seen and all hell let loose in the outer yard. Hands swung out to smack the horse's rump and, willingly or not, Addis galloped out beneath the portcullis.

Moira turned away with relief, only to find angry, cunning eyes glaring at her from atop the stairs. Another hand pointed, this time Simon's, this time at her. The red-haired knight began descending toward her.

"Out now, and run, girl." Sir Richard muttered, walking in front of her. "I'll see you get through the gates."

Blood pulsing with fear, she turned on her heel and dodged through the buzzing crowd. In the outer yard the crowd slowed her progress, but she elbowed and nudged and squeezed to the gate. Popping through, she could not see Addis on the lane ahead. Despite the excited stream of townspeople pouring around her, she decided it would be safer to skirt along the back lanes in case that red-haired knight still followed.

She darted behind the ovens and aimed for the town buildings, trying to stay in the shadows beneath eaves. Would Simon send men after Addis now? The whole town was in an uproar, and people spilled into the side lanes where she sprinted.

Shouts and yells began piercing the general noise. Horse hooves clamored on paving stones not far away. Addis on a horse might get through the town gate before Simon ordered it closed, but she on foot might not. She wondered what Simon did to people who foiled his plans and felt a renewed surge of panic.

The sounds of a horse grew louder, trotting down a side lane in her direction. She ran for her life. The hooves followed in pursuit.

He was upon her in moments, cutting off her path with the bulk of his animal. She heaved breaths of exhaustion and closed her eyes in resignation.

They opened to find a strong forearm bound by a gold armlet stretching down to her. She looked up at the dark head limned by the bright sky. "Up quickly," he ordered. "Unless you want to grow old with me in one of Barrowburgh's dungeons."

She grabbed his arm and he swung her up behind him. She had barely landed before he spurred the horse to a gallop. People gawked and peeled out of the way while they flew through the narrow lanes.

"Do they follow?" she yelled into his back while the horse's rump jostled her.

"Damned if I know. Would you like to stop and see?" he shot back. His angry tone reminded her that his delay while he searched for her had increased his danger. "Not yet on horse, if they do. None saddled in the yard for them to use."

He turned into the main lane and headed for the gate. Its portcullis was just beginning to lower. People saw them coming and many raised arms and cheers while they passed. Addis streaked beneath the descending iron edge and out into the silent countryside. Moira's whole body went boneless with relief.

He didn't slow until he entered the woods. They trotted along its paths until they came to the clearing where her cart waited. Addis swung his leg over the horse's neck and jumped off, then grabbed her and hauled her down.

"I told you to wait here." A tight fury poured out of him. He grasped her firmly around the waist and she angled away in resistance.

With relief had come her own annoyance at his foolish boldness. Now his tone made her patience snap. "You also told me that he would not try to kill you." Her mind saw it all again and his carelessness made her livid. She smacked her hand into his chest to relieve her exasperation. "What were you doing up there? Standing forever like that? You know his mind! Tempting the devil, that's what! I'll wager that you challenged him directly when you spoke too, didn't you? Told him outright that you would come for him one day. Gave him fair warning, like the chivalrous"—*smack*—"noble"—*smack*—"stupid man you are!"

He caught her hand and whipped it behind her back, pulling her closer, arching her body. "You could have gotten us both trapped in there!"

She flattened her free palm against his chest and pushed back from him. A firm arm circled her waist and forbade her release. "You were safe enough once you got through the castle gates. And that bolt was your own fault, daring him like that with your conceited boldness. Do not blame me for any danger you faced today."

"Should I have ridden out and left you within those walls? That is all I need now, for Simon to discover who you are and use his hold of you against me."

"If he had caught me, what would he have had? A bondwoman. One serf more or less will not affect the outcome of this, and that man is smart enough to know it."

She glared at him, hot with anger. She wanted to smack him again, but her free hand had become imprisoned between her body and his chest. Gold lights flamed down at her from absorbing eyes embedded in a stern face.

"That man is smart enough to surmise that you are much more," he muttered, forcing her closer, sealing her against his body. His mouth claimed hers with a punishing kiss.

Surprise made her resist and she twisted her head away. His mouth scorched her neck, finding spots where its heat seemed to flow directly into her blood, arousing visceral sensations that channeled the anger and worry into emotions just as tempestuous but offering a different release. He liberated her hand but captured her head, holding it to his assault, commanding submission. Blood already riled by excitement burned hotter, pulsed faster. Their shared danger and heated confrontation had left her raw and exposed. The relief and worry and anger of the last hours merged into a blind need for reassurance and she mind-lessly relented and joined his passion and the venting it offered.

He took her mouth as if he sought to consume her, but her own spirit responded with something more than pas-sive consent. She broke her arms free from his domineer-ing hold and circled his neck, bowing against him. Her tongue and lips met his in contention, continuing their argument with a wordless sparring, refusing subjugation. Desire prickled her skin, weighted her belly, and pulsed above her thighs. Her mind dulled to everything except the feel of it all and the reality of him, alive and whole. Their passion ascended to a savage peak before slowly subsiding into a clouded valley of vulnerable connections.

She found her head against his chest, his arms wrapped around her body, his lips pressed against her temple. "Of-fer your life to him or anyone like that again and I will strangle you," she whispered.

He laughed quietly. "I said before that you are a vicious woman." He gently separated from her. "We must go, Moira."

She did not want to leave their embrace and lose that brief, wordless joining of friendship and desire. She moved away reluctantly and forced her emotions into sensible or-der. "Do you know the village of Whitly?"

"Aye, it is just across the border into the lands of the neighboring Dominican abbey. Some of our people live there."

She told him about Sir Richard and his advice. Addis nodded. "Richard was my father's steward. If anyone at Barrowburgh can be trusted, it is he. And if Simon fol-lows, he will not risk the uproar that an attack on an abbey village would cause." He looked to the cart. "We cannot delay by bringing it. Get what you need, and we will try to have someone retrieve it later."

She ducked into the trees and found her sewing basket. She plucked some clean veils and shifts from one of her trunks and stuffed them inside. He mounted the horse and took the basket from her, then extended his arm again. Once settled astride behind the saddle, she slid the basket over her arm. Holding on proved a little precarious with her burden, and she tottered with the animal's gait.

Addis took the paths leading to the road south, then moved to a faster pace. She looked at the strong back in front of her face, knowing that she had complicated things again by permitting that kiss.

Do not let these feelings overwhelm you, she chastised. Remember who he is and will be and what must happen a few months hence. Picture him on those stairs, and never forget what it means. He will stand there again someday, and at his side will be another Claire. Whatever passion he shows for you now is the result of danger and proximity and convenience. Have no illusions about this.

She continued laying it all out, her common sense forcing harsh reality atop her heart's quandary. She felt confused and emotionally naked, and very glad that she would not have to speak or meet his eyes for a few hours at least.

After a few miles Addis left the road and headed across country. She was sure she would be bounced off the horse now. Unexpectedly, he reached behind and lifted her right hand from its grasp on the saddle. Pulling gently, he led it around his body and placed its palm on his abdomen.

The movement brought her forward against the support of his back, and after a few moments she let her shoulders and head relax against him. She succumbed to the comfort of listening to the muffled beat of his heart. The new position steadied her and made the horse's gait less uncomfortable. He did not release her hand, but kept it flat under his throughout their journey, pressed to his body.

+ + +

The sun hung low when they approached the village of Whitly. Addis paused at its outskirts.

"Three manors share it, but it is on abbey lands," he explained. "Close to half the people are ours."

Moira peered around his shoulder at the longhouses and cottages. "Help me get down, please. I am sore from riding."

He offered the support of his arm while she slid off her perch. She smoothed her skirt and stepped away. He knew that it was not soreness that had made her dismount. She did not want to ride in behind him and face the assumptions that might raise. He glanced to her careful expression while they moved forward. He would have trouble with her still. She did not accept it yet, did not see the inevitability of it.

The houses emitted sounds of families eating their supper but they were noticed at once. Men appeared in doorways and women at windows. A few boys darted up the lane. By the time he stopped his horse near the church a knot of men was waiting.

"I seek Lucas Reeve," he said while he dismounted.

A white-haired man lumbered over from a nearby threshold, wiping his beard on his sleeve. "I be Lucas."

Addis turned. He let the gray eyes examine him and watched the shock of recognition when the gaze slid along the scar. "I am just come from Barrowburgh. Sir Richard, my father's old steward, suggested I stop here tonight. He said that I would find a welcome in this village."

"Saints be praised," Lucas muttered with widening eyes. A broad smile slowly broke across his weathered skin. "Saints be praised!" he hooted. He threw out his arms to the growing crowd. " 'Tis the lord's son, the one what died!" He flashed a toothy grin and winked. "Of course, I'm hoping you didn't die for real since you be standing here now and if you are dead that makes you a ghost or demon, don't it?"

The villagers swarmed and word passed up the lane. Lucas gestured Addis toward his house. "Come and eat and drink. There's food waiting and there will be more once we get the women cooking again. We will feast your return and pray our thanks to God for delivering you and sending you home to us. The people of this land are badly in need of you, that's for sure." He ushered Addis into his house and pressed him down onto a stool. "Come from Barrowburgh, did you? I'd have given my eyeteeth to see that devil's face when you rode in those gates." He pushed a wooden bowl of soup at him. "Meat, wife! Send the boy out to kill some fowl."

Men followed and the chamber became cramped. The next few hours filled with ale drinking and food arriving from neighboring homes. Lucas's wife held court by the hearth, supervising the celebration. Addis could tell from the meager offerings that Simon's greed had left these peasants with little to spare. Still, sounds of revelry filled the building and its croft and toft. The sun set while the villagers squeezed to the table to fill Addis's ears with complaints about Simon and his oppressive fees and corrupted hallmotes and disregard for common rights.

To refuse the hospitality would be an insult to these people, and so he suffered it. Moira had melted away from his side at the church, and now she sat among the women. More than a few curious glances had slid her way at first, and Addis had no doubt that she had read the question of everyone in the house. She answered it by ignoring him. Her garments made her a part of them, but her lady's manner and speech set her apart, and to be on the safe side they finally decided that she must be the latter.

The ambiguity that she successfully established regarding her relationship to him was borne out by the smiles eventually cast his way by a tawny-haired girl named Ann. Inviting smiles, and eyes that focused on the right side of his face and managed not to see the left. The village slut, he surmised.

"My daughter and her husband have gone to a fair, and their cottage is empty," Lucas explained at one point. "They would be honored, I know, if you made it yours. 'Tis the new one at the far end of the lane, and I'm sure that all is right, but we will see it is prepared for you."

The last thing Addis wanted was the whole village accompanying him to that cottage. Nor did he want Moira's disinterest to convince them that she was so separate from him that she required a bed in one of their homes. Suppressed desire simmered in his body and he maintained his patience with these peasants only through concentrated effort. "My woman will take care of it," he said.

Lucas glanced to her. The ale made him bold. "She is . . . ?"

"She is a bondwoman of my manor at Darwendon. She has business to the east and I escort her since I head that way too." It was the God's honest truth, but he trusted Lucas to get the message.

Lucas absorbed this without comment but his gray eyes flickered. No villager would approach that cottage this night or next morning. A sharp glance from the reeve and the slut's expression dulled. Addis turned his attention to a man asking the lord to bless his children.

There were rules regarding hospitality that one could count on in any village, and Moira waited for the offer of a bed or pallet in one of the women's homes. When the night wore on and the offer did not come, she admitted that despite her attempts to convince them otherwise, these people had reached certain conclusions about her and Addis. Her own behavior had been indifferent toward him, so the only explanation was that Addis had said something to the reeve and Lucas had silently passed the word. She resisted believing that because of what it implied, but the petulant retreat of tawny-haired Ann provided the final evidence.

Despite her averted eyes she had been very alert to him the whole time and now the knight at the table began to press on her awareness. The knowledge of what he planned to do to her began to intrude on her thoughts with astonishing explicitness. Despite the seductive memories attached to those images, despite the man commanding her attention through the sheer power of his presence, the shadow and bondwoman sadly recognized the disaster for her life that his intentions would create.

She tried to rehearse the denials that she had worked out two days ago, but in light of that kiss today she doubted that they would carry much weight. She could explain away that first transgression as an accident. Today had been something else. Welcome. Necessary. Born of an uncontrollable euphoria that had existed separate from the practical plans that she had made for her life.

What could she say to him? *I lost my head because I was relieved for your safety.* Partly true. That had possibilities. *If you think about it, it was merely a kiss of friendship.* Aye, and pigs have wings. *I will not do this thing with you, Addis, I am most firm about that. My resolve is like steel.* Unless, of course, you kiss me again, in which case I will melt into a puddle of lust and abandon every shred of common sense.

The memory had her melting already. A heady warmth tingled in her hips and flushed through her limbs. Hollow, hungry sensations streaked through her core. She quickly looked at the handsome face and saw it again above her while he summoned her passion as if it were his to demand at will. He had not given her any more attention than she had him this evening, but she had sensed his consciousness of her over the hours as surely as if they still faced each other in that embrace.

She turned and found Ann eyeing her critically, as if she measured the competition. I forfeit, Moira responded with her eyes. Truly. Do not listen to Lucas. Be bold. Think of the benefits to you and your family if you please the lord. He might even let you live in the castle until he marries again.

Moira looked over to see Addis bending his head toward a man but his eyes found her. His gaze struck her as invasive as ever despite its shielded warmth, and more than a little dangerous. For a few beats of timelessness the whole chamber emptied of everyone but the two of them and his expectation of what lay ahead. An unwelcome thrill spiraled down from her neck to her loins and a low, fearful excitement blotted through her.

Ann, deciding the lord's largesse was worth a few risks, ended it by stepping between them, carrying some ale. His attention shifted to the lithe young body approaching. Moira felt like a cornered rabbit suddenly liberated by the hunter's distraction.

Ann was well practiced in getting a man's attention, and her breasts grazed his arm while she smiled vivaciously and filled his cup. Addis's lids lowered. A few of the men smirked. Moira's good sense heaved with relief, but her heart felt a foolish spike of jealousy.

"Pity, ain't it?" a voice said quietly at her shoulder. Lucas's wife, Joan, had closed in for some confidential gossip. "His face, that is. He was the most beautiful boy."

Moira never noticed that scar much, at least not as something so unusual. It was just a part of him, like his eyes and hair. Of course, she had seen him when the wound truly cut his face in half, so this remnant appeared to her a minor thing.

"They say the hip is worse," Joan continued, bending closely to encourage confidences. She had drunk her share of ale this night. "I know some of the women who tended him when he returned. Horrible, they said. Sure he would die, they were."

She had seen that wound at its worst as well. "Not so horrible if he walks and fights still."

"Aye, a miracle of sorts. Perhaps his young bride prayed for him and God listened. Didn't do much else, from what is told. Rarely saw him all those months, and never helped with his care. Surprised us all that the wedding was held at all. A proud and selfish girl."

"Not so proud. And young and frightened. Lady Claire was my friend."

Joan pursed her lips, sorry to lose that topic to misplaced loyalty. "They said he'd never walk right again."

I know.

"Better off dead, some said."

Aye. Including Addis.

"But even before he was healed, he ordered them to help him stand. As soon as he returned here. Despite the pain, he would walk the length of his chamber holding on to servants, several times a day, back and forth. They cried describing it, those men who helped him did. Like watching a man being tortured, they said. Would beg him to stop, but he would not. Some say the hip healed different because of it, that it kept him from being crippled. I say it was the prayers of his father that done that, and maybe of his lady, if she bothered to pray for other than herself, that is. He went on that crusade before he was whole, you know. Still weaker than he should be, and the wounds still mending inside. Said he went to repay God for sparing him."

Is that what he said.

Joan looked at her meaningfully, hungry for details.

Moira could not oblige her even if she wanted to. She had not been at Barrowburgh during those months, had not even come for the wedding. The last she had seen of Addis had been his broken, bandaged body lifted into the wagon that would take him home. Beside him had sat Claire, her face a mask of duty and obligation. *Not proud. Young and frightened.*

She did not want to talk about this. She groped for a way to change the subject only to realize that she didn't want to talk about anything. In fact, she didn't want to be here any longer. Ann had managed to squeeze herself among the men at the table where she could give Addis her full attention. Lucas looked a little embarrassed by the girl's boldness. Addis neither encouraged nor discouraged her.

"You don't mind?" Joan asked, glancing to them both.

"It is not for me to do so."

"Nay, with such a man . . . still, a woman has feelings."

"I do not mind." That was not true. While she had no intention of giving him what he wanted, she still resented the idea of his bedding Ann instead.

Well, she couldn't have it both ways. Her good sense had been praying for deliverance since she got on that horse even if another part of her had not, and now redemption from her own weakness had been sent in the form of an eager girl with tawny hair.

Joan had told her about the daughter's cottage, and Moira stood abruptly. "I will go prepare the house," she said, wondering if Addis would bring Ann there and if she should just bluntly ask Joan if there was a pallet in another house that she could use.

"She and her mother have their own place a few doors down," Joan explained kindly, lighting a candle and handing it to her.

Moira slipped through the crowded room toward the

door. At the threshold an invisible connection touched her like a hand on her shoulder. She looked over her shoulder to see those dark eyes noting her departure.

She found the little cottage without difficulty. Its new thatching and clean plaster announced it the home of newlyweds. She opened the door and her candle's flame pierced the gloomy interior. Finding the window over the bed, she threw open the shutters to the moonlight.

Buckets stood by the hearth. After lighting a low fire, she collected two and made her way back to the village well. Sounds of revelry still poured out of Lucas's house. She carried her burden back to the welcome silence of the cottage and set the water near the hearth.

Lucas's daughter was an impeccable housekeeper, and the cottage needed no preparation. In fact it possessed an organization and cleanliness that made Moira uncomfortable. It reminded her of her own cottage at Darwendon, and nostalgia for those four years with Brian flooded her.

It had been almost like having a real home and family during that time. She sat by the hearth, using some of the warmed water to wash, fighting the bittersweet mood that those memories evoked. A real home. A secure place. She hadn't had either since she was thirteen years old. A child to love and care for. A spot of stability and warmth in an indifferent, angry world.

The thoughts weighed on her, emphasizing the loneliness that she had known in her life so often that it had become predictable. Worse after Edith died. Excruciating with Claire's passing. Unassuaged by that brief marriage, but wonderfully dulled for four years by caring for a child.

She wanted that balm again. She yearned to feel centered and grounded in one place, with a purpose that mattered and a small world that belonged to her forever. Not the Shadow, but, for a few people at least, for her family, a source of light.

The reflections saddened her and she tried to cast off the mood. When that didn't work she walked out of the cottage to escape its strange power. The little house stood at the edge of some fields, and just past its croft she spied the high roof of the open structure that protected the hay mound. She picked her way through the neat garden toward it.

The sweet smell of hay wafted to her on the cool breeze. She shifted some this way and that, making a ledge on which to sit. Lying back in its springy support, she could watch the half moon and the starry dots sprinkling the velvet darkness.

She began counting those little marks of brightness and her mind wandered through memories recent and old. Her heart grew full and vulnerable. She became isolated from everyone and everything except this little ledge of hay and that vast sky propelling her consciousness freely through space and time.

CHAPTER 7

❧

NOT PROUD, JUST young and frightened . . .

The passageway smelled cool and damp and the stones absorbed the faint scuffle of her shoes. No sounds here, like so many places in the castle this day. The whole household had grown subdued, holding its breath, waiting for death.

She had already tried all of Claire's other hiding places. The chapel, the east tower roof, the nook beside the hall hearth. Now she peered into the shadow under the stairs rising from the kitchen. Her candlelight reflected off a cascade of blond hair draping a huddled body.

A head moved and blue eyes looked up, wide and frightened and then relieved. "Thank the saints it is you."

She bent down over her friend. Two years older than she, but a child again suddenly. "You must come."

"I cannot," Claire breathed, shaking her head slowly, looking to a spot on the floor.

"You must. Your father sent me to find you. . . ."

"I cannot!" She glared up. "Have you seen him? Have you?

Cut to pieces. My God, he had no face left, and his body . . ." The words sliced, full of horror. The tone was close to hysterical.

"Wounds always look worse at first. My mother says it is the bruising that deforms his face, that no bones were broken. She will tend him. There will be a scar, but all knights have scars. . . ."

"He will be crippled and he looks monstrous." She said it bitterly and her eyes glazed, looking inward. What did she see in her soul? A betrothed girl lacking the strength to do her duty toward her intended? A spoiled girl angry that fate had played such a trick on her? Both most likely, but a man suffered upstairs and Moira found that she had little patience all of a sudden with Claire's delicacy and selfishness.

"He is asking for you. Whenever he becomes conscious he says your name. You must—"

"I must, I must! Who are you to tell me what I must? Go back and tell them that you could not find me. Say that you did but I am ill. Do whatever you choose, but I will not come with you. I cannot bear to look at him." Her body began shaking, a slow shiver at first, but then jerking movements that made her cross her arms over her belly. She shook her head and careened like a mourner, heaving dry sobs. "Oh, my Addis. My beautiful, beautiful Addis . . ."

Moira gave her one last glance. So, this was love. What a thin, fragile, self-centered thing it could be. She turned on her heel and ran back up the stairs.

Sir Bernard paced outside the chamber, as worried as if the young man behind its door were his own son. "Where is she?"

"I . . . she is very ill. Prostrate with pains in the stomach."

His eyes narrowed angrily and he glared down the passage at the void where his daughter should be approaching. Shaking his head, he took her arm. "Your mother is going to open and purify his hip. God willing the pain will put him out, and he is mad in his head from the fever, so perhaps . . ."

She resisted, not wanting to go in any more than Claire had.

His fingers closed more tightly. "Stand by his head, girl, and speak to him while it is done. Maybe he will think it is she."

She found herself pulled into that torture chamber. Her mother looked up expectantly, then pursed her lips when she noted Claire's absence. Moira pleaded with her eyes to be spared this horror, but Edith was all business suddenly, laying a dagger in the coals of the low fire.

The space smelled of corruption and sweat and the noxious odor turned her stomach. Raymond and two other men stood alongside the bed. She forced herself to walk around them and look at the man lying there.

Bandages swaddled half his face where Edith had sewn the cut. They covered part of his swollen mouth and so his fevered ramblings came incoherently. Pain and bruising distorted the face she could see, thinner than she remembered, the bones looking very sharp, the youth looking suddenly old. Sympathy for his agony shredded her heart and her resistance.

They had stripped him, and she glanced down to the festering wound slicing diagonally from his waist through the top of his thigh. Someone had sewn it roughly on the field, to cover exposed bone and hold his stomach in, they had said. Edith suspected the sword had nicked the gut, causing the corruption to set in quickly.

She moved close to his head. Raymond shot a questioning look at his father, who remained stoically nonexpressive. Edith rose from the hearth and came forward with the dagger, its hilt wrapped in a thick cloth.

Someone had placed some water on a table near his head. She dampened a cloth and wiped the battered face as gently as she could, hoping she could give some small relief, feeling his pain as if her own body had been ravaged. Oh, Addis. My beautiful, beautiful Addis.

He felt her touch and grabbed her arm. The unbandaged eye opened to reveal a dark pool aflame with golden lights burning out of control. He peered at her and something like rational *awareness flickered over his expression. He looked down his body at the men flanking him, and the hideous wound, and Edith with her dagger. His jaw stiffened.*

Someone brought a stool and she knelt on it. She leaned forward and stroked his hair, cradling his head against her chest. "I will stay with you," she whispered, hoping he would think she was Claire but knowing from that look that he would not. Still, the comfort seemed to soothe him.

Bernard nodded and four pairs of hands pressed down to hold him. Addis pulled his right hand free and sought hers and grasped it tightly to his chest. Edith bent over the hip.

He twisted his head toward her violently with the first hot cut and clutched her hand like a dying man. She pressed her lips to his temple and battled for composure and whispered prayers and poems and songs of love while he smothered his screams in her breast.

She became aware of his presence slowly, sensing it before the body leaning against the post took form in the shadows. He did not startle her. His reality simply emerged out of her thoughts like a seamless continuation suddenly given substance. How long had he been there?

Not now. I will have little strength now.

His shoulder pressed against the post and his arms crossed his chest. She might have been dreaming into the sky but he had been contemplating her and his attention created a disturbance in the breeze that had alerted her to him. She did not speak to let him know she had seen him, but waited desperately for the perilous mood of her memory to pass.

"I thought that you might have fallen asleep," he said.

How could he be sure she hadn't? He could not see her face well in this darkness. Perhaps he heard the slow, hard pounding of her heart.

"Do you think to stay out here all night?"

"I had not planned to, but since . . . why aren't you with Ann?" It just blurted out, sounding more petulant than she felt.

He did not answer at once. He just stood there, filling the night with a subtle danger, making this hay mound a much less peaceful place all of a sudden. "I am not with her because I do not want to be."

"It would simplify things if you did."

"Would it? I don't think so. For this night perhaps. No more."

She sat upright on the ledge of hay and looked out to the dark fields. His arrival had started a visceral throbbing in her that seemed to affect the whole night, as if the air and the crops absorbed a rhythm from her. The sensation was both unsettling and alluring. He hadn't moved, but his own pulse became noticeable in the space between them, as if his life force were adjusting to hers, seeking to join it beat for beat. Instinct mumbled warnings in her ear, but her spirit, hungry for unity of any sort, responded with an astonishing yearning.

"What do you want with me, my lord?" She sighed the question, emphasizing the *me*.

"You have not called me that before. Do not start now."

"I think it best if I do. It is a reality that I forget at great cost."

"As your lord, I forbid it." He walked toward her. Common sense demanded that she jump away from him. She didn't.

He settled onto the hay beside her and all of her senses snapped alert. She should have made the ledge larger so she could scoot away and his hip and shoulder would not graze hers like this, raising that horrible, wonderful friction.

"Right now I want only to sit with you in this perfect

night under this glorious sky. It has been a lifetime since I have shared such peace with a friend." He angled back a little, relaxing against the hay. She could not see his face now, but she felt his warmth a mere two hand spans away from her back.

"When I was in the Baltic, I would sit under skies like this, knowing the same moon and stars shone above England. There was both comfort and pain in the notion."

She could well imagine the loneliness he had endured there and empathy twisted her heart. "Does it work the other way too? Both comforting and painful to know that this sky looks down on those people?"

"A little."

She had surmised as much. "They enslaved you."

She felt the slightest pull on her scalp. He had found one of her errant strands of hair falling down from under her veil and must be touching it. She could not feel his fingers, but their casual movements prickled up to her head, causing tiny shivers to echo through the skin there.

"Aye, and it makes no sense. It is a strange thing, what happens to one in that situation. The first year my whole being was full of hate and anger and scorn. I planned escape after escape in my mind at night. I saw only their barbarism and all of the differences from us. But one can live like that only so long. In time, the strange becomes familiar. Life finds a pattern. I never surrendered to the slavery, but I could not remain separate and angry for six years. The similarities started becoming apparent. We have our barons, they have their *bajorai*. We have our priests, they have their *kunigai*. We burn our heretics, they burn their sacrifices."

"We have one God, and they worship many."

"Their gods and our saints have much in common. The distinction we make is lost on them."

"And on you? That is heresy, Addis."

"I merely came to see it how they saw it. Oddly enough, it is coming home that has made me understand them more clearly. I find that I walk through the land of my birth much as I did at first through that land, like a stranger encountering odd things. Customs and ideas that I took for granted I suddenly see afresh."

He still absently fingered the hair. Her neck had become alive from the emanating sensations. His pulse had met hers now, as if their blood beat in time together and the whole night joined in. The intangible connection was more dangerous than a caress and its compelling power mesmerized her. "And you, Moira. What of your life during those years?"

"My life? What a question! No adventure there. I lived a typical life, not at all notable."

"Raymond said that you married a gentry knight."

Still that gentle play. Her shoulders quivered from the subtle contact. She felt an appalling urge to circle her head and purr like a cat. "You knew him. Sir Ralf, who had a minor holding from Bernard. Bernard arranged it so I would be cared for. He even gave me a dowry. Bernard got it back, of course, in return for my swearing away the widow's dower. It was only right to handle it thus, since Ralf died at the wedding banquet, so it had not been a true marriage."

"Did Bernard also give you to the second man?"

"Nay. That was after he died. Raymond was lord then, and . . . well, I decided it was best to leave Hawkesford, although Raymond permitted both my mother and myself to stay. Edith was sick already, and my own place there had become awkward. James was a wool merchant from Salisbury. He would come after the sheep were shorn every year. He seemed a decent man, and demanded no dowry, although he knew about Edith's house and field and expected it to come to him through me. He had a grown son, so the contract left little for me if he died and I was childless. Still, with no dowry . . ."

"Raymond said that you were not married long before he also died."

"Aye. He fell ill a month later and died soon after. I tried to mourn him and felt guilty that I could not, but he had been much a stranger still. And if my motives had been practical, his had been more so. I think that he had calculated that the cost of keeping a wife was cheaper than the hiring of a servant and the buying of whores. But for the fact I wanted children, I might have found a way for him to continue doing the latter."

"Did he hurt you?"

"Nay. He bored me. What a terrible thing to say of the dead, but it was true. He sought to be a very pious man. He would pray all evening and then come into bed determined not to succumb to the sins of the flesh but his piety sometimes failed him. Sharing his bed was not loathsome, just . . . tedious." Why was she telling him this? Now she was the one being tedious. And yet, somehow, in this night with the rhythm of the whole world tying them together, it seemed natural to speak of it.

"I put up with it because I was his wife and because I wanted children. Not because of the security their birth would bring me when he died. I wanted a family. And my own home, I liked having that too. Simple things really, what every woman has. There was little affection between us in so short a time, but I was contented. I should like to know that contentment again."

So here she was after all, broaching those arguments that would underpin her denial of their passion, and he had led her down the path to do it. It came out easily though, a confidence between friends.

"Caring for Brian made you delay that."

"Aye, but I do not regret it. I do not resent one whit

those four years. But now it is time to make a life for myself."

She expected a retreat from him with this more blatant implication, but instead his hand wound more obviously in the long strand of hair.

"With a freemason."

"Or another such man. A good man, who will be a good husband and father and make a home with me. Such a man will not have me if I have been bedding another."

It had to be said and faced, but she felt something in the aura behind her change in response to the bluntness of it. A small flaring of power that made his presence surge and surround her, shuddering with . . . what? Protection? Possession? Anger? She did not understand it, but it felt as if he had thrown an invisible cloak over her. Within that cocoon their mutual rhythm continued, but his beat pounded steadily stronger, taking control, timing the pulse and demanding that hers conform. The sudden shift astonished her and she sought in vain the strength to cast off his effect.

"Not all men are so pious as James," he said as if nothing had changed.

Why did it sadden her to explain it? She hesitated, reveling for one hungry moment in the way their spirits adhered to each other. "Nay, but all men are proud. They do not want wives whom others whisper about. Do not want a woman who has been the lord's whore. Whoever he is will probably ask about you just as James asked about Raymond. I want to be able to answer truthfully next time as I did with him."

He straightened and sat flush beside her. The movement startled her and she almost jumped away from the warm body looming tall beside her now.

"And what did you say to James when he asked?" His tone sounded light and curious, but something else was happening below the banter of this conversation and her body and soul knew it. Wariness swelled, commanding her to get away. Her feet dangled just inches from the ground, and it would be an easy thing to hop down and run. Run to where though? That invisible cloak seemed to swaddle her tighter, holding her in place beside him. She couldn't move. She could barely find her voice, let alone respond in her own casual tone.

"I said that I had never been in Raymond's bed."

"That sounds very imprecise. An intelligent man will spot the other possibilities. Considering the time we will have spent together, you will have to be more blunt with your mason."

She felt her color rise. "I will say . . . Addis de Valence was never my lover."

He laughed softly. "Still a bit vague, Moira, and in part a bit untrue. Nay, you will have to make it very clear. You could say, for example, that my lord has never had me."

That laugh heartened and reassured her a little. Perhaps her caution had gotten the better of her. "Or get most precise yet. Swear that I have never fornicated with you."

"That should do it."

She laughed herself. "You are a kind man, Addis. To understand and even to jest about this."

He did not respond. She turned her head to find him looking at her. Despite the dim moonlight she read, nay she felt, his expression, and her heart turned over with an alarming jolt.

"Is that what you think this has been, Moira? A jest?" His arm slipped up her back and eased her toward him. "Nay, lovely lady. It has been a negotiation."

His lips took hers before she could marshal any resistance. Gentle but firm, that first kiss spoke a determination that said nothing less than a pummeling struggle would stop him. Weak objections briefly drifted through her mind before she succumbed to the sweet beauty of it. That invisible cloak wrapped them both now, so comforting in its warmth and protection. The delicious connection overwhelmed her, and the careful explanations just articulated disappeared along with all of her thoughts, carried away by the night breeze.

His tongue entered her, probing, savoring, controlling. He dominated that pulse, drawing hers into his. Flushes of heat cascaded through her, burning away any remnants of denial and resolve. She embraced him, anxious for the feel of his solidity, and he pressed her closer until her breasts crushed his chest with tantalizing contact. The speed with which her passion vanquished her solid sense frightened even as it exhilarated. She lost control, helpless to the dangerous sensations and yearnings trembling through her body.

He ended the kiss and caressed her face, his fingers drifting behind her ears to the pins holding her wimple. He slid the cloth off and pressed his mouth to her neck before carefully going to work on her veil.

"You asked what I want with you, Moira," he said while he kissed and bit and licked her ear in ways that made her shake. "I want everything. I would know every inch of you, every part and thought. I want to take you every way a man can have a woman, and I will not pretend otherwise." His hand moved down her body with a firm caress that articulated his desire. "But I do not seek to seduce you to something against your will. I do not deny that I want you completely, but I will settle for less."

His bold words summoned shrill streaks of desire. She barely heard the offer of restraint as he submerged her in another kiss. Long. Absorbing. Demanding. His hand pressed her stomach as if it could feel the blood strumming there.

His arm encircled her neck, his hand slipping down to the lacing of her gown, meeting the other at the knot. He kissed her temple and hair while his fingers worked. She looked at the crossing strands being pulled through their holes, level by level, down past her breasts. The memory that she should not permit this flashed and she stiffened.

"Nay, Moira," he chided, gliding his fingers along her collarbone and down her chest. "I only take what you have already given to me."

His hand slid beneath the fabric to cover her breast and all of her senses reeled with the warm contact. Engrossing kisses and confident caresses methodically eroded her pitiful defenses. She tensed, struggling not to lose everything in the absorbing pleasure flooding her. His fingers began playing with her nipples in devastating ways. A throbbing hunger awoke between her thighs. A low moan escaped her and she lost her hold then and became cast adrift in rising swells of passion. Only Addis existed in this world of sensuality, his presence more real than her own, his strength a raft to which she tethered herself.

He slipped the garment down her shoulders, easing the shoulder bands of her shift along with it. He pushed the fabric down her arms to her elbows so that her breasts were exposed. The cool breeze tickled her skin like a teasing breath. The garment restricted her arms, binding them against her sides, leaving her to accept his kisses and caresses without a return embrace. His captivity of her body both aroused and frustrated.

He bent low, his body obscuring the night sky. His breath mixed with the cool breeze before his mouth warmed her breast. His arm supported her wanton arch of offering. Her whole body shuddered with indescribable cravings while he licked and kissed and drew on her.

No thought now. No yesterday or tomorrow. No sense

and no plans. Just sweet bonding and high-pitched pleasure and piercing, growing need.

He grazed her nipple with his teeth and her little groan melted with the sounds of the night. He took her in his mouth and sucked and her rapid, frantic breaths filled his ear like an audible voice counting the beat of his heart. The whole night joined in. The sounds of insects, the flow of air, the spirits of the rocks and trees acknowledged their primitive intimacy.

He moved them both, resting against the hay and lifting her onto his lap with her back against his chest so they could both watch the night sky and he could see her moonlit face. He took both her breasts in his hands and her lids lowered and lips parted. He teased at those dark tips and felt every movement of her body's response. The rhythmic pressure of her hips and buttocks. The sinuous stretching that asked for more. His joy in her pleasure astonished him. The comfort and peace of holding her awed him. The stars seemed to sparkle with the pattern of her sighs. Amidst them the half-moon glimmered. *Go find your own woman, Menulius. This one is wholly mine.*

Her rising passion produced little groans of need. Her legs had parted and he bent his knee so that she rode his thigh. The intimate pressure completely undid her. The garments still bound her but one hand flailed, seeking contact. She gripped his other thigh while her whole body pressed into his and a begging cry warbled low in her throat.

He wrapped his arms around her, holding her close with his lips pressed to her cheek and his crossed hands still arousing her breasts. Sanity debated with hunger. If he took her she would not deny him now. The soft trembles beneath his arms said that much. It had been his intention, even while he cajoled her with promises of restraint. Suddenly, however, he did not want to mar the perfection of sharing her passion. He needed her completely willing. He did not want to face her regrets afterward.

The stars and breeze swam around him. The spirits urged him to finish the rite of possession. His own body echoed the demand. Menulius gazed down, his vague shadows forming a mocking half smile.

He shifted and slid his arm under her legs. "I am taking you to bed now, Moira." He lifted her and carried her through the croft to the cottage, away from the spirits and elements telling him to use her.

Low lights, cool and warm from moon and hearth, filtered through the shadows. He laid her on the bed beneath the window and she appeared ethereal in that light. He sat beside her and kissed her while his hands went to work on her garments. A small sound of protest emerged while he pulled the gown down her legs. The smallest frown puckered her brow, as if the bed and undressing reminded her of her objections. He shamelessly caressed her back from the intruding denial, playing at the sensitive peaks of her breasts until she slid the straps of her shift from her arms so that she could embrace him.

The sensation of her hands on his shoulders and back immersed him in bliss. He rested his face against her breasts for a moment, reveling in the serenity she brought. Then he pushed the shift down, his kisses following the linen over stomach and hips and thighs. He paused there, inches from the scent of her arousal, and resolve wanted to crumble. Somehow he leashed the animal hunger and rose from the bed.

He gazed at her while he removed his belt and tunic. She looked so beautiful. Moonlight washed her pale form and reflected off the clarity of her eyes. Despite the shadows he saw confusion looking back at him. He pulled off his shirt and lay down beside her.

If she demanded it he would find contentment just sleeping with her in his arms. He would try to hold her to him with that intimacy alone, but he wanted more secure bonds. He had learned a thing or two during those years of competing with a god for Eufemia's passion. He knew something about the power of pleasure and how it worked on a woman's soul.

She embraced him, but he felt hesitancy in those arms. He caressed her length and wariness and embarrassment tinged her shudder and sigh. If he left the choice to her she might well sleep on straw in the croft. She did not know what she wanted and needed, did not comprehend what waited for them if only she accepted it. He made the decision for her with possessive finality. He would not take her, but he would have her.

He used his hands and mouth until she rocked against him, clutching his back, burying her cries in his shoulder. He took his time, enjoying endless kisses, riding the torturous pleasure with her. With searching hands he explored her body, here firm and taut, there soft and yielding. In her aching need her own hands moved, first shyly but then with more confidence. Her fluttering caresses burned into him and the heat of his blood rose to a blinding level.

He pressed her against his length and caressed to the top of her thighs. With his first touch she lost all control. Beautiful sounds of pleasure and need poured out of her until she spread her legs with abandon. She hung around his neck and clawed a hold on his shoulders when the convulsive end neared. A violent tremor quaked and a shocked cry erupted. She grasped him like a fearful child seeking shelter as the release shook her.

He held her huddled body and buried his face in her hair while her slowing breaths soothed his own painful need. She lay silently, nestled in his embrace, with the night air cooling their ardor.

"Why didn't you . . . ?" she finally mumbled against his chest.

"I said I would not."

She burrowed deeper, as if facing him would embarrass her. "At the end . . . why did you do that?"

"To show you that sharing my bed will not be . . . tedious. Didn't you like it?"

"Aye. Too much. But even so, I will not be sharing your bed, Addis."

"You are sharing it now."

She raised her head and looked around the cottage. "Not your bed. Not the lord's bed. Much more like my bed at Darwendon."

She looked so captivating with the moonlight making a little glow along her profile. If she wanted to believe that she could contain this within this cottage and this night, he would let her think so for now. "Aye, not the lord's bed. This night it is just Addis finding solace with Moira."

He sat and removed his leather hose and cast them aside. He stretched out wearing only his braes, letting the breeze cool his skin. Her warmth contrasted deliciously and he pulled her against his chest and legs, alert to every inch of connection. Her palm stroked his face, firmly caressing along the scar as if that thick ridge of damaged flesh did not exist. Shifting slightly, she embraced his shoulder with one arm. Instinctively, naturally, as if he had done so a hundred times before, he rested his head against her breast and an indescribable peace rinsed his soul.

He slept deeply, but she did not. She lay holding his body, looking over his shoulder out the window at the beautiful sky, thinking it was painfully sweet to be close to someone like this, if only for a short while.

Her fingers drifted over the muscles of his shoulders. A strange man and a stranger night. She doubted that this lovemaking had brought him much solace despite his last words, even if he slept like the dead now. She had given her whole life, and she recognized giving when she saw it.

Not selfless though. Nay, not without a charge. He probably already knew what she slowly accepted while she held him. A woman cannot do that with a man and remain aloof. She cannot sleep naked like this afterward, holding him all night, and pretend that nothing binds them in the morning. This strange lovemaking insinuated that he expected something far more dangerous than her services as his lehman. It would take all of her strength to refuse him now, whatever it was that he wanted from her.

The reasons for doing so seemed very distant. Common sense and carefully laid plans counted for little in this intimacy. Confused thoughts scrambled through the fitful sleep that finally claimed her.

Dawn's light woke her. She lay on her stomach under the wool blanket Addis must have thrown over them both. His arm was slung over her back. She opened her eyes to find him awake on his side, head propped on hand, watching her. His raven hair fell around his head in a thick cloud disheveled from sleep. The bronzed shoulders and chest lay a hand span from her nose. The gray light cast his face in severe planes, emphasizing the slash of mouth and the long ridge of scar, making him look stern. She remained motionless and her soul instantly understood his expression.

He rose up on his forearm and slid the blanket off her body revealing her full nakedness to the early light and his eyes. He bent kisses to her back, creating a thrilling trail of heat. He stroked down to her buttocks and his fingers grazed the cleft with startling intimacy. His eyes met hers. "I had six years to learn lessons in continence, but seeing you this morning destroys my resolve of last night. I am going to take you this time. If you want to deny me, you had better run away now."

Deny him? That would take a voice and hers had disappeared because her heart was in her throat. She would need a body that could move, and hers had become immobile with screaming anticipation. He did not wait long for her to decide. Turning her over, he moved on top of her, dominating her with warm strength and hard flesh.

No restraint this time. A different Addis with a different intention. Kisses and caresses that bespoke his need and prepared her to accommodate it. He led her up a rapid spiral into a primitive, hungry passion.

Drumming quietly echoed in her head. It took a while to realize that it was not the beating of her heart or the pulse of his power. It did not even emanate from within the cottage, but poured in the window above them. She tried to block it out, but it only grew louder.

"Hell," Addis muttered, looking over to the front of the cottage and the sounds of a small troop reining up in the lane.

The aura of bliss split as if someone had slashed it with a knife. The door burst open and a blond youth appeared in its light. "Aye, this be it!" he called, backing out with a laugh. "But we came too early. He still be topping a whore."

The men were in high spirits and ribald shouts of encouragement filled the air. Moira shut her eyes to the reality bouncing its sounds around the walls. This night of beauty was to be followed by a dawn of shame. Her good sense suddenly rose tall, stiff from its long subjugation to her impulses, and filled her with scolds. It really wasn't fair. She hadn't even done the crime but she would still pay the price.

She found some composure and raised her lids to find

Addis looking down at her, reading her embarrassment. He rested his palm on her cheek to soothe and reassure her.

"It seems Sir Richard did not come alone." He swung up and reached for leather.

She dressed quickly, pulling on shift and gown and hiding her disheveled hair beneath a veil. Away from his embrace and the bed, she experienced a growing awkwardness with him. The morning air began to dilute the scents of their intimacy. The rising sun burned away those sweet connections. She watched Addis don his garments and fasten the knight belt low on his waist, assuming again the lordly presence of yesterday. She glanced around the little cottage, foreign now in the light of day and looking starkly, relentlessly *real*.

He turned to the door but she hung back. He came over and held her head to a kiss. "You either walk out at my side as my woman or in my shadow as my slut, Moira. Let it be the first way. They will show you respect in order to honor me."

He took her hand and led her through the threshold. Sun gleamed off armor and weapons. Men and horses and wagons jammed the lane. A quick silence fell when they emerged. Seven pairs of eyes scanned down to where Addis still clasped her hand.

Sir Richard strode forward, flickering an apologetic glance to her. While he passed the men his hand swung out and without even looking he cracked the blond squire across the face so hard that the youth staggered. Not missing a step he advanced until he stood an arm's span away and beamed a teary smile up at Addis.

"Well, now, 'tis a glorious morning, 'tis it not, my lord."

Addis released her to accept the embrace of his father's

steward. She eased along the shadow of the house, away from the male drama.

Richard gestured to the others. "Alan and Marcus insisted on coming. And that there's Small John, Big John's son. As true as his father, I promise you. There are others, but we left them back there. Might be more useful inside, and I like the idea of that bastard worrying about whom he can trust." He walked to the carts. "Come see what we've brought you."

Moira realized that the rear one was hers. "Found some villagers bringing it here this morning," Richard explained with a point. "But look you here. Your father's armor and such. And some coin. Not much, since that whoreson found most of it despite my hiding it in ten different places. And we've Patrick's destriers down the lane a bit. Still the devils they ever were and just as hard to control. Ah, and there is this." He reached into the cart and pulled out a long, heavy weapon. "The family sword. I took it when your father died. Thought maybe Simon would try something, what with you dead and the boy just a babe. Figured he might take the land but I wouldn't let him have the rights."

Addis took the old Norman sword in his hands. His face was a severe mask of composure, but Richard was not so contained. He grasped the hilt below Addis's fingers. "We here never swore to him, not in our hearts. Only to the lord, and he was never that."

Addis hesitated. They all stood like a frozen image. He looked across the knights and squires, seeking until his eyes met hers. He glanced at the cottage, through its doorway into its dim depths, and then back at the sword pointing down at the ground. Resolve set his expression. Resolve, and maybe resignation. He lowered the weapon. Sir Richard followed, kneeling to swear his oath of fealty.

She slipped back into the cottage, blinking away stinging tears. Well, that was that. It had begun, and it would end with him dead or triumphant. She was glad that Sir Richard would be at his side. He appeared a man whom Addis could depend upon. He would need such a friend with him.

The sounds of other oaths drifted to her while she busied herself tidying up the cottage, trying to fill her sudden hollowness with practicalities. When she had finished she looked around the little space. A broken pitcher held some wilted flowers on the crude table, and she darted outside to pick some new ones without anyone noticing. She smoothed the coverlet over the bed, noticing the careful stitching of its piecework. Other details, like the carefully scrubbed floor and the neatly stacked crockery, absorbed her attention.

She had no trouble picturing the young couple who lived here. They loved each other. One could just sense it. Happy despite their poverty of goods. Secure in their hold of each other. It had been the ghost of that love that had unsettled her when she first entered last night.

She found her basket and thumbed a shilling out of the leather sack and slid it under the pillow. A body obscured the light from the door and she turned to see the blond squire standing there.

"My lady, my lord said to tell you that we are ready to leave."

She faced him, holding her basket against her stomach. He had addressed her the safest way, but he eyed her curiously, wondering just who and what she really was.

"I am not a lady," she corrected, reminding herself of the essential fact of her relationship to Addis. "My name is Moira Falkner, and my mother was serf born."

CHAPTER 8

THE ROAD BECAME CROWDED when they neared
London. Travelers moved in both directions, forcing their
retinue into a long line. Moira drove her cart at the
rear and Addis rode far in the front. She had planned
it that way.

The four-day journey had been a quiet hell presaging
her future as the lord's whore. Addis had made his interest
clear, and the knights and squires showed their respect for
him by ignoring her. They helped her in a formal,
guarded way, but no one spoke with her much. It struck
her as the way men had treated Edith when Bernard was
nearby, and reminded her of the very different way they
often treated her when he was not.

Sometimes she would find one of the knights looking at
her with an expression that indicated the respect for Addis
did not truly extend to her. It is so because he wants it thus,
those eyes would say, but you and I both know what you
really are. A woman like you could as easily be mine this
night as his, and when he tires of you it might yet be so.

Sir Richard demanded all of Addis's attention, but then in this troop of men she hardly expected him to bother much with her. They exchanged no more than a few words each day, and from early dawn until they made camp each evening nothing distracted her from thoughts that debated the alternatives awaiting her at the end of this journey.

If he had left her alone completely she might have felt calmer about what she had decided to do. But the second day she had woken to find him beside her in the cart where she slept, squeezed to her side under the blanket while he held her. Each night he came again to lie by her side. She had clung to him last night under the starless sky, wishing she could hold him forever but knowing in her heart that she could not. His world would never permit that, nor had he ever indicated that he even wished that it would.

It will be much worse later if I wait, she reminded herself firmly while she carefully drove her donkey amidst the other carts crowding her sides as the road widened.

The town walls could be seen now and she scanned their endless breadth with astonishment. London was huge. She had heard as much, but never expected anything like this. The town had outgrown its walls, and spread along her road in a collection of inns and houses of every size and description. Noises and smells increased with each step until all of her senses were assaulted by the density of people and activities. A massive, sculpted gate loomed at the end of the road.

Addis and Richard neared the gate and some guards emerged to meet them. The line of travelers began halting and bunching. A wagon pulled up alongside her and the old man driving it rolled his eyes at the jam developing. "Damn knights," he muttered.

"What is happening?"

"Don't like armed retinues coming in, even small ones. City is on the outs with the king, and doesn't want too many of his men inside at once. Just bide your time, woman. They'll move 'em out of the way soon."

The guards gestured Addis and Richard over to the wall of the fortifications. "Will they refuse them entry?" she asked as the crowd inched forward.

"Depends on who they be, don't it? Have to ask their questions first and such."

More guards had arrived. A general confusion cramped the road. Moira looked at Addis being peppered with inquiries. Blinding yearning swept her. Emotions she had harbored for half a lifetime almost made her turn her donkey. She locked her gaze on him and branded her mind with the sight, losing herself in anguished regret.

The jolt of her cart jerked her alert again. Travelers surrounded her, separating her from the squires, and the line began edging toward the gate.

She forced her eyes away from him and faced the square hole of freedom. His knights and squires pulled aside to join Addis and Richard. She stayed in the line and let the crowd move her on, away from him and the alluring, disastrous passion he offered.

The shadow of the gate fell across her and she faced a guard, but his attention found the little altercation alongside the wall more interesting than her. His arm swung out and she passed through the wall.

The incredible confusion on the other side stunned her and she almost turned her cart around and headed back to Addis. So many people and lanes and shops and animals. Screaming children and squealing pigs and barking dogs kept darting into her path. Colorful signs swung over her head and buildings loomed and jutted above them, some three or four levels high. Carts and stalls jumbled with foods from gardens and hearths, with craft work and leather, clogged the spots where the main road absorbed little side lanes.

She felt immediately lost and overwhelmed, and sighed with relief when she spied the tall spire rising above it all in the distance. In Salisbury the cathedral served as a general meetinghouse and marketplace, and she assumed it would be thus in London.

The street widened in front of the cathedral. The square was full of vendors and people of every degree doing trade or just passing time. She jumped down and led the donkey into the milieu. She skirted the edges, looking for a friendly face.

A fat woman selling baskets eyed her cart and frowned. "Not near me, you don't."

Moira examined the woman's simple but neatly woven wares. "Nay, I have not come to trade today."

The woman's curiosity got the better of her. She huffed around her own cart and peered into Moira's. "Fancy weaves. This one is interesting. Not exactly round, is it, but deliberately not." She lifted it out and turned it upside down. "How do you get the colors? The red and purple?"

"Berries. I make a tub of juice and water and soak the reeds."

"Ach! Well, no berries growing in London, that's for sure, or for miles around except on the king's hunting grounds probably. What there is gets picked and eaten. You'll be wanting a pretty sum for these. Have better luck over in Westminster where the court ladies walk about. They come here too sometimes, and there's merchants' wives who would pay your price, but these be ladies' baskets if you ask me."

Moira stored away the advice. Their common trade had formed a bridge and the woman seemed kind enough. "Can you tell me of an inn where I might find a chamber."

"There be inns aplenty in London, and across the bridge in Southwark. Depends on the kind you want. Some's for ladies and some's for pilgrims and some's in between."

"A clean place, where I can have my own chamber. Run by honest folk."

"Well, if you have the coin there is a small one run by Master Edmund's wife. He is a tanner, and the place smells a bit since his trade is there, but then all of the city smells, don't it? She is a God-fearing woman and runs a clean place. Usually gentry types stay there when they are in town, but you talk and walk like one so maybe they'll take you."

Moira asked for directions to Master Edmund's place. "You take care," the woman warned in parting. "Pretty thing like you in this city better watch your step. There's lots of wolves in this town glad to take a bite of country chicken."

Within an hour Moira had settled herself into the small, plain room leased to her by Goodwife Elsbeth. Her cart and its belongings were stored in a stable in back. Edmund had assured her they would be safe since the city quickly hanged any thieves, so few took up the vocation.

Sitting on her straw mattress, she collected her thoughts. She doubted that Addis would look for her, and if he did he would never find her in such a large town. It would not be necessary for her to hide, but perhaps for a day or two she should avoid the main streets and market-places just in case.

She tried not to picture his face when he realized she had run away. How would he react? With the anger he had promised? With surprise? With indifference? Perhaps the last. Barrowburgh would occupy him now, and in this city he should have no trouble finding a woman willing to share a knight's bed.

The city din breezed through her window and she pictured him all the same. Not angry or indifferent, but looking down at her, his eyes alight with warmth, turning his head to kiss her. An aching hollow emptied her. It had been a delicious dream, sharing his friendship, tasting that passion, touching that spirit. Had it been thus for him too? If so, would he understand that she rejected heaven in order to avoid hell? She doubted it. Men never understood the cost of these things to women, because no one ever asked them to pay the same price.

The emptiness filled with a wash of loneliness and fear. Her good sense had never made her this miserable before.

Elsbeth called up, inviting her to share some ale, and she went down to the kitchen, grateful for the distraction.

"You plan to live here then?" Elsbeth asked while she poured out the ale.

"Aye."

"You brought more coin than I saw, I hope. 'Tis a hard town for them's that's aliens, not citizens in the law, and doubly hard on a woman alone. No shop for you. If you mean to sell those baskets, it will be on the street."

"I have some more coin. Not much, but enough, I hope." The leather sack and ruby were stowed in her sewing basket in her cart. Safer there where Edmund could see who entered the stable than in her chamber. "This inn of yours is very attractive. What does such property cost in this town?"

Elsbeth settled on a stool. "You think to buy property? Your husband must have been good at his trade."

"James was a wool merchant in Salisbury."

"Wool merchant or no, I doubt he left you enough to buy a house like this. One hundred and fifty pounds this one cost. My man saved long for it, close to twenty years."

Moira thought the ruby was worth that much. She had always intended to use that jewel to help Brian establish himself. The plan had been a simple one. He would train to be a knight with Raymond, and she would provide the funds for his horse and armor when he earned his spurs. Now she would use the ruby to establish herself instead, and property made the most sense. A man would understand the value of an inn that earned income more readily than the vague worth of a small red stone.

"Now a craftsman's house in a north or east ward, maybe you could get one of those for fifty. We are near the Cheap and the river, which makes a difference. And if you want to lodge pilgrims, your best choice is to go across river to Southwark. That's where the pilgrims stop on their way to Canterbury."

"I knew a woman who came here a few years ago. She spoke of working in a pilgrim's tavern owned by her cousin. Would that also be across river?"

"Aye. The city discourages the pilgrims coming in. Too many of them. They mostly stay in Southwark."

She had intended to look for Alice after she settled herself, but if finding her might prove easy perhaps she would do that first. In the rare event Addis should find her it would be good to have Alice's testimony about Bernard's freedom. And although she and Alice had not been close friends, it would be reassuring to have a familiar person to turn to in this busy, strange town.

"You come looking for a husband?" Elsbeth asked bluntly. "If so, there's plenty of men looking for a wife. With enough coin or property, you could even get one with the city's freedom, a citizen. The going dowry is one hundred pounds with them, but you have a craft of your own and are pretty enough, so for you maybe it would be less."

"I am not looking for a husband." Her response surprised her. Of course she was. Quite specifically. Confiding as much would ensure a steady stream of eligible men to this house. The notion of facing that right now, the very insinuation of what marriage meant with that unknown man, vaguely repulsed her. She had always assumed that she could tolerate bedding her next husband just as she had tolerated James, but now . . . She would find Alice and then a property and make some more baskets. Later she would place herself on the marriage market. By then maybe Addis would be dead to her again.

She returned to her room, feeling tired but also reassured. Things should work out fine. She had managed in Salisbury, hadn't she? Not nearly so big, but a town was a town. She laid down to rest, sorting her plans for tomorrow. Images of Addis at the gate entered her head, and she wondered if he had even gained admittance to the city.

Southwark was no London. It possessed a transient, unstable mood, as if no one on the streets had been born there or planned to stay long. Haggard pilgrims swarmed amidst footloose squires and apprentices looking for strong drink. It did not take Moira long to guess the profession of the many women who strolled the lanes and sat at windows of certain houses.

Elsbeth had explained that Southwark was not part of London but a separate town, and one with loose laws and a bad reputation. She had advised Moira not to go at all and to guard her purse if she did. Thinking it could not be that bad, Moira had come anyway but brought only a few pence with her.

She had thought that she would find Alice in a snap. After all, how many taverns could she need to visit? Dozens, it turned out. She popped out of one late in the evening, thinking that she should have begun this search earlier in the day. She had waited until late afternoon in the hope that crossing paths with Addis or one of his men would be less likely then. But it had taken longer to reach Southwark than she expected, in part because she kept pausing to examine houses that might serve as likely inns. Now she hesitated in the street and noted dusk's arrival. She would have to come back tomorrow.

She walked back to the stone bridge and made the long crossing. Guards were closing the city gate just as she slipped through.

She retraced her way back to her inn, lost in her thoughts, following her route without much real awareness of anything more than the darkness and the silence. And so, when she turned a corner and stepped right into a pool of dazzling brightness, she gasped in surprise.

Three men carrying torches stood chatting by the side of the street. They heard her and turned.

"Well, now, what do we have here?" one of them said.

She tried to walk past but they blocked her path.

"Coming from a job then?"

"You be a long way from Cock Lane, girl," another said.

She glanced from face to face in confusion. They peered at her in the torchlight, looking very stern and official.

"Let me pass, please."

"Now, we can't do that. It's our job to patrol this ward and be sure the likes of you stay where the city has put you. When you came through the gates you knew the risk if you were found," the first one said.

"I just returned from Southwark. I live inside the gates."

"Do you now? The wardens will want to hear about that. Whores aren't allowed nowhere in the city but Cock Lane." He took her arm in a firm hold.

They thought that she was a . . . it was too ridiculous! She had seen enough whores this day to know she didn't even remotely resemble one. "My good men, you are quite mistaken. I am simply trying to get to back to my inn."

"Ooo! She's one of them fancy-talking ones who goes to the job instead of him going to her."

"Don't be absurd. Do I look like . . . like a . . ."

"In the dark all women look the same. You should know that."

This was taking a preposterous turn. "See here—" she began in annoyance.

"Nay, you see here," he said. "You are walking the streets alone after curfew against city law and in my experience there's only one reason a woman does that. It's Tun prison for you."

Prison! "This is outrageous."

The man who gripped her arm eyed her more closely. He hesitated, then shrugged. "Aye, well, you explain your story to the magistrate tomorrow. My job is to collect the nightwalkers and whores off the street and you be both as I see it. So, let's go. It's a bit of a ways to the Tun."

"You cannot be serious," she cried as he began dragging her away.

"Don't give me trouble now."

"Unhand me," she said lowly. "I will walk with you. Do not dare to touch me again."

The man looked back at his companions and laughed. "She's good. She's very good. Has that snooty tone down pat. I'll wager that this one's expensive."

Moira peered at the eyes glowing in the torchlight. They belonged to the head guard of Tun prison, the round fortress where London incarcerated those arrested for night crimes. The guard had taken one look at her and ordered her brought to this windowless chamber instead of a prison cell.

Grateful for his consideration, she accepted the ale he offered her and then poured out her explanation of why she had been walking the streets after the city curfew. "I told the night constable about Elsbeth and asked him to send for her," she concluded. "She knows that I am new to the city and its ways."

"He will tell her if he can find her. Doesn't mean she will come, does it? You have kin or such here? Anyone else who can pledge for you, or bring the coin so you can stand surety?"

She would rot in this place before she asked anyone to look for Addis. Besides, he might not even have been allowed through the gate.

The guard leaned against the wall behind his bench and patted his thick girth thoughtfully. "The thing is, and it is amazing I tell you, but none of the women brought here are really whores. Night after night the city makes the same mistake and rounds up some females and all of them, every one, have stories much like yours. It grieves me to see what is done to them on the morrow, the ones who can't get out during the night."

"What happens to them?"

"Well, if the magistrate doesn't believe them, and he almost never does for some reason, the woman is put in a cart and dragged through the streets for public mockery. All the way to Newgate, which is on the other side of town. The crowd can get a little rough, I tell you. Then she's left on Cock Lane outside the gate with the other bawds."

That didn't sound *too* bad. Not like a public flogging or being locked up in this damp, stinking place for months.

" 'Tis worse than one would think, being humiliated

like that. Branded a whore forever, she is. The whole city has seen her face. And there's records kept too. The city likes to keep records on everything. 'Tis a long way to Newgate, and the men sometimes get lewd on the way, especially the young ones, though the women ain't much better to my eye. And she can't return to the city. If a woman is found more than once plying the profession here, the next time her head is shaved before she is carted." His bright eyes appraised her. "We guards here hate to see it. We do what we can for the poor things."

Moira recognized the opening ploy for a bribe when she heard it. "You said that some women get out during the night. How is that permitted?"

He flickered an appreciative glance. "Sometimes someone comes and makes a pledge and offers to pay a fine. The way we see it, it saves the city a lot of expense and trouble that way."

"What is the fine?" She had all of three pence.

"For you, I'd say it would be about two shillings."

Two shillings!

"You look to be an expensive sort. You tell me your man's name, and I'll send word to him. He'll pay it. 'Tis his job to do so. No point in sharing with a man if he doesn't come up with the coin when this happens."

He hadn't believed a word she had told him. The door to the chamber was closed but the acrid smells of the prison managed to permeate the walls. Nausea churned her stomach and helplessness overwhelmed her. "I have no man. I am not a whore," she said, burying her face in her hands.

She waited with resignation for him to call the other guards and have her taken away. Somehow she would get through this night and tomorrow.

"Well, now," the guard said in a smooth tone that caressed the silence. "If you've no coin and won't send for your man, there's another way. You've a lady's way about you, and a body most men only touch in their dreams. Might be worth two shillings at that."

Her empty stomach heaved with disgust. She forced down the bile before she raised her head. "Nay."

Two sparks of lust flickered in the torchlight. If this man decided to force her she would have no escape. Collecting herself, she faced him down with one of Claire's noble gazes. Absorbing that manner had served her well over the years with men of every degree, but she worried that if this one dreamt of bedding a lady it might only prove provocative.

Anger and insult flared but soon subsided. He stood and took her arm and dragged her to the door. "Have it your way, woman. We'll see how proud you still are when you get to Cock Lane."

CHAPTER 9

ELSBETH CAME THE NEXT morning but with one glance Moira worried it had been a mistake to ask for her. The tanner's wife bore a hard expression that spoke her embarrassment at being summoned to a whore's trial.

No hallmote would judge her and the others waiting for swift justice. Only two bored magistrates who looked as if they had heard every story before waited to decide her fate.

They barely glanced at her and considering her condition she was just as glad. A night in Tun prison had reduced her to a snarl-haired, half-broken, stinking image of the basest type of person. The prison held one large cavern for all the women, with no benches or stools to sit on, just foul straw on a filthy floor. During the night, one by one, the real whores had disappeared when their men paid their bribes. By morning only she and one other woman remained.

They let her plead her case but no one asked any questions. She finished her tale and it even sounded thin to her. She hopefully identified Elsbeth as someone who could pledge that she spoke the truth. The magistrates called the goodwife forward.

"It is as she told me," Elsbeth conceded.

"Do you have any independent knowledge that it is true?"

"Sounded true enough at the time. An odd manner, I thought. Too refined for her degree. Alone, that was sure. Asked me how to get to Southwark. Said she knew a woman who had gone there a few years ago."

One magistrate pursed his lips and glanced knowingly at the other.

"Asked about buying a house in the city," Elsbeth continued helpfully. "One with chambers enough to serve like an inn."

"Indeed," the magistrate mused sourly.

Moira groaned at the conclusions these men were drawing. Better if the goodwife had stayed at home.

Elsbeth recognized the interest her revelations engendered. She warmed to the attention. "Said she wasn't looking for no husband. *Very* sure about that."

Moira got the impression that that fact, more than any other, sealed her fate. She listened to the punishment meted out, so tired that she almost didn't care.

They brought her to a chamber until the rest of the cases were heard. At midday a guard took her and the real whore out into the yard where two carts waited. A group of men carrying timbres and pennants and drums collected near the wall.

The gate stood open and people drifted in to watch the preparations. While a crowd gathered someone draped a smelly yellow-and-white-striped robe over her shoulders and placed an unlit candle in her hand before pushing her up into the cart.

A sea of attentive faces assaulted her. Unfriendly

expressions of scorn and mocking interest examined her. Hooded eyes glowed with self-righteousness and lascivious speculation.

An unfamiliar horror woke her numb spirit. This was going to be much worse than she had imagined. They were all strangers, but by the time it ended, the humiliation might prove devastating. A public flogging might be preferred.

She tried to steel herself but the sleepless night had left her with little strength. The pointing fingers and knowing nods of the crowd seemed closer. The cart had not moved but already she felt something inside her crumbling.

"You should have told me it only took some coin to assure your compliance, Moira. I could have been using you for weeks now and I did not even realize it."

Addis. She swung around and her heart jumped with relief and then thudded with fear when she saw his expression. Her throat tightened in response to the fury leashed beside her.

She suspected that his mood had little to do with finding her like this and everything to do with her running away in the first place. Her depleted spirit could not bear this now.

"Will you enjoy watching the woman who refused to be your whore displayed as one to the world? I have had all night to contemplate the jest and it ceased to amuse me many hours ago."

"Your memory fails you. I never offered you a whore's price. And you refused me nothing."

"Go away, Addis."

He grasped her chin. "Right now it is unwise to speak with disrespect to your lord, woman."

She needed no reminders of the trouble she faced with him. It leaked out of his body and shot from his eyes. She turned to see the whore ready in the cart behind her. A guard sidled up and gathered the reins of her donkey, preparing to lead the little pageant of shame. The mummers with their timbres and pennants took up positions.

Addis strode forward and his hand landed on the guard's shoulder. The man cringed when the strong fingers crushed his flesh. "Go and get the magistrate," Addis ordered.

The guard hustled off. Addis returned to her. "Did you really think to hide from me in this town?"

"It is a very big town."

"Not big enough. Nor will it be the next time if you think to try again." The crowd had begun making protests about the delay. "Perhaps I should give you to them, Moira. I tire of your rebellion. Perhaps this day I should let you taste the freedom you insist is your due. It will be easier than convincing the magistrate that an error was made."

"Could you do that?"

"Give you to them?"

"Convince the magistrate."

"Noble blood counts for something even in this city." He tilted her chin up with one finger so she looked at him. "You will have to behave like the bondwoman I tell him you are though. And you must swear that you will not run away again."

The mummers swung pennants and tapped timbres to appease the crowd. Through the gates Moira saw bodies lining the street, leaving only a narrow path for the carts. Some guards parted the mob to permit the passage of one very annoyed magistrate.

"Swear it," Addis ordered.

"I will not run away again. I swear it," she whispered.

The magistrate huffed up alongside the cart. "What is this? I am told a knight demanded I come. What is your interest in the whore?"

"I am Addis de Valence, Lord of Barrowburgh and kinsman of the late Earl of Pembroke. This woman belongs to me. She is serf born, and bonded to my land at Darwendon."

"Then you can have her after the city is done with her."

"Does the city punish innocent women just to entertain its people? She arrived here yesterday in my company and became separated when we were delayed at the gate. She is no whore, but only a country woman ignorant of city ways."

The magistrate sneered. "Separated, eh? Run off, more likely, and looking to find a bed the easiest way women know how." He turned to her. "What say you, woman? You did not speak of this before, even to be spared punishment. This cart may not look so bad if you ran away and he takes you now."

The people nearby had quieted while they strained to hear the conversation at the cart. If she were not so dirty and tired and numb she might have refused this public declaration, but in her current condition the protection Addis offered carried a wretched appeal. "He is my lord," she whispered, her throat burning with suppressed tears.

The magistrate pulled the robe from her shoulders. "Then show these people that he is so I don't have a riot on my hands because they think we let some knight buy a whore's freedom."

It took a moment to understand what he meant. Too spent to care overmuch, just desperate to be done with all of this, she dropped the candle, climbed out of the cart, and walked around to Addis. Blocking out the staring eyes and refusing to look at Addis himself, she knelt in front of him.

"Take her, and be sure she behaves while she is within these walls," the magistrate said, scowling. Addis hauled her to her feet. Sir Richard appeared out of nowhere to take her other arm. The two of them dragged her through the crowd.

Some in the mob were not to be denied their sport. Shouts of "whore" and "harlot" rang out, and other voices urged Addis to punish her with a rod or strap. Ripe fruits flew and one landed with a squashing thump on her back. Only after they got through the gate did the mob forget her, and then only because the other cart began to roll.

They pulled her to a side lane where two horses waited. Addis grabbed her waist and threw her up on the saddle and then swung up behind. Richard mounted the other horse but turned to ride in a different direction.

They began trotting through back lanes.

"How did you find me?"

"I talked with basket sellers at the markets." His cold tone made her cringe. The Lord of Barrowburgh would not quickly forget the trouble she had caused and the insult she had given him. Certainly not before they arrived at his house. "I assumed that your wares would have been noticed by them, and I found a woman who had spoken with you yesterday. She sent me to the house of Master Edmund, and he told me where his wife had gone this morning."

That simple. Stupid of her to think that she could disappear even in a town of this size. "My cart is still with Edmund and his wife," she said, suddenly worried about her belongings and especially the sewing basket. The biggest danger of being carted to Cock Lane hit her. If she could never reenter the city, she would have lost everything, including the ruby.

"When Richard returns I will send him for it. The city would allow only the two of us in. The others stayed across the river last night and he must see to their board."

He rode through the low gate of a long two-leveled house and into a small yard. Stables flanked the paved court on the right and a long hall faced it on the left. The overgrown mess of a neglected garden rose up in the back, surrounded by the remains of a stone wall.

She twisted to look back at the block of the house facing the lane. Of good size, with at least five or six chambers, she judged. Her first reaction was that after some desperately needed repair it would make a fine inn.

Addis pulled her off the horse and dragged her by the hand into the hall. She tripped after him while he strode to its end and barged through a door. He swung her forward and she stumbled into the kitchen. An old skinny woman stirring a pot in the large hearth rose in surprise at their abrupt entrance.

"Give her a bath, then send her up to me. Burn the gown," he ordered.

And then he was gone, his retreating boot steps echoing through the hall.

The old woman wrinkled her nose. "Where'd he find you?"

"Tun prison."

"Ach, that explains it. You smell like a devil's fart."

"Since I spent the night in hell, I am not surprised."

"Made a lot of trouble you did, Moira Falkner. My man is still out searching the city for you." She thrust a thumb toward the door. "*He* be ready to kill you, I think. Brave of you to cross a man like him." Stupid of you is more like it, her expression said.

"Who are you?"

"I'm Jane, my man's name is Henry. We were his mother's people. Stayed here after Sir Patrick died, though everyone else left. Not of Barrowburgh bond, but of her family's lands, and besides, we'd been here long enough for the freedom." She bent her stiff body for some buckets. "Come and get some water with me for this bath. Won't help you much if we keep him waiting on you all afternoon."

Moira took several buckets and followed Jane through a side door that gave way into the garden. A well stood a few feet away and they filled their buckets and returned. Together they rolled the big wooden tub away from the wall, toward the hearth. Jane set her buckets to heat by the low flame while Moira emptied hers into the tub. She made several more trips for water, then waited with Jane for the water to warm.

"How have you lived?" she asked Jane.

"Was a bit of coin hidden and we found it. That lasted a while. Mostly we've been selling pieces of furniture. 'Twas some nice chairs in the hall with backs and they brought good coin. Lived off each one for four months. Didn't want to strip the place, but we had to eat. Sold things what wouldn't be missed much. No shame in sitting on benches even in the best halls. I kept telling Henry, What's the point? The house had been forgotten. He wouldn't hear me. Insisted on doing his best to keep it up, but he's old and so the wall's half down and the stable needs a roof and . . . well, you'll see soon enough what's what." She glanced in the direction of the house. "*He* ain't noticed yet. Showed up in a black mood 'cause they wouldn't let his men in but mostly 'cause you'd been lost. Worried at first, then angry in a cold way when he decided you'd run off. You be in for it, Moira Falkner. 'Tis a rash thing you've done."

Moira grimaced agreement and tested the water in the buckets. She poured them into the tub and began stripping off her garments, glad to be rid of their filth and stench.

Jane appraised her body while Moira climbed into the tub. "Well, with that loose robe gone it makes more sense, don't it? Wondered why he had brought a bondwoman all the way from Darwendon, Henry and I did. Curious that he stopped everything to find you, we were."

Moira sank low in the tepid water. "Do you have any soap?"

"A bit. You'll be wanting to wash that hair. Looks like a rat's nest. We'll get you clean and pretty again and maybe it won't go too badly for you."

Moira did not want to contemplate what awaited with Addis nor how badly it might go. Maybe very badly, but she felt little fear. The only emotions her battered spirit could muster were an edgy resentment and sad resignation. She had publicly declared him as her lord and sworn not to run away, and had thus accepted the shackles that she had vowed never to wear again. She had entered Tun prison still secure in who Moira Falkner really was, but had left with that identity repudiated. He had exploited her weakness and vulnerability to make her do that, and it said a lot, too much, about what existed between them and what did not.

Living in Claire's shadow had given her ample opportunity to observe how men like Addis treated women for whom they held affection, and how they treated all the rest who merely caught their eye, highborn or base, wives or villeins. Affection tempered a knight's inclination to dominate and possess, to subjugate and vanquish. She almost hoped that he would beat her as the mob had urged. It would put that night firmly behind them. Maybe it would force her to hate him a little. She was counting on his helping her to do that and from his mood she suspected that he would not disappoint her. The only question was the means by which he planned to demonstrate her submission.

She scrubbed her hair and ducked under the water to

rinse. Her head emerged just as Jane gathered up the gown and shift from the floor and tossed them into the hearth.

"Nay!"

"He said to burn them."

"They are all I have until someone gets my cart."

"I'll get you a blanket. Bit warm for it today, but better than those. Not fit for a beggar, they ain't."

"Could you lend me a gown, just for today? I am larger but if it is loose, at least . . ."

Jane turned with hands on hips. "Look you here. You may disobey and run away, but that's between you and him. I ain't seen that man since he was a boy but I know something of lords and that ain't one to cross. Where would Henry and me go if he got angry and turned us out? If he says burn the clothes I burn them. Unless he says to give you one of my gowns, I don't do it. Only have three and as I see it one of two things is going to happen when you go up those stairs. He's going to beat you or force you and either way any gown won't come out in one piece."

She could do without old Jane so bluntly laying out the options that she herself had refused to face. Perhaps it need not come to that. Surely she had not completely misjudged him when she saw a kinder side.

Jane brought over some ale and bread. "You eat something. Will make you feel better."

The food revived her a little. "Tell you what," Jane soothed while she handed her an old linen towel. "There's some strawberries out in the garden that I found yesterday. You come here after and we'll have some. I've some salves too if you need them. You dry yourself now and I'll use my comb on that hair."

She sat on a stool and stared at the charred remains of

her gown while Jane worked the comb. It had been over an hour since she arrived but she doubted that Addis had forgotten about her.

Jane fetched a blanket from the house. Moira wrapped herself in it. The billowing wool reassured her a little, and the bath and food had returned some strength. Deciding that she could not avoid this confrontation any longer, she followed Jane's directions through the hall and up to the solar.

He was not there. She sighed a prayer of thanks. Deciding that she would wait a few minutes just so that she could honestly claim later that she had, she stepped inside.

The solar was really more of a large bedchamber. At least one chair had not been sold by Jane and Henry, and it faced a table near the window overlooking the street. A curtained bed and some stools and chests made up the other furnishings.

She slipped over to the window and gazed down at the city. She wished that she were back at Darwendon where people knew her. London was too big, too busy, too cruel. But she was stuck here now, cut off from every life she had ever known. She had sworn not to run away.

If she gave the ruby to Addis and bought her freedom at the high price he had set, would he agree that ended the oath she had made? Free women do not run away, they just leave. What then? Free in this city with no property and little coin, how would she live? How could she get back to Darwendon alone, and if she did, what kind of life awaited her there? Darwendon had been a place to protect Brian and plan the future. Could she live in that cottage forever, without the hope that the red jewel had always provided?

He would not insist on keeping her forever. With only two old retainers in this house, he needed her now, but that would end one day. Perhaps in time . . .

A sound broke through her thoughts. She swung her head and then jumped back with a start when she saw him standing on the threshold. She moved from the window into the wall's shadow, as if she could disappear as she had done so often in her life.

"You do not have to be afraid," he said.

Aye, I do, she thought desperately. For she had seen the expression on his face while he watched her, and had known in that instant that if she was not very careful she might never be free again.

CHAPTER 10

"YOU DO NOT HAVE TO be afraid," he said, but she did not believe him. She had caught him watching her, and had seen the emotions that the relief of having her back could not completely appease. She pulled the blanket closer and hugged the wall. He smelled her fear and it sickened him to admit that she did not worry without reason.

He had spent the last hour trying to purge the dangerous tumult that wanted to control him. A day and night of worrying about her safety and seething over her flight, of facing the ghosts of this house without the anchor of her peace, had almost made him a madman. In the darkest hours his resentment that she had abandoned him had revived the scathing memory of another abandonment by another woman. Finding her at the Tun had incited him anew with the evidence that she had chosen to face the city's scorn rather than call for his help.

Not trusting himself near her, he had left her in the kitchen and strode out into the city, hoping to walk off the worst of it. His pacing had brought him into a little square faced by the parish church. It was an ancient building with thick walls. He had entered the deserted cool nave barely lit by a few splotches of light falling through the high small windows.

It smelled of the incense and rituals of his youth, pageants of faith and reconciliation in those days. Desperate for a breeze of grace to calm his turmoil, he walked to the altar and waited.

What had he expected? Light to break through the stone and a ghostly hand to reach into his heart? The vision of the church's saint telling him that all would be well? He did not know, but he had counted on leaving that shadowy space less disrupted than when he entered. It did not happen that way. He stood there hungering for the old reassurances. Instead he only experienced that eerie sensation of being a man out of place and time, now visiting the temple of a foreign cult.

He had returned to the kitchen and listened through its closed door to the sounds of water splashing. He pictured the lush body hunched in the tub, sleek with water, clear eyes turning to his approach. And then other images showing acts of love and punishment, of tender pleasure and harsh profanity, crashed through his mind. He had almost entered and thrown Jane out so as to assert his possession and demand her submission as his blood raged to do.

Instead he had forced himself from the door and walked outside to where the garden once spread in neat beds and pruned orchards. In its current condition one could imagine it was a field far from this city. Weeds reached his thighs while he strode to the back, as far from her as possible. The sounds of town life dulled here, and the buzz of bees and scratching of rodents could be heard. He lay down in some grass and wildflowers and looked up as he had done on days during his enslavement when he sought to pretend that he was home.

The sky god Perkunas's endless domain had stretched cloudless like a serene lake, a cool eternity that could absorb any earthly strife. Slowly, imperceptibly, like so many inaudible murmurs, the spirits of the garden began their rhythmic chorus. Not dead or silenced in this land after all, as he had learned that night in the hay mound. Just so restrained that only a soul open to them would ever feel their presence. Their whispers soothed him, like old friends accepting his fury without argument and thus gently defusing it.

Not an abandonment, he had finally acknowledged. Not like Claire. This one owed him nothing except a serf's obligations which she had never even accepted as his due. A quiet voice carried in the breeze said to let her go, that he could bind her no more than garden walls could hold these spirits, but the last hours had proven that he could not do that now. His physical hunger might be relieved by some other woman, but his soul would find solace with no one else. Recognizing the weakness of his need alarmed him. He had survived six years of enslavement because he had learned to need no one and nothing, and now that he was free and restored to his homeland, unexpected chains weighed him more surely than any slave bonds had done.

He had finally climbed the steps to this solar, following the wet footprints that marked her recent passing. The hunger and rage still trembled but its roar was low and contained now. He had found her standing near the window, limned by soft light while she watched the city street, draped like a mendicant in her brown blanket. He had watched her while she contemplated her private thoughts, realizing that he did not know what to say to her. And then she had turned suddenly and caught his naked gaze and seen more than he would have liked.

She looked so beautiful and vulnerable there with damp waves cascading to her hips. She clasped the blanket together above her chest and only a small triangle of skin showed at the bottom of her neck. Bare feet and ankles poked out below the flowing folds. He had never noticed before how lovely her feet were. Slender and delicate like her hands. Her clear blue eyes watched him cautiously from the shadows.

Part of him still wanted to vent his outrage that she had insulted and betrayed him. Another part wanted to ask how she could have left him bereft of her comfort and peace. But the man who had been a slave knew the answer to that already, not that he would ever admit the dependency that the question revealed. The resurrected Lord of Barrowburgh might be furious, and the knight adrift in his homeland might be injured, but the slave of the *kunigas* understood her far too well. She had seen her chance for freedom and had taken it.

She moved one step forward, a brave woman prepared for the worst. "Let us be done with this, my lord."

"Be done with what?"

"Whatever your reason for demanding my presence here. If you intend to punish me, let us be done with it."

"I said that you do not have to fear me. I never thought to punish you," he lied.

"Nay? Then you perhaps want to command me in my service to you. I can see that this house needs work as you thought it might. It will take time, but with Jane and Henry's help I will get it in order so that it befits you. Do not trouble yourself that I might not understand my duties. I know my place."

"It is good that one of us does. Is that why you think I have you here? To punish or to command?"

"I pray so."

"You pray in vain."

Dismay broke her composure. She licked her lips and lowered her eyes. "Aye. I feared as much. I beg you then not to misuse me, my lord," she said softly.

Her sudden fragility and deference wrenched something inside him. Her plea had been an old one spoken since time began by the weak to the powerful, but hearing it from this proud woman tore at him. "What makes you fear that I plan to, Moira? I have not done so before."

She passed a hand over her eyes, as if her vulnerability embarrassed her. "Perhaps it is because I stand here naked but for this blanket, at your insistence. Jane would not loan me one of her gowns after she burned my clothes."

He had been so absorbed in just looking at her that he had not realized that she was naked, nor wondered why she had wrapped herself in a blanket on a summer day. "I will have your cart gotten soon. Are there garments in it?"

"There is a gown. Between today and that day when those men . . . my others have been ruined, but I have a little coin and will buy some cloth."

With the cost of cloth, it would take whatever she had to buy some. He walked to the chests along the wall and opened one. "Come here."

She hesitated, then emerged from the shadows and obeyed.

"This chest holds some of my mother's things. Take what you need. Take it all."

She knelt beside him. She curiously lifted the edges of folded cloth, then bent and began methodically stacking the garments aside, examining them one by one. The movement caused the wool to creep down her shoulder, exposing the top of her creamy back an inch from his knee.

"It is all too fine. Silks and such."

I would see you in silks and jewels every day. "Better they are worn than that they rot."

"They will not rot if cared for. When you marry, your lady will be glad to have them." She began putting them back in order. She still clasped the blanket with one hand, but the other arm moved back and forth, causing a gap to form. Little flashes of breasts and thighs fluttered beneath the moving edges of wool, inflaming him.

"If I marry I will have the wealth of Barrowburgh with which to buy more. Take them. I do not have coin to waste purchasing simpler things if we can use what we already have."

She knelt back with a linen robe in her hand, considering it. The loosened blanket fell back off her shoulders. Skin and chestnut hair hovered beside his thigh, mesmerizing him. He lightly stroked the bare shoulder with his fingertips.

"I do not think to punish or command or misuse you, Moira. I would have you at my side by day and in my arms at night."

She stiffened, then rose quickly and faced him, casting the robe aside. "Better to punish, my lord. The strap's sting ends."

"You speak coldly for one who was so recently an affectionate lover. Has one day of freedom changed your heart so much?"

"Nay, because in my heart I was always free. 'Tis a few hours of bondage that have chilled me."

His hand still rested on her shoulder. He drew her forward. "Then let me warm you."

Something at his core groaned with relief when his arms closed around her. Her feminine softness seemed to absorb the worst of the sharp emotions that had been driving him this day. He splayed his hands over the hills of her curves and tasted the fresh cleanliness of her pure shoulder.

She *was* chilled, whether from the bath or exhaustion

she could not say. The strength and warmth of his arms promised an enticing comfort. She tried to squirm in resistance against the sudden embrace, but somehow the movement transformed into a pliant molding against his chest.

Lips brushed her hair and temple and cheek with careful gentleness, as if he sought to prove that the danger she had glimpsed did not really exist in him. A soulful yearning cried inside her when he pulled her closer. Firm palms caressed her bare back and found her skin through the gap in front while he pressed kisses to her neck and finally her mouth.

She let him, reveling in a glorious, final taste of what could never be. She let the sensations cascade through her body, evoking the bittersweet longing one feels at any parting.

"I have spent the hours since I rode through that gate to find you gone asking if I had misunderstood somehow," he muttered into her hair.

She closed her eyes to savor the strokes of his hand raising wonderful heat on her thighs and buttocks, sorry that he had spoken so soon. "You misunderstood nothing, but I want us to stop this," she whispered, blinking back tears.

He pulled away to look at her, but he did not release her. "Can you say that these hands misuse you, Moira, and that you are not willing?"

She sorrowfully extricated herself from his hold and stepped back. She hitched the blanket back on her shoulders and grasped it closed. "I am weak to the pleasure, but what you offer me will someday bring misery and I will not endure it. I swore when just a girl that I would not be any man's whore, least of all one to a knight or lord."

Gold fires flamed. Dangerous fires, that spoke of more

than thwarted desire. "You say that often, and insult me with it. 'Tis you who misunderstand, and who think the worst of me without cause. Those garments are not meant as a bribe to buy a bedmate for a few nights. I do not seek to make a whore of you."

She had suspected as much when she saw him at the doorway. Better if he did only want her for brief pleasure. "What you call it will not matter. All others know such women for what they are."

He paced away, his face set in stern planes of confused annoyance. He shot her a glare over his shoulder that flashed with those emotions she had glimpsed when he entered. "What of Edith? She lived with her lord in affection. All could see what was between them. Is that how you knew your mother? As Bernard's whore?"

"It is how *you* knew her, do not deny it. What you and all the others called her, if not to her face then among yourselves. My mother knew more than affection, she knew love with Bernard. She was his lehman but she had more than most wives do of her man's heart. She had it the best that such a woman can ever have, but still she was shamed."

"None will shame you if they want to keep their tongues."

"They need never say a word for me to know their minds. Please listen to me and hear what I say and try to understand. You cannot even give me what Bernard gave my mother. Bernard had his son and was growing old. He had done his duty to his family and honor and chose not to remarry. He could treat my mother as his lady because no real lady presided at Hawkesford. It will not be thus for you and you know it. The Lord of Barrowburgh is no Lord of Hawkesford, but the king's man with a position of superior prestige and no serf-born woman can sit at your high table. And you are still young. If not for more sons then for the alliance that will secure your hold on your honor you will marry again, Addis."

He could not refute the truth of it and she was grateful that he did not try.

"She will accept it. She will have to."

"*I* will not accept it. I will not be the woman kept in the south tower, waiting for the lord to steal time from his family and duties to lie with me. I will not be the lehman whose children are bastards, desperate for the lord's recognition."

"Can you doubt that I would care for any child of my blood?"

"I will not be the bondwoman fretting while she ages that the lord's eye will be caught by a younger woman, or growing jealous of the affection that he shows toward his wife."

"I too will be aging, Moira."

His insistence threatened to erode her resolve. "I will not be denied a home of my own, a place in which I know love and security. I have lived on the margins of other people's lives too long, Addis. I will not knowingly choose to do so again, not even if that life is yours and not even for the passion you can make me feel. I am tired of being the shadow."

He walked to the window and gazed out, crossing his arms over his chest. When he finally turned back to her she looked in those deep eyes and knew that he understood, but that it counted for little in whatever compelled him.

"Do you expect me to accept this, Moira? To forget the peace and contentment that I find with you in my arms? To ignore the hunger I have had since I first saw you in that cottage?"

"If you cannot accept it then let me leave! Send me

back to Darwendon at least. Release me for good and forget about me! Some other will give you that contentment soon enough."

"You go nowhere but with me!"

"Then what, my lord? You put us into an impossible position. Or will you force me and thus corrupt the affection that we have shared?"

He did not offer the reassurance she desperately hoped for. He only looked at her so long that she began to feel naked despite the blanket. Her arguments suddenly seemed meaningless as that gaze grew invasive in the old way, summoning memories old and new, demanding that she remember their intimacy and passion, raising images and sensations that her tired spirit tried to reject with little success.

She was waging a battle that a part of her did not really want to win. Her body responded to that probing connection with a flush of warmth and anticipation that both frightened and seduced. Her fortitude began crumbling. Yearning filled her reckless heart.

"I do not think it will come to force," he said, as if he had seen into her mind and assessed the weak forces commanded by her good sense. He held out his hand. "Lie with me now, Moira. You will see that all will be well."

The order jolted her with shock and something terribly like excitement. She looked away from the strong hand reaching for her. "Nay."

"Remove the blanket and come lie with me. I would see you and take you in the full light of day."

Saints help her, she almost released her hold on the wool. "I will not invite what I have just rejected."

"Should I command you as your lord so that you can blame your compliance on obedience instead of desire?"

A little flare of resentment reinflamed her prudence. "I am grateful to you for reminding me of who we both are, my lord. As I once said, I forget it at my peril. The free woman foolishly succumbed, but the bondwoman will not."

"They are the same person."

"Nay, they are not to my eyes. I do not deny that I felt the sweetest pleasure with you. But the heaven that you offer is a form of hell, especially with such chains attached. You have bound me to you with an oath and submission that I cannot undo, but it will not be as you think. Unless you force me, it will not be so."

She really thought that he was going to come and test the truth of her brave words. Tension shrieked between them and her body responded in a shocking way that said the future was out of her hands because if he crossed that space there would be little forcing to it.

He turned away and she almost collapsed with relief. "Then let us both pray that I learned continence in the Baltic as well as I thought, Moira. Take some garments and leave now."

She heard a warning in his order and did not wait for another. Plucking the linen robe from the chest, she hurried from the chamber. The last vestige of strength deserted her on the steps. She clutched the wall, struggling to choke down the sob strangling her throat.

She did not see much of Addis the next few days. He left the house early with Sir Richard to ride to Westminster in daily missions to see the king. Sometimes they did not even return for the midday meal, and she and Jane and Henry would take their dinner alone at a table in the cavernous hall while they rested from the day's chores.

They worked sunrise to dusk. Jane and she scrubbed all the chambers and laid down new rushes. She and Henry managed to mend the holes in the stable's roof and patch and whitewash the plaster on the buildings, but the stone wall and hearth needed a craftsman's hand. She decided to delay asking Addis for the coin since his time at Westminster usually left him angry and silent. He did not speak of those visits with anyone except Sir Richard, but she knew from his mood that they were not going well.

The house had four chambers besides the solar. For her own space she took a tiny one on the first level, far from where Addis slept. Sir Richard had retrieved her cart and she set the few belongings along the walls. Her labors exhausted her sufficiently that sleep claimed her instantly when she retired. She was grateful for that. It would have been horrible to lie there thinking about the man above debating his options regarding Barrowburgh and Simon and all the rest.

A week after their arrival he returned from Westminster in time for dinner. He entered the kitchen with Richard, looking for some ale.

"He avoids it, I say," Richard remarked, continuing a conversation as if she were not present.

"Perhaps. Or he has never been told."

"Do you believe that? You go and wait every day for a week and the man does not even know you are there? You are not some bachelor knight whom his clerks can ignore."

"The Despensers and their people are thick around him, like circles of walls guarding a keep. I think that none enter the gates unless that family permits it. If Hugh Despenser is Simon's friend I may rot sitting in that anteroom."

Richard shook his head. "Fine thing we have in this realm, if the son of Patrick de Valence . . ."

"It is because I am the son that I will rot. Who knows what stories Hugh poured in Edward's ears when he arranged for Simon to get Barrowburgh? Who knows if

Edward is even aware it has happened? It is said he has no love for governance, that he prefers tilling soil like a yeoman and rowing on the fens to attending to state."

"Fine thing we have in this realm . . ." Richard muttered again with disgust.

"I will have to find another way to meet with him, that is all."

"Impossible if those gates are manned as you say."

"I must find a way for the king to order them opened."

"You could petition when the next parliament meets."

"I will not wait on a parliament. I will know where Edward stands before then."

Moira and Jane hustled to lay down the meal in the hall. Addis and Richard sat with them, continuing their conversation at one end of the table. Moira munched her bread and salmon stew and examined the luminous walls of the chamber. She and Henry had finished painting it this morning and it gleamed fresh and clean. She doubted that Addis had noticed the changes in the property.

"There is a tournament seven days hence," Addis mused.

"Edward seeks to appease the barons with sport and a large purse. Stupid, if you ask me. A chance for like-minded men to meet."

"But under his eye and with the Despensers' spies everywhere. Not so stupid maybe."

"Think you of entering?"

"I have already done so."

"Will be good sport, but all for naught if you don't win. You'll just be one of a score of combatants then. Even if you are the champion, there's no saying it will get Edward's attention. He does not care much for weaponry, and will pay little mind even if he is present. Once the pageantry is over he will most likely nap."

"If the king enjoys pageantry, then perhaps one should try and get his attention during the pageant," Moira interjected.

"Oh, aye," Richard mocked. "There will be riches aplenty displayed, girl. A royal tournament is not some country melee. The knights bring their finest garments and gold-painted armor and long retinues of squires and grooms. The Pope himself would get lost in such a fete, and Addis has not even a squire to lead his destrier."

"Then perhaps one should not compete with such richness," she said. "Perhaps simplicity is the way to stand out. Or novelty."

"You suggest that if I ride in that pageant dressed like a simple knight the king will notice? I think not," Addis said.

"Not as a simple knight. As a Baltic crusader."

Addis looked quizzically across at Richard. The old steward shrugged. "Could work, couldn't it? Men always talk of joining the crusade but never do. There is prestige and glory in it, and stories of adventure to be told. Edward may be intrigued."

"The question is, how do I show that I am such a man?"

Moira learned the answer the next day when Addis sent Henry to fetch her to the solar. She found him standing near the bed, wearing the buckskin garments that he had not put on since Barrowburgh. Colorful cloth was strewn around the chamber. She recognized the silks and wools from his mother's chest.

He lifted a red surcotte. "You have not used them as I told you."

"I took some of the simpler things. One does not clean stables wearing velvet."

His jaw twitched. "You should not be cleaning stables."

"If not me, who? Henry is too old to do it all himself. Please, my lord, enough of this. Serfs work, it is why lords have us. Now, is there some way that I can serve you?"

The red silk flowed from his fist. "I do not need you to serve me, but to help me. You suggested that novelty might gain the king's attention. When I attend the tournament, I will be very novel indeed. A knight dressed like a barbarian should at least raise some talk and speculation."

"You will go thus?"

"Aye. Richard has honored me by offering to carry my weapons, but I need someone to lead my horse." He raised in question the scarred eyebrow.

"Will ladies be doing so for the others?"

"Not this time. More novelty."

"I am no lady and all will know it. I will look a fool, as will you."

"You will look beautiful, and when we are done you will look exotic as well. It will be a spectacle that the king cannot ignore." He thrust out the silk. "Put this on, Moira."

She took the garment and held it up. She had no intention of changing her clothes in front of him. " 'Tis not a gown, but only a surcotte."

"Aye. No sleeves. The daughters of the *bajorai* dress thus in warm months." He looked at her thoughtfully. "Your hair unbound, I think. You will cut some of the amber from this tunic to make a headdress to hang across your forehead."

She would appear more barbaric than he. Most likely she would look like a war prize brought home by the conquering crusader.

"Will you do it?"

When she proposed the idea she never thought to be asked to play a part in it. Still, it might work and get him an audience with the king. Until that happened things were at a stalemate, for Addis would never move independently until he knew for certain that Edward had abandoned his family.

"I will do it."

He stepped forward and slid the gold armlets off, then took her hands and pushed one, then the other, far up her arms. "You will wear these as well."

She gazed down at the thick bands etched with intertwining serpents. Pagan images on barbaric gold. Their worth would support her longer than the ruby if she disappeared during the tournament. It disturbed her to realize that he believed her sworn oath enough to trust her with them. "They are beautiful. Where did you get them?"

"The daughter of a priest gave them to me."

Not a Christian priest if he had a daughter. He had said he was enslaved by a *kunigas*. That man's daughter then.

"She helped me to escape," he added.

The meaning of the gold bands seemed very clear. "She must have loved you very much."

"The daughter of a *kunigas* cannot love a Christian slave."

She lifted the silk surcotte from his hands. He stripped off his tunic so that she could take it to cut the amber. He looked very primitive suddenly with the buckskin sheathing his legs and his bronze chest bared. The long scar marked him like a painted line worn to increase his fierce appearance.

The priest's daughter had seen him thus every day. Had they been lovers? He spoke of continence learned in the Baltic, not abstinence. She felt a peculiar jealousy toward that unknown woman, but also deep gratitude that he had not been completely alone during those long years.

Memories of their reunion and journey, of that day

near the lake when she last saw him thus, invaded her. The flat muscles of his chest, the sinewy strength of his arms, the cords of his abdomen . . . she realized that she was looking at him too long, and that he had noticed. A warmth glimmered in his eyes, inviting her, nay, daring her, to reach out and touch the body a hand span away.

"I will try to look as barbaric as possible," she muttered, turning away from him and temptation. So easy to misunderstand the meaning of passion. A woman's soul yearned to do so. Men had probably exploited that since time began.

He was right. The daughter of a *kunigas* cannot love a Christian slave. And the son of an English baron cannot love a serf.

CHAPTER 11

ADDIS DUCKED THROUGH the threshold of the tavern and surveyed the throng of pilgrims. Ale had been flowing for several hours this hot evening. The crowd of petitioners heading to the tomb of St. Thomas at Canterbury had long ago drowned the restraints of their disparate degrees and collected into a noisy, high-spirited party.

He walked over to the keg. The man guarding it thrust a crockery cup into his hands. "Two pence."

Addis paid. "I am looking for a woman. I was told that she lives and works here. Her name is Alice. I wish to speak with her. It is worth her time."

"She be in back, through that door there, washing."

He carried his ale to the back chamber. A stout woman bent over a tub of murky water, swishing cups and mugs. Heavy dark brows bridged a prominent nose. Wisps of black hair escaped her kerchief. It had taken Richard almost a week to track her down amidst the taverns of Southwark.

She straightened and turned and peered at him. He moved closer to one of the candles lighting the chamber. Shock widened her eyes.

She crossed herself three times in a row. "Holy Mother!"

"I am not a ghost, Alice."

"Holy Mother!"

"I wish some time with you."

She backed away. "I have been here the year and a day!"

"I do not seek to return you to Hawkesford, but if I did you could have lived here ten years and it would not matter once you were back there." He let the threat sink in, then set a silver mark down on a table next to the candle.

"I don't do that anymore. I have a man now, and he wouldn't like it. There's women out in the tavern though. . . ."

"I only wish to talk."

She made a face indicating that sounded most peculiar to her. Addis settled himself on a stool and after a cautious hesitation she took another one.

"You left Hawkesford after Claire died?"

"Seemed as good a time as any. My cousin had gone some years before and I knew he was here. Raymond is not a bad lord, but with Claire gone I wouldn't be serving a lady anymore, just be one of the regular women again, so I left."

"You were present at Bernard's death?"

"Aye. Claire had gone home to see him before he passed. I traveled with her from Barrowburgh."

"And what did he say while he lay dying? About Edith?"

" 'Twas tragic to see their love and sorrow. I was pulled in to witness his words to her. Gave her and her people the freedom. About time, what with him setting her above everyone like a lady when we all knew she was no different than the rest of us. Should have done it years before if he meant to. What good was the freedom then, with herself sick already and not long for the world?"

"Was a priest present?"

"Aye. And we all made our marks on some parchment."

"You are very sure that he included Edith's people? Her daughter?"

She nodded. "Spoke of Moira like his own. Wanted her free. Makes sense. She hadn't lived like us for some years, had she? Hard to go back to that once you know better. I certainly couldn't, for all the work here."

He thumbed in his purse and slipped a shilling next to the mark. "You are very sure that he included the daughter?"

Alice looked up in surprise.

Another shilling topped the other. "Positive? You could swear it?"

She licked her lips. "It was some years ago. Whether I could swear it . . ."

A third shilling joined the stack.

"Seems that wasn't so clear, now that I recall. Spoke of it, but it wasn't on that parchment, I don't believe."

Addis nodded. She slid out a plump hand to scoop up the coins.

He grabbed her wrist before she got them. "I think that you should join the pilgrims traveling to Canterbury."

"Make a pilgrimage! There's too much to be done here. I might be gone a month, walking all the way down to the shrine and back."

"Think of the benefit to your soul. There is coin enough there to pay someone to help your cousin while you are gone."

She considered that. "Aye, well, I've always wanted to make the pilgrimage, if truth be told. One hears of such wonders from the others. It is said the cathedral is like heaven itself."

Addis added another shilling to the pile. "Perhaps you will say a prayer for me at the shrine of St. Thomas."

"Certainly, my lord." She glanced to the coins. "Will that be all? I've these cups to wash and . . ."

He pushed the candle closer to her. Not a clever woman, and too frightened to lie effectively. "Nay, that is not all. I want you to tell me about Claire's time at Barrowburgh after I left. I want to hear about Brian's birth and my father's death."

The thick brows shot up into half circles. She met his gaze warily. "Not much to tell."

"All the same, I will hear it."

"Better to let the dead lie in peace."

"Start with the boy. Did she show affection to him while she lived?"

Her eyes narrowed to slits. "As much as could be expected. He was conceived in violence, wasn't he?"

He heard the condemnation that even her fear could not hide. "Is that what she said? If my wife confided that to you, perhaps we need to start earlier. I would hear what Claire told you. I would learn all of it."

Addis stared at the stack of coins on the solar's table. He had found them beneath a stone in the hearth, in the hiding place his mother had once shown him as a boy. Joan and Henry had missed this little cache.

Thirty pounds. It would not go far in hiring an army.

His thoughts drifted back to the coins left in the tavern with Alice. A high price to pay for a woman he could not bed. The mark alone would have hired a knight for a month. Well worth it though, if it got Alice out of Southwark for a month or so. He should feel guilty about bribing away Moira's pledge about Bernard, but his need for her would not let him. The story did not release her of her obligations to Darwendon for the reasons he had explained at the hallmotte, but he did not want to tangle over legalities with her now.

Alice had not wanted to speak of Claire. She might easily betray Moira, the bondwoman who had been raised above her natural place, but she had not wanted to discuss her lady. Nor had he wanted to hear it. He had only suffered it because he needed to know now. He had already surmised much of the story and little that he had heard this evening had surprised him. He should have felt more sympathy when Alice described Claire's loneliness and isolation, but a part of him had been glad to hear that the woman who had let him face hell on his own had seen something of it herself.

He let himself picture her for the first time in years and the memory of her beauty almost seduced him into understanding. A woman whose appearance could devastate the strong had little need of internal strength. The Claires of the world took without asking because everyone insisted on providing whatever they wanted. Small wonder that she had no practice in giving, and had been incapable of it even under the demands of duty.

The memories created a bitter taste in his mouth. He turned back to the coins and his calculations of how many men they would hire and for how long. Selling the gold armlets would make a considerable difference, but if the king failed him and he had to lay siege to Barrowburgh he would need war machines and a large force and possibly many months. Even so, his chances of success were slim, and any victory might be short-lived if Simon procured aid from the Despensers.

A woman's sharp scream suddenly shattered his contemplation. He listened alertly but heard nothing more. It had sounded like Moira. He was out of the chamber and down the stairs even before he had decided to move.

In the torchlight of the courtyard he saw her by the gate. She twisted in an unnatural way and it took a moment to realize that a man held her body, with his hand over her mouth. Addis strode toward them, reaching instinctively for his absent sword.

"Unhand her," he ordered.

The man looked up from where he had been speaking in her ear. He wore long dark hair tied back at his nape and the plain garments of a London townsman.

"I could not risk her slamming the gate," the man explained. "My apologies for frightening you, madam, but tonight's business will not wait for morning."

"Release her," Addis warned again, tightening his fist in case the man refused.

A bright smile beamed. "Pity to have to. She is a nice armful at that. You will not scream again, will you, madam?"

She shook her head and the man stepped away. "You are Sir Addis? I must ask you to wait here a short while. I need to get the others."

The man slipped back out through the gate. Several minutes later he returned leading five men. One dressed in clerical garb led the others. "Addis de Valence?"

"I am."

"My name is Michael. I am clerk to John Stratford, Bishop of Winchester. Myself and the others would like to speak with you. I apologize for the hour but it is essential that none other knows that I am in London."

"Let us go into the hall. Moira, have Jane pour some ale for these men."

"She has retired. I will do it."

Addis brought the men into the hall. They settled themselves around a table. "I would know your names," he said. "If you seek me out at night I assume that your reasons are not friendly to the king."

Michael nodded. "You are an intelligent man, Sir Addis. It is a relief to deal with one for a change. Nay, our errand is not friendly to the king but it is most friendly to the realm. There is no harm in your knowing our names, but I must ask you to swear to speak to no one about this meeting and what we discuss here."

If they wanted an oath it would be treason that they discussed. He should send them off at once, but his days of waiting for the king's attention had not left him in a very loyal mood. He swore as they wanted.

Michael pointed around the table. "This is Sir Robert, Lord of Cavenleigh in Yorkshire. Thomas Wake, son by marriage to Thomas of Lancaster. Peter Comyn, cousin of Elizabeth Comyn, who is one of Lancaster's heirs. Sir Matthew Warewell, once of the king's royal household."

Addis noticed that the man who had held Moira was not introduced, and sat a little aside as if he were not truly a part of the group. When Moira arrived with the ale he got up to help her. The cleric's servant, he guessed.

"There are many others," Michael said. "You are not alone in your dissatisfaction with events in this realm. Robert here was forced to sign a note pledging that he owed Hugh Despenser twenty thousand pounds in order to keep his land. Peter's cousin was imprisoned until she made over a similar obligation and relinquished two estates. Sir Matthew's brother was executed even though he played no part in the rebellion. Unfortunately his lands adjoined those of a Despenser favorite. The king's men flout all sense of law and custom and know no shame. It will be the same for you."

"Perhaps. I have not spoken with the king yet."

"You have tried for several days. We know of your efforts. It will come to naught. Look at what happened to your kinsman Aymer. The Earl of Pembroke spoke for compromise and tried to influence the king to the right path. He became an inconvenience and was murdered while he sat on a privy."

"I am aware of all that you describe. I have not sat in the king's anteroom and walked through this city with my ears covered. I also know that it is not just the barons who are disgusted, but the town burghers and the common people as well. No one is pleased with Edward's choice of friends and the influence that they wield over him. If you have come to tell me about my country and warn me about these men, do not concern yourself."

Michael spread his hands. "I can see that you are a man who likes to get to the point. Let it be so. I am just come from Hainault, where the bishop is in exile with Queen Isabelle. He is there like the bishops of Hereford and Norwich because his life was endangered when he was made bishop over the king's choice, and because he spoke for decent governance to men who do not know the meaning of the word."

Addis had learned all about the exiled bishops. Stratford was an ambitious man, but he was known for good counsel. He had tried to support the king until circumstances and conscience demanded that he speak out.

"The queen has betrothed her son, Prince Edward, to Philippa of Hainault, the daughter of the count. In return the count has promised aid to Isabelle. She has said that she and the boy will not return here while the Despensers are in power. We got rid of them once, but when the rebellion failed the king brought them back and their influence is greater than ever. The return of the queen and the prince cannot be effected until the Despensers are removed again, but a parliament will not achieve it this time."

Now they were getting down to it. Five pairs of eyes searched to see his reaction to this overture.

The long-haired man still sat aside, drinking his ale. Moira entered from the kitchen and set some fruit on the table, then disappeared back through the door. The disturbance at the gate must have pulled her from her room while she prepared to retire because her hair was unbound and uncovered. She wore one of his mother's linen robes, a simple green one that scooped at the neck and stretched across her breasts before flowing freely. The servant's quiet examination was not missing any of it.

"I trust that you are not going to ask me to kill Hugh Despenser," Addis said, trying to ignore the attention Moira was provoking. "It would be almost impossible, and solve nothing."

"Nay," Sir Matthew blustered. "If any kill him, it will be me, and Lancaster's brother, Henry, will hone the ax."

"We only ask if you are with us should other steps be taken," Michael said.

"That depends on the steps."

"Isabelle is raising an army. The Count of Hainault is aiding her. Some time soon she will be ready."

"You speak of an invasion? It had better be the largest army known to man."

"Perhaps not. Edward has lost the confidence of the barons and the townsmen. It is a small group who still are loyal to him. If the country welcomes Isabelle . . ."

"Do you think that Edward will not fight?"

"There is no standing army. He will not have time to call a levy, and if he does few will come."

"You speak of deposing a king."

"We speak of setting aside an incompetent, corrupt ruler, and placing his rightful heir in his place."

"Let us consider frankly what that means. The prince is underage. If a way is found to depose the king and crown his son, there must be a regent. It is said that Isabelle has openly taken Roger Mortimer as her lover. Even when I was a youth he was known as a grasping, ambitious man. If he is regent, or she, we could have another Hugh Despenser."

"It will be a council, not one man, who advises the young king. Any power Mortimer accrues will be short-lived. The prince is fifteen," Thomas Wake said.

"It is a rash thing that you propose."

"It has been done before. There is precedent. Did not his own father set aside a king of Scotland?" Thomas asked.

Addis considered the audacious plan. If the people supported it, it could work. If it failed, everyone who touched it would be cut into pieces and hanged from crossroad gibbets. They had all better be reading the mood of the country correctly.

"We came for a reason," Michael said. "You are not known as one of us, and we will see that you never are. We have need of someone who can move about without being followed. In two weeks Isabelle will send word saying where and when she will land. The messenger needs to be met on the coast and the instructions brought back here. We thought that you might do that."

"Why me?"

"It will be a man from Hainault. A merchant. He will not know any of us. Your scar . . . it cannot be faked. If I say only speak with you, he will know if it is the right man."

So someone had finally found a use for his badge of identity.

They did not press him for a decision. The conversation shifted to more descriptions of the Despensers' excesses and to stories of families destroyed by their greed and injustice. All the while Addis contemplated their request. His father would not have approved. Patrick had believed in diplomacy and took his oath of fealty to heart. But Addis had never sworn to Edward, and would not do so unless Barrowburgh was returned to him.

Moira arrived with some bread and cheese. The long-haired man observed her subtly as she bent to place it on the table. Addis shot the man a warning glance which he did not see as he angled to watch her walk back across the hall.

"Will you do it?" Thomas Wake asked.

"I will consider it."

"When will you know? Michael must leave in three days."

He would give Edward whatever time was left. "I will let you know before then."

Michael looked dissatisfied with that. Out of the corner of his eye, Addis saw the nameless man rise casually and meander away toward the kitchen.

"Who is he?" he asked Thomas Wake, gesturing to the now empty stool.

"His name is Rhys. A London citizen. He knows the lanes well and moves us about at night. The mayor is with us, but we do not know all the constables and he can get us here and there without torches and such."

"He has proven helpful in other ways," Sir Peter added. "He works at Westminster and he has a way of hearing things while going about his craft. There are those who don't notice servants and such and things get said. He heard the king himself swear to kill Isabelle when first he sees her again. Carries a knife in his boot just for that."

Addis twisted a look at the closed door where Rhys had gamely pursued Moira. "He is a craftsman?"

"He works on the fabric of the new chambers at Westminster. Serves the master builder and does the window tracery."

Serves the master builder. Carves the window tracery. Addis twisted and glared at the door again.

Damn. The man was a freemason.

Moira contemplated half of a meat pie left from supper, wondering if there was some way to cut it into seven pieces without having the offering look too poor. It was embarrassing to have knights and barons arrive at the house and have nothing with which to show hospitality.

"Is your well water good?" a voice asked. "I have had enough ale for the day."

She looked up into the blue eyes and friendly smile of the man who had barged through the gate. She bent for a bucket. "Aye, it is good. I will get some for you."

He took the bucket from her hands with a questioning look. She pointed to the door leading to the garden and returned to her deliberation of the pie.

"You are a kind mistress to let your servant sleep and do her work for her," he said when he returned. On his own he found a crockery cup and dipped out the water.

"You misunderstand. I too am a servant."

He propped himself on a stool, as if he planned to stay awhile. He examined her with curious eyes and she wondered how she could ever explain the peculiar, confused life that had brought her here as a bondwoman but also given her the manner that made him think her mistress of the house.

"My name is Rhys. What is yours?"

"Moira."

"You are new to London."

"Is it so obvious?"

"I live in this ward. I have not seen you before."

"I go out to market, little else. I do not like your city much, Master Rhys." She had no idea if he was a master, but counted on his correcting her if he was not. He looked old enough for it, close to thirty years old.

"It is big and noisy, but full of interesting things. With time maybe it will not frighten you and you can enjoy its pleasures."

"I do not think that I will have time for that. It is only me and two old servants here, and there is much work to do." She considered the pie, and then the nice man keeping her company. "Would you like some? There is not enough for everyone."

"Thank you."

She cut a large slice and handed it to him. "You could have just asked entry tonight. You did not have to push your way in."

"I did not want to be seen at the gate overlong. I am sure that Sir Addis will explain to you later that this visit never happened and that those men were never here." He smiled charmingly. A nice-looking man, she decided, with shoulders and a chest that spoke of physical labor. While he held her she had felt the strength in him. Not a merchant then.

"This house had been all but empty for several years," he said, glancing around. "There have been those in the ward who sought to buy it, but the old man here said it couldn't be sold."

"It was neglected. Addis was gone on the Baltic crusade, you see, and then . . ." She halted and flushed. Rhys had blinked a subtle acknowledgment that she had not referred to Addis as "my lord" or "Sir Addis," but in a familiar way. "I have known him since I was a little girl," she added too quickly.

He rose and came over to her. "Can I have more of the pie? It is very good."

She gave him another slice, grateful that he had cut off the prattling, confused excuses and explanation that had wanted to tumble out of her mouth.

"If you live in this ward, you must know the tradesmen here," she said, moving to a stool near his.

"Almost all of them."

"Then perhaps you can advise me. The stones in the wall and hearth need work, and the stable requires a whole new roof. Can you give me some names of men who would do this for us?"

"Wood is expensive. Probably better to secure the frame and then thatch the roof. I know some boys who will do it for you. As for the wall, it will take a mason. That is my craft, as it happens."

A mason. "If you move with such men as are in the hall, you must be very established. Such simple work as this . . ."

"I am established enough, and employed right now at Westminster. But in the evening I have some time before it turns dark. I will come tomorrow and see what needs to be done." He swallowed the last of the pie. "If Sir Addis only has you and two old servants, he must be short of coin. But a house such as this should not be left in ruin. Tell him that I will do it for supper. Someone here is a good cook."

"And your wife is not? She will not appreciate your staying away because our meat pies are better."

He smiled and brushed his hands, then rose. A nice-looking, soft-spoken man. "I have no wife, and I tire of eating in taverns. I will come tomorrow."

He began to leave but Addis entered first. He appraised Rhys and the mason returned his own measuring examination. A strange silence pulsed that made Moira feel a little ridiculous.

"They are ready to go," Addis said.

Rhys moved to the door, then hesitated at the threshold. "Sir Addis, a small retinue arrived this day at Westminster. White and scarlet banner, with a gold falcon. I was told it was led by one Simon of Barrowburgh."

"How large a retinue?"

"Only four knights that I saw. No doubt they came for the tournament."

"No doubt. Did one of the knights have red hair?"

"Like flames."

"I thank you for telling me this."

Rhys shrugged, flashed a warm smile at Moira, and walked out with Addis in his wake.

Addis saw his visitors off and then returned to the kitchen. Moira was wiping the cups and pretended not to notice him.

"Does he know who you are?" he finally asked.

"He asked my name and he knows that I am a servant here."

"Does he know that you are mine?"

She carried the cups over to the wall shelf. "He will fix the wall and hearth and asks only supper in return."

"Very generous for a freemason who already assists master builders."

"Aye, it is generous."

"You will tell him that I do not need his services."

She faced him across the kitchen, her back against the wall. "You do need his services. The stones are half down and anyone can enter. If those men came to discuss what I think they did, you may well need a strong high wall around this property. If Simon followed you here, you most certainly do. I can clean stables and patch plaster, but I cannot mortar stone."

Three strides brought him over to her. "You will tell him who you are."

She glared a challenge up at him. "I will tell him that I am a bondwoman, if that is what you mean. He already thinks so anyway, since I am not of London."

He pressed a hand against the wall near her head and hovered closer, his face a hand span from hers. Something flickered in her eyes. Alertness to their proximity. Fear of it. After seeing her smiling at that mason he didn't give a damn.

"You will tell him that you are *mine*."

"I will not. It is not so."

"It *is* so." His other hand braced the wall so that he entrapped her. No part of their bodies touched but her warmth easily filled the tiny space between them, alerting his skin, summoning responses that he barely kept in check even without this closeness.

He looked down at her, forcing her gaze to meet his. The interest shown by the mason had provoked a primitive possessiveness and he let her see it. She returned his stare belligerently, as if she dared him to try and make her submit. It inflamed his body and blood with a furious desire and he held on to his control by only a single, thin thread.

Her expression changed, softening. A vague tremor wobbled through her. She suddenly looked fragile and vulnerable. He sensed her own arousal, and her fear of it. It only made him want her more.

"Do you think that I will stand aside and let some man woo you?"

"You speak nonsense. He only wanted some water."

"He watched your every move. He has already found a way to come back."

"Even if you are correct, you have no right to interfere."

"I have every right."

"You do not!"

He couldn't help himself. He dipped and his lips brushed hers. A gentle caress, no more, but his whole body yelled an affirmation that staggered him. The need to clarify his possession ripped with a slashing determination. "I have every right. You are mine. Your passion is mine. Do you think my forbearance has meant it is not? I only wait for you to accept it."

"Nay."

"Nay? Let us test the truth of that. Let us see how indifferent proud Moira has become."

He kissed her again, tasting and biting and urging her open. She tried to twist away and he held her head in both hands so she could not. Something broke in her, as if a rod of resolve had snapped. With an anguished sound of dying protest she accepted him, parting her lips.

He probed her soft mouth and pulled her to him and clung to her soothing warmth. A submerging flood of needs rolled through him. He cupped his hands over the curves of her buttocks and pulled her against his swollen phallus and took her mouth again in unrestrained exploration.

"Please do not . . ."

Her whispered protest sighed between the gasping breaths of their fevered kisses. Her passion joined his even while her words denied him, and his hunger ignored the little plea. Holding her limp body in one arm he sought the full softness of her breasts with his hand. Hard peaks pressed his palm. He circled gently and her hips flexed against him. His arousal roared at the familiar rhythm.

Little thought now, and no constraint. He bent and grazed a nipple with his teeth. Her whole body, whole being, stretched in response. His mouth wet the cloth until it adhered to her, a thin obstruction through which he sucked until her lovely low moans sang.

He carried her to the table and sat her on its edge. Her head lolled against his chest while he unlaced the gown's back. Fire glow gleamed off her skin as the fabric fell down to her waist. He pushed her hair back and looked at her.

Beautiful. Lovely. Skin taut over shoulders and inviting breasts. Passion made those clear eyes sparkle with incredible lights. He slid his hands up her dangling legs, bringing the skirt high, and caressed the softness of her exposed thighs. He brushed the curls of her mound and pictured her lying back on this table in the dancing firelight. Bending those knees to accept his body. Clinging to him in pleasure as she had in Whitly, only with him buried inside her.

Accepting him, all of him, and the union still left incomplete by her pride. Wholly his.

He held her breasts and flicked caresses with his thumbs until she closed her eyes and bit her lip against the sensations.

He bowed her back and teased with his tongue while his hand sought her thighs again.

He began easing her down, lifting the skirt yet higher. She resisted, grabbing on to his arms.

"Then come up to bed, or into the garden."

She looked up with parted lips and blurring eyes, the image of a woman entranced. Even so, she shook her head.

"Did that merchant leave you in fear of it? There is pleasure in the joining too, Moira. I will not hurt you."

Her forehead sank against his chest and he held her

with one arm while he caressed close to her intimate warmth with the other hand. Wetness touched his fingers and the scent of it drifted around them like a musky fog.

"It is not that. You know it. Do not pretend that you do not," she muttered with a wavering voice. "You said in Whitly that you do not seek to seduce me against my will, but you do so now."

He heard her accusation and admitted its truth, but a part of him angered and darkened at this denial. He wanted her to the point of madness and yet even when besotted with pleasure she held to her damn pride. The hunger coiled dangerously inside him. He stroked the cleft of her mound.

Despite her sharp inhale, her hand stopped his and tried to pushed it away. He pressed his lips to the top of her head and felt her quick heart against his chest. He kept his hand to her, gently exploring and probing the soft folds. Shivers of pleasure spread through her with his touch.

She really could not stop him unless he let her. Afterward she would see the rightness of it. Of them together. She belonged to him, after all. By the time he was done she would not call it force, or even seduction.

His better half reasserted itself, aghast at the path he justified. An ancient one, well trod over the ages by lords and their bondwomen. This was Moira, not some serving wench of no account.

If you do it this way, you will never really have her.

He resented that voice of reason. He glared at the arms strained against him with their weak resistance. He suddenly hated the births and blood and pride and realities that kept them apart. He could sweep them all away and make a new reality. She could not stop him and didn't really want to. She would accept it.

Two minds and two souls battled inside him, and the

urge to own and possess and hold her forever began to win.

She lifted her head and moist, clear eyes looked right into his. A regretful, quavering smile turned up her mouth with an expression that said she had no concerns about which way he would go. Her trust reminded him forcefully of who she was, and what she meant to him, and what he really wanted from her. The danger began uncoiling.

"Let the mason come," he muttered. "Let him know you and see the truth of it, even if you do not."

He turned and left abruptly as if angels drove him away.

CHAPTER 12

RICHARD HAD BEEN RIGHT about the wealth and honor gathered for the tournament. Jeweled surcottes, painted saddles, colorful pennants, gleaming armor . . . the richness overwhelmed the eyes. In the midst of it all Addis's animal skins and exotic woman stood out as a distinctive oddity, making the knights and crowd curious.

Moira had practiced with the dangerous destrier whose reins she held. Addis had decided to forgo a palfrey and so sat atop it, controlling the animal with his legs more than she did with her hands. Behind him Richard carried the weapons and shield of Barrowburgh, a knight of high status in his own right proudly assuming the role of squire for his lord.

Among the combatants and the nearby crowd it was working. Whether a king jaded by novelties would notice was another thing.

"Stay nearby after we pass through the lists," Addis said. "As it is, half these men will be following you home like so many dogs."

He sounded annoyed. She thought that took some gall
on his part, since it had been his idea to display her thus.
The red surcotte reached to mid-calf, leaving part of her
naked legs exposed. The silk's soft flow implied more of
her body than was immediately apparent, and the scooped
neck and sleeveless cut looked indecent without a gown
beneath it. All of the other women wore veils over bound
hair, so her flowing locks alone were startling. Little lines
of amber beads beat on her forehead, a thin gold chain
stretched across her chest, and the armlets circled her upper arms. Addis had placed all the wealth on her, and she
had glanced in a polished plate and admitted that she
looked very exotic indeed.

The pageant moved forward and they took their place
among the retinues. She passed in front of the crowd. A
blue pair of eyes several heads back caught her glance and
she realized that Rhys was here. He had come to the house
for two evenings now, working the stone before partak-
ing of some supper in the kitchen. Yesterday she had told
him about her role today and he had expressed mocking,
exaggerated shock when she described the costume.
Now he smiled in a reassuring way and she was grateful
for that.

They moved slowly toward the tented raised gallery
where the royal family and retainers sat. A shock of red
hair caught her eye. It moved and dipped at the back of
the platform and she stretched to see better. Her blood
pulsed as she recognized the knight from Barrowburgh,
and beside him none other than Simon himself.

She looked back anxiously at Addis and he gave her a
calming nod that said he had seen as well. Then he turned
and formally acknowledged his king.

Edward appeared royal enough, but she had expected a
man larger than life, not the very ordinary face and short

beard and normal brown hair. His garments were sumptu-
ous, but then so were all of the robes and tunics surrounding him. He sat with no lady, but between two men who
were clearly related. One was of middle years, and the
other appeared to be his father. She guessed that they
were the Despensers about whom Addis had spoken.
Edward examined the barbaric-looking knight passing by
with obvious interest, pointing and speaking quizzically to
the younger man on his right.

They proceeded on to the tents in the field where the
knights would prepare for the combats. Richard had already secured one and the armor and lances waited within.
Addis jumped off the destrier and Moira gladly relinquished the reins.

"Do you think it worked?" she asked.

"Aye. Whether it worked enough for him to ask for me,
we will see later."

Her role finished, she turned to walk away.

"Stay here, Moira."

"I want to watch the tournament."

"Before my turn Richard or I will take you there, but
do not go alone."

"If you worry about the gold, I can leave it here."

"It is not the gold that might get stolen."

She went to sit in the shade of the tent. She had not
raised *that* much attention and interest. This was her first
tournament but it did not appear that she would have the
day of fun that she had anticipated. She had counted on
mixing with the crowd and enjoying the vendors and en-
tertainers who ringed the field, not sitting for hours under
Addis's watchful eye.

She wondered if he had seen Rhys in the crowd. Let
him come, he had said, but she was never alone with the
mason in the kitchen. Jane or Henry always managed to

have some work that required their presence. She strongly suspected that Addis had instructed them to act as guardians.

She glanced up and caught him looking at her. She suddenly felt very exposed in the red silk. Since that night in the kitchen he had treated her with restrained courtesy, but his deep gaze would catch her sometimes like this and summon that intense connection that seemed to charge the air between them. She should resent this other hold he had on her. She should especially resent the knowledge he had demonstrated that night of how little of her will really stood between him and the passion he wanted from her.

He turned away. She ruefully admitted that her burning face and pounding heart had nothing to do with resentment.

He had chosen forbearance that night. He had known that the hands halting his caresses would not do so for long with that aching pleasure seducing her. He had stopped, but these looks said that he merely had decided to wait for her to accept that she was his. His contemplation of that filled the house whenever he crossed its threshold.

It was a long, hot day. Because of the hours needed to fit Addis's armor before his turn, she only got to see four knights meet in the lists. She tagged along when Addis himself fought and watched from amidst the squires with Richard close beside her. He cuffed a few bolder ones who tried to speak with her.

"You need not hover near me like a nursemaid, Sir Richard. Those boys are hardly dangerous," she muttered while she observed Addis ride into position and face off against his first opponent.

He wiped his sweating bald head with his sleeve. "Nay, but my lord is. Almost did not let you come once he saw you today. Came close to giving up the plan right there and then. If the day wasn't so damn hot he'd have you swaddled in a cloak, he would, or sewn up inside that tent. Wouldn't do at all if he saw something he didn't like and rode over here with that lance instead of where he is supposed to tilt."

"He exaggerates the allure of a few beads and some red silk."

"He exaggerates nothing, woman. Take it from a man who is not too old to notice. Now you stay by me or these young stallions will be holding a different type of tournament to impress you."

Addis unseated his opponent on the second pass and Richard nodded approvingly. "Pray he keeps it up or it will take one of those armlets to buy back the forfeit of his horse and armor."

He did keep it up. She watched proudly as he triumphed in tilt after tilt. Eventually it ended and his name was placed among the finalists who would compete the next day.

A royal page approached their tent while Richard finished unstrapping Addis's plate. Moira was returning with some water for washing and observed the brief conversation. She set the bucket down just as the page left. Addis sluiced water over his head.

"Well?" she finally asked with impatience.

He shook the water off and accepted a towel from Richard. "The king sent a summons to visit him before the jousts tomorrow."

"It worked then. That is good news."

"Aye, it worked."

"You do not appear overjoyed."

"I will be asking for justice from a king who does not understand what the word means, Moira. Hugh Despenser will stand by his side, speaking in his ear, and Simon will stand behind Hugh. The king may not know why I have come to Westminster, but Hugh and Simon do, and they have been working on his mind. Edward can give me justice, but I think he will not do so."

"Still you must try."

"Aye, I must try."

"And if he forsakes you?"

He gestured around the field. "There is much discontent here. One feels it in the air. Meetings are being held in some of these tents. Rumors spread among the squires and grooms. The strife is deep, and many have stories like mine. Hugh Despenser and his father have gone too far in their greed and Edward is helpless under their influence. I have heard that in some regions there are those who pray to Thomas of Lancaster as a martyred saint. If the king forsakes me I will have much company."

"I have heard grumbling when I go to the markets for food. It seems that no one speaks of Edward with any warmth or loyalty."

"He curtailed some of the city's freedoms," Addis explained. "A stupid man as well as weak. Londoners are inclined to support their king against the barons unless they find themselves threatened. We will see what the morrow brings, Moira, but I am not optimistic."

He would not speak of it to her. Danger awaited him if the king refused his petition. Horrible danger. He had not told her what transpired that night when those men came, but she had heard enough and surmised even more. The situation with the king had reached the point where unthinkable alternatives had become acceptable. One smelled it on the streets and read it in the unspoken words underlying vague comments in the market. Everyone was waiting for something, much as she had waited that day in the courtyard at Barrowburgh.

Would he join those men? She watched him prepare to

depart, contemplating thoughts he did not share with her. If Edward rejected his claim, he might decide that he had nothing to lose.

She tried not to think of the cost if he joined a move against the king and lost. She had heard of the horrible deaths such men faced, and had seen the parts of bodies hanging from gibbets after the rebellion. Sick dread turned her stomach at the image of them desecrating his body that way.

Richard emerged from the tent with some plate and weapons and began to pack them on the extra horses they had brought. Addis shrugged a tunic over the padding that he wore beneath his armor. He swung her up on a saddle to begin the ride home.

"You looked beautiful today, Moira. It was you who captured the king's attention." He took her hand and kissed it, startling her. "I thank you. For all of the ways that you help me."

Addis twisted on the bed, unable to find rest. The choice that he had always suspected he would face would be met tomorrow. In some ways it had already been made but for the king's decision. Only if Edward proved worthy of loyalty could he give it.

Tomorrow one of two doors would open, and a man whom he did not know, a man reported to be unfit for the crown that he wore, held both keys. His spirit churned with deliberations about the imminent decision facing him. At times like this he wished that the old prayers still sustained him.

The night was hot as the day had been. He stripped the sheet from his body and lay naked, seeking a breeze. He stretched an arm across the empty space beside him to where the linen felt cooler. He thought of the woman who should be lying where his hand rested and his body tightened, adding a new torture to this sleepless night.

He wanted her. Hell's blood, how he wanted her. He had tried to be satisfied again with the contentment he felt just having her nearby, but it was not enough anymore. He would sit down the table from her, eating his meal while his mind engaged in elaborate, detailed loveplay. He had mentally taken her in every chamber of this house, in the garden, at the well, in the bath, everywhere. He constructed sophisticated arguments to refute the practical realities she had thrown at him, but they were not sufficient to sway her so he did not speak them. She had decided that the cost of what he wanted was too high for her and his conscience ruefully acknowledged the truth of that. He suspected that even if he had Barrowburgh again and could gift her with pearls and jewels she would still find the cost too high. Just his luck to hunger for a proud woman with so much common sense.

Who would have expected the quiet, plump girl to see so much from her shadows? Children should not be that perceptive. She should have been delighted with the betterment of her life and enthralled by the luxury brought by Edith's place with Bernard. Instead she had seen the hooded looks, the silent scorn, the isolation of a woman plucked from one world and put in another merely because she pleased a man.

Bernard's whore. Had he ever called her mother that? Most likely. But the daughter had not read every mind and look accurately. She had seen the veiled disapproval and heard the squires' lewd snickers, but she had missed the envy many felt when they saw the joy Bernard shared with his bondwoman.

He glanced down at the prominent evidence of his arousal, and threw himself from the bed. He pulled on the buckskin leggings and strode from the chamber and out to the courtyard. The utter silence of the city assaulted him. So strange that the hellish confusion could disappear with the sun.

Faint lights glowed through some windows in the house from night candles in the chambers. He had deliberately not learned which one was hers because he did not need to be imagining her there, but now he paced back into the house and the short passageway on the ground level.

He knew instinctively that she was at the end, as far from him as possible. The choice of a woman afraid, but of what? That the lord might claim her service in the ancient way? If so, that night in the kitchen probably had not reassured her much. Nor him. The son of Barrowburgh was sometimes still tempted. With a different woman it might resolve things, but this one would only be embittered, even if he cajoled her to pleasure and passion. He wanted her willing, which she might never be.

He pushed open the low door to the tiny chamber. Her chests and stools cramped the walls, and her pallet lay in the position her bed had at Darwendon, with its foot near the door. An empty bit of floor stretched near her head, where Brian would have slept. She lay serenely, naked beneath the old sheet that made shadowed valleys between her breasts and legs in the dim light.

She slept deeply, not stirring at all. Did she dream of that mason? Intelligent and skilled and on his way to becoming a master builder. Just the man she had described as her ideal. He was proving smooth and skilled in other ways too, timing his work to end after the household had eaten so he could have her attention in the privacy of the kitchen where Addis could find no excuse to be. He had resisted the urge to warn the man off, but every time he saw that dark hair emerge from the garden to wash at the well he had wanted to. Rhys courted her for marriage, of that Addis had no doubt.

The silk surcotte was folded neatly on top of one chest. She had looked stunning in it and he hoped she would keep it. His footsteps did not disturb her as he walked around her pallet to look at her face. Sliding his back down the plaster wall, he sat on the floor in Brian's spot and calmed within the serenity that she gave unknowingly and he accepted without questions.

The page led him through stone passages and chambers to a door giving out on an enclosed garden. Courtiers dined from plates of fruits and pheasant beneath neatly pruned trees and beside tidy hedges. A few women enjoyed the meal, but only men hovered around the king, who sat on a low bench topped with turf.

Edward glanced up with his approach, at first with confusion and then disappointment when he noticed that Addis did not wear the barbarian garments. He had attended this meeting as Patrick de Valence's son, and his surcotte bore his coat of arms.

Hugh Despenser had been speaking with a man near the wall, but he eased over to arrive near the king when Addis did. Edward accepted Addis's greeting and raked his appearance with his eyes.

"Your face. It is a cruel scar. Did you get that with the Knights?"

"Nay. I have marks enough from those years, but I brought this one with me."

"It is a badge of honor if won in battle, but I expect the women do not like it much."

"Like children, most women find it frightening, but a few have not minded overmuch."

"Aye, but then some women like to be frightened." A

few courtiers laughed obligingly when Edward grinned as if he had made a joke. "Sit and tell us about it. How goes the crusade against the pagans? Hugh here speaks of going next year but I have explained that the realm cannot afford his absence."

"The Knights would be grateful for Sir Hugh's valor," Addis said. Men like Hugh Despenser never went on crusades, especially ones in the Baltic where the Teutonic Knights took all the spoils and land. He settled himself in the grass in front of Edward and spun a half hour of adventures, ending with the fatal bravery of the crusaders in the *reise* that led to his capture.

"You were held by them? The pagans?" The notion fascinated Edward. He lowered his lids suspiciously. "Did you recant your faith to be spared martyrdom?"

"They never asked me to. It is the Christians who seek to convert the conquered."

"Still, you must have seen things. Witnessed rites that no Christian should." The idea of forbidden rituals titillated him.

"A few simple rites. No one required that I attend any rituals or offerings."

"It is said that they burn men. Knights whom they capture."

"I saw one such sacrifice. The knight was in his armor and on his horse. He had been drugged and did not know his own end."

"But they did not burn you."

"Nay. Their gods do not like scarred faces any more than women and children do."

Edward looked around at his entourage. "We must find a way to honor Sir Addis. He has suffered much for God's war."

"I seek no new honor, but only that which is mine by my blood and my birth," Addis said carefully.

Edward appeared confused. Hugh Despenser bent and whispered in his ear. His words only made the king ill at ease.

"Your father, Patrick, was one of the contrarians who rebelled against us," Edward said sympathetically, as if breaking bad news that Addis had never heard. "His lands were forfeit."

"He unfurled no banners against his king."

"There are witnesses who say that he did," Hugh interrupted.

"For coin and land men often bear false witness. Did they swear to this before the peers?"

"Your father died. There was no need, not that such formalities are necessary with such blatant treason," Hugh coolly instructed.

"The charters say they are always necessary," Addis responded directly to the king, ignoring Hugh's usurpation of the conversation.

"Not if a man takes up arms against his liege lord," Hugh tartly inserted.

"That is so," Edward nodded. "The rebellion threatened our person and the realm. The barons received God's justice. My councillor says the lands were not broken apart, that they remain whole, and given to your brother. We have been more generous than warranted."

"He is not my brother, but the son of my father's second wife, and not of our blood. I petition you to undo the injustice."

Edward's eyes glared with sudden anger. "Injustice? Injustice? These barons presume to demand I relinquish royal prerogatives. They dare to instruct *me* in whom I choose as my councillors. They draw up charters and lists of rules for me, and seek to put men I neither like nor trust at my right hand. God's breath, they murder my dearest friends in the name of rights that derive *from me*.

They ferment rebellions and raise armies against me, and then speak to me of *justice*? Lancaster and the others received their justice as ordained by God when I was anointed king!"

His own outburst seemed to surprise him. He calmed under Hugh's hand on his shoulder and continued whispers in his ear.

" 'Tis a grave misfortune that your father forsook his oaths to his king while his son fought for God. A brave man should not suffer for the sins of his father, but it is always so. Darwendon is yours, however, secured by your marriage. And there is a manor in Wales that we will give you, to honor your valor and ordeal in God's holy war."

Wales. Despenser territory. Addis doubted that he would ever be allowed to enter that manor's gates. He would refuse to do so if it meant swearing fealty to the self-satisfied man pulling the king's strings.

He rose, experiencing a new tranquillity about his course. He had learned what he needed to know and the king's decision liberated his conscience. "You are too generous, for a true crusader asks for no reward but what God might deliver when he dies." He smiled. "I am grateful that you heard my petition. I must ask your leave now, with your permission. I should prepare for the tournament."

His courtesy brought a warm smile back to Edward's face. "Fare you well, Sir Addis. I will watch for your performance today."

He turned away and saw Simon standing near the garden portal, stretching to observe the conversation near the turf bench. "You have come for the tournament, Simon?" Addis greeted him when he neared.

"Aye, and who thought to see you here, Addis? In truth I come to visit my future bride, but the festivities drew me as well."

"You do not compete, however. Nor does Owen."

"Owen longed to, but I have other duties for him."

"I am sure that you do."

"Who was the beguiling woman who led your horse yesterday? A fetching piece."

"Just a woman whom I know."

Simon gestured toward the king and leered a grin. "He spoke of nothing else at the evening meal. You should have brought her today."

"I do not think that Edward found her so beguiling as that, Simon. He may have got four children on his wife, but that ordeal is over."

Simon's face fell. "It is treason to insinuate thus."

"Then the whole realm is treasonous. I care not whom or what any man beds, but it should not affect his judgment."

"You are displeased with his judgment?"

"As you knew I would be. Your friend Hugh will tell you all, I am sure."

Simon held out his hands. "You seem becalmed all the same. Let us put this behind us, Addis, and join hands like brothers. It is not my doing or my fault that things happened thus."

Addis gazed down at the outstretched palms that would as easily grasp a dagger as offer reconciliation. "Go and find your bride, Simon. The friendship of a man like Hugh Despenser needs constant vigilance."

"That purse will help," Richard said as they led the horses down the lanes toward the house. "Appropriate that a crusader won. Maybe God has finally decided to repay you a bit on this earth."

"They arranged for me to do so, and you know it."

"Now, I'm not so sure about that. . . ."

"They permitted the king's champion to advance to the

final round even though three knights could have defeated him earlier. He was still half-drunk from a night of debauchery, and my guess is that they arranged that too. They wanted the king's man to fall to the son of a family whom Edward had broken. The message may have been lost on the king, but not on Hugh Despenser."

"If they chose to do so, just as well it was you. Like I said, that purse will help, and paying the forfeit of horse and armor certainly would not."

"Exactly. Another message. One of friendship and this time to me."

Old Henry hurried over to take the horses when they entered the courtyard. Both Addis and Richard joined him in unpacking and grooming the animals. Twilight was dimming when Addis finally emerged from the stable. He and Richard had supped at a banquet on the field, and the household would have eaten by now. "See if the mason is in the kitchen," he instructed Henry. "Tell him I would speak with him."

While he waited he strolled over to the garden. Someone had begun trying to clean out the growth. A bed near the front had been weeded so that the summer flowers could spread and the surrounding hedge had been cleaned of grasses. Moira, trying to impose some order on the wildness, just as she kept the least tame of his own inclinations in check.

Rhys took his time coming. Deliberate, that. A wordless reminder that as a citizen of London he need answer no lord's call. He finally emerged from the hall and sauntered over to the garden's edge.

"You know how to find Michael, Stratford's man?" Addis asked.

"He is in the city. I know where to go."

"Tell him that I have agreed."

Rhys turned to leave.

"Why do you do this?" Addis asked.

"Do what? Help these men or woo the woman you want?"

Now that was blunt, and either very brave or very stupid. "Help these men. The city cannot protect you if things go wrong."

"Nor you. Before they come for me half the barons in the realm will be drawn and quartered."

"Our grievances are heavy ones."

"And ours are not? I may not have lost a great estate to these men, but I have my reasons for wanting them brought down. We all do."

They stood facing each other, the growing darkness dissolving their forms. Rhys did not move, as if he waited for the rest of it. For some reason he had invited the confrontation and Addis could not hold his tongue.

"You know that she is bonded," he said.

A smile flashed in the night. "So she says. An accident of birth, just like yours and mine. She is a proud woman with a strong heart. A man could do worse."

Much worse. "When I leave here, she will return with me."

"Perhaps."

"I will not release her."

"I did not think so. Still, there's things you can control and things you cannot, even as a noble and a baron. Her birth and yours are two of the latter, and so is her character. 'Tis her body and eyes that catch a man's attention but her pride and honesty that keep him coming back. Those are what will form her decision, and it does not bode well for you, does it? Your birth means that you cannot offer her the dignity that she counts more valuable than pearls. I do not think that you have bought her yet, nor will you when this is over. Such a woman would not be swayed by half of Barrowburgh as a price."

She already has half my soul. Half of Barrowburgh would be an easy gift.

"A part of me hopes that you force her," Rhys said, turning to leave. "It will end whatever hold you have on her more surely than death."

He disappeared into the night. Addis circled the garden and entered the kitchen through the open well-door.

Moira sat with her back against the hearth wall, lost in thought. She wore a weary expression, as if she contemplated something that saddened her. Dark hair fell around her body and he wondered if she always displayed her glory while the mason ate here. Jane was nowhere to be seen.

She heard his step and looked over with a resentful glare. Suddenly Addis understood. The man had touched her, kissed her. *It will end whatever hold you have on her.* Rhys had sensed what existed between them.

He dropped the king's purse on the table. A smile lightened her expression. "You won? You were the champion?"

There had been little satisfaction in the competition, but he took pleasure in the sparkle that the news brought to her eyes. "Aye. Take what is needed to pay the mason."

"You will need the coin, and he said . . ."

"I know what he said, but I will not be indebted to him. Use some of it to buy what is needed to make this a proper house for the Barrowburgh honor. We may have visitors in the future. And hire another servant."

"Jane and I can manage."

"Hire one." *Hire ten, damn it.*

"And the king?"

He shook his head. "He offered me a manor in Wales instead."

"As big and rich as Barrowburgh?"

"You can be sure it is not. Still, if he had not accused my father of a treason that he did not commit, if I did not feel the ghosts of my father and grandfather reminding me of my duty . . ."

He felt a soulful need to hold her in his arms all night and tell her about it. Choosing one's course did not mean the journey would be easy.

She came over and lifted the purse. "How much is it?"

She stood so close that he could smell her scent. And another's. "Fifty marks."

"A lot. But not enough?"

She did not miss much watching from the shadows. "Not enough."

She opened the purse and plucked out three coins. "There will be a way. A marriage alliance perhaps."

He gritted his teeth. Proud, practical Moira. "If it comes to that, do not blame me for it," he muttered.

"It would make more sense to blame the wind for moving the leaves, my lord. It is always thus for those of your rank. In some ways you are less free than the villeins who till your fields."

She spoke as if she articulated an argument that her mind had been weighing. Had she been debating the realities of their respective births when he entered? He wished that he knew what had transpired in this kitchen between her and the mason this evening. Just how practical had she decided to be?

"Are you going to do it? Help those men who came here with Rhys?"

"Aye."

She inhaled a deep, composing breath. "I fear for you, Addis."

Addis. At last, his name again. "I have nothing to lose now. All the coin in the realm would not secure Barrowburgh while the Despensers rule in the king's place."

She kept looking down at the purse, poking absently at it with her finger. "Still . . ." She faced him abruptly with glittering eyes full of warmth and concern. Suddenly they were just Moira and Addis again, separated from the world, riding a cart alone through the country. "You will tell me? When you must do something dangerous, if you might not come back . . ."

He brushed the hair near her face with his palm, relishing the moment that she would not let last but that he yearned to stretch into eternity. "I will tell you."

She looked up at him with a trembling lip and puckered brow. He took such joy in her worry that he thought his heart would burst. "You will not do anything stupid, will you? Rash and noble and brave like at Barrowburgh? You will not . . ."

"Nay." And it was true. He would not. He would carry the expression in her eyes with him to ward off the insidious temptation he had felt at Barrowburgh. No matter how weary his spirit might be, he could not know such reckless despair again while she was in his world.

He sensed her pulling back from the sweet unity threading them together. As if she feared it. He battled the urge to embrace her and demand its continued life. *It is so. I know it and the mason knows it. Why don't you?*

She held out the purse. "I have what I will need for now." When he made no move to take it from her, she let it drop back on the table and walked away.

CHAPTER 13

MOIRA SAT SURROUNDED by the riot of late summer color filling the garden. She pulled a reed from a vat of water and nimbly wove it into the basket taking form on her lap. The patch of ground where she rested still shot high with overgrown grasses, but the rest of the garden had been cleaned, its hedges pruned and its paths redug.

Addis had worked this transformation. No longer required to spend his days in the king's anteroom, he had joined the efforts to improve the house. The morning after the joust she had risen early to help Henry in the stables, only to find the work already done. Day by day the garden had emerged from the weeds. It was not fitting work for a knight and Sir Richard was appalled but Addis did not seem to care. She suspected that he merely sought activity to occupy his body and mind, but it had relieved her of the most strenuous chores and so she was grateful.

She had time now to make some baskets and would come out here after the midday meal to rest. She found herself drawn to this back section which Addis had inexplicably left wild. It seemed removed from the house and the city, a little spot of open country within the civilized garden.

She turned the basket and worked the pattern, singing to herself, losing awareness of the city sounds outside the wall as the strands of her craft and voice spun a private world. And so she did not notice him right away.

He stood in the shadow cast by a tree near the wall. He was dressed for riding. She looked to the courtyard and saw Henry and Richard and two horses. The day suddenly lost some of its warmth. Her voice died away.

He seemed preoccupied by distant thoughts and a slight frown hooded his eyes. He could not have been there long, but she knew that he had been watching and listening for a while.

"You do not sing much anymore," he said, stepping closer and settling on the ground beside her. His tone carried speculative undertones, as if he had just realized this change from years past.

"That is not true. I often sing. I used to sing Brian to sleep every night. I sing to myself while I work."

"But not for others."

"I sang at Darwendon."

"A religious song. Not the romances like you often did at Hawkesford. And only because I commanded it."

"I sang at Hawkesford because Bernard wanted it, but I never liked doing so." That was a blatant lie. Those moments in the hall had been the only recognition she had received in that household and she had savored them. But she did not want him asking her to entertain during their dinners here. She did not want to sing love songs while Addis de Valence sat at the table.

"So it is a private thing now, something that you own that cannot be taken from you."

"Aye. A private thing." With private memories attached to those melodies and words. Hidden yearnings and childish dreams, mostly, but also some heart-wrenching emotions that the sounds could both evoke and soothe.

She could see Richard peering toward them. "You are leaving?"

"Aye. I said that I would tell you."

"How long?"

"Three days. Four. No more than a week."

"I am glad that Sir Richard goes too."

"He insisted."

She lifted a reed and began plying it so that he might not see her worry. "If someone found out . . . if this journey became known to the king . . ."

"No one should know. Few have been told, and their own safety would be at risk if they were indiscreet. There is some danger, but not much."

She wished that she could believe that. "You are not going to tell me where Brian is, are you?"

"Nay. He is safer than you could ever make him and I'll not have you living your life protecting a child who is not your own."

"The choice should be mine."

"Perhaps, but I have made it for you anyway."

She forced a smile. "I may live my life resenting the choices you keep making for me."

He laughed. "Few enough, Moira. For a bondwoman you are not so easy to control." He leaned forward and kissed her, holding her head so his lips could linger. It was a sweet kiss of farewell and nuanced longing that could break a woman's heart. "If something goes wrong, you will not be harmed. Bondmen are not punished for their lord's actions," he said while his mouth brushed her cheek. It sounded more like a reassurance to himself than to her.

He rose.

"Fare you well, Addis. Take care and be safe."

He looked down a moment, then left to join Sir Richard.

She watched him until he passed through the gate, and then picked up her basket and resumed her work. Full of emotions and fears that she dared not acknowledge, she began absently singing a love song from her youth. It was an old one that she had not sung in many years. She thought that she had forgotten the words, but they just emerged without thought, undamming the poignant memories attached to them.

She sat in the shadows, half-alert even while she dozed. Restless movements on the bed had become normal sounds, and so she jerked awake when they stopped.

She peered toward the body dimly limned in gold from the single candle, its left knee bent and propped over a pillow. Her gaze moved up to eyes gleaming in her direction, and elation surged. Finally, after four days, he had woken.

"Who is there? Come here where I can see you."

She approached the bed and he gestured for her to move the candle closer. Doing so quelled her happiness. The watery shimmer of his eyes said he was conscious but not really awake. The flushed dryness of his skin indicated the high fever still raged. This sudden recovery was an illusion, merely the brief tranquillity at the center of a storm. If he survived he might not even remember it.

"Ah, it is Claire's Shadow. Did my wife fear her prayers would disturb my rest?"

"She just left. I took her place while she went for some sleep."

"Do not lie to me, little one."

"Truly, she has—"

"She has never been here. Did you think I would not know

it? Even when they butchered me, a servant woman held my head and hand. I remember not who it was, but I know it was not Claire."

She could find no response to that, so she poured some ale and moved to lift his head to the cup.

"*Help me to sit.*"

"*You cannot. The wound—*"

"*I am stiff from lying here, damn you! I will sit.*"

"*Perhaps I can raise your head at least.*" She found a blanket and together they bunched it under his shoulders so he only half-inclined. He looked down his sheet-shrouded body and yanked the covering aside.

She had seen him naked many times while she helped Edith care for him, but not with him aware of it. Her presence became insignificant, however. He examined the bandage tied at torso and thigh, covering most of his left hip. He flipped the sheet back with a sound of disgust.

"*Sit. Nay, not over there. Get the stool and sit here.*"

She obeyed and settled beside the bed. His gaze seemed both to see and not see, to scrutinize and to wander. Eyes half-conscious and half-mad peered over the brim of the feverish sea that had submerged him. They both existed as part of a wakeful dream. How long before the waves pulled him back down?

"*How fares the lovely Claire?*"

His bitter tone made her wary. "*She is not so well, Sir Addis. Weakened from worrying and praying for you.*"

"*You lie well, little Shadow, but not well enough. If she prays, it is for my death.*"

"*That is not fair.*"

"*Such loyalty. She is fortunate to have such a friend, but I hope that you do not expect similar loyalty returned. Has she spoken with her father yet?*"

Claire had indeed spoken with Bernard and had pulled Moira along for support. Images of that horrible meeting flickered through her mind, scenes of Claire imperious, then *pleading, finally hysterical as Bernard for the first time in her life refused his daughter her request.*

Addis read the conclusion in her eyes. "He would not agree to annul the betrothal?" The bandage had been removed from his face and the raw sewn cut twisted with his vague grimace. "Nay, Bernard will not seek to undo that which has been consummated."

She blinked in confusion, which amused him. "I have bedded her. Before I left. We were neither of us too discreet. Bernard knows. The whole household knows. The one time in her life Claire was generous, and it has led her directly to hell." He glanced toward the destruction hidden by the sheet, then lifted his fingertips and traced the thick line on his face. "Poor Claire." Bitterness again, but a note of sympathy too.

He looked away with eyes glittering so brightly she feared he would succumb to madness. Enough time passed that his voice startled her when he spoke again. "This I can live with." He gestured to his face. "But the hip . . . it pulls so I cannot straighten my leg. Will it always be thus? Am I condemned to walk bent forever?"

"No one knows. No bone was broken, but the fiber . . ."

"Remove the pillow."

"It is not yet healed."

He stretched to reach down and his face tightened in pain. She quickly pulled the pillow from beneath his knee.

He ripped the sheet away again, and tore off the bandage, exposing the ghastly scarlet wound that carved his stomach and belly along the line of his hip from waist to the middle of his thigh. The sight of it made him pause. "Can't say that I blame her," he muttered. Gritting his teeth he slowly pressed his leg to straighten it. She could see the threads along the wound stretching, pulling, resisting his efforts. His eyes darkened but he persisted until she could not bear it any longer.

"Nay! You will tear it open!" She rushed to the end of the bed and pressed her weight against his shin, forcing him to stop.

He sank back, closing his eyes against the defeat. She waited until she believed he would not try again, then replaced the pillow under his knee and covered him.

The stressed breaths calmed and his eyes remained closed. She hoped that he had fallen asleep, but in time the lights glimmered at her again. Not all golden this time, but mingled with black fires in an expression that disturbed her.

"Has he had you yet?"

The question stunned her. "Had me?"

"Raymond. Are you yet a maid?"

"Of course. You are mad from the fever. Raymond is like a brother to me."

"He may be like a brother to you, but you are not a sister to him and he knows it. He saw you with new eyes when he came home last year."

Addis de Valence had barely spoken to her over all these years, and this sudden personal conversation unsettled her. He was in a delirium after all, just articulate instead of rambling. He spoke what entered his mind, oblivious to normal restraints.

Something in his aura bothered her too. A strange mood emanated from him, like a heavy presence born of dark emotions. Hatred for Claire?

"He is to wed soon," she said, trying to shake her sudden unease.

"Aye, but the lady does not suit him. He will do it as Bernard requests, but she is not his choice. He thinks to find better pleasure with you, little Shadow. He would have you like Bernard has Edith."

"You are mistaken."

"He watches and waits, Moira, but you are what, five and ten now? You will have to decide soon. He has told the squires that you are his, and the village boys."

She had noticed Raymond warning boys off, but had assumed it was a brother's protection. "You are wrong, but if you are not it will not be so."

He shrugged. "You are probably wise. Raymond is a good man, but such women have no rights. A man's mind changes and his lehman is cast adrift, scorned by her own people and forgotten by his."

She needed no instruction on that. A lehman's daughter knew the same insecurity.

"Should you not rebandage it?" he asked, gesturing to the hip.

She fetched the basket of clean rags. He watched as she washed the gash and pressed cloths along it. He held the basket while she found lengths to cut for binding and took the knife from her when she had finished with it. That indefinable dark presence seemed to grow, like something thick and misty exuding from him. She bent to tie the binding around his thigh and his phallus swelled with her close touch.

"Damn," he muttered. "Still, it is good to know that the sword did not unman me."

Face burning, she quickly finished her work and covered him. He did not seem embarrassed at all.

"Too much to hope that my wife would come ease me." He smiled. A strange smile. Hollow. He watched her carefully and she did not like the dark fires taking over now. "Do you know Eva, the whore who lives by the foundry? Go and tell her that I ask her to come."

"You cannot . . ."

"Go and get her, girl. I will find no rest now."

"You are very ill."

"I am damned uncomfortable and since Claire is praying and you are a maid . . . go and get her."

The fever had made him irrational. "You cannot move. How can you . . ."

"She will use her mouth, little fool," he snapped.

She swung away with shock and embarrassment.

"I am sorry. I am not myself and forget you are a good girl. But go and get her, Moira. It is my bidding."

If it would ease him and bring rest, who was she to lecture on virtue? Reluctantly she nodded and walked from the chamber. At the door she looked back and saw him staring blindly at the ceiling with a peculiar, determined expression.

In the passageway, free of the oppressive air of the chamber, she saw that expression again. It loomed sharply in her head while she began descending the stairs. Suddenly, as if a door opened, she understood it, and understood too that odd mood that had been issuing from him. He did not really want Eva. He wanted her gone so as to be alone!

Turning on her heels she ran back.

She found him leveraged up on one arm, the sheet cast aside, the bandaging knife grasped while he pressed fingers to the inner flesh at the top of his crooked leg, seeking the mortal vein.

"You will not!" she cried.

He glared at her, then continued his search. "Be gone, girl."

"Nay!" She lunged, throwing her weight against the arm that held him up, grabbing at the hand that held the steel. It swung away and the blade flew, skittering across the floor when it landed. He thrust her off and collapsed, cursing her.

She cowered on the floor beside the bed, choking on tears of shock. An awful silence filled the chamber.

A hand touched her head. "Go and get it for me," he ordered softly.

"Nay," she mumbled into her knees.

"It is better this way. Normally such things are handled by comrades on the field. How many crippled knights have you seen?"

"You do not know that you are so badly maimed. Your leg was straight when Edith sewed the wound. Once the skin heals, maybe it can be straight again."

"You will not help me? Then go and get Claire and tell her what I want. For this she will come."

She raised her eyes to his and shook her head. Dark fires consumed him. He pushed up despite the pain and swung his good leg to the floor. She jumped up and forced him down and he proved too weak to resist for long.

"I will not get her. Nor will I leave here again, unless my mother takes my place. You are too sick to know your mind and too weak to fight despair." She sat on the bed beside him, her arms imprisoning his shoulders. "Rest now."

"Damn you!"

"Rest."

He stared with anger but slowly, under their connected gaze from which she would not flinch and with which she announced her determination, the dark fires extinguished one by one. It seemed half the night had gone before the last one died.

"Maybe it can be straight again," he said into the silence. "We will see." He closed his eyes. "Sing, Moira. Not a religious song though. I am not feeling friendly to God this night. Lie beside me and sing. Perhaps I will rest then."

Her voice could fill a hall, but now it only traveled the small space between their heads. She stretched alongside and embraced his shoulders and sang about love until his fevered face nodded against her breast and he sank back into his oblivion.

She shook into awareness. The basket in her hands was finished and she did not even remember completing it. Through blurred eyes she examined it for mistakes.

A movement. A presence. A man intruded on her dreamy mood. She looked up into kind blue eyes.

The wrong man.

Her smile of welcome hid her sigh. She had never known living could be this hard.

Rhys handed her a small sack and she quizzically looked inside. "Cherries! Where did you find them?"

"Best not to ask. They should stain your reeds as well as berries though."

"I dare not waste them so. Jane and I will make them into a pie and you must have some."

"They were for your baskets, but a pie would be nice."

He sat beside her. "Do you not rest on Sundays, Moira? Even peasants do."

He subtly criticized Addis with the question. "Peasant *men* do. Someone must still cook and clean. Besides, I am resting now. These baskets are not work."

He stretched out on his back, his wiry strength propped on his elbows. For the hundredth time she examined him and told herself how fortunate she would be to have such a husband. Decent and good and sober and skilled. She should welcome his attention and look forward to these visits that had continued even after the repairs were completed. He still came despite that night in the kitchen.

His embrace and kiss had turned her to stone. She had wanted so desperately to want him that she had invited the intimacy, only to experience no warmth at all when it happened. She might have been the virgin bride in James's bed again, passive and objective and embarrassed. Feeling some excitement would have simplified many things, but her lack of response had been so obvious that she had not even had to ask him to remove his hand from her breast. He had simply done so, separating just as Henry entered with Addis's summons.

They never spoke of it, but still he returned.

"He has left?"

"Aye. You knew it would be today?"

He nodded. "It will get dangerous from here, and this journey is the least of it. What will you do if something happens to him?"

"I have a freeholding at Darwendon. Perhaps I will go back there. I will probably look for Brian. He is a child I cared for when we thought Addis was dead. He has hidden him, and will not tell me where."

"Sir Addis's son?"

"Aye."

He hesitated thoughtfully. "And yours?"

"Nay." She told him about her place at Hawkesford and Simon's threat, and how she came to live with Brian.

"That explains much, but not everything," he said. "I came here today for a reason, Moira. I knew that he would be gone and thought that you might speak freely. I have been thinking that you would make a good wife, but I sense that your place here is not the normal one. I would know the truth lest I make a fool of myself. What is between you and Sir Addis?"

A gentle way to ask the question, much kinder than James's blunt query. She had answered with indignation to James, but she could not do so with Rhys.

She thought of the responses she and Addis had playfully tested that night in the hay mound. Only the last would suffice. "We have not fornicated."

He appeared amused, which relieved her tremendously. "An odd answer. Amazingly precise."

"It is, isn't it." They might never wed, but she could not lie to this man.

He swung up to sit cross-legged in front of her. "Moira, you are not a girl and I am not a boy. It is not lack of a home or work that has left me unwed, nor greed regarding a dowry. I have bided my time because I sought no ordinary woman. I like your manner and honesty and I think that we could make a good marriage. I would have offered already, but for Sir Addis."

"It does not sound like you offer now either."

"Nay, I do not. It is not a judgment, Moira. I expect no explanations and hold you to no blame." He took her hand. His was strong from grasping a mason's tools. "For good or ill, what begins with his journey today will resolve very quickly. A month from now we will be either dead or victorious. The chance for the former is reason alone not to offer. If by some fate I live and he does not, this may be

an easier thing. I will even accept the boy Brian into our
home if you wish it. But if he lives, he will leave here soon
after and you may have to make a choice because then I
probably will offer. I will make this marriage happen if
you accept me, no matter what his claims on you."

She smiled at him with true affection. A clever, honest,
understanding man. He meant what he said. He would
make it happen somehow, even if it meant giving Addis
one hundred pounds. No words of love though. Nay,
Rhys would not lie to her any more than she would lie
to him.

There was nothing for her to say. She merely nodded,
and he lay back down and talked to her about simple
things, a practical man tilling soil for which he might one
day have seed. A patient man biding his time, counting on
her pride leading her to the only sensible decision.

CHAPTER 14

MOIRA WAS KNEADING BREAD DOUGH when Richard entered through the garden door. She stared at him and then at the empty threshold, straining hopefully to hear the approach of another man.

"Where is he?"

Her voice conveyed her concern. He had been gone longer than she had expected, longer even than the week he had said would be the limit of the journey. She had not slept well the last few nights while she agonized over fantasies of him cut down on the road or being tortured in Westminster's dungeons.

Richard lifted a reassuring hand. "He was wounded but he lives."

"Wounded!"

"We were attacked on the road back."

"Why didn't you bring him here? If you left him I will—"

"He lies in a house in Southwark. He thought it best not to enter the city gates right now. He asked that you come."

Asked that she come! As if the entire King's Guard could keep her away!

"Carry a basket and pretend that you go to market, Moira. I will wait for you at the pier west of the bridge."

He left and she hurriedly washed her hands and scrambled to decide what she should bring. Had his wounds been cared for? Were there salves in that house? Did he need clean garments? She cursed Richard for disappearing before she could quiz him.

Stuffing a few washed garments into the basket along with a salve to ward off corruption in cuts, she hustled to the courtyard. Wounded. How badly? Not too badly if he was giving orders. She knew that wasn't true, that a man could suffer mortal wounds and still be conscious, but she clung to the piece of illogical comfort just the same. Not that it helped much. By the time she found Richard at the pier she had become a mess of agitated excitement.

She jumped off the boat even before it had been securely moored at the Southwark docks. Richard escorted her past the small houses of the stews in which prostitutes conducted their trade. Marcus lounged outside one near the end and stepped aside so they could enter.

"Small John and Marcus knew of this place," Richard explained. "It is a ways from the town, and easier to defend."

"He is in danger then?"

"We do not know yet."

The house was crowded with knights and squires and two women, all relaxing with drink and gaming. Passionate sounds came from behind a curtained corner. Richard flushed and glanced an apology and gestured her to a door leading to a back chamber.

Addis reclined on a bed and a skinny blond woman of middle years sat beside him, feeding him soup. His arm was bandaged and his left leg rose bent under the sheet.

The woman placed the bowl aside, rose to test some water warming by the low hearth, and then returned to continue the meal. She leaned closely and whispered something to Addis that provoked a stiff smile. Some soup dripped from the spoon onto his naked chest and she bent down with a sly smile and licked it off.

Moira instantly felt ridiculous for those nights of worry.

Richard cleared his throat loudly.

Addis looked over and muttered something to the woman. The whore raked Moira with her eyes and rose. When she and Richard had left, Moira walked over to the bed.

"You look comfortable enough, my lord. Very comfortable, in fact. I feared that you might not be receiving proper care but I can see that I fretted for naught." She crossed her arms over her chest and paced around him, nodding with approval. "Aye. Well fed, well bathed, and well rested."

He grinned. "Well enough."

"Indeed, these ladies seem to have you very well in hand. Completely so. Is there some reason then why you called for me?"

"Not to bathe and feed me."

"Clearly not." She faced him with hands on hips. "If I learn that you have been lying in this pleasure house for days while I worried across the river, that arm will not be all that needs healing."

With a laugh he grabbed her wrist and pulled her to sit on the bed beside him. "I only arrived this morning, and I called for you because these women are so soft-spoken and gentle and obliging that I feared they might be angels. Your sharp tongue reassures me that I am still on earth among the living."

"No doubt such a place is a knight's idea of heaven."

He gave her the warmest smile she had ever seen. "Not mine."

That flustered her so much that she lost hold of her annoyance. Relief and joy flooded to take its place and she felt embarrassed at having greeted him so poorly.

"I am heartened to see you alive and whole."

"Not entirely whole."

"You said a week, and when you did not return . . ."

"The wound slowed us."

She gently touched the bandaged upper left arm. It had been bound with strips of cloth to the side of his torso. "What happened?"

"An arrow. Some men were waiting as we returned."

"Then it is known why you went? If so, even this house will not be safe. Perhaps you should go back to Darwendon."

"We will learn soon enough what was known. No one in London has been taken, which is odd. It is possible that Edward plans some elaborate trap, but maybe some other game is being played. I will stay here a day or so and then return to the city if nothing develops. Whoever is behind this received word I had not died, several days before Richard and I got back. Time enough to send guards to arrest me on the road."

"You are not making much sense."

"The more I think about it, the less sense it makes. The men who attacked intended to kill me. Edward should want me alive, to learn what I had been told about the queen's invasion. So perhaps it had nothing to do with the king at all."

"Simon?"

"Or someone else."

"How many were there?"

"Five that I saw. But I sensed a sixth one hiding in the trees."

"You are wounded but Richard is not." The implications of that sunk in. Richard would fight to the death to spare his lord one scratch. She narrowed her eyes on him. "You met them alone, didn't you?"

"Do not scold, Moira. I had no choice. I sent Richard away. One of us had to try and get back with the message, and to warn Thomas Wake and the others that they might have been betrayed."

"It is a miracle that you are alive, isn't it? You walked into a trap not knowing what would be faced. Noble and stupid and brave. You promised me. . . ."

"It was not like that. Not like Barrowburgh," he said softly, touching her cheek. "It was not."

The full impact of the danger that he risked in this scheme hit her. Five against one. It truly was a miracle that he was alive.

The warmth of his hand touched more than her skin, adding an anguish to her relief with its tangible reminder of what had almost been lost. She had grieved for him once. She had almost had to grieve for him again. She might yet grieve in the days ahead. Her eyes began to blur. She hid her reaction in an examination of his arm. "Has it been cleaned and sewn?"

"A physician tended it. It had become so useless that I thought the bone had been hit, but he said it had not. He bound me because he did not trust me to keep it still."

"He must be a good physician if he knows a knight's mind so well." She turned to the bent knee. "Another arrow?"

"Nay. Just a blow like on the road from Darwendon, but worse. My insides have knotted. It has happened before. I can not straighten it, and it will be thus for a few days. Warmth helps."

"Then we will give it warmth." She fetched the heated water and some cloths and moved a stool beside the left side of the bed, glad to find some way to help him that would also busy the hands that wanted only to touch him and revel in the reality of his safety.

She pushed the sheet up the side of his hip. For the first time she saw the remnant of the wound that she had tended at its worst. Like the scar on his face, it might have shocked her if she had not seen its raw, corrupted birth. Now the long jagged welt of damaged flesh did not dismay her, but the large discolored bruise surrounding it did. She gently caressed the damage with her fingertips.

The hand of his bound arm grasped her wrist, stopping her. She flushed and reached down to dip a compress into the hot water. "I am not surprised you cannot walk."

"It is not the bruise but the muscle underneath."

She laid a towel alongside his hip, then pressed the warmth to his skin. "The blow could have broken the bone, just as the arrow might have shattered your arm. For all of your scars, Addis, you have been lucky in your wounds."

"That is true, Moira. I have been lucky."

She dipped the compress again to renew its warmth. He watched her with a serious expression. She smiled, just enjoying the quiet pleasure of being with him again.

"Has he had you yet?"

The question stunned her. It took a moment to remind herself of their current time and place. "You have no right—"

"Has he?"

"You lie here in a bawd house being licked by a whore and you question my virtue? You have a lot of—"

He grabbed her wrist again. *"Has he?"*

"Nay."

He released her. "Not for the lack of wanting you though. Did he take full advantage of my absence?"

His insistence exasperated her. "He only visited a few times. Once the day you left and then recently. Since I was sure you were dead I found the distraction welcome."

He missed her sarcasm. He cocked his head with a curious frown. "How many days passed without your seeing him?"

"Five . . . six . . ." She suddenly saw the meaning of his question. "You cannot think . . . Nay, Addis, surely not."

"He knew when I left and where I went. He knew it all. The men who attacked me were hired swords and not very skilled. The man who sent them did not fight himself. Hugh Despenser could afford better and know where to find them."

If I should live and he dies, it will make this easier. "You are wrong. He is a good man, and would not betray the plans being laid over this."

"Even good men will dare much to clear a path to their goals."

I will find a way to make this marriage happen. "You do not understand. It is not like that. There is not such between us that would make him kill. The goal is not that important to him."

"We will know soon enough."

"I will not have you harm him because of me."

"If he paid those men to interfere with my return, whatever his motives, I will be the least of his danger. I will not accuse him, but Wake will learn soon enough if he left the city."

"He has been here? Thomas Wake?"

Suddenly he looked ill at ease. He glanced away too deliberately. "He came to learn the message I brought back."

The oddest emptiness trickled through her, like a brief

echo of what she had felt when Brian departed. "Only for that?"

He looked down, lips slightly parted, and remained silent so long that she thought he would not reply. The sensation trickled again and again, like rivulets of loss wanting to form a hollow sea. Finally he raised his eyes to hers.

"He also came in friendship, and with an offer of help."

The emptiness engulfed her, filling her whole chest, choking out her breath. "With the bond sealed in the usual way? With a marriage?"

"Moira . . ."

"It is a wonderful thing, my lord. Such a man and family . . . I said some way would be found, did I not? Thomas Wake is married into Lancaster's family, isn't he? If this plan succeeds they will be as powerful as before. I am relieved to know you will have the alliance needed to regain Barrowburgh."

She prepared the compress again even though the water had cooled. Her methodical actions masked the unexpected devastation ripping her apart.

This was the last time she would help him. She would serve him at the house, but that was not the same. When he left London she would beg him to let her stay, and even turn to Rhys if she must, but he was not so cruel as to expect her to serve him in his marriage. In a matter of weeks he would be dead for her again, and this time she would not even have Brian to care for in his memory.

Her eyes stung and she stared at her hands holding the cloth to his flesh, grinding her teeth and willing composure. Perhaps if she were not so raw from worry she would not react so strongly. She had known this must happen eventually. She had been the one to remind them both of it. But eventually was later and this was *now*.

His hand closed over hers. "Enough now. It is feeling

much better, but whether from the warmth of the water or the comfort of your friendship, I do not know."

And she was the one who had denied them both the full comfort that friendship could have brought. It had been a sound decision, as this news clearly proved. She let the cloth drop into the bucket and sat miserably on her stool, gazing blindly at her lap, wondering if she hadn't been far too sensible. But how much harder to hear these words if she had acted differently? Then again, maybe not harder at all. She had never guessed that the pain of this inevitable reality would slice her into pieces like this.

"Come and sit beside me, Moira. Over here on my good side. I would rejoice in being alive with you for a while."

She looked up to find him smiling. She really thought she would weep then. Forcing a smile of her own she circled the bed and settled beside him.

It seemed the most natural thing to ease down under the arm that circled her shoulders, and lie alongside him in the still afternoon. They lay in the sweet connection she had not known since the night before London, and its poignancy both eased and deepened the pain.

"I think that I envy your mason," he said.

"Sometimes you speak nonsense."

"His simpler life has a kind of freedom. No ghosts of ancestors whisper in his ear. His choices are for now, not the past and not the future. But it is not just that. I envy him because he is whole."

"You make too much of a few scars."

"I am not speaking of scars or wounds. I think I was bitter about them once, at the beginning, but that was long ago. Nay, he is whole in other ways. Complete in himself. It is that I envy."

She turned on her side so she could see his face. It also brought her closer to his body and pressed the skin of his shoulder against that of her cheek, which felt very nice. "You are complete."

"Nay. I feel as though there are two half men inside me, two worlds and two souls. I am only whole sometimes, like now. There is no peace without that completeness."

She only partly understood him, but she sensed the peace of which he spoke. They lay together with a quiet contentment that produced a type of bliss. Even the anticipation of loss that shadowed her heart possessed a certain beauty. He had said that he wanted to rejoice in being alive with her and she felt very alive and unnaturally alert to each specific precious moment.

She turned her head and pressed her lips against his skin, wanting to taste his tangible reality. She laid her hand on his chest, touching his heartbeat. She inhaled deeply, memorizing his scent. *Probably never again.* She snuggled closer, savoring his physical closeness. Aye, she rejoiced even while she cried.

Her hand edged along the bindings tying his arm to his body. Her searching caress traced the hard muscles of shoulders and chest and abdomen, branding the details in her senses. She rose, absorbed in the nowness of him, no past or future whispering in her ear, free in her choice to know him as completely as possible before losing him again.

"Moira . . ."

She ignored him and bent to kiss his chest, letting her lips follow the meandering explorations of her hand. She licked as the whore had done so that woman would not have known more of him than she did. A profound stirring saturated her, richer than mere excitement, a pleasure that filled her heart and overjoyed her soul.

She moved and felt and kissed and absorbed, not thinking about anything at all except knowing him, *having* him for this first and last time. His fingers caressed tensely into her hair. She glanced to his watchful eyes and returned to her discoveries.

She slid the sheet away while her mouth followed the scar's line down and the heat of her breath offered comfort the way the compresses had. She kissed the damage as a mother might when trying to ease a child's pain. Her fingers pressed and learned the sinews of his thighs and knees, his hard belly and hips, finally the smooth surface of his erect phallus.

Total knowing. Completeness. Brief possession. She did not think or question or consider. She explored and learned, the evidence of his pleasure bringing her astonishing happiness. She felt the want pouring out of him, hungering and waiting, and her own arousal spiraled. Aye, total knowing. Her kisses followed her hand as if the progression were essential.

His sharp breath penetrated her constricted awareness. She let his subtle reactions guide her and immerse her. His tension encompassed her, straining beneath his grasp on her shoulder. She sensed it shaking, crumbling. "Enough," he gasped, pulling her up, pressing her mouth to a fierce kiss while the release flexed through him.

She drifted in the moment, tasting him, suffused still with the heady passion of it, feeling his tautness seep away.

A tilt of his head separated their mouths. She opened her eyes to see fires blazing at her.

He was furious.

He kept her head so close that their noses almost touched. "What was that? My betrothal gift?"

"I only wanted . . . I needed to . . ."

"You wanted? You needed? I have been wanting and needing for weeks, Moira, and now when half my body is crippled you serve me this passive, solitary pleasure. I will not take gifts from you any more than you take payment from me."

His anger could not make her regret it. "Do not yell at me, Addis. The gift was to myself. Besides, you could have stopped me."

"A man does not stop a dream come to life, even if it is incomplete." His hand pressed against her head, drawing her still closer to his severe, intent face. "Then let us finish it, to the extent you have left me capable. You look well content with your control of this want and need you had. I do not plan to leave your passion so contained."

He kissed her again with slow deliberation, provoking her sensual stupor to a sharper alertness. He would not let her move, but kept her breast crushed to his chest and his fingers splayed on her scalp, holding her while he carefully ravished her mouth and neck and ear. He was right. She was content in her containment of her need. She was not sure that she wanted this. She feared the pain waiting on the other side of ecstasy.

"Better if you did not . . ." she said.

"You would have me take pleasure and not give it? You are too generous, Moira," he whispered in her ear while his teeth and tongue explored ways to send her body trembling.

" 'Twas not generosity. Not really."

"Nor is this. Not really. Do not worry. You are safe from me for a while at least. Your mouth took care of that too well."

"Then it makes no sense for you to . . ."

"Ah, but I want to. Need to. Like you." He caressed around her arm to the outer swell of her breast, defeating her protests with suggestive strokes that raised anticipations of sensations that she remembered far too well.

She capitulated. Angling across his chest she accepted the kisses turned to her mouth. Shifting on her side she invited the deft touches on her breast. Her body treated the delicious feelings as if it nibbled at a savory. Soon she was thinking of nothing and just experiencing the building intensity of it.

"Take off your gown."

"I don't think—"

"*Do it.*"

He helped her sit on the bed's edge and untie the lacing along her back. She slid the loose gown down her body until it sank to a pile at her feet. She sat a moment, her eyes closed, trembling with an expectation that pierced clear through her.

He caressed along her thigh to the hem of her shift. "This too."

She looked at him. His eyes burned with desire of a different kind, with a passion only partly physical. She understood it. Recognized it. Not generosity. Not really.

She slid the shift off and sat naked beside him, the small of her back against his waist. He gently stroked down her back and she bowed into the heady contact. With two clumsy shifts he eased his body over, making a bit more room for her.

"You are so beautiful, Moira. Kneel here so I can see you and touch you."

She climbed beside him and knelt, sitting back on her feet. Examining her as she had him, he traced along her edges and curves, drawing her body, exploring hills and valleys, crevices and swells. The journey of his hand raised such pleasure that her eyes blurred and her throat dried. Impatient craving trembled its demand in her breasts. Thick moisture dampened the pulsing hunger growing between her thighs.

He eased her toward him until she had to brace her weight on hands flanking his head. She bent a kiss to him while he continued to arouse her hovering body, flicking and rubbing her nipples as if he heard their demands for attention.

Her conscious world began to constrict to just him and her and the crying desire titillating her with its sweet torture. Her passion broke out of any containment. He sensed it and began driving her mercilessly higher until she mindlessly uttered small cries that marked the rhythmic need throbbing through her. The passivity of her position both frustrated and excited her. Only the immobile arm and bent leg kept her from straddling him and pressing herself against his length. Except for the dulled memory that she had rendered him incapable, she would have sought the joining that her body demanded.

He pressed into her back, moving her down and forward until he could take her breast in his mouth. She gasped in relief and then dissolved into sighs and cries. The pleasure became twisting and tense and sharp. He licked and sucked and teased while his caresses moved to buttocks and thighs, to belly and back and she became frantic for more. He gave it to her, sliding his hand between her thighs. She parted them for him and groaned when he ventured where her whole body begged him to go.

Drawing on her breasts and tantalizing with his hand he led her from frantic to desperate and into delirious until the want and need overwhelmed her. The desire started stretching, seeking, reaching. . . . He released her and she rocked back, burying her moans in his shoulder. He used a touch that sent the exquisite release crashing through her like a cataclysm.

She collapsed, managing to remember that half his body was infirm. He pulled her into the comfort of his arm, her cheek and hand sealed against his chest.

They lay there for hours, neither sleeping nor moving, adrift in a little world of sweet comfort and peace. They barely spoke the whole time, as if both knew that words had no place or reason in this precious "now."

It is love, she thought. *Denying its name does not dull either the beauty or the pain.*

She nestled closer and watched across his chest as the afternoon sun grew long shadows on the chamber's walls.

CHAPTER 15

MATHILDA WAKE WAS BEAUTIFUL, small, and frail, with a pale radiance that illuminated the spot of courtyard where she stood. She kept her eyes lowered modestly while Thomas introduced her. Addis frowned down at her elegant blond head. His first reaction was that the girl accepted her duty but knew her worth far too well.

His second was that she reminded him of Claire.

Her creamy lids fluttered and she scanned up his length. It was a slow, long journey before her pretty head tilted back and she saw his face. Thomas must have warned her about the scar, but her smile still wavered.

"You are very tall, Sir Addis."

He had to admire her clever recovery. "And you are quite small, my lady."

"It is thought that I might yet grow, but I do not think that you will shrink."

"If you would prefer that I do, I will try." The banter

flowed easily. He knew how this game was played. He'd once been a champion at it, a lifetime ago.

"Oh, I do not think that I would care for a small knight, Sir Addis."

Thomas beamed beside her. The father's obvious pride interested him more than the girl's obedient demeanor. Did Thomas indulge her? Could she bend him to her will? If she begged to be spared from this match, would Thomas relent?

The possibility should make him concerned, but he found himself hoping it was so. The side of himself that acknowledged the need for this alliance kept battling the side that resented the coercion of duty. A perverse temptation to find ways to frighten her kept pricking at his better intentions.

He led the way into the hall. Pleasant smells floated up when their feet crushed the herbs mixed with the rushes. Summer flowers hung in abundant clusters from the beams and window headers. A crisp new cloth covered the head table and the chair from the solar had been moved down to the lord's place. Piles of colorful fruits substituted for more costly adornments but added to the hall's fresh, cool effect, as if someone had decided silver would be too heavy and formal on this late summer day. Three musicians sat on stools in a corner.

He had ignored the impending visit but Moira had not. She had demanded to know the day and then had prepared for it, badgering the coin from him to purchase the food and objects and services befitting a dinner where he met a kinswoman of a great family, economizing where she could and spending where she must. She knew from her years at Hawkesford that one did not stint on such an occasion. Every detail would be a manifestation of his honor. He scanned the delightful results and wondered if the child by his side could even appreciate the efforts a bondwoman had made on her behalf.

She was not in sight, nor would she be. She supervised in the kitchen, he guessed, or maybe rested out in the garden now that all had been prepared.

He wished that she were present. If Thomas saw her lush body and clear eyes he would wonder and eventually he might ask. Then he could let the father know that which the daughter must eventually accept, that the bondwoman who served him in London would always be with him. That when he sought friendship and comfort it would be with the Shadow and not the tiny sliver of light to whom he was bound. If he had his way he would seek more than that from her, not that he expected success there.

A bittersweet mood had tinged their last week together. She visited the Southwark house every day that he lay there but the intimacy had never again turned physical. The night that he returned to London he had waited, hoping that she would come to him, all the while knowing that she would not. He supposed he had known even while it happened that her passion had been a final, sweet acknowledgment of what had occurred and what might have been.

Thomas had explained that Mathilda was fourteen but she barely looked that old despite her elaborately plaited hair and costly gown. Addis hoped to God that no one would expect a quick marriage between him and this child. Perhaps he would entertain her with explicit descriptions of his scars and how he had attained them. That should help delay things until she matured more. Maybe it would delay things forever.

Henry and a hired servant delivered the food in stages and Thomas's squires served it. The musicians played softly. Richard and a widow lady he had been courting joined them at the table. Mathilda graciously accepted the choice meats that Addis offered her along with his attention.

She talked a lot. She managed to turn every topic back to herself. Claire had been like that when a young girl. Later she had acquired the finesse to make others gladly do the job for her. He wondered if this child was clever enough to figure out the shrewdness of permitting that.

He learned all about her pony, who had run off in the spring, and how half the estate had searched for five days before finding it. He was treated to an elaborate description of the new silks her mother had recently purchased. She reassured him that she prayed often to her favorite saints, but that her special devotion was for the Virgin Mother.

Between her disorganized stories and Thomas's commentary he managed to receive a complete list of her many virtues and womanly skills. He reflected that he had learned more about Moira during the long silences of their journey from Darwendon than he could ever acquire about little Mathilda from all these words.

Moira. What was she doing now? He considered complaining about some dish so that she would be obligated to show herself. He could use her soothing presence. Little rumbles of resentment in one of his souls kept threatening to fracture the courteous composure of the other one.

"The musicians are skilled," Thomas commented toward the end of the meal.

"Aye, they are," Mathilda agreed. "It is too bad there is no minstrel. I so love to hear song."

"Then the next time I will be sure to steal the best from the king's court," Addis said, smiling.

"Methinks one of the best is right here in this household," a squire said absently while he poured wine. His lord glanced sharply at the lapse of etiquette and the youth flushed.

"You've a minstrel but he does not perform?" Mathilda asked. A petulant frown showed her hurt that the man trying to impress her would not offer every pleasure at his disposal.

"I have no minstrel, I assure you."

Thomas appeared confused and twisted to his squire. On the spot now, the youth flushed more deeply. "Not a minstrel. My apologies, my lord, but I heard the lady singing in the garden and it was very sweet and I . . ."

"A lady?"

"Not really a lady. The servant woman from the kitchen."

Mathilda decided to test the sincerity of Addis's interest with this point. He well understood the little pout, the intimations of unhappiness, the signs of a girl checking just how malleable her charm could make a man. An expert had used these ploys on him many times.

It was Thomas who succumbed. He patted her arm. "If it is a singer you want I am sure that this servant will agree to it. Is that not so, Addis?"

He looked at his intended. After they married she was in for some shocking surprises regarding his susceptibility to women's wiles. "She is not a performer."

"But we are a small group," Mathilda cajoled, venturing a touch on his hand. "If you require it she must do it."

Thomas smiled expectantly and Mathilda widened her eyes in a beseeching way. To them it was a small thing. Refusing the child her simple pleasure would seem surly and insulting. He got the sense that the future of Barrowburgh hinged on his giving in to the spoiled girl on this first, small request.

The resentment thundered. If Moira were agreeable to singing she would have planned to do so. It was a private thing for her now. He hesitated long enough that Thomas's face fell. At the other end of the table Richard rose. "I assume it is the woman Moira whom you want, my lord."

Addis glared a glance at him and Richard returned one of his own. Will you risk so much for this? the steward's eyes scolded.

Would he?

Richard did not wait for his agreement. He strode to the kitchen. Thomas reassumed his smiling demeanor. Mathilda seemed very pleased with her small victory.

Richard returned alone and Addis wondered if Moira had refused. No doubt Mathilda would expect that he go beat her.

"She wants to wash first," Richard explained.

The conversation moved to other things and so when Moira finally entered the chamber no one noticed her at first except Addis. She had bound her hair in a thick plait that dangled along her back from beneath her veil. She wore no wimple and the light color of her headdress and linen gown contrasted with the bronze of her skin. Eyes as clear as rippling water pierced him with resentment.

"It is the Lady Mathilda's pleasure to hear you sing," he said when she approached the table.

"I am honored, my lord."

"She is devoted to the Virgin Mother. Do you know a song about Our Lady?"

"Of course. At least twenty. Is there a preference, or may I choose on my own?"

"As you prefer."

She retreated to the musicians and spoke to the lute player.

"I thought she was a peasant," Mathilda said. "She doesn't look like one. She doesn't look much like a servant either."

"Do the women who serve you look like peasants and servants?"

"Nay, that is true. But then, they serve a lady and there is no lady here."

Aye, there is. As noble as you will ever be. "In her life she has been closer to ladies than your maids are to you."

Mathilda pondered that while her mind tried to reconcile the dignity and linen gown of the kitchen maid preparing to sing. Addis turned to Thomas Wake and knew that man had drawn certain conclusions that would explain everything. He shot Addis a man-to-man look of forbearance and understanding.

Moira sang beautifully even though she did not put much effort into it. He could tell that she was uncomfortable and resentful at having the attention focused on her. She sang two songs to the Blessed Virgin, the second a very long one that surely should satisfy Mathilda's devotion.

"We must get a woman singer," Mathilda said to Thomas. "The minstrels are not nearly so lovely of voice." She looked slyly at Addis. "Does she only know religious ones? Something gayer would be nice. A love song perhaps."

"I do not think . . ."

Mathilda rose and gestured. "A love song now, Moira. To raise our spirits."

"I do not think the woman knows any. See how she hesitates, my dear," Thomas said quietly.

"Of course she does. Everyone knows them."

Moira nodded. "If it would please you, my lady." She said something to the lute player and they began.

Except for overhearing her briefly in the garden that day, Addis had not heard Moira sing the romances in years. She did not look at anyone in the chamber. Rather she fixed her eyes on a spot near the windows while she let her voice flow.

More emotion and expression colored this song. It displayed her voice's beauty in ways the religious works had not. Addis listened and a very strange sensation suffused him. It had been years, but still he sensed that he had heard her sing thus very recently and very frequently, that he knew every nuance and detail in the way her voice touched the notes and enunciated the words.

Somewhere, tantalizingly out of reach, vague ideas and ghostlike images wanted to attach to this melody. Soothing memories stirred in some hidden corner where they slept. That made no sense at all. Moira had sung at Hawkesford at meals he attended with Claire, and recalling Claire never brought peace. The experience unsettled him with a gnawing, groping sensation that he should be remembering something.

Her voice mouthing those loving phrases undammed a saturating serenity. He felt his face against her breast and the warmth in her arms and the contented solace of care and love. He stared at her profile pointing toward the window, his whole essence stretching for the memories that would explain if her music called up fantasies or facts.

Sing it to *me*. Somewhere in my dreams or my life you once did so. I can feel it. Forget the others and do so again. One glance only, so I know that you feel what I feel, so that I know that you accept it is so.

She finished without turning her face, leaving him with a profound disappointment. He had lost awareness of his guests and so the girlish voice to his right startled him. "Her voice makes one want to cry or swoon." Mathilda clapped with delight. "Another!"

Moira tensed.

"I am sure the woman has other duties," Thomas said.

"Oh, surely one more."

"It is enough, daughter. I tire of song now."

She tried a halfhearted pout but decided not to bother. "Please, some coin so that I may gift her."

Thomas thumbed ten pence out of his purse and Mathilda called Moira over. "This is for you, in appreciation for sharing your lovely voice." She pressed the coins into Moira's hand. "Perhaps I will have many opportunities to listen to you in the future," she added in a whisper that everyone heard.

Moira looked at the specie and then at the lovely child beaming at her. She smiled kindly. "You are too generous. It was my honor." She addressed Addis without looking at him. "May I take my leave now, my lord?"

He gave it gladly, wishing that song had left him as self-possessed as it apparently had Moira.

She huddled in the garden, balled up behind the largest tree, listening to the sounds in the courtyard of the Lady Mathilda departing. Uncontrollable sobs racked her body and she buried her face into her knees to smother them.

She had finished her duties before collapsing into this overwhelming grief. Somehow she had held together through the nightmare of singing that love song for the two of them. She had directed the final service and even helped Jane with the washing. She had left the sounds of talk and laughter in the hall while the guests took their leave and had walked beneath the afternoon sun, toward the wall, telling no one where she had gone.

It wouldn't stop. The cries ravaged her to where she gasped for breath. Her chest would surely burst. She grasped her legs so tightly that she hurt herself and tried to will her body back into control.

She had prepared this day for him even though he had resisted it. She had tended to the food and flowers and musicians, but she had sworn that she would not see it. She had arranged things so she need never enter that hall and meet the young maid who could give him back his honor. She would help him as she always had when she could, but she refused to watch with heartache from the shadows again.

She peered over her knees at her hands and slowly opened the one that held the ten pence. The coins marked her palm from being grasped so hard. She stared at them through blurring tears and thought of Mathilda's words to her.

She couldn't do it. Not just the singing. She couldn't do any of it. Serve them. See them. Watch their children born.

He did not intend to release her. She just knew it. Lehman or not, he planned to keep her with him. It made no sense. The girl was beautiful, radiant, cheerful. He had never looked to the shadows beyond Claire's light. Why should he want to now?

The sobs calmed to choking bursts amidst deep breaths. From the courtyard she heard the sounds of horses finally moving. Some boot steps scraped the stones and silence fell.

She trusted that he would not look for her. He had plans to make and a marriage to consider. She prayed that the regretful expression on Richard's face when he came for her would be the only apology she would ever receive for being commanded to sing at this feast. If she faced Addis again today she would fall to pieces once more and he would see it. She could not bear that humiliation.

Calmer now, she rose and peeked around the tree. The garden and courtyard were empty. She skirted the flower beds and walked to the house, seeking the privacy of her chamber.

Maybe later he would change his mind. Maybe, after he married, after he had Barrowburgh, he would relent. But she could not endure this that long. As a girl she had done so, but she had little choice then. She was a girl no longer, and she had the means to end it.

She sat on her pallet and pulled her sewing basket into her lap. Ripping at the lining, she plucked out the ruby. She had thought to buy an inn and a husband with it, but her mason had talked of marriage without asking her dowry. Rhys would not miss that which he never expected to get.

She stared at the soft brilliance of the jewel. So costly and so small. Valuable because it was rare. Desired because it was beautiful. Like some women.

Enough, then. Too many years had been spent on a childish infatuation. Too many memories imprisoned her. Enough of the past. Let it go.

Addis looked for her in the kitchen and garden and concluded that she had probably gone to the market to replenish the food stores. He left word with Jane to inform him when she returned and then retired to the solar. He hoped that she would not be gone long. He wanted to thank her, and to apologize.

The feast had tired him in indefinable ways. The girl had made him feel old and world-weary. More than years separated them. A lifetime of experiences that she would never learn about lay like a chasm between them. He doubted that passion or time or even children could bridge it, mainly because he had no desire to do so. His body might join with hers to sire sons, but his soul would never be able to bond with her. Not because she was young and vain and a lot like Claire. Not because of who she was at all. The real problem lay in who she was not.

He paced to the window overlooking the courtyard, hoping for the flutter of light linen that would say she was back. He saw again her gracious acceptance of Mathilda's coin and her stiff composure while she sang that song. She had not looked at him during those love lyrics, even though every fiber of his being had urged her to. Just as well. It would have drawn attention to his reaction. As it was he suspected Thomas had noticed.

He threw himself on the bed. He felt empty, adrift, as if he could not connect his mind to his body and his body to this chamber. The little storm of resentment kept churning and rumbling. In some ways he had been a freer man when a slave. No duty set his course for him there. Yokes set upon your shoulders were easier to bear than responsibilities born in your blood.

He found himself wishing that he had met Moira then, that she had been captured in a raid into Poland and brought to the slaves' compound. Would he have been able to love her during those cautious years? Would the peace have been there then, peeling open the heart hardened for survival as easily as it had done upon his return? If offered his chance for freedom, would he have forgone it if it meant leaving her?

A scratch at the door broke his reverie. Jane poked her head in.

"She is back?" He swung off the bed to go to her.

"Nay." Jane stayed near the door, twisting her hands in her skirt. "She said to wait until tomorrow before giving it to you, to say she rested in her chamber this evening, but I thought as how you might want to know now."

"Know what? Give me what?"

She appeared fearful enough that foreboding began dripping through him. She scooted over and dropped something on the table.

"She said to tell you she's buying the freedom. With this. She said to tell you it should cover the price you set. Said she is not forswearing her oath because a free woman does not need to run away."

He strode quickly to the table. A ruby twice the size of a robin's egg lay atop the parchments.

Jane licked her lips. "She said it'd be more use to you than her now. Said you could use it to hire archers and such."

"Where is she?"

"Said to tell you she cannot do it, whatever that means. Said even in friendship and love she could not, and that—"

"Where is she?"

She jumped back. "Don't know. I swear, my lord, I do not. She left awhile ago and said she'd send for her things later. Just took a big basket is all. I should have come at once, I know, but it took me a time to realize what she meant and what she planned to do and then Henry said I should . . ."

He stared at the ruby, not hearing the explanations flowing from Jane beside him. An astonishing pain strangled him.

He gestured blindly. "Leave."

"Do you want Henry and me to look . . . ?"

"Just go now."

She ran off. He fingered the jewel. Its deep brilliance and shadowed planes mesmerized him. Rich color, dark depths, subtle lights. Beautiful. Solid despite its clarity. Like her.

Where had she come by it? From Edith, undoubtedly. From Bernard. She had possessed it all this time. While at

Darwendon and on the journey here. It was her dowry, but leaving him had become more important than going to a husband with such a marriage prize.

Tell him that I cannot do it.

Nay, she could not, any more than he could. If someone said that he must watch her daily with another man, he could not do it. Not even if she needed him nearby. Not even in friendship and definitely not in love. Perhaps even while he demanded that she admit the love they shared, he had been counting on her never accepting it. He could ignore the hurt he planned to give her if she kept denying it.

Admitting that left him raw. He took the ruby over to the chest where he stored the coin. He lifted the lid and the two gold armlets glimmered at him, glowing as if they demanded his attention. He picked one up and fingered it, examining the engraved serpents. Moira's words in this room haunted him suddenly. *She must have loved you very much*, she had said of the priest's daughter.

Eufemia's face loomed in his mind. Had she? He saw her sitting by her house and her passion illuminated by the moon. He remembered her bony frame walking away and her last look from amidst the reeds. After six years of looking at her, he saw her truly for the first time. And in her solemn, controlled expressions that obscured the emotions that he did not share, he saw Moira too, but not just the woman. Moira the girl, watching from the shadows.

His throat burned like fire and the ruby blurred in his hand. He knew everything, just sensed it, even though the history and details were lost to him. Holy God, in his selfish need what had he been doing to her?

When he fantasized about meeting her when a slave, he had asked the wrong question when he wondered if he would have forgone freedom if it meant leaving her behind. Eufemia had demonstrated the real strength of love and friendship. The true test would have been whether he could have sent her away to her freedom if meant staying behind himself.

Jane did not know where Moira had gone. Well, he did. He strode to the door. It would not do at all if a pagan witch woman showed more fortitude than a Christian knight.

CHAPTER 16

❧

EVERYONE IN THE WARD knew Rhys and she
found his house easily by asking for directions. It was a
modest dwelling on a short spur of a lane. No one answered her scratch and she settled down on the door stoop
to wait.

Skinny tall houses crowded shoulder to shoulder
around the little finger of pavement. A furrier and a
weaver worked at windows across the way. They examined
her, as did the women and children milling by doorways.
She hoped that Rhys would arrive back before nightfall.
She certainly did not want the constable finding her here.

He turned onto the lane an hour later, carrying his
tools in a sack over his back. He noticed her immediately
and she pushed to her feet.

He showed pleasure at seeing her, which helped enor-
mously. The emotions that had driven her here had dulled
a little and the logic of coming did not seem so clear now.
He had not visited since Addis returned, and she knew
that he had been questioned about the attack on the road

from Hastings. If the interrogation had been rough he might blame her for it.

"I brought you some supper," she said, lifting the basket.

He took it from her and opened the door.

He did not need the front chamber for a shop and so the table and stools were there. The house looked comfortable enough, but was furnished sparingly. It struck her as exactly what she expected for an established mason who had not married yet, but who intended to someday. At a loss for words and suddenly shy, she unpacked the food from the basket.

"It looks like someone had a feast," he observed as she set out the white bread and hare stew and venison pie.

"Aye." She carried the stew over to the hearth. Rhys relit a low fire and she set the earthen bowl nearby to warm.

"Thomas Wake visited." She knew that she did not have to say anything else. He had been to Wake's house. He would know about Mathilda and would guess the reason for the feast.

"I trust that your lord's wounds are healing? Sir Thomas sought me out last week. Wanted to know where I had been the last days."

"He asked it of all of you who knew where Addis had gone."

"But Sir Addis thought that I was the one who followed, didn't he?"

She nodded.

"And what did you think, Moira?"

"I told him it could not be you. That you would not try to see him harmed."

"You give me more credit than I deserve. I will not say that it did not cross my mind."

"I know that you did not do it." Actually she did not

know that for sure at all, since the evidence did not indicate that it had been the king or the Despensers who sent men after Addis. She just did not believe that he cared for her in the way that might drive a man to kill.

He shrugged. "Nay. He carried important information. This chance may not come again."

"Do you think someone else betrayed you all? That the king knows?"

"Possibly. It may be that when we leave this city to join the queen a whole army will await us on the road."

She did not want to contemplate that danger again. It had not been far from her mind the last week while she tended Addis in Southwark and lay awake into the nights listening for the sounds of soldiers at the gate.

When they sat to the meal she did not eat much. She kept trying to picture herself here, sitting with him every evening, living in this space, bound to him.

"Are you going to tell me why you are here?" he asked while he poured some ale.

"Perhaps I just wanted to share my supper with a friend."

"Perhaps. But you are not sharing the supper and you look distraught."

"I am just tired, that is all."

"You prepared this feast today?"

"I was glad to. It is an important alliance that he makes with Thomas Wake. It will get him the help that he will need." She tried to say it lightly but the words wavered just enough that he looked at her very intently.

She still walked a narrow precipice in holding on to her composure. She took a deep gulp of ale. "I bought the freedom today. He had set a high price, but I paid it. I had saved enough . . . I had hoped to . . ."

"How high?"

"Too high."

"You need not have done so."

He meant that he cared not whether she was bonded or free and she felt grateful for that. "I did need to. I had sworn not to run away. Anyway, it is done."

"Do you think he will accept this?"

"He set the price and I paid it. A son of Barrowburgh does not go back on his word."

"I wonder if he will view it so plainly, Moira. You see a different man than I do if you believe that."

She did not want to debate Addis's character. It would be best not to think about him at all right now. Even the mention of his name set her tottering on the brink of tears.

She chastised her foolish heart and plunged forward with resolve. "Despite what I paid, I still have some coin. I also have my freeholding at Darwendon. It is a whole virgate, and a cottage and its croft." It did not sound like much now that she listed it.

He poked some bread at his stew. "Are you explaining your dowry, Moira? Have you come to propose a marriage?"

"I hear that the dowry for citizens is one hundred pounds. I doubt the virgate is worth that much. For a mason like you who owns a house and works at Westminster it is probably a lot higher. Scores of fathers probably approach you all the time."

"Aye. Scores." He grinned. "Hundreds."

"But I have my craft too. Ladies pay good coin for my baskets. And if you marry, you would not have to eat in taverns anymore."

"That is certainly worth something."

"And while this is a fine house, it is not really a home for you. You might even take on apprentices if you had a wife to care for things."

He propped his head on his hand, amused with her

recital. "You need not convince me of your worth. I told you that I had been thinking to offer for you myself. I had already decided that whatever dowry you brought would be sufficient and that I could use a wife. Nay, the only problem that I see is a different one."

"What is that?"

"You do not want to sleep with me. There are few things that will turn a marriage bad as quickly as that."

The blunt statement left her speechless. She had not expected to actually speak of that. She dropped her gaze to the table planks.

"I was not married long and am still inexperienced in these things. A new man's touch still startles me. But I was an obedient wife to James even in our bed."

"I do not want obedience. If that is the dowry that you bring me I will not take it."

The day had exhausted her and now the last of her wobbling strength broke beneath a gust of discouragement. It had been a mistake coming here. He did not want her. She should have realized that the end of his visits meant he had reconsidered.

She rose to go, dreading returning to Addis's house. Maybe she could avoid him and after she slept she would be able to think clearly about how to live in this city on her own.

He reached for her arm and stopped her. "Is that the only way you can know a husband, Moira? In obedience?"

"It is what men want."

"Not me."

Nay. If this man only sought a dutiful wife he would have married years ago. Too emotionally numb to know embarrassment, she spoke her mind.

"I am here, aren't I? I came today of my own choice. I do not know if I have what you want, or if we can make a good life. We neither of us loves the other but we have friendship which is as much as most couples ever find. I thought we might begin to see what could grow between us. I had not intended to go back, but I will if I must."

It just poured out, sounding more desperate than she wanted. He examined her thoughtfully, then got up and came around to her. "Nay. You will stay and I welcome you."

His head dipped and he kissed her. It was an offering of friendship as much as passion. She accepted the brief warmth and tried to ignore the quiet cry that filled her chest.

He carefully embraced her and she let herself relax into his arms. The wrong arms, but she drew some comfort from their strength. She half hoped and half dreaded that he would do more than kiss and embrace. She would begin to discover pleasure with him, she resolved. With time she might find a passion that would obliterate all those memories.

A shadow slid over them, distracting him from another kiss. They both turned their heads to the doorway.

Addis stood there, looking dangerously tense. His eyes flashed over them and whatever coiled inside him seemed to suddenly wind tighter.

Rhys released her but only so he could thrust her behind him. "Do violence in this house and you will answer to the city courts."

"I only come for what is mine."

"She is a freeman now."

"Not yet."

She could see Addis and had no trouble reading his mood. She knew that taut conviction and where it could lead and a breathless alarm seized her. "Nay, Rhys, do not . . ."

His arm swung out to prevent her walking around him.

"If you go back he will not let you leave again. Even if it means your death, I think."

She placed her hand on his arm. "That is not true. You do not know him. He is not dangerous to me."

"Nay, I am not," Addis agreed, stepping inside and unsheathing his sword. He lifted it until the point rested on Rhys's throat. "But I am dangerous to you. Do not interfere. You can have her when I am done with her."

"You are already done with her. She is done with you."

"Not yet. Come, Moira."

Turmoil poured out of him and she feared what he would do if Rhys continued this confrontation. "Put up the sword, Addis." She pushed Rhys's arm out of her way and walked to him. "You have no argument with this man. You know that I came here of my own choice. You will not harm him because of me."

He glared at Rhys with a primitive hostility. She stepped closer and placed her hand on his sword arm. Pressing against its resistance, she coaxed him to lower the weapon.

The worst of his fury unwound from his body. She could feel it loosening. After a few moments he resheathed the sword.

He still glowered at the mason, who still stood his ground.

"You will come with me, Moira. Sleep where you wish tonight, but you will come with me now."

Rhys shot her a look of warning. She returned one of reassurance. He means it, she tried to convey. Trust me. I know him. Rhys's reaction displayed neither understanding nor acceptance.

Her gaze swept back to Addis. He looked away from Rhys and their eyes met. His expression almost stopped her heart. Anger still, but also a pain that she never thought to see in him again. A deep, soulful awareness of loss that matched her own fierce grief.

Rhys ceased to exist. There were just the two of them looking at each other, acknowledging what had been and what must end. The declarations never spoken now flowed inaudibly between them. She knew that whatever his reasons for following her here, it had not been to force her back to him. She ruefully admitted to both gratitude and disappointment in that.

She stepped toward the door. A quick movement made her turn in time to see Rhys lunge for Addis. His arm swung and Addis answered the challenge, landing a blow on the mason's face that sent him stumbling back against the table.

He grabbed her hand and pulled her into the street. With long strides he dragged her into the main lane. She stumbled after him, struggling to lift her skirt so she would not trip.

"You did not have to hit him," she snapped.

"I'm glad he gave me the excuse. He got off lightly. I almost took his head when I saw him embracing you."

She resisted his pull, but to little avail. "You lied then. You said that I could go where I would."

"I did not lie. When I am done you are free to go back to him. But knowing he has you is different than seeing it, Moira. I can be excused some jealousy, I think."

He hauled her along, never slackening his determined pace. She realized that he did not head back to the house.

The street disappeared into an open square. She looked up in confusion at the high towers rising in its center from the huge mass of the cathedral. Addis pulled her across the stones toward the portals, through the remnants of vendors closing down their stalls.

Inside the nave he paused, surveying the tables at which

scribes and lawyers offered their skills. He gestured for a cleric passing nearby. "Go and ask one of the priests to come."

He led her over to a table against the east wall. The man working there had begun to gather his parchments.

"You know the law?" Addis asked.

The balding, plump man nodded. "I do."

"I want some documents. Legal and binding."

The lawyer hurriedly set out his quills again. "Certainly, sir. What must the documents convey?"

"I am Addis de Valence, Lord of Darwendon, and this is Moira Falkner, a bondwoman of those lands. Write the language that gives her the freedom."

The lawyer began scribbling. "You will need three copies. One for each of you and one for the Church."

"Do it then."

The cleric returned, leading a member of the cathedral chapter. The priest advanced with curiosity. "I am giving this woman the freedom," Addis explained. "I would have a priest witness it."

They all waited silently for the half hour it took the lawyer to pen the documents.

"It will be legal this way," Addis muttered at one point.

"Aye. Best if it be legal," she mumbled back. She avoided his eyes and carefully studied the cathedral decorations. Being near him kept chipping away at her fragile hold on her battered self-control. She had known many partings from him, but this final voluntary one promised to be the worst. A horrible sensation filled her, similar to what one experienced during a death watch.

The lawyer presented the copies for Addis's acceptance. He read every word on each one, then put his name to them. The priest and lawyer witnessed and Addis rolled one and placed it in her hands, formally declaring the end of his hold on her.

She stared at it and the tears wanted to flow so badly that she dared not move. The priest drifted away, but Addis turned to the lawyer again.

"I need another document now. A charter this time, for property. It is to transfer ownership of a house in London from me to Moira Falkner in return for a jewel, a ruby, which she has given me."

Her mouth fell open. "That was for—"

"The price was cruelly high and even so its purpose failed. I sought an amount you could not find. Since you found it anyway, there is no point in insisting on it."

"Still, it was yours to set. You need not give me the house."

"I could just return the jewel, I suppose, but it will be easier to sell than the house, and for you the property makes a better dowry."

"They are both your right to keep."

"I will not take a single pence for your freedom, Moira. If I had not forced you to resume the bonds you would never have known them again. And I will not see you go to him with less than other women could offer. The house will be yours to keep or sell." He turned back to the lawyer. "Write."

It seemed that they waited a long time for this document. The lawyer conferred with Addis on occasion and she waited to the side, awed by an anguished melancholy that refused to permit any other emotion. She looked at his face as he bent over the parchment, and thought that she saw sorrow in him too. That only made it worse. He was giving her the freedom and her inn and a freemason waited to take her to wife. Everything she had planned and wanted would come true soon. Instead of satisfaction she knew only nostalgia and heartache.

Finally it was done and she wished it were not. She would live in this nave forever if it meant not having to walk out those doors and have it truly end for good. In some ways his death had been easier to absorb than this.

He walked beside her to the portals. She tried to revel in the reality of him one last time, but the awareness was so colored by pain she could not bear it. They paused on the porch, standing so close that their bodies touched, holding the scrolls of parchment that documented the ties he had severed.

He looked down at her. She saw his face through a wash of tears. So handsome. Not a cruel mouth at all, but kind and generous and gentle in its kisses. If only . . . She sighed. So many if onlys stood between them.

"You do not have to go to him," he said. "You need not if you do not want it."

"It is time to make a life for myself. To start anew."

He looked around them with a blind, frustrated expression. Something broke in his face, as if an internal battle had just been decided and he was relieved for the victor.

"Start anew with me then. Say the words and make your life with me."

She looked at him in confusion.

He smiled and gestured to the portals. "This is where it is done, isn't it? By the peasants and townsmen. At the church door. There is a priest inside if you want his witness, but we do not need it. We only have to join hands and say the words that make the sacrament."

She thought that she would break apart from the love and sorrow that ripped and clashed through her. The tears flowed, rivers of saltwater streaming down her cheeks.

He gently brushed their wetness with his hand. "Say the words with me, Moira."

She clutched his hand to her, turning her face to taste her tears and his skin. "You know it can never be. It means turning your back on your place, your blood, the means to regain it all."

"I will live with it."

"I will not let you. The regrets will be a weight all your life. You could not be satisfied with Darwendon any more than I could be satisfied in bondage."

He began to argue. She placed her hand on his mouth to stop him. "It is impossible, Addis. But I will love you forever for asking."

She turned quickly. Her feet moved beneath her. Somehow her body followed. She tore herself from the portal and from the steps. From him.

She wandered for some time before seeking the way back to Rhys. She licked at the love filling her, savoring both its quiet joy and poignant sorrow. She immersed herself in it while she blindly walked the lanes. Finally, when the evening grew old and the buildings cast long shadows, she kissed the sweet memory and then carefully placed it in a chamber of her heart and closed the door.

Rhys was not alone. She entered his house to find a blond woman dabbing at his face with a wet cloth while he sat at the table. She paused in the threshold and they both noticed her. With a sharp look in Moira's direction, the woman handed Rhys the cloth and walked toward the back of the house.

"She is a widow who lives next door," he explained blandly, pressing the cloth to his face. "She heard the argument."

Moira decided to accept that, although the woman's look had implied more than a wall existed between the neighbors. She sat beside him on the bench and placed the parchments on the table. "He would not accept any payment for the freedom. He gave me the house in return for the price I had paid."

"It must have been a very high price."

"It was."

He put the cloth aside and fingered the parchments. The blow had raised a bad swelling on his face.

"I am sorry that he hit you. You only sought to protect me."

"You keep giving me more credit than I deserve. I did not go for him only to protect you."

They sat in a stretching silence that unsettled her. She began to feel like an unwelcome intruder in a stranger's home. He looked at her in an intent, hard way that made her even more ill at ease.

"Why did you come back here?"

The question startled her. "I thought we . . ."

"So did I. But I saw the way that you looked at him, Moira, and now I do not think that we can. When I asked you what was between him and you, you did not answer as precisely as I thought. I had not seen you with him much, and that was a mistake I think."

She began emptying out, as if everything between her neck and her toes started to disappear. "It is over. Completely." She held up the parchments in a crushing grip. "I have the freedom! I have more property than any of those fathers ever offered. He is gone from my life and has no hold on me!"

"Is he? Doesn't he?" He rose with a disturbingly cool deliberation and stepped behind her. She felt his warmth close to her back and then his hands on her shoulders. She stiffened against the intimacy. He caressed down and cupped her breasts and she gritted her teeth.

"Doesn't he? The wrong man, Moira. The wrong hands."

He spoke the words that her heart felt. She broke. Collapsing with a horrible misery, she buried her head in her arms on the table and succumbed to the sobs that vanquished her exhausted control.

He sat beside her and patted her shoulder and said something soothing which she did not hear. The flood of emotion began retreating. She straightened and wiped her face with her hands.

"You are not being fair. With time I am sure—"

"Perhaps, but I am not inclined to take that chance. I did not expect love, but I would prefer to marry where it is at least a possibility. It is a lifetime that we speak of. I am not so foolish as to wed a woman whose heart is owned by another man."

She wished that she could refute him. She could not. He was right. Addis did own her heart. He had for half her life. Eight years of being dead had not loosened those bonds and she could not claim that time would destroy them now.

A crushing bleakness immobilized her empty body. She foresaw a future of existing half-alive, of moving and eating and tending her inn while a part of her, the part capable of love and joy, slept an eternal rest. Rhys was right. Even if she made a marriage and gave some man her body, a part of her would never be touched again.

"I do not know what to do," she mumbled.

He shrugged. "You are free and you are wealthy. You do not need a marriage to secure your future. You need no man to feed you. You can do whatever you want."

"Whatever I want."

"I cannot imagine you ever being more unhappy than you are right now, Moira. If I were to know such pain, I would want it to be for a reason."

For a reason.

Footsteps treaded on boards back in the kitchen. The sounds of the widow moving a pot clanked in the silence.

She turned to him, her lips still trembling from the tears that wanted to spill. But slowly the emptiness began filling with a peaceful, glorious possibility.

He smiled kindly at her. "If you find yourself with child, you can support it. This city takes such things in stride. You will not be the first woman living thus."

A spot of wetness snaked down her cheek. She wanted to weep still, but for different reasons. A wonderful lightness suffused her as she closed the door on her pain for a while, and reopened another that would give the grief reason and meaning when it emerged again. A shared love, at least for a while. Memories to complete the others. Maybe enough happiness to sustain a lifetime.

He placed the documents in her hands and rose. He walked to the passage leading to the kitchen where the widow waited. Stopping, he spoke without looking back at her.

"Go home, Moira."

CHAPTER 17

❧

"I JUST TOLD THE MEN to come in one by one over the next few days, and now you are saying that we leave and go to them. You are not making any sense," Richard said.

Addis continued packing his belongings into horse bags, trying to suppress the chaotic thoughts and seething frustration racking him.

Damn her pride. Damn her relentless realism. Damn her!

Dark had fallen. Was he undressing her now? Holding her full, perfect breasts? Licking their hard tips, or other places where his own tongue had only ventured in his imagination? Would that mason take the time to give her pleasure, or just use her the way the wool merchant had? Would she truly give herself to him, or just permit her body to be claimed?

"Why pay for a Southwark inn when there's all this space here? If it's because you want to avoid seeing the child Mathilda, you needn't worry. Wake is sending his family out of the city till all this is over."

He saw her tears glimmering, increasing the clarity of her water-blue eyes. Like tiny pure pools they looked up at him, reflecting his own awareness of loss. So sad and so happy that last look had been. He saw her trembling smile while she pressed his hand with lips he wanted so badly to kiss. She had walked away straight and strong, taking with her the only thing that truly mattered to him, leaving him with the first declaration of what they should have admitted weeks ago. *I will always love you for asking.*

He wiped his mind of the torturous images, wishing he could purge his heart as easily. Nothing left but duty. No course but to complete his responsibilities to the same blood and honor that formed an iron wall between them. He would see it through in the name of his father, but he did not really care if he succeeded or failed right now.

He opened the chest with the armlets. "It is time to trade these for coin. Did your lady know of some merchants who will give an honest price?"

"I asked her, as you wanted. I've the names. Now, about this sudden notion to go across the river, it is not smart. Think about it. If nothing else, it means we have to cross back once things start just to ride north and there's just a few bridges and they can be blocked. Better to be in the city anyway, especially if something goes wrong."

"I am not some green squire who needs lessons in strategy."

"Of course not, my lord. Just I don't understand this sudden decision."

He handed Richard the armlets, then dropped the ruby amidst them. The temptation to keep it, like a token from her, struck him. Best to let it and the memories go. "This too. Tomorrow at first light, sell them all."

Richard frowned down at the riches in his hand. He plucked up the ruby. "One of your mother's jewels? Should have told me you had it. I've been recruiting the men to pay with the gold is all. This will make a big difference."

"Not my mother's. Moira's. I traded this house for it."

"Moira's! Who would think a bondwoman would possess such a thing! Doesn't seem right, somehow."

"She is not a bondwoman. I gave her the freedom today. And the house. I think that she plans to make it an inn."

"If so, she should be glad for us to stay. What with the others, we will fill the place."

"I doubt that she would be glad to have *me* stay, and I know that her future husband would not."

"Future hus . . . you mean the mason?"

"Aye."

Richard chewed on this revelation. "Seems to me that you are making plans as if you know that woman's mind in ways you might not. Perhaps you complicate things for nothing. Better to stay here, and you know it."

"I know her mind on this, I promise you. We leave at first light."

"Well, if you don't mind, I think I'll check with her just to be sure. If she intends to make this an inn, her feelings may be hurt if you take your trade elsewhere."

"You'll not find her. She has left."

"What are you talking about?"

Addis shuffled together the parchments on the table. His hand paused on the newest ones. "She is with him."

"Nay, she is not. Hell, I saw her just before I came up here."

He froze. "Where?"

"In the courtyard. She'd just run in and we jested

about how she almost got caught out after curfew again and—"

"Was she alone?"

"From what I could see, but I was just passing by the gate."

"How did she look?"

"Hell, she looked like Moira. How should she look? 'Twas dusk and hard to see, but she appeared normal enough to me. Bit out of breath is all. What is this about?"

Addis strode to the door, arguing against a desperate hope. The place was hers, after all. She had every right to return. He was the intruder and she probably had expected him to be gone by now. Rhys had most likely come with her. They probably planned to enjoy the luxury of the solar's bed tonight. He had no trouble finding many reasons for her reappearance, none of which had anything to do with him at all. Still the hope spread like a childish excitement that he could not control. He probably should not go to her, but of course he had to.

Richard's voice followed him down the stairs. Out in the silent courtyard he looked around. Instinctively he knew that she was not in her chamber nor in the kitchen. He walked to the edge of the garden and peered into the darkness.

A light figure moved in the back, gliding ghostlike between the trees. He walked quietly along the wall, trying to see if a man strolled beside her.

She was alone. He stopped and watched her from the shadows while she paced thoughtfully, fingering a leaf here and plucking a flower there. Her hair fell around her body, making dark streaks down her pale gown, swaying to veil her face when she bent to smell a rose.

She appeared very serene in her solitude. She looked

like a woman well contented with how things had turned out. The hope crashed into a wall of disappointment.

Even so, her presence soothed him and the turmoil and regrets of the last hour receded. He would stand here a while and savor the gift of peace one last time and then fetch Richard and go.

The soft flow of the pale robe stopped. For several heartbeats she did not move. He had the sensation that the whole garden had halted in time. Then she plucked another flower.

"I have been in love with you since I was twelve years in age."

She spoke it as if she merely continued a conversation that needed finishing before they parted.

He moved toward her, grateful to have an excuse to be closer. She paused on the path until he drew up beside her. Neither hope nor disappointment now, just comfort in walking beside her for a while.

"It was cruel of me not to see it back then, Moira. I fear that I hurt you without even knowing it."

"There was more joy than hurt in it. I will not deny the pain of seeing you and Claire at times, but I was happy for your happiness. And for hers. Even with the heartache, I embraced the love. It gave my young life purpose in a way."

"I find myself wishing that you had said something."

"Claire's Shadow declaring her love? You would have laughed, or treated it like the childish thing it probably was at first."

"Maybe. I would like to think I would have been kinder than that."

They reached the far wall and she rested her back against it. She fingered the flowers of the little bouquet she had gathered. "The whole time you were gone I loved you. I did not contemplate it much, but it was there.

Strange, isn't it? I expected it to fade once you had died, but when you came back I knew it was still in me. A dangerous thing, love. It is that that I ran from as much as the bonds."

And what she ran from still.

"Did he come with you?"

"Rhys? Nay. He decided that he did not want me. Even the value of this house could not sway him."

"He is a fool."

"Not at all. In fact, he may be the most sensible man I have ever met. He knows that I still love you. He knows that no jewel can buy freedom from that."

He leaned his shoulder against the wall, wishing he could see her expressions. He felt both anguish and pride in hearing her speak so calmly of loving him. Her voice sounded even and controlled, as if she spoke from some inner resolve. His own blood and emotions were churning. "If a lawyer's document could settle that freedom the way you wanted, I would gladly procure one for you."

She laughed and poked the flowers at his nose. "I think that you would."

"There will be another man. You are beautiful and now you are well propertied. And you have a good heart. There will be plenty of men who will count themselves fortunate to have you."

"I do not think I will be marrying anyone, Addis."

So there it was. The statement that killed the small chance that she had reconsidered his offer at the cathedral. He could not believe how empty it made him again. Proud, practical Moira. Describing in one breath an endless love and reaffirming in the next its impossibility.

It would be hell to walk away, but staying any longer promised a worse torture.

"I thought that you would not be back tonight. I had

planned to leave before you returned tomorrow, but Richard and I will go now."

"There is no need. The solar is yours, now and whenever you are in London. Besides, it would be very unchivalrous of you to leave after I have set aside my pride and good sense and come back."

He stared at the profile sniffing the flowers, trying to see her face in the darkness.

He almost dared not ask because he feared the answer. "Did you come back to your property or to me?"

She turned her head in surprise, as if the answer should have been obvious. "Oh, I most definitely came back to you." She placed her hand on his chest. "For whatever time we have left."

Gratitude and relief washed in a torrent. He lifted her hand and kissed it, then grasped her into his arms. Sweet perfume rose as the flowers crushed between their bodies. He buried his face in her hair and savored the feel of her fingers against his chest. Her last words tempered his joy for a only a moment before the sheer pleasure of holding her again banished the concern for a later time.

She tilted her head to invite a kiss and the willing gesture undid him. A hunger more soulful than physical drove his hard response. The sweet taste of her lips sent a ferocious desire tensing through him. The tip of her tongue swept his in symbolic acceptance.

He surrounded her, afraid she might disappear if he loosened his hold. He wanted to bind her to him, seal their bodies, absorb her into him. His exhalant phallus pressed against her belly and he probed her mouth in a simulacrum of the joining he craved. With a sharp gasp she broke the devouring kiss but slid her arms from between them to join the embrace.

He ate down her neck until he found the heavy pulse

beneath her ear. His mouth locked on the hot beat, connecting her life rhythm to both their hearts. She gasped again, rising on her toes with an abandoned stretch.

"I want you. Need you. Completely. Now," he muttered against her skin.

"Aye."

Her breathless affirmation made him burn. He almost pulled her to the ground. "Where? Your chamber?"

"The solar. Your bed."

"Your bed now."

"Our bed now."

He had to release her to get her there. He took her hand and led her through the garden, not bothering with the paths, tromping over flowers and pushing through hedges.

She tripped along behind his determined stride much as she had on the way to the cathedral. Her gown caught on a bush and a courtyard torch dimly lit his expression when he turned and snapped the branch with his fingers. Her heart lurched. She had felt very bold and secure while she ran back here and spoke her love in the garden. Seeing his desire and expectation made her excited and nervous and not very self-possessed at all.

He handed her up the stairs and followed a step behind, his tension warm on her back and a guiding hand on her hip. She entered the solar and walked to its center, noticing the packed bags and tied weapons. Despite her decision she felt self-conscious suddenly, and a little fearful. He closed the door and looked at her, then took the candle from the table and dipped its flame to several others in the chamber.

"You do not have to be afraid," he said with a vague smile. "I am not going to devour you."

"Do I have your word of honor on that?" She laughed. He cocked his head thoughtfully, then shook it. "Nay."

"Well, no one can ever accuse you of not giving fair warning." Giddy and wobbly, she sat on the edge of the bed and watched flame after flame briefly illuminate his face, exaggerating the hard planes and the golden-lit eyes. He wore the Baltic animal skins and she was glad he had changed from the lordly garments of the feast.

"You remind me of my obligations under chivalry. I suppose since you have surrendered that means I should give you terms." He replaced the candle on the table. "But I find I do not feel much like a Christian knight at the moment."

Nor did he look like one. "After such a long and patient siege, I did not expect to get quarter."

"Good."

He stripped off the tunic and she did the devouring, with her eyes.

He walked over until he stood in front of her. Each step quickened her blood, flushing her with excitement.

The chiseled muscles of his chest hovered a hand span from her nose. The smallest gap separated her legs from his thighs. She looked up into his severe intensity. Thudding anticipation tremored through her.

She reached with trembling hands and caressed his chest, admiring his lean strength, loving the sensation of his skin beneath her palms. He let her, looking down. She reveled in the feel of his taut abdomen and waist, and ran her hands along the sides of his hips, splaying her fingers over the buckskin. Leaning forward she pressed her lips to him, closing her eyes, tightening with a strumming expectation.

He stretched his fingers through her hair, holding her face to his body, kissing the top of her head. "I have never taken a woman in love before. Not really."

That was not true, but if time and anger had dulled his

memory of the last time she would not remind him now. "Are you saying that you love me, Addis?"

"Aye, and it needs saying. I love you with both of my souls. I am only whole with you."

He raised her up and turned her so he could undo the closures on the green gown. He lowered the garment, his hands skimming her with titillating brushes while he slid it down her body. He gathered her long hair to her back and turned her to face him. He slipped the shift from her shoulders and it slinked down her curves until she stood naked in the candlelight. He barely touched her while he looked at her, just grazed her softly with his palms. Finally, handling her like a fragile possession he led her onto the bed and discarded the rest of his garments until they lay skin to skin beside each other.

Fingertips and gaze drifted over her breasts and hips and thighs. "You are very beautiful, Moira."

She did feel beautiful. The most beautiful woman in the world. Valuable and rare and perfect in his eyes. The equal of all the Claires and Mathildas of the realm. The love of half a lifetime swelled, filling her with happiness.

He broached her with soft, tasting kisses and slow, contemplative caresses. His hands and mouth moved over her body like he savored the exploration and memorized the passages of pleasure that he discovered. Desire rose in little sparks and tremors, a gradual delicious stimulation. She stretched and arched, thrusting her breasts toward his attention.

"I had planned to spend half the night on this loving, living out my dream, but it appears you may not let me." He smiled, giving the caress she sought. His circling touch provoked heavenly pleasure. "Nor will my own need, I think."

"Next time," she barely breathed.

He gently squeezed her nipple between thumb and finger and bent to flick the tip with his tongue. An arrow of tense excitement shot down to the itching moisture already pulsing its demanding torture. "Aye, next time. And the next. And the next. I had many dreams."

Even so, he took forever, honoring her with intimate caresses, teasing her breasts with his tongue and lips, kissing her with controlled fervor. He guided her into a frenzied tumult of sensuality. She grasped him to her and every spot of her body and consciousness pleaded for more. She reached for him, taking the hard length of his phallus in her hand, using her knowledge of his own body like a challenge against his restraint. He responded by caressing down to the cleft between her legs. A focused heat and hunger burst with his gentle massaging of her inner thighs. She lost conscious control of her body. She undulated with abandon, frantically begging for what he withheld.

He spread and bent her legs, splaying them until the palms of her feet met. Cool air and desperate voracity produced delicious shivers. He touched her open vulnerability and a moan of wonder and gratitude escaped her. He rose up and looked down at her and his fingers began driving her mad. She rocked into the gentle touches and rubs, body and mind knowing only a single craving that pitched higher and higher. The exquisite sensations deepened the hollow hunger that demanded filling. As if he heard its urging he slid a finger inside her and she cried an affirmation, bowing her body in grateful acceptance. The relief was too brief. Almost instantly it became a tantalizing promise more than a fulfillment, making the hunger worse.

"I like to see your need of me," he said. "I like to see you feel what I feel and want what I want."

He sucked on her breast and used his hand very deliberately. She bucked and cried with a delirious burst. Surely she could not bear any more.

He moved over her, settling between her legs, taking his weight onto his arms. She reached down and guided him to her, impatient for completion, almost unhinged with a wanting that threatened to shatter her. She grasped his buttocks and lifted her hips to absorb him. A thread of control snapped above her. He thrust with a force that shook both their bodies and she cried from the startling sensation that she had been split. The shock cleared her senses.

He hovered over her, shoulders and arms tense and expression serious. Her body began to relax, accommodating the invasion. He must have felt it because the veil of concern left his eyes.

"I will withdraw at the end so you do not get with child."

The feeling of ravishment faded, leaving only a blissfully tight fullness, as if he physically permeated every void in her. She caressed his face and pulled his head down for a joyful, welcoming kiss. "Nay. Do not. After all this time, let it be complete."

He moved carefully, easing the fullness in and out of her, emphasizing his possession with controlled retreats and advances, pausing sometimes until her body moved with entreaties for more. The feel of him inside and all around her, the connections of body and skin and intimacy, left her emotions so saturated she wanted to weep. She held on to his strength, accepting, begging, absorbing, immersed in the precious reality of this long-awaited loving.

She thought that he had fed her hunger, but slowly its insistent warmth reemerged, trembling through her limbs, reawakening sensations where they joined. Her sighs of contentment shortened to gasps as her desire escalated again. He sought her mouth in a probing kiss that matched the rhythms of his body, then lowered his head to take her breast in his mouth, sucking hard while he drew her into a higher passion.

He bent her legs and leveraged up to move deeply. Less gently now, he gave her pleasure while finding his own. He answered his own need while summoning hers again. His body ravished hers with quickening rhythm and increasing force. The release of power left her breathless and her consciousness focused on the summit they approached. He thrust harder and quicker. Demanding. Claiming. Profound sensations quivered through her in response. Tension poured out of him, into her, spiraling down to their jointure. Her arousal shuddered with an intense physicality that then soared, split, and spread, shaking her with unearthly exhilaration. He joined her in it, surrendering with a climax that ravaged them both.

His spent body covered her and she surrounded him with arms and legs, holding on to the union and savoring the rippling ecstasy, realizing she had never known such peace and completion. Such wholeness.

I feel as if I am in a new world. I feel as if the earth, the air, every plant has changed.

He rose up slightly with a peculiar look and she realized that she had spoken aloud. His inwardly searching expression passed quickly. She smiled at what she saw in his eyes then. Definitely love. Surely contentment. Undoubtedly happiness. But also something else. Possession and ownership. *Mine*, those eyes declared.

And it was so. His. Not by bonds of birth, but by free choice.

He moved to her side and pulled her into an encompassing embrace. She snuggled against him, still holding him with one arm and leg. They lay in silent peace for a long while before he spoke.

"I think that your wool merchant prayed too well. But for the maidenhead you might indeed have been the virgin widow. You should not have been so impatient. I did not have to hurt you."

"You hardly encouraged patience." She giggled. "James and I wed during Lent. It is why I was called that. He died soon after Holy Week and it was assumed we had forgone consummation until Easter, as is customary. He was not so pious as that, however."

"Nay, not with such as you in his bed. So he succumbed on a few occasions to irreverent pleasure but made sure you did not enjoy the sin. I do not like the man much. Not just because he had you first, although I will admit some resentment at that. Despite what you said in the hay mound, I think that he did hurt you, and not because you were impatient."

"I was his wife."

"Another reason to dislike him." He gave her a mischievous glance. "I should warn you that I am not much given to prayer at all. In fact, you may regret taking a crusader and prisoner to your bed."

"I will never regret taking this one. Besides, you will not convince me that it has been eight years."

"Nay. Only two. Which is too long for any man. But for your gift in Southwark, I might have impaled you against the garden wall tonight."

She looked at his handsome profile. He had the opportunity for all kinds of gifts while he stayed in that bawd house. She had just assumed. . . .

He rose up on his arm. He caressed down her body and his thoughtful gaze followed his hand. "If ever two people belong together it is you and I, Moira. But you are not going to stay with me, are you?"

"I am here now."

"You do not intend to come with me to Barrowburgh though."

"I will come to see you enter its gates, but nay, I will

not live there with you. I have not changed my mind about that, Addis. I will be your lover until you retake it or marry, but I will make my own life here."

"What if you bear my child?"

"Then I will raise your child and be glad for it."

"If it is a son . . ."

"If it is a son he may prefer the life of a craftsman or merchant. Not all born to the blood are suited to be knights. Our king is evidence of that."

"You must let him decide that, Moira. And me."

"When he is of age for service, he and you can decide. At the age when he would leave for apprenticeship under any case. But I'll not give up a child before that, Addis. Do not expect me to." *Do not expect me to give up all that remains of you before I absolutely must.*

He muttered a curse. "I do not understand your pride in all this. You give yourself to me but with conditions of time and place. You will share a bed with me but not let me take care of you as either a wife or mistress. You say that you love me but in the next breath say you will leave me. I do not know if I can accept this."

"You must promise me that you will. You must let me go when it is time. What I said to you that day in this chamber has not changed. Nor has your duty and the life that you were born to live." She caressed his frowning face and smiled. "Let us enjoy the peace of being whole these days that we have. Complete in this time and place, with neither the past nor the future whispering in our ears. For a while at least I am wholly yours. While we can, let us just be Addis and Moira loving each other. I am so happy. Do not let what must occur a month or so hence ruin it."

"So winning back my honor means losing you. It will be a bitter victory then."

She would have trouble with him when the time came. Still, he seemed to accept it, and the kiss he gave her sealed the agreement. The intimacy deepened and he hardened against her hip.

"I said at Whitly that I wanted to know you completely, every part of you. When I said that I wanted to take you every way a man can have a woman, I expected to have a lifetime, not a few weeks. If you will only be mine for a brief passion, then so be it. But no negotiations this time, Moira. No quarter."

He gently turned her body and bent her forward so that her bottom snuggled against his hips. He carefully entered her again and filled her motionlessly. He bent his body around her while his hand cupped her breast.

"Being inside you is so right. Perfect. Better than any dream," he muttered against her shoulder. "Tell me again, Moira. Say that you are completely mine."

It *was* right and perfect. "I am completely yours, Addis."

His kisses on her back and nape and his fingers playing at her breasts quickly had her desire twisting again, seeking assuagement. The sensations of traveling the path to passion with him inside her from the beginning astonished her. With a needful whimper she wiggled against his hips, encouraging the fullness to move.

A firm hand stilled her hip. "Nay, love. Let me go slowly so it lasts."

And it did go slowly. A long, sweet loving full of alertness to each other, her body curved into his as if they made one form. The joining became normal and separation an unthinkable severing. The beauty of it lulled her to something much deeper than pleasure, even when he reached around to caress the spot sure to bring her release.

Three times he took her before they slept, each union a different dream with its own pleasure. After the last she collapsed on top of him, boneless with sated exhaustion. Her last happy memory was lying with her cheek against his chest, his strong arms holding her tightly.

CHAPTER 18

MOIRA SQUEEZED BETWEEN the bodies jamming the wall's battlements and gazed down on Addis.

He stood beside the mayor of London, surrounded by aldermen and nobles, patiently looking down the Strand, toward Westminster. Londoners crowded the wall flanking Newgate, cramping the archers positioned to give their leaders below protection.

She was grateful that he had not ridden north as planned when word came that Isabelle had landed. The mayor had discovered that Richard had recruited over two hundred men from the shires surrounding the city, and decided that this unexpected small army would be more useful protecting London than joining the barons rushing to the queen's side. When he and Thomas Wake had asked Addis to remain and lend his help to the citizen guard, Addis had agreed.

It had proven an intelligent request, but not for the reasons envisioned. The city had received the news of the imminent fall of their king with an orgy of jubilation. But a triumphant people can easily turn into a riotous mob, and only the many armed men wearing the city's colors on their sleeves had helped maintain any semblance of order. Periodically the army of Addis de Valence had been forced to subdue violence. He had been gone long hours the last two days helping command and deploy the watch, only returning to the barricaded house for short spots of sleep. When he came, day or night, she had taken the opportunity to lie beside him while he dozed.

The Strand, the street connecting Newgate to Westminster, appeared deserted. Moira jostled her way next to a tall archer.

"Can you see anything?"

"Nay. Not yet. If he's going to come it will have to be soon though. The last messenger said the queen is only a half day away now."

"Perhaps the king does not know his danger."

"He knows. He's got spies and messengers same as us."

"Maybe he will fight at the castle."

The archer grinned. "With whom? Them that works in the town say as soon as word of the queen's landing reached us, the courtiers began bleeding out of Westminster as if the buildings were on fire. Hardly anyone left with him now and there's no army waiting for his command. Nay, he'll try to find sanctuary in this city."

She gazed down on the raven head of the tall man standing patiently beside the mayor. He had not worn armor and his only weapon was the ancient sword of Barrowburgh strapped to his body.

"Will the mayor and others be safe, do you think?"

He shrugged and patted his crossbow. "The gates don't open no matter what happens down below. Us up here are the best the city has, my lady, and we've orders to take down all of them except the king if the mayor and lords are attacked."

Knowing that Addis would be promptly avenged did not reassure her much. She knew why the mayor wanted him down there. It had less to do with the fact that he commanded two hundred men who helped protect the city walls, and more to do with the fact that he was the son of Patrick de Valence and kinsman to the late Earl of Pembroke, both high nobles with holdings directly from the crown. His blood made him a formidable presence in any confrontation with King Edward. Still, she wished he had not been at the house when the summons came and that he now monitored developments at some other gate besides this one.

"There they be, my lady. Coming slow like, as if the devil wasn't on their tails the way he is."

She did not bother to correct the way he kept addressing her. She had looked the part of a lady for over a week now because Addis had commanded that she wear the silks and velvets folded inside his mother's chest. She squinted at the entourage in the distance.

The group outside the gate had noticed the riders. Addis twisted and looked up, found her amidst the crowd, and made a motion instructing her to move back from the battlements.

She ignored him. She did not plan to lose sight of him for one instant. Her heart swelled with love and worry while she watched the king and his richly adorned councillors come.

It had been a beautiful week of love before the city began to disrupt. For two days it had just been the two of them, before Richard began sending the men over from Southwark. Even then they had time together, enjoying the lengthening cool nights in each other's arms, squeezing a lifetime of passion and talk into the precious time allotted them.

Certain memories made her blush and smile. Those

nights had been filled with incredible pleasure as Addis indeed sought to know her every way a man could have a woman. Sometimes courtly, sometimes primitive. Frequently astonishing. Always careful. He never hurt her but he made no requests either as he commanded her body and her passion and explored the rights ceded to him during this temporary possession.

She had missed him the last two days. She would miss him much more very soon. Even as she stood here, Richard made the preparations for the army to leave the city.

She could see the king now. He rode between the Despensers, resplendent in a long jeweled robe the color of sapphires. He held himself straight on his mount but even from a distance one could practically see the fear and outrage quivering through him.

The whole wall silenced. Maybe fifty riders stopped twenty feet from Addis. Word spread and in the streets behind her the din of celebration noticeably dulled. Beside her the archer pushed for elbow room and sighted his weapon.

A herald hailed the mayor. "The king demands entry to the city."

"I do not advise it," the mayor replied. "Disorder has broken out. His person might not be safe."

"Within your house he will be safe enough."

"I cannot guarantee that. A mob killed his friend the Bishop of Exeter yesterday. Dragged him from his horse and beheaded him with a butcher knife. I fear that no house is secure enough, not even mine."

Edward paled at this news. The elder Despenser became furious. "Open the gates! Your king commands it! I'll find and deal with the murderers of Exeter!"

"The city will deal with them," the mayor said

smoothly. "And these gates do not open. If a war must be fought, let it be fought elsewhere."

Hugh Despenser scanned the walls. "There's soldiers within. I see some," he said to the king. He examined the lords arrayed before him and his gaze settled on Addis. "Your men?"

"My men."

"You dare to raise an army without the king's permission?"

"I expected to have a good use for one."

Hugh chewed his lower lip. "How many?"

"More than enough to deal with the knightly prowess of fifty court administrators."

"No doubt also enough to deal with a citizen guard composed of craftsmen and apprentices. Come stand by your king's side, Sir Addis, where you belong. Your army is already within the gates. Order these merchants to do their duty by their king."

The mayor startled at that, and looked at Addis with concern.

"My king chose to have another stand by his side, but I do not see him there now," Addis said.

Hugh made a face of disgust. "Simon is a coward. Couldn't run away fast enough. Know your blood and put a short end to this foolish pageant. Your kinsman the earl never forsook his king."

"Nor did my father. And it is true that Aymer chose fealty when the opposition moved to rebellion, and even commanded the army that crushed them. His loyalty got him a dagger in the heart."

"By God, man, do your duty by your king! 'Tis treason if you do not. He demands it of you!"

"I have not heard him demand anything of me."

Edward had been silent during these negotiations for

his refuge, but now he spoke. "Barrowburgh is yours again, Sir Addis, and much more if you aid us. I know loyalty to my friends."

"I do not doubt it. But the father and son flanking you now know loyalty only to themselves. Look what they have brought you to. Petitioning for entry to the crown's own city." He stepped forward. "Send them away. They are dead men, but you are yet the king. Give yourself into my protection and I will see no harm befalls you. There are two hundred inside who will aid me at my order. We will escort you to the assembled barons."

"Do not hear him," Hugh hissed. "Men loyal to you prepare themselves. They will rise up and stop this blasphemous outrage."

"None rise up. We receive messengers many times each day. No army musters for you to the west or the south and your queen rides with an army of her own from the north."

"The French she-lion!" Edward yelled. "I will have her burned for such treason!"

"Give yourself into my protection. You will be safe until you see her, and I will hand you to the bishops and not the queen herself."

Edward appeared to contemplate the offer.

"Aye, he will give you protection," Hugh Despenser sneered. "As his kinsman Aymer protected Gaveston."

"The king is not the one who needs to fear Gaveston's fate," Addis said.

But Hugh had hit his mark with the reference to the king's long-dead lover, and his abduction from Aymer's protection and subsequent execution fourteen years prior. Edward's expression tightened into something that almost approached strength.

"We will leave these gates, and remember well the insult to our person by this city," he said. "We will join with the people and barons loyal to us and crush this rebellion like the last. Every man blocking this gate now will suffer the fate he chose with his treason."

He turned his horse. His retinue split to permit him passage and then funneled behind him. Only when the last opulent robe had disappeared amidst the buildings flanking the Strand did the heavy portcullis of Newgate begin to rise.

Moira waited for Addis inside the gate. The mayor held him in conversation a long while before he could break free and come for her.

"He does not want us to leave, but I explained that the worst is over. The people will return to their trades now," he explained while they walked to the house. "This day made the difference. If London had supported Edward, the queen's position would have been made more difficult. It is a foolish king who does not understand the value of this city to his power, and it is said that Edward has antagonized its citizens throughout his reign."

"So it is over?"

"Not over, but done. It will not be over until the barons decide what to do with him."

"Will you follow him?"

"Some suggested that we do, but there is no need. His path west can be mapped by the manors of lords in debt to him and Hugh. We can only hope that whoever finds him remembers that they deal with a man who still is the lawful king."

They entered the courtyard. It teemed with men preparing weapons and packing belongings. In the center Sir Richard shouted orders to squires and servants regarding arrangements for carting food and equipment. The city had found beds for many of Addis's recruits, but fifty men had cramped the chambers and hall and camped in the yard these last few days.

Richard walked over. "I've sent word to the others. We can be off in a few hours."

She turned to Addis in shock. She had known he was leaving, but had assumed it would be a day or two hence.

The arm holding her shoulders tightened in reassurance. "Call for me when all is prepared. I will be in the solar."

When they were out of sight on the stairs he stopped her and cupped her face with his palms. "It will be no easier on the morrow. As it is, I could find a hundred excuses to never leave here if I permitted myself that freedom."

She should have known he would do it this way to try and spare her the anticipation of pain. He had done the same when he took Brian away.

"You have not been here much these last two days. You have not slept a solid night, but only in bits and pieces while you helped this city. Surely it cannot hurt to wait."

"We will ride out to join the queen today. I would have her and the prince see that Barrowburgh is with them."

She accepted the sense of that, but still she felt miserable. He took her hand and led her up.

"Come lie with me, Moira. It has been bliss holding you while I slept my short rests these last days, but now I want to love you before I leave."

It was a heart-wrenching loving. Sweet and slow, with the pleasure suppressed by other emotions. Her soul savored every touch and sensation as much as her body did. When they finally joined he moved as if the pleasure of connection meant more than that of the completion.

She did not find her release with him, but she did not care. She held his head to her breast when he had finished, her arms encircling his shoulders, and just absorbed the nowness of him.

He shifted and caressed her thighs but she stayed his

hand. He rose up and looked down at her. "It would be unchivalrous of me to leave you thus."

"I only need to hold you. I am content."

"But I am not." He twisted her hand off his wrist and stroked her nether hair. "It would please me to watch you in your pleasure, like I did that night in the cottage and that day in Southwark."

She opened her legs. "Well, we would not want you displeased, my lord."

"Nor would we want you ill-pleased."

He watched her but she did not watch him. Her eyes closed with surprise at his first touch. He did not stroke that spot of pleasure but flesh farther down, where they had joined. It still pulsed from the pressure of him. The quick ecstasy shocked her and sent her senses reeling until she was clawing a hold on him, trying to both stretch into and away from the intensity of it, gasping pleas to him and to heaven.

The release came violently, shaking through her, evoking a cry that the whole household must have heard. The extraordinary contractions echoed through her belly long after her body had relaxed.

"That was really wonderful," she sighed, snuggling against him.

"Aye, wasn't it. I'll have to remember that for later," he said, laughing. "Now give me the peace of your love, Moira. Perhaps I can sleep a while before I have to get in the saddle."

He slept but she did not. She embraced his shoulders and focused on the weight of his head on her breast, never loosening her hold, trying to stretch each moment into a lifetime. And so the time passed slowly, but it passed nonetheless. Two hours later she stood by his side while men-at-arms mounted.

"Richard heard that he headed west as expected.

Nowhere else for him to go but to Wales and the Despensers' lands," Addis said while he surveyed the horses bunched in the courtyard. His foot soldiers milled outside in the lane, waiting to march from the city. "Henry of Lancaster will anticipate that and be waiting for him."

He spoke of practical things, as if that would make this departure less significant, but Moira saw in his eyes that he felt what she felt.

"You will follow after all?" She nestled under his arm in the threshold of the hall, wishing this leave-taking could be more private. She wanted to hang all over him and weep and give vent to the emotions screaming below the calm demeanor she tried to maintain.

"We will still ride north to the queen first but then head west to join with Lancaster. Henry hungers for vengeance because of his brother's execution. I will feel better knowing there is a calm voice present when the king is taken. We must convince Edward to abdicate. There is no precedent for executing a king, and if he is killed the whole realm will be torn by war. And while in the west I must stop at Hawkesford and Darwendon and see how things sit there." He gazed around the buildings and smiled. "Your inn will be suddenly empty after being crammed with men. After all of the work of the last week, perhaps you should rest before letting any chambers."

"A few good nights' sleep for a change and I should get my strength back." She grinned weakly, trying to make light of their imminent parting. Their intimacy had left her feeling dreamy and sated but that only added poignancy to the sadness. She dreaded those nights alone without his love holding her. Lonely nights, and days empty of the sound of his boot steps.

He pulled her back into the shadows of the hall and lifted her into an embrace. "I will come back as soon as I can. You said that you are mine until I retake Barrowburgh and I will hold you to it. You will come with me when I go there, so make arrangements for someone else to run your inn."

Aye, he would come back, but many weeks between now and then would pass with him gone. There had been so little time for happiness thus far, and not much more remained. Would it be enough to last the lifetime she faced without him?

"Will you bring Brian back with you?"

"I had not thought to."

"He should see his father's triumph when it comes. He will not get in the way. I will care for him."

A frown creased his expression. "He is safer where he is."

"Please, Addis. I will not see him again after . . . He is your heir. I would think that you would want him by your side when you reentered those gates." He did not look pleased with her request and she hesitated before pursuing it. "Perhaps if you share this with him you can learn some love for him."

His face tightened, but so did his embrace. "Do not blame me if I cannot warm to him. When I look at his face I see betrayal."

He saw Claire is what he meant. Brian had her coloring and face and radiance. Everyone else responded to the beauty with a smile, but she knew the reasons for Addis's scowls. His heart had shut on Claire eight years ago, and he had learned never to think of her. These last days he had spoken of many things, of his crusade and enslavement, of the woman Eufemia, of his father and family, but never had he mentioned Claire and what had occurred between them. Nor had he been receptive to discussions of Brian, who was a reminder of that pain. Hopefully the Lady Mathilda would love the child, because his father never might.

"I will promise that you will see him again, Moira, but I will not be bringing him to a siege camp. It is dangerous. I would not bring you either, but for my need of you."

She tucked her head against his chest and inhaled his scent and relished his breath on her hair. "Will I receive word of you?"

"I will ask that you be told whatever is learned of me, but I face little danger. The whole realm has abandoned Edward. We only have the tragedy of a king hiding in his own country now."

"Still, it is a big country. You might be gone a long while."

"Aye, a long while."

He lifted her chin to a kiss of gentle sadness. "I leave all of my heart with you, Moira. My body will be in Wiltshire and Wales, but my thoughts will be here with you."

She abandoned any pretense of dignity and clung to him while her quiet tears flowed. She looked up at burning eyes moist with yearning. He smiled, caressed her face, and stepped away. Assuming a warrior's expression of duty and resolve, he walked into the yard.

It was Rhys who brought her news over the next weeks. He came as a message bearer but the second time she asked him to stay for supper as a friend. While they waited for the meal she showed him her inn, and the changes she had made to the chambers. When they emerged into the courtyard again he noticed Henry hauling water to the trough by the stables.

"You should think about sinking another well out here. If those ten beds fill with visitors, bringing water for all of the horses will be a burden."

"Aye, and I am saving to expand the stables as well.

Next summer for both, I think, if I have the coin. Right now, with the court disbanded, there is not much trade for inns."

"That will change, and soon. Word is that Lancaster prevented Edward from entering Wales. He and the Despensers are in the western shires, and the net is closing on them."

"Do they have an army with them?"

"You worry for your knight? Nay, just a small group, not enough for a battle. No more than seventy, it is reported, and with Wales closed they lose some every day. Addis will come to no harm."

She leaned against the inn's wall, glad he spoke so easily of Addis. He had hesitated accepting her invitation, but she was happy he had. She suspected he had offered to bring her the messages so as to check how she managed alone, and perhaps to see if she needed a friend. She did.

"You appear happy," he said.

"I am happy. And sad. But you were right. The happiness gives the sadness some reason. He will be back, and I yearn to see him, but his return begins the end, doesn't it? It brings a soulful pain to think about that."

"You have decided to remain here?"

"I will go with him while he fights for his home. He is going to tell Thomas Wake that he wants no betrothal until it is regained, that he will not bind Mathilda to a poor knight, but the match has been agreed to and Wake will lend his aid because of it. But once it is done, once he sits in the lord's chair again, I will come back here."

"Surely he will visit London."

"When he does, the solar is his. And my friendship will always be here for him. But he knows that it ends at Barrowburgh and with his marriage."

" 'Tis a hard course that you set, Moira. Are you sure it is what you want?"

She had been asking herself that same question frequently the last few weeks. "It is the only course that permits me to wish his happiness in the life I will never see. Our love has been beautiful and whole and I'll not live my years grasping at its remnants. Nor will I let the shadow of that love interfere with the contentment he might find with his new family. Aye, it is what I want." She pushed away from the wall. "Now come and see how the cook I hired suits you. It is a man, and he is lately come from a manor is Kent."

Rhys raised an eyebrow. "A runaway?"

She feigned surprise. "Heavens, I wouldn't know! Do you think it is possible? I never thought to ask. I just noticed that his meat pies surpass mine and knew you would never forgive me if I didn't take him on."

He came again the next week to say that the elder Despenser had surrendered at Bristol, but that the king and Hugh had set to sea from Chepstow, just ahead of the advancing army. Word came soon after that both had been captured when they landed in Glamorgan. Hugh Despenser had been sent north to Hereford, but Lancaster was bringing the king east.

She had been living as if in a wakeful dream, going about her duties with a dull spirit and an inactive awareness. Now her heart and body awoke. She knew not how long it would take for that army to travel the breadth of the realm, nor if they came to London, nor if Addis would have other duties that might delay him after they handed the king over to the barons. She only knew that he was coming back. After two long months she would see him again soon.

She waited two weeks before allowing herself to expect him. Then she prepared the solar and took care with her appearance every day, and her gaze drifted to the gate whenever she entered the yard. Time slowed because of how hard she waited.

The last leaves fell from the apple trees. Frost withered the flowers. The first snow fell. The city erupted with stories about Hugh Despenser's execution and Edward's imprisonment.

She waited some more.

CHAPTER 19

MATTHEW, THE NEW GROOM, found her at the well.

"There's four knights in the courtyard asking if we have beds. I told 'em we are full, but they said that they would sleep in the hall if need be."

Moira set the bucket on the ground and pulled her cloak against the biting wind. Rhys had been right about her trade improving. With King Edward imprisoned at Kenilworth, the barons had begun congregating at Westminster to debate his fate as soon as the holiday of the Nativity had passed. A parliament had been called to begin in a fortnight. All of the inns in London and Southwark had long ago filled.

She gazed out at the garden stripped of flowers and leaves and full of winter's chill. Barren, like her life. She bit her lip and valiantly made a decision.

"We will put them in the solar and I will use a pallet in the kitchen."

She had resisted giving up that chamber, but had finally

accepted that the man for whom she saved it would not be returning.

Her excitement had desperately defied that reality. It had not dulled a whit during the additional weeks of waiting for him, of looking for his tall body every time she heard a noise near the gate. But it had never been him, nor Richard, nor anyone with word of his expected arrival.

The anticipation had transformed into worry when she learned that he had not accompanied the king to Kenilworth. After repeatedly badgering Rhys for information, the mason had reluctantly admitted that he had heard that Addis was spending the holy days at one of Wake's manors in Yorkshire. Both excitement and worry had vanished in one horrible heartbeat. With sick acceptance she had drawn the obvious conclusion.

Thomas Wake must have pressed for the early betrothal after all. When Addis had promised to come back he had not anticipated that. It would be madness to antagonize Wake in order to enjoy a few more weeks with Moira the innkeeper. She had decreed there would be an end and she could not blame him if circumstances had forced it sooner than she had expected.

After all, what choice did he have? The course was obvious, sensible, and practical. If asked she would have urged it on him. Of course. Certainly. If it plunged her from heaven into hell sooner than she had expected, that was the cost of such things.

Her heart admitted no anger, just a void of loss. Accepting the sense of it, the inevitability, did not make the disappointment easier to absorb. She carried a grief inside her like a weight, and had begun to wonder if it would ever lighten.

"There should be room in the stable if they have horses," she said, forcing her mind to the practical details on which she now hinged her life. "Tell Jane and Henry to make pallets for the solar."

"When you said that chamber was always mine, I did not expect to share it with other than you," a quiet voice said from the doorway.

She swung around, her heart flipping with a surge of joy that she battled to contain. She barely suppressed the impulse to throw herself into his arms.

She had never expected him to return here so soon after binding himself to Mathilda. She faced him awkwardly, determined to hold on to her dignity.

He stood tall and dark, a simple cloak floating over the buckskin garments. He appeared a little thinner for his travels, as he had when he first came back. Golden lights danced in his deep-set eyes while he inspected her reaction carefully.

"Go tell my men that we will stay here, in the hall if need be. And tell Henry to see that a bath is prepared in the solar," he ordered the groom.

Matthew hustled off and Addis turned to her. "We both knew it would be a long while, Moira."

"Aye. I did not know it would be this long though."

"Nor did I, but duties kept me west."

Duties.

"I received no word of you this last month. Just rumors."

"What rumors?"

"That you were with Wake and spent the Nativity with him and . . ."

She bit off the bitter sound of her words and blocked her mind from memories of her own lonely feast day, spent with the servants while she pictured him charming little Mathilda in front of a merry household.

This was exactly what she had hoped to avoid. The jealousy. The desperate desire to probe for reassurances. It demeaned them both. She had not realized how difficult this would be, but then she had expected to have more time to prepare for it.

"She is just a child. A pretty, frivolous girl. I found her . . . tedious."

"She is your lady." *And she will have you her whole life! Was it so selfish to have expected a few weeks more before that?*

She hated herself like this. The combination of surprised relief and seething resentment kept her immobile. Addis observed her with perplexed annoyance.

"You are wounded and I am sorry for it, Moira. Let us go to the solar and I will tell you why I was delayed."

The last thing she needed was to hear the details. "The solar is yours as I promised. You know where it is." She lifted her bucket and turned to carry it around to the stables.

Three steps had him blocking her way. He pried the bucket from her grip and threw it aside.

"What is this? Have three months turned you cold?"

"I am not cold. I am joyed to see you, but . . ."

"Has some man been wooing you? The mason again? If so he can damn well wait. . . ."

"Rhys proved a better friend to you than to me. He heard where you were, who you were with, and tried not to tell me."

"I could not refuse to go with Wake, no matter what my heart preferred."

"I know that. I do. But those duties in the west, as you call them, have changed things, haven't they? Do not expect me to live as if they had not occurred. She is your lady now. Do not expect me to pretend she is not, and go on as if—"

He reached for her and cut her off with a firm kiss. "You are still mine, Moira." Not a question. A statement. Actually, a command.

"I told you that I would not—"

He kissed her again. "Come to the solar. You will see that nothing has changed."

Just like a man to think pleasure could heal all wounds. "I will not. You have made the marriage, Addis."

He pulled back with a frown. "I can see that I have some explaining to do."

"Not at all. You need explain nothing. . . . Oh!"

She confronted his face one moment and his back the next as he lithely scooped her up and slung her over his shoulder. They had entered the kitchen before she realized what had happened.

"Put me down, Addis!"

"Nay. I can see that we will talk in circles and if we do, it will be in a chamber where there is a hearth at least."

"I will walk."

"You will argue."

"This is embarrassing."

"This is efficient."

He strode through the hall and she closed her eyes against the stunned looks on the servants and knights. Jane scooted close behind and stuck her face up.

"Matthew said you be wanting a pallet in the kitchen."

"Aye."

"She will not," Addis said, not missing a step.

The man had forgotten who owned this house. "Make one up."

"You waste your labor," Addis advised.

"Do it." Moira commanded, attempting to rise so she did not dangle so ignominiously.

Out in the yard now. The new groom and cook stared gape-mouthed. "Water for a bath," Addis ordered while he breezed by.

Up in the solar he dumped her on the bed. "That is more like it. If this city did not close its gates at night I would have arrived while you were abed, naked as my mind saw you all during the last days of riding."

"Perhaps you would not have found me alone."

It was a spiteful thing to blurt, revealing that maybe she did blame him for those duties in the west after all.

Well, damn it, she did!

His expression hardened. "I would have killed the man, Moira. Do not doubt that. If I learn that some lover has been stealing what is mine I will—"

"I have not been unfaithful," she admitted miserably.

The servants arrived with buckets of water in time to see his anger flickering. Henry smiled a nervous welcome, glanced at Moira for reassurance, and quickly supervised the preparations. They couldn't get out fast enough, and left some water heating by the roaring hearth.

Moira began to rise.

Addis unbuckled his sword belt. "Stay there."

"You will not," she announced testily, very annoyed by his assumptions. She had expected him to argue against their agreement when the time came, not simply ignore it as if he held some lifelong right to her. Letting herself blame him for not delaying Wake helped her maintain her anger. And ignore the simmering excitement of lying on this bed with him standing over her.

"Not yet. I am befouled with a week of horse and camp life. I will bathe and then I will take you."

Just like that.

In a pig's eye.

He stripped off his cloak and tunic.

Three months' abstinence and multiple memories and the hidden happiness of seeing him again combined to shudder desire through her. She mentally caressed the exposed muscles of his back.

He stretched his hands to the fire. "I am not betrothed, Moira. I did not visit Wake to make the marriage."

Relief burst. Love broke free of the restraints she had carefully forged this last month. Only a reprieve, but she welcomed it with giddy exuberance.

"He agreed that the girl should not be bound before I take Barrowburgh. Even with his help I might fail. I went to discuss and plan that help, but before that I visited Darwendon and Hawkesford. I spoke with Raymond."

"How is Raymond?"

"Angry. I told him about us. If he joined me on the field, I did not want him to learn it there."

"And will he join you?"

"I do not know. When I left it did not appear so. In fact, it would not surprise me to find him under Simon's colors."

"I doubt that he was as angry as that, Addis."

"He has wanted you for ten years. The youth's lust turned into something else long ago."

"Not love."

He shrugged. "He would never call it that."

"Nay, Raymond Orrick would never call feelings for a serf-born woman that."

"I cannot speak for his heart. Only my own. If he feels only one tenth of what I do, then it is love whatever he calls it, and he may not forgive me."

"It would be a pity if I caused you to lose his friendship and its aid."

"Not your fault if it happens. Anyway, we will see." He lifted a bucket and poured its warm water into the tub. She made to go and help him.

"Stay there."

Making a face of demure obedience she kept her place. He emptied the rest of the water, glancing to her in a considering way. "I cannot decide," he said, laughing.

"Decide what?"

"Whether to have you serve me in the bath or lie on that bed where I can watch you."

The notion of caressing him with soap sounded like a fine idea to her. "The bath."

He studied the tub. " 'Twould be a long soaking but little washing, I think, and it does not look large enough for us both."

It looked plenty large to her. Now that her misgivings had been vanquished she yearned for his embrace.

He began pushing off his leggings. "The bed, I think. Naked."

He stripped himself and she watched the hard body emerge, imagining its strength under her hands and over her length. The memories flushed prickles down her limbs.

He settled in the tub and washed his hair. He combed the wet locks back with his fingers and cocked an eyebrow at her. "You are still clothed. I said naked."

She knelt and plucked out the lacing along the front of her wool gown. Her breasts itched to be free of the garments and warmed by something besides cloth.

He lathered an arm and her senses vicariously experienced the progress of his hand on his skin. The anticipation of touching all of him, of feeling him with her and in her . . . it was almost too delicious and left her trembling. He smeared soap on his chest. White wetness glistened on sculpted flesh. She itched to draw patterns in it.

She slid the gown down her body and his gaze followed the fabric's journey like a firm caress along her length. She sat and slipped off her winter hose, first one leg then the other, and his eyes slowly traveled the knit stockings' long descent to her feet.

He propped a foot on the tub's rim, not paying

attention to his actions while he observed her. She envied
the fingers scrubbing the bent, well-formed leg, moving
higher to knee and thigh. Serving him at the bath really
would have been very pleasant.

Her hands rose to her shift straps and his lids lowered.
She recognized that serious intensity. She surrendered to
an urge to taunt him. She removed the straps one at a time
so that she could keep her body covered. She lowered the
fabric down her breasts as slowly as possible.

"You really can be a vicious woman, Moira," he said.

She smiled and made no effort to speed the process.
Caressing him in the bath would have brought quicker
satisfaction, but this distant pleasure was incredibly
arousing.

Naked at last, she knelt high and lifted her arms to
undo her hair. Her breasts spread and rose with the movement and she took her time, watching him watch, enjoying the effect so obvious in his eyes. The long tresses
cloaked her body like a tattered mantle through which her
breasts and hips poked. She crawled away for a pillow and
her hair swung down, revealing another erotic view. She
reached for a pillow, set it on the edge of the bed, and
stretched out on her stomach in front of him.

Washing movements ten feet away continued, but his
attention never left her. "Have you heard any news of
Kenilworth?" he asked as if they did not mentally make
love across the span that separated them.

"Rumors of the king's health and spirit. Nothing else.
It is said he is in a deep melancholy."

His gaze meandered along her shoulders and back, over
her buttocks, and down her legs. She propped up on her
elbows and he did not miss the side swell of breast she
exposed.

"At least there are rumors. That is a good sign."

He wet his chest with a cloth. She fantasized that her

tongue licked along his breastbone. Then lower. "You still worry for his safety?"

"His death would be convenient. Turn over."

She did, lying out, watching him watch. "What will the barons do about him?" It took effort to maintain a conversational tone. Tweaking tremors of excitement preoccupied her attention.

"That will depend on him, I think. He must be very frightened. I would be. He has no doubt heard how Hereford executed Hugh. It was as brutal as the indignities that Gaveston suffered. The Archbishop of Canterbury has finally acquiesced to the inevitable and thrown his support to the queen. He will not be king a month hence. Sit now."

She barely heard him but her body obeyed. Her legs dangled down the side of the high bed. He washed the body invisible under water and her mind's eye assisted. Not long now. She did not think it possible to be this hungry without a single touch.

He left the tub and dried himself before the fire. She feasted on the sight of his body glowing beside the hearth and tingled deliciously at the magnificent evidence of his desire. She could tell from his expression that Edward's problems had disappeared from his thoughts.

"In my mind I held you every night while I was gone. I pictured you thus, on that bed, your eyes bright and your breasts full and hard, waiting for me. It did not do much for my rest, but all day I looked forward to it. Did you dream about me?"

"Aye." She glanced down at the two hard nipples pointing erotically, beckoning him. She cupped her breasts' lower swells, directing their fullness in offering. "I dreamt of you. Your hands, your mouth. Here. Everywhere. I dreamt of everything. All of it."

He cast aside the towel and walked over.

She still held her craving breasts. He grazed one protuberant tip with his fingers. "Like that, love?"

The sensation almost lifted her off the bed. "Aye."

His thumb rubbed gently. "And this?"

Warm tension twisted below her belly. "Aye."

His palm lightly teased while he leaned down to kiss her lips, carefully biting and probing in a display of the restraint he intended. All of this indication of the long lovemaking awaiting only made her arousal spread with a luscious burst.

His head dipped to the uplifted request. "And this?" His tongue flicked over each nipple, then circled one seductively.

She thought she would die. Embracing his waist she urged him closer. "Aye. And this."

Anticipating her, he stood tall. Still it surprised him when she enclosed his hard desire in the valley between her breasts, holding him next to her heartbeat.

"And this." Her tongue teased at him as he had done her.

"Ah, Moira, you *are* vicious," he said, sighing, and he used his hands to show her cradling breasts more attention.

They gave each other pleasure until she was rocking with need. She released and embraced him, rubbing her cheek against his abdomen and splaying her hands over his back. "I cannot wait any longer," she muttered.

He knelt, spreading her legs so their bodies were close. The exposure of where she pulsed only made it worse and she grasped his head and shoulders in an entwining embrace and ferocious kiss.

"I think you will have to wait nonetheless. I had all these dreams, you see. Months of them. Would you deny me the chance to make even one real?" He cupped her breasts this time, lifting them to a mouth and tongue that aroused her without mercy. Impatience gave way to a delirious acceptance and she closed her eyes and experienced the sensations for their own sake.

"You are so warm, Moira." He caressed around her hips and over her thighs, brushing the damp curls almost pressing his chest. "Wet. Ready. Tell me that you are completely mine."

More than ready. Starving. Her body pulsed with astonishing demand, leaving her aware of little else. She told him, barely hearing her own words.

He spread her thighs wider. "Lie back."

She gladly did so, grabbing his shoulders, urging him up to her. He laughed quietly and released her hold. "Not yet. Not until you are screaming for me."

His mouth and hands found the way to make her do so. Soon anxious, needful sounds poured out of her, a chorus of passion muffled by her dulled hearing. Primitive sounds transformed into begging cries. They escalated until he came up over her to give the union for which her body shrieked.

He settled himself and then bent her knees up to her chest. Extending his arms he rose up and looked down the gap between them, watching his entry. Their concurrent sighs quivered their bodies.

"You feel so good, Moira. Perfect."

Again and again he fully withdrew before penetrating again. Forceful waves of relief and anticipation alternated, driving her close to the edge of endurance. The howling first streaks of release began spreading and she urged him down, wanting more.

"I'm glad you will be with me at the end this time," he said, his voice low and ragged by her ear. "Complete together."

His passion broke in a burst of intensity, inciting her own, pulling them into an oblivion of shared sensation.

He stayed on her afterward. Her breasts pressed against his chest and her legs embraced his waist and he savored the contact of her moist body beneath and around him. He made no effort to move off her and she signaled no discomfort with his weight.

He tucked his face into the crook of her neck and breathed deeply, inhaling euphoria along with her scent. This drove his lovemaking as much as the pleasure. It was like a taste of heaven, and the glory of calm and love that the priests said one found there.

He wound his hand in the long tresses streaming over the bed. Love, aye, but with its conditions. He remembered her cool resolve when he met her by the well and felt less peaceful all of a sudden. He had trusted, nay, he had prayed, that she would not be able to turn from him when the time came. Today had shown that she meant what she had said, she would hold him to that agreement she had forced.

He rose on his forearms and looked down at her. Creamy lids fluttered and blue eyes narrowed while she smiled. Her upstretched arms, still encircling his neck, rubbed his jaw. He turned to kiss their soft skin and then stroked his face along the valley of her breasts.

She did not know how much he needed her. If he could find the words to explain it he would try to, but what existed inside him did not have names that he knew. The whole time he had ridden with Lancaster's army he had felt a man apart, watching a dream unfold. His body knew the right moves, his voice said the right words, but his soul felt that by some magic it had been placed in the wrong body. The sense of being a foreigner in his homeland had eased over the months while he was with her. Riding at the head of an army, being addressed as the Lord of Barrowburgh, being apart from her, had made it surge again. Time had not brought the familiarity he had thought. That had become clear when he left this house and city and her.

The worst part was that his soul knew not in which body it really belonged. Not Addis the slave, although the spirits still lived for him. Not the son of Patrick de Valence, even though custom and honor dictated his decisions.

Only with Moira did he possess any secure sense of who he was, and then because his image reflected off her love. He even accepted his duty mostly because she expected it of him, even if success in regaining his honor meant losing her. The two halves did not totally forge into one when he was with her, but the division ceased to matter much at all.

Losing her. His essence rebelled against the expectation of that. It would be like being flayed. He held her face with his hands and tried to peer through those clear eyes into her soul and discover if she truly would find the strength to leave when the time came. He saw only the pure love of a serf-born woman who had been taught by life to expect nothing.

The open way she looked back touched him as it had so often since he entered her cottage at Darwendon. A provocative nameless something nudged at him, as if a friendship older than these past months and a connection deeper than even this love and pleasure bound them. It unsettled him now, poking persistently.

He kissed her with a passion and possession that had nothing to do with desire, then moved aside and, as he almost always did, laid his head on her breast.

He could not let her go, of course. When the time

came, he would find a way to keep her. When she was nearby he lived in a different world. Everything changed. The earth, the rocks, every plant . . .

Her firm arms embraced his shoulders in that comforting habit of hers. His face pressed against the softness of her full breast. *I feel like the earth, the rocks every plant has changed.* Her words, whispered that night after they first made love, confusing him because they sounded so familiar.

His mind stretched for something lost behind fog. He noted again this frequent embrace.

She held him the way one might hold a child.

Or a person who mourned.

Or someone broken by pain or despair.

CHAPTER 20

THIS IS NOT going to work."

"It appears not. The cot is too small."

"It is not the bed, Addis. Even on the ground . . ." She began to giggle. "Where do you get these notions?"

"In my dreams." He laughed, untangling the confusion of limbs he had created. It took some doing.

She stretched and embraced him over her body and heart. She enjoyed his playful experiments, but in truth they both took a special pleasure in this simplest form of lovemaking.

He settled himself, filling her. Spring's earliest smells seeped into the tent with dawn's first light. "I saw the abbot speaking with you yesterday. Did he scold you again?"

"A very mild scold. Since your army camps on his lands he feels obligated to do his duty to condemn sin. He saves the worst for the camp whores, but even then his heart is not in it."

The profound contentment of being inside her suffused

him as it always did, and he resisted the urge to move. "He wants to be rid of Simon as a neighbor badly enough to overlook much, I'll warrant. He did not argue when I brought the letter from Stratford ordering the abbey to let me use their lands."

She ran a finger up his back, making him suck air through his teeth. "It was fortunate the bishop chose to help you."

"Not just good fortune, Moira."

"How so?"

Hunger conquered his patience. "I will explain some other time."

Later she walked with him through the damp field and crisp air to the top of the hill where six sentries waited. They had caught one of Simon's men last night. Spies from Barrowburgh fanned out through the region daily to try and locate the army that Simon knew must be coming. So far none of the men who had found the camp had been permitted to return and Simon did not know that fate literally waited on his threshold.

Addis sent the prisoner to the abbey's dungeon after questioning, then turned and looked out over the encampment.

"It is impressive," Moira said, scanning the tents and fires stretching into the distance. He embraced her and she nestled her back against his chest and snuggled under his surrounding cloak. Together they watched the bright blur of the rising sun burn away the low mist.

"Impressive, but not decisively so."

"Still not enough? Even with the queen's footmen?"

"Barrowburgh is formidable. Wake should arrive soon but even with the army he brings and the archers sent by Lancaster nothing is certain."

"The aid of so many is an honor to your family."

"In part. But like Stratford's help, it is also to repay me and also, mostly, a bid for my support should I succeed. Already the powers in the realm realign and new factions form. It will be thus until young Edward can wear the crown on his own."

"So even with one king gone and another crowned, nothing has changed." She shook her head. "I felt sorry for them both, the father facing the end and the boy facing the unknown."

She felt sorry because she had seen them both. He had brought her with him when he was chosen to join the entourage that traveled to Kenilworth to press for abdication. Not only nobles had faced Edward that day, but representatives of the entire realm. Priests and monks, peasants and merchants, magnates and craftsmen had urged their isolated king to step aside for his son. Edward had fortunately agreed, but Moira had not been the only one to weep at the sight of a man destroyed because fate had condemned him to be born to a life for which he was not suited.

"The boy faces the unknown, but I think he has the heart for it," Addis said.

"Aye. Only five and ten, but one can see it. I saw him watching his mother and Roger Mortimer and the way they assumed the crown was theirs even though he wore it. He did not seem to miss much."

Nor did Moira. He had brought her to the coronation too, dressed in his mother's velvets and looking as much a lady in grace and demeanor as any lord's wife. She had not wanted to go, but once there the excitement of attending such a great event had obliterated any awkwardness. An accident of birth, Rhys had called a person's status, and it had never been more true than in that great hall or been proven more clearly than by the events of the last weeks.

"He is cut of the same cloth as his grandfather. Soon he will come of age to rule on his own. Until then the queen and her lover will have a council to deal with."

"I do not think they will listen to the council," she said.

"Nor do I. Nor does our new king. He spoke with me and some others. He found a way to pass a few words privately."

She turned in surprise. "You never told me that before."

"He said very little. It was more his expression and tone. In fact he began by admiring your form. He may only be five and ten but he has an appreciation for a pretty armful of woman when he meets one."

She laughed and jostled him with her elbow. "Seriously, what did he say?"

"That my lady appears to have the most magnificent breasts that ever a man—"

"Addis!"

"I swear that I quote him directly. And then he looked at his little Philippa and said that Mortimer had reassured him that although she did not come from a great house and was not a beauty that her broad hips meant she would be fertile. He smiled like an old man and added that Mortimer had misjudged the true value of the count's daughter, which would lie in her loyalty and love, and that his wife would be his first and most formidable ally. And then, having just mentioned allies, he asked how my preparations progressed for Barrowburgh, and offered to ask his mother to provide aid."

She peered toward the tents that flew the royal colors. "You mean it was young Edward and not the queen . . ."

"It was the queen, but at his suggestion. I doubt she knows he mentioned it to me. So she thinks she has bought my loyalty when in fact I know the true source."

He led her down the hill and through the awakening

camp. They stood by the fire outside their tent and he wrapped her under his cloak again. She felt so good and right next to him. He wondered if she had experienced the same bittersweet mood when they made love this morning. Soon this army would move. They never spoke of the parting which she still assumed would occur when Barrowburgh fell, but it was never far from his mind. He had greeted the arrival of every man with a combination of relief and resentment.

A horse suddenly clamored through the quiet morning. A sentry pulled up beside them and pointed south. "A troop. Maybe a mile away. Seems to have circled around from the west."

That would be Wake. "How many?"

"Maybe fifty to seventy."

Addis frowned. Thomas was supposed to bring two hundred at least. Wake had not liked Moira's visibility during the last few weeks in London, but had let Addis know that he understood. Still, although marriage alliances were practical arrangements and many men retained mistresses, Wake might have rethought everything if he concluded that Addis's devotion appeared too strong.

If so, why bother coming at all? Nay, more likely he had split his men so they would attract less attention. Part of him felt disappointed with this obvious explanation. He needed Wake, but if the man himself retreated from the agreement . . .

He gestured for the sentry's horse and the part that secretly wished that would happen and damn the consequences drew Moira toward it.

She resisted. "I will wait in the tent."

"You will come. He knows about us already. He will be in this camp for several days before we move and I will not have you hiding." He mounted and pulled her up behind.

"You are a fool to make such a statement through my presence behind you," she hissed into his back.

Perhaps. But during the time left he'd be damned if he would deny her, or let discretion create any separation, or treat her as less than she was to him.

They trotted through the camp and he waited at the southern edge. The arriving troop broke into view at the crest of a low rise of land. The leader saw them and galloped ahead.

Long blond hair flew back from the rider's head. He slowed when he neared, and paced until he sat along Addis's side. Blue eyes scanned, pausing on Moira, and several heartbeats of utter stillness passed.

Raymond smiled and threw his arm back toward the approaching men. "Could only raise sixty, what with it being near planting time, but at least these men are seasoned in battle. You might consider waging your next war during the growing months like everyone else, brother."

Addis had not missed the reaction contained in that encompassing look. No longer angry, but not approving either. He reached out his arm and Raymond did the same, joining in a clasp of friendship. "I am grateful that you have come."

"Couldn't pass up the chance to see that snake get skinned. Too sly by half. Never liked him, even as a youth, and dreaded whenever we found ourselves at your father's board together. Besides, we both know Bernard would leave his grave to haunt me if our family did not do its duty by yours."

"It is good to see you again, Raymond," Moira said as they turned to ride back to the camp.

"And you. Love makes your eyes even brighter, Moira. I can see this knight suits you."

It was said with a forced joviality but it broke the awkwardness just the same.

"Aye, he suits me well," she said, laughing.

At the tent Moira made an excuse to leave. Raymond watched her walk away. "You must suit her very well if she lets you give her velvet gowns. She would take nothing from me."

"They are my mother's things."

"Do not get annoyed. I am not suggesting that you have bought her. If a few gowns were all it took with her . . . She is a proud woman, is all. It must be a true love if she puts that pride aside."

She *had* put her pride aside. She walked through this camp as if living with a man who was not her husband carried no shame at all for her. Somehow she had decided that this brief time and particular place existed outside the normal world and its rules. He was the one who resented the occasional looks of disapproval sent her way, and the abbot's penitential warnings.

"I did not think that you would come because of it."

Raymond shrugged. "She always said that she thought of me as a brother. If those aren't the most dispiriting words women have ever spoken to men, I don't know what are. And I suspected that she had sworn never to be like her mother. But if she has changed on that with you, I have decided that perhaps it is for the best. Lady Mathilda will naturally prefer her own children when they come. It will be good for Brian to have Moira's love in your home."

"She has not changed. She intends to return to London when I am done here."

Raymond looked over in surprise. "With any other woman I would say that was just talk. You will permit it?"

"I can hardly imprison her." Not that the thought had not entered his mind.

Raymond grinned. "Get her with child and she will forget such nonsense."

God knew he'd been trying his damnedest, and only in

part for the bargaining ploy it might give him. He sensed that she hoped for it too, as if a child would be a manifestation of the union they had known. It would continue then, and live on even if they separated forever. When her flux had come last week he had silently shared her disappointment.

Warriors never talked long of women, and Raymond moved on to questions and discussion of the strategies Addis planned. But the whole time he enjoyed the camaraderie of his old friend, a small portion of his mind followed her through the camp. He knew her pattern of activity as surely as he knew his own, and mentally joined her in it every day while the sun relentlessly moved and the men continued to arrive, all of the routines propelling him toward the victory that he both craved and dreaded.

She waited until he had dressed and left the tent the next morning before rising herself. The night had been sweet and touching, just hours of blissful intimacy while they held each other and talked. He spoke of his plans for the next few days but the subject had not mattered so much as the sharing of warmth and words. It had been, she suspected, his man's way of trying to soothe the tensions that had arisen with the arrival first of Raymond and then of Thomas Wake. Yesterday both the past and the future had intruded on their "now."

Several times last night she had seen that look in his eyes that had appeared more frequently as the days passed. It contained the question that he would not ask and that she could not answer. *Will you really leave and end this?*

Her mind still held to her decision, but her heart had been waging a fierce battle against the good sense with which it had been made. In truth she had been ignoring that anticipated parting so that its shadow would not dim the glory of what they had now. Thomas Wake's arrival had reminded her that the moment would come very soon when her resolve would be put to the test. It would be a specific moment, she did not doubt it. A precise point in time when it was clear she must either leave or walk forward with him.

She put on a simple wool gown and cloak and broke her fast with some bread and cheese. Last night Addis had insisted she sup with him and the others, but she knew that her company, that any woman's company, had become inappropriate. She would make herself scarce today, and use this opportunity to do something she had been planning for some time now.

She brought a basket and stopped at the supply wagons to get a jug of wine, then made her way to the rough corrals where the animals were kept. A groom noticed her and walked over. She explained her requirements. By the time the sun had fully risen she was on her way, heading toward the abbey road in a small cart pulled by a donkey.

It took most of the morning to reach her destination because Addis's army camped in the southernmost reaches of the abbey's lands. She arrived at the village of Whitly just as men came in from the fields for dinner.

Lucas Reeve stepped to his doorway at the sound of her cart pulling up. Delighted surprise lit his eyes. "Joan, it be the lord's woman here!" He tied the reins to a post and helped her down. "Just in time to eat, Moira. Come in and tell us how Sir Addis fares."

She presented the wine and accepted the place of honor at their humble table, but ate sparingly so Lucas's two sons would not suffer from her unexpected visit. When they learned she had spent the last months in London, they peppered her with questions about the momentous events there.

"Well, now, it seems to me that with the king and his friends gone, these lands will have the lord whom God intended." Lucas smiled with satisfaction.

"The king's council has returned the estate to Addis, but Simon has not accepted the decision," Moira explained.

"I'm sure. He's been living like an earl, bleeding the people and the land to feed his luxury. If he hands it all back he is a poor knight again, with nothing. And if there's to be retaliations against the pigs who joined Despenser at the realm's troughs, he is better behind those walls."

"It explains the word we have gotten from the other villages," his eldest son said. "That Simon's been calling up those with guard obligations. Must be preparing for a siege."

Their eyes turned to Moira expectantly.

"It is no secret that Addis will come," she said. "He told Simon that he would."

"Aye, but the question is when," Lucas mused with a grin. "And if you are sitting here now, I find myself wondering where the lord is sitting."

It was why she had come, but she chose her words carefully. "Not on Barrowburgh lands, but near enough."

The information raised their excitement. "God be praised," Lucas muttered. "Has he brought enough? His grandfather built one hell of a fortress there."

"He says with the likes of Barrowburgh there are never enough."

"Tell us where he is and every man who can carry a staff will go to him. I served as a pike in the Scot wars and can do so again despite this white hair. Damn, he should have called for us."

"He will not risk you. If he fails you will be at Simon's mercy."

"We'd rather die like men than slowly starve. Hell, a fever could take us all tomorrow. Word of the king's fall came weeks ago, and people are itching to have it out with the bastard hiding in that keep. Point us to Sir Addis and by morning there will be hundreds on the road offering to tear those walls down with their bare hands."

"I cannot tell you. If word spread, Simon would hear and Addis wants his march to be a surprise. But when he comes you will know it, and if word were sent to the other villages . . ."

"It will be done, Moira. We might not be of much use to him scaling walls and such, but every pair of arms can help and an extra thousand men filling that field will put the fear of god in Simon, which alone makes it worthwhile. Every farmer loading ballast will free a trained soldier for the walls."

She dipped a crust of bread into her soup. "He does not know that I came here. He might not like my interference."

He grinned and patted her arm. "None at this table will say anyone told us to prepare. Who is to know that what weapons we have were sharpened in advance? Lords don't count us as whole men in their wars, but we have made the difference before. You are one of us, Moira, and know that even bonded men have rights worth fighting for. " 'Twill be a fine revenge to stand with Patrick's son, be the result victory or death. He may not expect us or think he needs us, but when we come he'll be glad for it."

Lucas and his sons began planning for messengers and Moira turned to Joan for simpler conversation. Men began passing the cottage to return to the fields but a sudden commotion of horses disrupted the lane.

Commanding voices called families out of their homes. Everybody at the table silenced and tensed. Lucas peered around a shutter and cursed. "From Barrowburgh. Six of them, with that red devil Owen at their lead."

Owen! He might recognize her. She glanced frantically around the small cottage, but there was no place to hide.

"All of Barrowburgh bond out in the lane." Harsh voices yelled the order over and over. "Out in the lane or your home will be burned." Joining the commands came sounds of people being pushed and women screaming.

"Stay behind us all, Moira," Lucas said. "Whatever they want it should be over soon enough."

He and his sons stepped outside and formed a wall to protect the women. Moira eased into position behind Lucas and kept her eyes lowered. She prayed that she looked like any other serf despite her linen wimple and veil and the fine wool of her gown. With luck none of these men would even see her.

Her throat dried as the lane fell quiet and Owen paced down its length. He stopped in front of their little group, but then Lucas was Barrowburgh's reeve in this village. She glanced quickly at the flaming hair and steely gray eyes and tried to shrink still further into obscurity.

"Good day to you, Sir Owen," Lucas greeted amiably, as if six knights roused the villagers every day.

"I am come with a message from your lord," Owen said. "The men in this village are to bring all horses, donkeys, and livestock into Barrowburgh before nightfall. Also any grains left from last year's harvest still stored here."

"It is an odd request, sir."

"Not a request at all," Owen snarled.

"It is not within the customs and obligations—"

Owen's swinging fist cut off his words with an impact that doubled the reeve over his knees. Briefly exposed, Moira lowered her head yet more.

"All that is here is his. Your life is his if he requires it.

Any villager found hoarding will lose the hand that dared to steal from him."

He spoke to Lucas but the villagers had closed in to listen. A thick circle of watchful eyes peered over the swords holding them back.

Lucas straightened and met Owen's glare. "And what would Sir Simon be wanting with all the grain and animals? Does he plan a feast that will mean the starvation of every man who serves him?"

"His reasons are none of your concern. Worry only about the obedience of your neighbors. As the lord's man here you will be held responsible for seeing it is done."

"Aye, it will be done. And you are right. I am most definitely the Lord of Barrowburgh's man in this village, and honored to be so counted."

Moira bit her tongue at the true meaning of that declaration. Lucas's acquiescence eased Owen's belligerence. "By nightfall," he repeated in a calmer voice.

She could see his boots on the ground. They began to turn away. Holding her breath, she waited with breaking relief for the danger to pass.

He paused. It seemed that Lucas and his eldest son tried imperceptibly to move their bodies closer together. The boots turned back and stepped forward. Heart pounding with renewed fear, she gritted her teeth and prayed to disappear.

The boots stepped closer yet. Lucas and his son were yanked apart, creating a chasm of shrieking peril that she suddenly faced alone. A hand grabbed her chin and jerked until gray eyes peered into her own.

His other hand pulled off her veil so abruptly that the pins flew in the air. An amused smile broke across his hostile face.

"Well, now. I wonder what the Baltic slave princess is doing so far from London and her master."

✦ ✦ ✦

It was mid-afternoon before Addis realized Moira was not in the camp. When she did not join him at dinner he had assumed that she had decided to leave the knights to discuss war without a woman present. As was his habit, his eyes had searched for her after that whenever he walked through the camp but she never appeared. He told himself that she prayed at the abbey or visited the sick, but with each hour a gnawing worry grew. It finally led him to the men tending the animals.

There he learned that she had ridden off in the early morning.

Numbness instantly soaked him. Right there in front of the nervous groom his body became a shell devoid of feeling or sensation. The small part of his mind that did not succumb existed separate from any physical awareness.

She would not be back. He just knew it. She had left as she had said she would, but sooner than she had warned.

He had expected to feel anger or pain when it happened, not this horrible vacancy. He stared at the groom, vaguely noting the man's increasing discomfort. His senses scattered and his dulled mind tried to understand why she had not waited the few days remaining.

He should not have left her this morning. He had seen how the presence of Raymond and Thomas Wake unsettled her at last evening's meal and had spent the night trying to soothe her. Both men had been very courteous, but each one stood for something in her mind and he could feel her spiritually withdrawing into the shadows even though she held her smiling composure to the end of the supper.

At least, he thought, both men had been courteous. If he learned that either Raymond or Thomas had said something to hasten her departure, he would kill the man.

Doing so right now would not even raise his blood. Because he had no blood. Or bones. Or substance.

The groom eased his weight from foot to foot, anxious for dismissal. The movement brought him back to some comprehension of where he stood. "Did she take anything with her?"

"Just a basket."

No trunk or garments. Nay, they were his mother's things. She would not take them with her. Just a basket. Knowing practical Moira, she could live for a month out of a basket.

"Did she say where she headed?"

The groom should have asked, and now he shrank while he shook his head.

Addis strode away and his disembodied legs took him to the top of the hill. He scanned blindly, knowing there was nothing to see anyway. She had been gone for hours. He would send a man to the abbey on the small chance she had gone to speak with the abbot, but he knew she would not be there.

His senses began righting themselves. The parts of his body began reawakening, finding each other. Emotion trickled into the void. He narrowed his eyes and peered toward the road she must have taken.

An unholy fury suddenly split, like lightening streaking to the ground. Not a word. Not a sign. She owed him that, damn it! They owed each other that. Even if she had guessed that he would fight to dissuade her, she owed him the chance to do so. Did she think this was only about her life and her future and her choices?

He grasped on to the anger because he knew the danger of the sea in which it served as a raft. He had felt that numbness before. Recently at Barrowburgh. Once in the Baltic lands. Long ago in dreams remembered only as journeys in despair. Not a tempestuous sea but one of seductive calm, warm and welcoming, with eddies so soothing it could lull one into an eternal sleep.

He remembered looking down at her before he left the tent in the morning. She had appeared peaceful and serene, her skin luminous beneath the abundant chestnut hair. She had stirred and noticed him there, and held up a limp hand that he kissed. . . .

If that was to be the last touch and sight of her, he had a right to know it. If last night was to be the final hours, she should have told him so that he could speak of things that had meaning.

He glared at the hundreds of men spread out below him. He had been dreading this battle because victory meant losing her, but now he itched to have it done. He would tear those walls down if it meant being finished with it. He would sit in his father's chair and claim the rights of his birth. He would secure his hold and make his power known.

And then, when he had done his duty, he would find her.

He stomped down to the camp and roused some men to search for her and sent another to the abbey. Hopeless, of course, but he would make sure she had not returned. Seething with frustration and disappointment he circled through the camp, informing the knights and retinues that they would move on the morrow. Like a spoon stirring a pot, his progress churned the army into an activity of preparation.

The anger sustained him until the night, when he found himself sitting with Raymond by the fire outside his tent. His old friend had been smart enough not to comment on Moira's absence or his change of temper. They spoke of the morning and the plan to be executed, until Raymond left.

Addis stayed by the fire. He had not entered the tent all

day and did not want to now. It contained garments bearing her scent and other objects of her life. If he saw and touched those remnants of her presence he might lose hold of the raft.

In the distance a small commotion inched down the hill. Like a tiny whirlwind it entered the camp and scooted between fires and tents. Addis watched it come, distracted for a moment from his thoughts. As it drew nearer it materialized into Richard and Small John pulling a peasant between them.

"Caught another one," Richard gloated, throwing the man to the ground. "Simon must be running low on spies if he's using his farmers. Wouldn't answer our questions. Said he was of Barrowburgh bond and would speak only to you."

The man stared around wide-eyed, his gaze finally locking on Addis. He was a young man, not much more than a youth, and Addis thought he looked familiar. To his surprise the spy crawled forward and knelt.

"I am not from Simon, my lord. I am Gerald, son of Lucas, from the village of Whitly."

"I remember you. What are you doing here?"

"Looking for you and this army."

That was not a welcome answer. "How did you know the army was here?"

"I didn't, my lord. Not for sure. She said it was near and that we would know when you moved and I thought about that and decided it must be south of Whitly if we would know first. . . ."

He froze as the rushed words made sense. "She?"

"Aye. The woman Moira." Gerald thrust his hand beneath his tunic and pulled out a cloth.

Addis opened it over his knees. A veil. One of hers. Relief and fear drowned the vestiges of his anger. "Where is she?"

"That's why I've come looking for you, my lord. She was in the village when Owen came and he recognized her and took her. My father too . . ."

Addis rose and walked into the night before Gerald finished. He pressed the veil to his face and inhaled the shadowy smell of her hair. She had not left, but had only gone to visit the village where it had all started.

And Owen had found her there. Simon had Moira and she knew the army's location. He might use torture to get that information if he guessed that she possessed it.

A profound joy churned in him, mixed with heartfelt guilt that he had so quickly misjudged her and a soul-shaking terror for her danger.

He called for Richard.

"How long to get to Barrowburgh? Just the men. The wagons and supplies can follow. A forced march."

"Five hours about."

He scanned the heavens. The night had begun black with clouds but they had broken to reveal the bright disk of a full moon. "Before dawn then, if we left soon."

"Certainly before dawn, but surely you cannot think to march at night."

"I do think it. Spread the word. I want every man ready as soon as possible. We do not wait for the morrow. We go now and we carry what we need."

"It has been threatening rain and even if it holds off we could lose half the men in the dark."

"The moon has come out. We will not lack for light."

Richard looked close to exasperation. "The clouds could cover it again in a snap."

Addis gazed up at Menulius. "They will not." He turned and smiled at the perplexed steward. "The moon will shine for us this night. As it happens, he owes me this small favor."

CHAPTER 21

SHE KNELT IN THE SOLAR like a supplicant. Simon paced around her in furious frustration.

"He is still in London," she said again. The words came as a mumble through her swollen lips.

His temper flared and he glanced meaningfully at Owen. She braced herself. The knight swung and another slap landed on her face, unbalancing her with its force.

Soon it would be a fist instead of a palm. They had spent hours trying to beat the information out of Lucas while she watched. She had come close to speaking to spare him, but the reeve's eyes had begged her to be silent.

They had carried his unconscious body away and then turned to her.

"She knows where he is," Owen said flatly. He was enjoying this. An unhealthy glow lit his eyes even as he acted almost bored with his duty. "She was his whore in London and if she is here now she came with him."

"Nay," she argued, fighting a wretched fear that urged her to grovel for mercy. "He tired of me and I head back to Darwendon and my home. I stopped to visit in the village, is all, and seek shelter until the morn. . . ."

Another blow cracked across her face. Pain split through her head and she tasted blood.

How much longer until dawn? If she held out long enough, perhaps any move that Simon made would not catch Addis unawares. The army at the abbey greatly outnumbered Simon's forces, even swelled as they were by his anticipation of trouble, but an unprepared army could be devastated by many fewer men.

Simon's eyes raked her. "Darwendon, eh? You are bonded to him then, but you don't appear to be a serf. If he had cast his bonded slut aside she would not still be wearing that wool robe, woman, or linen on her neck."

"They were gifts. He let me keep them. He is not ungenerous."

"Well pleased, was he? Aye, I can imagine he was."

Her blood ran cold at the leering smirks that smeared both men's faces. "Apparently not pleased enough, since I was left to make my own way across the realm with naught but the garments on my back." She tried to look resentful and peeved. "And this gown is small compensation for what he cost me. I lost an entire crop because of his insistence that I serve him in London. If he were anywhere in this shire, I would gladly point you to him."

Simon studied her in his sly way. "Where did you learn to talk like that? Your manner is far above your place."

She could not decide if explaining would help or hurt, so she said nothing. Owen stepped forward and yanked her hair so cruelly that she thought her neck would break. He lifted until her knees left the ground.

"Hawkesford," she gasped. "I lived at Hawkesford as a girl."

"Hawkesford?" The answer surprised Simon. He grabbed her chin and lifted her face. Dangerous, shrewd eyes inspected her. He looked long enough that she saw something inside that gaze. Fear. Beneath his bluster and anger, within these walls and his power, Simon tried to hide the terror of a hunted man. The insight gave her heart.

"Hawkesford," he mused again. "Lady Claire had a friend there who was serf-born. She spoke of her sometimes. Would that be you?"

She refused to answer. He stepped back and smiled. "Aye, it be you. If you were of that household and her friend, I think that you know about the boy. Where is he?"

"What boy?"

Owen pulled her to her feet and slammed her against the wall. Two faces, one pale and impassive, the other florid and impatient, glared down at her. "Her boy. Brian. Where is he?"

She felt grateful that Addis had never told her where the sweet child hid. They might break her but her weakness could never help them ensnare Brian. "I do not know."

Owen slammed his fist into her body and her consciousness reeled. If not for the wall's support she would have fallen. "You waste your time," she breathed. "I am no one. Nobody. A bondwoman of no account. Addis de Valence does not confide to his whore when his army moves and where his son is hidden. You know how it is with such as me. If I knew anything I would tell you and at most bargain for some coin."

Simon's face pressed closer. The smell of onions on his breath and of fear on his body made her bruised stomach heave. "You know. Claire spoke of your loyalty. When she went to bed to birth that boy she asked you be called to care for him if she died. Serf-born or not, I think you knew the doings in the households of Valence and Orrick. I think that you still know them. And if you lie to help him

now, I wonder if maybe you are not more than a whore
to him."

"You speak nonsense and beat a helpless woman for
nothing. Could a woman like me ever be more than a
whore to you? His birth is even higher than yours. A son
of Barrowburgh has only one use for baseborn women."

"She talks too much while answering nothing," Owen
said. "Let me deal with her. If he has come she will
tell me."

Simon considered her, debating his options. A prayerful
hope gripped her, dangerous because it acknowledged and
released the terror she had been fighting for hours. A
change in Owen's regard said that his predator's instincts
had sensed the new vulnerability that the chance of reprieve had created.

"She will tell me," Owen repeated.

Simon nodded and turned away. "Do not kill her
though. She might be useful."

Aye, he enjoyed it. Too much. He proved well practiced
in creating suffering without causing the damage that
would make her drop. She prayed for unconsciousness but
it never quite came. Shallow, methodical blows and slaps
quickly drove her to the edge of endurance. Obscene descriptions of what would happen next further assaulted
her steadfastness. Pain and weakness began pushing her
to the point where she might sell her soul to stop it.
Knowing she was about to break, seeing it coming, she
found a final drop of rebellious courage. Pursing her
cracked lips, she let the bile that choked her rise and she
spit into his face.

A retaliatory fist crashed into her. The chamber swirled
and the stone floor rushed up. Her mind knew red and
then white and then nothing at all.

✦　✦　✦

Menulius lit their way, holding back the clouds that tried to obscure his glow. They used no torches, but the feet and horses of six hundred men made enough noise in the still night that anyone looking could easily find them. When mile after mile passed and no raiding parties from Barrowburgh attacked, Addis grimly accepted that Moira had refused to tell Simon what he wanted.

He tried not to contemplate what might be happening to her in that keep. The abuse would not come from Simon. It would be Owen. The Simons of the world always found the Owens who enjoyed doing the dirty work. The image flashed of that flame-haired man hurting her, and he barely resisted the urge to spur his horse and let this army catch up as it might.

He looked to his left and right at the thick shadows accompanying them. Men had silently fallen into step when they had passed Whitly, tromping alongside in the fields. All along the way more had emerged from the trees and hills. No one had asked his permission. A growing sea of bodies had simply formed on either side of the road. Some carried staffs or rough pikes or even scythes, but most merely brought their two hands and legs.

"They have heard about the reeve and the woman, you think?" Thomas Wake asked from the horse beside him.

"Perhaps. It would be the final injustice to a people who have suffered many."

"You should send them home. They will get in the way."

"I do not think they would obey if I did so. They are not in disorder, and appear determined. Simon is their Hugh Despenser. Each of them has made a hard choice as you and I did not so long ago."

"But when we reach Barrowburgh . . ."

"They will not disrupt the plan, and we may be glad of their numbers if we fail."

A cantering horse broke through the rhythm of marching boots and Richard pulled up alongside. "Just a mile more over that hill if we go through the woods." He pointed. "That will bring us in from the west. There's time to rest here for a while."

Addis looked at the sky. Three hours until dawn, he judged. His gaze fell on the flanking shadows pausing and bunching to make a large shapeless ghost.

"A brief rest. We will not stop long."

"You are changing the plan? If we continue we will arrive too early and by dawn he will have deployed his men. Have you decided to make camp after all?"

"Nay, we will still march directly into an attack."

Raymond paced around Wake to join the council. "You are mad, Addis. Even with the moon a night attack is suicide. We'll not see who we are fighting and . . ."

"We go forward. He will not expect it even if he has discovered that we are coming, especially at night."

"Your concern for the woman is impairing your judgment. If he planned to kill her she is dead already," Thomas said.

"And if he did not plan to kill her?"

"Whatever he intended is done."

Raymond threw up an arm. "It will help her naught if you fail because you acted rashly."

"You know that attacking in the dark is a fool's strategy," Richard weighed in.

Addis turned his horse and began walking it toward the shadows beside the road. "That is true, but we will not attack in the dark, old friend. Our way will be lit by all of Barrowburgh's hearths."

What the hell are you saying? Make sense, man.

The harsh voice penetrated the fog from far away.

There's movement out there, near the distant trees to the west. Men and horses.

You say you've seen men by the trees? How many?

Closer now. A familiar voice. Simon's.

Not seen, exactly, my lord, not with the moon going in sudden like. Felt more than seen, though there seem to be darker shadows there, bigger than they should be.

Probably just the night playing tricks on you.

Not just me. The other guards feel it too. I'd not have come if we didn't agree. . . .

Send more men to the gates then.

Will you be coming, my lord?

Awareness of the chamber returned and she suddenly smelled the hearth. Her cheek recognized the hard texture of stone on which it lay. Screaming aches groaned through her body from the spots where she had been hit. Sliding back into unconsciousness held an enormous appeal. She heard movements, but enough sense had returned for her to resist the urge to look.

"I'll go to the top of the keep and see what's what," Simon gruffed. "Get back on the wall."

"What about her?" Owen asked as the guard left. She lay utterly still and hoped that they would leave her in the heap where she had fallen.

"See again if you can wake her."

Liquid splashed her face and she fought her shocked reaction even though she inhaled some of it. Wine dripped down her immobile face, burning her broken lips.

"Are you sure she is not dead? I told you not to kill her."

"She still breathes."

"Leave her. We will see about this ghost army the guard *felt* and then see if she can be revived."

She waited until silence surrounded her before she tried to rise. Her whole body from her neck to her legs felt deeply sore, and it hurt to move her mouth. Despite the pain she reached for the wall and pulled herself up.

She could hardly escape, but she would not wait in this chamber for the torture Owen planned. The guard's report had given her hope. Perhaps Addis had come.

She groped along the wall and peered out the door. Men to the west, the guard had said. She skirted through the passageway to a chamber near the end. Trying to ignore the agony of her knotting torso, she felt her way to the window.

She was high enough to see over the walls to the distant fields and flanking hunt-land. A brisk breeze moved clouds across the moon, breaking them up now and then to permit gray light to spread. During those brief illuminations it did appear that movement occurred near the trees, but probably it was just the night playing tricks on one's eyes, as Simon had said.

She rested against the window edge and closed her eyes with disappointment. Of course he could not come until he was ready, and even then he would not do so at night. It would be rash to risk so much, even if he knew she was here.

Which he might not know at all. When he had discovered her gone, he probably concluded that she had gone back to London. Could he have thought her that faithless? Faced with her absence, he might have found it the only explanation.

Her chest filled with a horrible ache. She did not want to picture that. She turned back to the window and scanned the battlements of the inner wall to distract her mind from images of him angry and hurt, believing she had forsaken him so cruelly right before his dangerous task. The distant fields grew very black as clouds completely obscured the moon.

A flicker caught her eye and a tiny dot of gold appeared far away. It moved. Two dots now. She squinted. Suddenly four. Now ten or more. She watched in amazement as the specks rapidly multiplied and enlarged, like stars emerging and growing not in the sky but on the horizon.

The noise of household and guards suddenly stilled and the fortress went utterly silent. Others had seen. The faintest rhythm oozed toward her on the breeze, and the stars, not so tiny now, continued increasing in number and size. They filled the field and began spreading right and left, encircling all of Barrowburgh. She stretched out the window, unmindful of her sores, and the closest spots materialized into torches and then disappeared from view beneath the mass of the wall. Their light cast a yellow glow in every direction, displaying hundreds of bodies. The brightest cluster surrounded a knight flanked by the banners of Valence.

Her heart lodged in her throat while she watched him come. The sounds of his army crashed through the stillness of the keep. He raised his arm and the movement ceased and he scanned the breadth of the fortifications. Instead of grouping to make camp, the army and the torchbearers lighting its way just waited.

Another gesture and the army suddenly split and men surged forward carrying scaling ladders. Their shouts shocked the whole fortress. She gaped as the hell of war instantly replaced the eerie silence. He was attacking!

He rode his horse back and forth, yelling orders lost to her ears in the din. The torches turned his armor orange, as if he wore steel still hot from the forge. Another man joined him and she recognized the bald head of Sir Richard. The steward took command of the western attack and Addis galloped south to where the wall extended to surround the town.

She tore her eyes from the spectacle, her pulse racing. He had come, but his arrival might have increased her danger. She trusted that Simon would be preoccupied with his defenses now, but she could not count on it. She needed a place to hide.

She turned to run but a thick figure barged through the threshold. Simon strode over and grabbed her arm, twisting her back to the window. His body pressed obscenely along her back and a sour smell assaulted her. Fear. He reeked of it.

"You should be flattered. You must have pleased him very well with that body of yours. He comes for you," he hissed.

"Nay. He comes for you."

"These walls have withstood more than he can have."

"He has over six hundred, all battle-hardened men. And it looks like every peasant man able to walk holds a torch out there. You should yield, and if not you should armor yourself."

"Owen will deal with him. He has killed him before. He will do so again."

"He failed before, and proved himself a coward in doing so. When it comes to facing Addis he will flee or surrender and leave you to face it alone."

"He will not. Owen is more a brother to me than Addis ever was."

"If he never showed you a brother's love it was because he knew what he had in you."

"He was too proud to befriend such as me! To share the wealth of Barrowburgh. I saw at once that I would get naught from him. Owen saw it too. We were all just youths, but it was clear that the son of Patrick scorned me."

"So you stole what would not be given freely!"

"A man either takes or he dies on a bloody field for

someone else's honor." He pulled her through the chamber. "You will come with me while we watch this army founder. He will not breach the inner wall. No one ever has. When this is done I will enjoy taking you, as I have taken everything else that is his."

His grip gouged her and she tried to keep up. "He does not have to breach the inner wall. The animals and grain are outside the first gate. He has only to wait until the provisions within are gone."

Twisting her arm behind her back he shoved her up the stairs to the roof. "And let you starve with us? That is why I would not let Owen kill you. For your sake, woman, I hope that you pleased him well indeed."

"Do we enter?" Raymond asked as the town gate swung wide. Figures scurried away and the torches showed five guards lying in lifeless tangles. "May not be a good idea to get caught inside. It could be a trap."

"Those were not soldiers running away, but craftsmen. The town has opened the gate, not Simon."

"Still . . ."

Addis paced his destrier forward. "The easiest way into any fortress is through the gates, Raymond."

"There's two more after this one and no townsmen to open them. We are close to breaching on the east. Best to wait."

Harsh and shrill sounds poured around them. The outer wall would fall, a casualty of the surprise attack, but the inner one would not be so certain. The thick circle of torches lighting the battle made it appear as if the entire scene took place within a giant hearth.

"If we attack the gate even while they defend the walls it might encourage them to withdraw. And it will force them to cover the south as well." He gestured for Marcus and told him to allow a hundred of the peasants to follow with the wheeled battering ram, then led a small force of knights and men-at-arms into the town.

The lanes were deserted and the buildings shuttered. Nearer the gate he could see the progress on the wall more clearly. Simon's men were greatly outnumbered and no reinforcements had arrived. Simon had decided to sacrifice the outer wall and its guard. It looked as if one section to the east had been taken and secured, but even so the superior position of the defenders meant this could last many hours.

He called the battering ram forward and dismounted. He and the others made a canopy of upraised shields to protect the farmers pulling the huge cylinder of wood. The rest of the farmers stayed out of arrow range, prepared to replace their neighbors as needed.

The repeated impact of the ram created a sound like the world's largest drum, crashing through the night. The sea of peasants surrounding the wall began cheering "Valence!" with each blow and the huge swell of noise seemed enough to crumble the walls by itself. A rain of bolts and arrows pounded into the shields with each surge forward, their whistling melody absorbed into the rhythmic battle song.

Suddenly the arrows stopped. Addis peered up to see Thomas Wake and his men fighting on the gate's battlements, but some guards had redeployed and moved in. He called for ladders and led Marcus and five others up while the ram continued its work.

He did not know how long he fought. His presence on the wall was noticed, however, and at least two archers came close to taking him down. At one point he glanced to the upper reaches of the keep and he saw Simon there, with a woman beside him. Moira. Something like the madness in the forest gripped him then and he knew nothing but the mayhem of blood and swords until a dead calm fell that said the gate was theirs.

The sound of the portcullis rising heralded victory, and any guards still standing surrendered. Addis hurried down to the outer yard while his men poured in.

Richard found him and gestured around the bailey. "Have you seen anything like it?"

The yard was crammed with animals and wagons and stores, collected to sustain the keep in case of siege and to ensure that Addis could find no provisions in the surrounding countryside. Simon would have burned the forests next to drive off the game.

"Have it cleared. Move it into the town. Quickly, or it will be fired from above."

Richard shouted the order and men began pulling the animals out while archers helped cover them.

"Think you to continue now? It will be morning soon and we can pick our time," Richard asked.

"What do you recommend?"

Richard wiped some blood off his head and laughed. "As if you need my council, or listen when I give it. Well, aye, I would take advantage of the confusion. The men are still fresh and can taste victory. And if there's to be help from the inside, it will be easier for them if we move before Simon has time to consider what's what now, and think too hard about who is where."

Addis gazed at the tall walls filling with knights and soldiers. The inner portcullis was solid iron and no battering ram would break it. He could starve them out, but it might take months. And Moira would suffer along with the others.

Let it be finished. Now.

He gave the order and Richard went to organize the attack. He looked up at the keep but could no longer see where Simon and Moira stood. He muttered a prayer for

her protection. Would the Christian saints help her, con
sidering the sin of their love?

Just to be on the safe side he made the same request o
Kovas, the god of war.

They could see it all from the keep's roof. Like god
watching from a high mountain, they saw the battle pea
and then suddenly end when the gate opened. Simon'
men pressed shoulder to shoulder along the battlements o
the inner wall and shot arrows at the army invading th
outer yard, but Moira could tell from Simon's expressio
that he expected no more fighting this night.

Her eyes never left Addis, even while he fought ato
the gate. She saw the moment when he noticed her, an
then the savage mayhem that followed.

"He will at least wait until morning to attack again.
expect he will want to parlay first," Simon said while the
watched the provisions being pulled out the gate. "I
will give me a few hours to discover what makes you s
valuable."

She fixed him with one of Claire's haughty glares but i
did not dull his leer. "He does not fight for me, Simon
There will be no parlay and no terms, and he will not wai
until morning. Do you see any camps forming out on th
field? Look you to Owen. He knows it is not over."

The red-haired knight paced around the wall's walk
checking the deployment of the enemy. Simon's gaze
found him. "He will see that Addis does not enter, or does
not live long if he does."

"You have great faith in your friend. Do you really
think he will die to protect your hold on Barrowburgh?"

"Nay, probably not. But he will fight to the death to
protect himself from Addis's revenge."

A sudden outpouring of shouts and yells drew their attention back to the yard. A ringing line of men surged forward and the attack resumed.

The fighting was closer now, and the blood and pain loomed horribly real. She could see faces rise above the wall and their expressions when swords dealt the death blows. But more kept coming, and more again, until some bodies breached the wall and the fighting spread along the walk.

It was like a scene from hell. Her blood pounded and her eyes teared from the scenes of carnage. Beside her Simon observed as if he enjoyed an interesting entertainment, but she could smell that fear on him still. She scanned for Addis until she saw the colors of Valence and his swinging sword where he fought for a foothold on the wall near the gate. Raymond fought beside him, and Small John too. They were trying to take this entry as they had the last, but Owen noticed and led reinforcements in their direction.

Addis and the others who had breached the wall found themselves isolated as Owen's men thwarted any further scaling. Outnumbered now, they valiantly held off attacks from both sides.

He would be killed. She just knew it. His sword fell with methodical precision, but there were too many. She silently begged him to retreat, to find a way back down, and looked away to avoid seeing the death blow that would find him soon.

Her gaze fell on the inner yard. Amidst the wavering shadows a group of nine men moved in thick formation, all wearing the scarlet of Simon's knights. They eased along the wall with swords drawn.

They slipped forward. Three disappeared into the gate and the other six mounted to the wall. Her heart almost burst with despair when she realized they headed toward Addis. There would be no hope now.

They joined the battle, but not in the way expected. Suddenly those armored arms were pushing men off the wall, crashing archers' heads against the battlements, clearing a path to the sword fight. Owen glanced over his shoulder and seemed to assume they were with him. When a sword from behind felled the man by his side, he realized the truth.

She had forgotten about Simon, but his livid curses drew her eyes to his astonished expression.

"Sir Richard said some had stayed behind," she said.

"Vipers in my own bed! I'll have them roasted alive!"

"It does not appear you will have the chance. Even I can tell that their aid has turned the tide on that wall and that the gate will be taken soon."

Even as she spoke, the grinding sounds of chains and wheels filtered through the din of battle. Simon's eyes glazed.

"Three went inside. You were so busy watching Addis that you did not notice."

His gaze locked on Owen fighting desperately, his position as hopeless as Addis's had been just moments before.

"Surrender. He cannot help you or even himself anymore. Yield. Addis is not without mercy."

Beads of sweat dotted Simon's brow and the hair of his mustache. A furious desperation lit his eyes and he turned away, pulling her with him. "I'll not be counting on his mercy."

He hauled her down to the solar where he plucked two fat purses from a chest. With an iron grip on her arm he forced her down the stairway. The sounds drifting from the yard changed abruptly. She could hear hundreds of bodies moving and yelling, but no longer the screams of death and pain.

"It is over. He is inside," she said, wondering if Simon had noticed.

He pushed her downward with determination. "Aye, but I will be outside."

"You can move more quickly without me."

"I think that you are a better shield than steel, and so are worth the trouble."

"Think you to walk across these lands and not be found?"

"Horses wait not far away. I had great faith in Owen, but I am not a stupid man."

He pushed open a small door at the northern base of the keep. The yard was shallow here, and filled with shacks for chickens and pigs. High above on the wall Addis's men were accepting the surrender of Simon's.

Simon circled her in one arm and gagged her with his hand. Staying in the shadows of the shacks, he dragged her toward the wall. His rough handling reawoke her sores and she submitted to avoid more pain.

If he got her outside her peril might be even worse than before. Desperate and vengeful, he might kill her when he had no more use for her. A rebellious fear spread. She struggled and fought and he twisted her head cruelly in response. Pressing against the wall, he felt for the postern door.

A string of lights began edging around the keep. Simon shrank farther into the shadows but the glow spread until no shadows existed anymore, leaving the two of them starkly exposed. A tall armored figure strode among the torches toward them. Blood smeared the jerkin draping his body and colored the sword clutched in his hand. He stopped ten paces away.

"Are you going somewhere, Simon? I might consider permitting it if you did not try to take what was mine with you."

She could feel the body pressed behind her shake.

Simon's hand jerked down to his side and the two purses flew onto the ground at Addis's feet. One of the torch-bearers crouched and poured their contents out. Gold coins and glittering jewels flickered in a heap.

"I was not speaking of the wealth you had amassed and hoarded these past years."

His arm embraced her more tightly and the pressure on her bruises made her light-headed. "She will stay with me until I am well away."

"She will stay here, and so will you. You have much to answer for."

"It was a king who gave me Barrowburgh, and a king's council who took it away. I will go and answer to them for not obeying, but I will accept no judgment from you!"

"Your disobedience to the council is the least of it."

Simon's whole body flexed, as if he tried to suppress a huge shiver. Moira couldn't blame him. Addis stood there resolute and dangerous, a blood-aroused warrior who had just accomplished an impossible victory. There was little of the kind knight whom she knew in this man. He had removed his helmet and fury flamed in his eyes.

"Where is Owen?" Simon demanded. "Is he dead?"

"You pray that he is, I am sure, but when faced with the choice he took the coward's way as he always has. No trees or hired killers to hide behind up on that wall. No enemy army on whom to blame the sword or the spear. When it came down to him and me in a fair fight he yielded. And then he talked as if his life depended on it, as indeed it did."

He paced forward and Simon tried to pull her into the wall. "When my father married your mother he did not have to take you into his home as he did. But his generosity only planted greed in you, and plans to take my place as his son. Moira once said I was fortunate in my wounds, and she was right. In his youth Owen proved inept. A squire among my companions should have been able to kill me, the second time if not the first."

She gasped and twisted until she could see Simon's face out of the corner of her eye. He stared wide-eyed with terror, sweat pouring down his face. It was true. It had been Owen who scarred that body, Owen whose spear left Addis for dead on the crusade.

His strangled cry echoed her thoughts. "It was Owen!"

"His sword. His hands. But your idea and your gain. A hungry youth's impatient plan. But even with me dead, my father did not embrace you as his new son, did he? And so Lancaster's rebellion offered a way to make your own fate, without my father's favor." Addis traced the ridged scar on his face. "This I might forgive. Even those years of slavery. But my father's death was from no natural fever, I think. Owen doesn't think so either."

Simon's arm had become a death grip, squeezing the breath out of her, crushing her sore ribs and torso. Little spots of blackness dotted her sight. His other hand fumbled. A sharp edge pressed into her neck and a dagger hilt bumped her chin.

"You will release her," Addis said.

"Nay. You are speaking madness and I will get no justice here. You have no proof on Patrick but it will not matter during the power of your victory."

"Release her."

"She comes with me. If you want to see her alive again you will not follow."

Addis looked away for a moment and then stepped closer yet. Simon's terror surged in a palpable way. The blade pressed, the arm squeezed, and she almost passed out from pain.

"Aren't you forgetting something?" Addis asked quietly. "She does not know where Brian is. You may have my woman, but I have your son."

His words stunned her. She tried to twist and see Si
mon's reaction but the gesture made the blade burn he
neck. She stared at Addis, hoping for a sign that h
bluffed, but he did not even acknowledge her reaction. A
of his attention centered on the face gasping sour breat
next to her ear.

"You will never harm the boy who might be yours,
Simon blustered.

"Not mine. And a Christian knight should not harr
any child, but I find myself feeling less of one with eac
passing moment. Harm Moira and there may not be
shred of such mercy left in me."

She could feel Simon's panic. Her own mind veere
from thought to thought, trying desperately to accommo
date what Addis said and the cold way he said it. Simon
son! He had used Brian as a pawn from the beginning
Her throat tightened from a mournful sorrow, stranglin
her breath.

"Claire said the boy was yours!"

"She lied, even to you it seems. But you suspected th
truth. He would not have survived if you had not, no mat
ter how well Raymond and Moira tried to hide him."

"You cannot be sure. . . ."

"I am sure."

Simon clutched harder, the last grasp of a desperat
man. The pain made her dizzy. Through her numbin
awareness she felt him resist, hover, and then plunge int
despair.

A violent push sent her flying at Addis. Her blotche
senses absorbed the impact of his body, the support of hi
strong arm, and then his own thrust as he hurled her away
She floated to the ground on a pillow of semiconscious
ness, only vaguely aware of the furious activity rainin
down around her.

Suddenly a deathly silence fell. Strong arms lifted he

up and her head lolled against a metal chest. Her insides felt as if they had been bludgeoned by that battering ram. Darkness sped by and she found herself gently laid on a soft bed.

Her tenuous hold on reality strengthened, but she resisted full alertness and the pains it would bring. Voices and movements swirled around her but her mind folded in on itself and followed its own paths through memories and emotions full of joy and sadness. She saw Addis in all of his faces, but most starkly in the new one revealed to her tonight in the yard. A profound disillusionment made her keep her eyes closed even when a woman came to wipe her face and check her wounds.

She pictured Brian riding off beside the man she thought was his father. But he was Simon's son, and Addis had known. That she had lived four years thinking she protected one man's child when in fact the boy needed no protection at all did not dismay her. The joy she had known giving Brian love could survive the knowledge that her great purpose had been a fraud. But the fact that Addis had taken that child from her and hidden him among strangers, had risked leaving Brian abandoned and alone should he die, had severed that spot of light from her life, all to hold a threat over Simon . . . her heart turned from what it meant about him. She did not think she could forgive him for using the child thus.

Sounds intruded more insistently and she realized that she lay in the solar. She could hear men talking and entering and leaving, and Addis's low voice giving orders. She turned her head toward him and forced her eyes open a slit.

He had removed his armor and thrown on a cotte. He sat in the lord's chair discussing something with Sir Richard. He looked as if the chair had been built for him. Proud and strong and powerful. A family like Valence did not hold on to their honor by being weak-hearted, and he was undoubtedly Patrick's son. She had been loving hidden parts of him that could no longer be acknowledged. The man whom everyone else had seen and feared would dominate now.

He noticed her looking and gestured Richard aside. She watched him come until he stood beside the bed. He caressed her cheek. "You are badly hurt, Moira, but the women say they do not think that you bleed inside. You will be feeling better soon."

She did not think she would ever feel better again. "Simon?"

"He came at us both with that dagger. A mad thing, since I wore steel. The blade caught your shoulder, but it is not deep."

"Did you kill him?"

"The peasants killed him. They moved as soon as he did, and he was dead by the time I got through to him." He bent down and kissed her forehead. "I must go down to the yard now, and see that the people get back their animals and such fairly. Rest, love."

"Will you ask Raymond to come? I want to speak with him."

He nodded and turned to leave.

She raised a hand to stop him. "Kiss me, Addis."

"I will hurt you."

"Please kiss me."

He carefully brushed her split and swollen lips with his mouth, and pressed the gentlest kiss on them. Tears burned in her closed eyes, and not because of any pain. He lingered there, her Addis, the vulnerable Addis of confusion and loneliness who had found love with a bondwoman. Their warmth connected them long enough that she almost lost her composure. She savored it, branding her mind with this final memory.

A sound interrupted them. She looked through moist eyes at Thomas Wake standing at the door. Addis straightened, suddenly the Lord of Barrowburgh again, the fearsome warrior who could conquer a fortress in three night hours and hold a child ransom in a game of power. The two men left her alone in the solar.

It was as she had known it would be. The string of his life had been retied. He did not need her anymore, not really. And the point had come, that specific moment she had been dreading, when she must either leave or walk back into the shadows.

The deep breaths with which she fought tears racked her bruised body. She only found some comfort when she forced her thoughts from the past to the future, and to the quest awaiting her.

By the time Raymond came she had made her decision.

"You have heard?" she asked.

He frowned and nodded. "He says he is sure."

"Will he give Brian to you? You are his uncle."

"I have not asked yet, but I fear not. The truth of his birth will always be ambiguous. Addis can repudiate him, but there is no proof except Addis's word. When he is of age, Brian can challenge it, and will be a threat to any future son's hold."

"A man would not repudiate his own blood. Surely Addis is right."

Raymond shrugged. "Presumably. But it might be his final revenge on Claire. It is said she forsook him, and I know she fought the marriage. If he hated her for that, he might not want her son as his heir."

Could he do that? He had not warmed to the boy, and said that whenever he saw Brian he saw betrayal. "Do you know where he is?"

"Nay."

Nor did she. But she knew the direction they had gone,

and the time it had taken to bring Brian to his hiding place.

"I want to leave here now, Raymond. Will you help me?"

That startled him. "You are in no condition for a journey, Moira. And Addis—"

"Today, Raymond. Now. As soon as you can arrange a wagon. Some of the farmers will take me where I want to go. You need not escort me."

"Moira, you are wounded and shocked. You loved the boy and this news troubles you. Wait to speak with Addis."

"Aye, this news troubles me, and so does the realization that he will want to leave Brian wherever he is, a child alone with no family's love. But I always intended to leave. I said that I would see him enter these gates and sit in that chair and I have done so. The news about Brian only reinforces my decision."

Raymond sighed and shook his head. "You have always had enough pride for three women, and it is a hell of a thing that you do. He will not forgive you, or me for helping you."

"Will you do it?"

"I will do it. In the name of my sister's friendship for you and because you sacrificed part of your life to help my nephew, I owe it to you. But will you not wait to see him again first? To make your farewell?"

If she saw him again she might never leave, even with the disappointments and misgivings filling her heart.

"I have already said farewell to the Addis I love."

CHAPTER 22

SHE DID NOT NOTICE him enter the chamber. She was bent out the small window, the golden light of the late afternoon coloring her veil and flooding her form, the thin wool of her gown draping appealingly over her rounded hips. He could see her profile from the doorway and watched silently as her blue eyes scanned expectantly, then sparkled when a lovely smile enlivened her face. She lifted one hand from the sill and waved, then straightened and quietly stood like a sentry.

She appeared to him as an oasis of softness in a harsh world, a ray of light illuminating the chamber more than the sunbeams. His two souls had begun to accommodate each other, but her presence produced the old serenity and he welcomed the soothing grace made even more potent by the memories attached to it.

She did not move, but he knew the exact moment when she realized that she was not alone. Even so, her gaze did not leave whatever she watched.

"How did you find me?"

He went to her. "You were not in London and your people there had not seen you since we left together in the spring. You were not at Darwendon, and Raymond finally convinced me that he did not hide you at Hawkesford. Then I remembered that you had lived in Salisbury when you were married, and I wondered if maybe you had figured out that Brian was here too."

He looked out the window. The house backed against the abbey wall, and from here she could see into its yard. A group of boys kicked a ball among themselves. The smallest one's hair gleamed pale and blond.

"The friars would not let me speak to him, but I watch him every day from this window. He knows I am here now, and looks for me when they come out to play. His little face lights with a smile that says he knows that he is not alone anymore."

He looked down on the child whose existence symbolized betrayals far worse than the act that conceived him. It really didn't matter anymore. Nothing did from that time except the love and loyalty and strength that the Shadow had selflessly given.

"He is not mine, Moira. I am not punishing Claire by repudiating him. Raymond accused me of that, but it is not true."

"Nay, it is not. There is nothing of you in him. I see that now. Little of Simon either, for that matter. He is all Claire's son. She lied to me about him. About you. She said that you had demanded . . . before you went on the crusade that you had . . ."

"Forced her. And you believed that?"

"At the time it was not so hard to believe. It was a bitter young man whom they carted back to Barrowburgh, with a bitter girl by his side. You hated her then, I think, even if you do not remember it."

He remembered it. That part he had never forgotten.

'I had known Claire since she was born. Aye, I hated her, but not because she turned from me as a wife and a woman. She turned from me as a friend as well. Those years should have left us with that at least."

"She was young and frightened."

"She was shallow and vain and could only love herself. A woman with your depths and heart probably cannot understand that people can be thus. I had begun to see it as I outgrew my youth. Her radiance could not blind me forever. Her behavior when I was wounded only made me face what my heart had known for some time already." She had not looked at him. She still watched the child. "It troubles me to think that whenever you looked at that boy, you saw a child born from violence. That the memory you held of me those years was of a man who would hurt his wife."

A small frown tweaked her brow while her gaze turned inward. "Not really. She described it thus, but I did not believe you had used violence. She was your wife, and I assumed that you had demanded her duty to you. To her mind it might have been force, but I thought maybe it had just been like James and me."

"It was not even like James and you. I know he is not my son because despite the wedding I never lay with her after my return. I could not undo the marriage, but she was dead to me and I did not want her in my bed."

She nodded, as if he had just confirmed her own thoughts. "I have wondered why she lied about such a thing. To claim the child was yours made sense, of course. But why accuse you of such cruelty?"

"The whole household knew how things stood between us. Perhaps she feared that if she did not give a story that fit those facts some would wonder about the child's parentage. Certainly my father would have found it curious, since he knew we rarely spoke and that I had not touched

her. An enraged husband forcing his rights on the eve of
his departure would explain the child no one expected to
see conceived."

"How did you know he was Simon's?"

"I suspected when it was clear that he had not searched
for Brian very hard at all. He knew about Darwendon
even if he did not know about you."

Brian gave the ball a wild kick. The boys raced around a
corner of the building to catch it. She watched him disappear and finally turned, those clear eyes seeking his.
"Could you have done it? Used him in vengeance against
his father?"

"In truth, I do not know. If Simon had killed you,
maybe so. What do you think, Moira?"

"I think not, but I do not know either. You are a complex person, Addis. You once said you feel as if two souls
exist in you, but sometimes I sense many more, and some
of them frighten me. There are times when I do not think
I know you at all and never really can."

"You know me, Moira. If anyone does, you do. You
know me as well as I know myself, which I will admit isn't
very well."

She dropped her gaze to the floor between them. "I am
glad that you came to explain it to me, Addis."

"That is not only why I came."

She looked a little frightened, and shot glances blindly
around the room as if he cornered her and she sought an
escape.

"This chamber is overwarm. Come down to the garden
with me so we can speak."

"I don't think so, Addis."

He took her hand in his. The delicate warmth made his
heart swell with relief and love. He had feared he would
never feel her touch again.

She resisted warily. He coaxed her with a firm tug,

gearing himself for a battle more vital to his life than the one at Barrowburgh.

She should not go. She should send him away and not listen to whatever words he had for her. Her good sense chanted this while he led her down the stairs and into the small walled garden filled with young plants.

Aye, she should not go, but she looked at the lean strong back beneath its brown cotte, and the fine, tanned arm stretching to hers, and the handsome face looking back. Her heart flipped as it had since she was a girl, and the part of her that had long ago abandoned good sense with him would not be denied this final, brief time, no matter what raw pain it renewed.

He found a bench against a wall where a hedge hid them from the curious eyes of the goldsmith's wife who owned the house. She pried her hand loose and restlessly smoothed the folds of her skirt. She felt him watching her. Sitting close beside him left her a little breathless.

"Is all well at Barrowburgh?" she asked feebly.

"Well enough. The crops look good and the people are content. Lucas Reeve has recovered, although he lost sight in an eye that night. I gave each of his sons a virgate, and have said they need not pay heriot when their father dies."

"You are a generous and fair lord. The villeins at Darwendon thought so too."

"It was an easy generosity."

"And Owen. What of him?"

"At my encouragement Owen decided to expiate his sins with another crusade. A very long one. And Simon's mother asked if she might retire to a convent and I gave my permission."

"So it is all done then. You have your life back. It is as it should be. I am joyed for you, Addis."

He tilted his head thoughtfully. "It is done. I should be more than content. And yet I feel little joy myself, Moira. I have my life back, and I am not so foolish or ungrateful as to forget the value of it. But that keep is a cold place, full of lifeless shadows. I do my duty as I was taught from birth, but my heart cannot warm to it. Sometimes I feel like a slave again, now serving the ghosts of my ancestors."

She could imagine that and her heart ached for him. Loneliness was something she understood and had come to know again far too well. "It will change. When you marry and have a family, it will be a true home again. Lady Mathilda will bring life and warmth to Barrowburgh."

"When I marry it will not be to Lady Mathilda. Thomas Wake regretfully told me that the girl does not think we suit each other. He knew even when he brought that army that there would be no marriage. Mathilda thinks I am not refined and courteous enough. She wants a knight who will write her poetry and hang on each of her many words as if they are pearls that drop from her mouth."

"She is a silly little goose!"

He reached over and brushed back some errant hairs that had escaped her veil. "Perhaps she suspected that the whole time she chattered in Yorkshire, I was making love to you in my mind."

The light touch and the look in his eyes made her tremble. She barely found a voice. "If so, that really was discourteous."

His fingers drifted to caress her face, gently moving over the flesh as if he were learning its structure. He summoned an anguished love in her full of poignant, impossible yearnings that said she would pay dearly in the days ahead for this visit. In the three months since she left him she had finally learned to dull the pain, but had also learned that the punishment of loving the wrong person lasted a lifetime.

"I want you to come back with me."

"Oh, Addis . . ."

He embraced her with one arm and kissed her into silence, his palm resting warmly on her cheek. "You will come. You must."

So tempting to sink into that embrace forever. "There will be another betrothal, another Mathilda. You speak of only a reprieve, and my heart can take just so many such partings before it breaks forever. You are proof enough that each of us lives several lives before we perish. There is wisdom in accepting when one ends and another begins. I love you, Addis. I always will. But there is no place for me in the life you have now."

"If that is wisdom, then I will never be wise. I do not want a life that has no place for you in it. You will come back with me and take the place that is yours in my heart. No obligations to the past stand in the way. We will marry."

He looked so serious, so determined, as if he spoke logic instead of nonsense. She caressed his face and his head bowed to her touch until they sat with foreheads pressed and palms on each other's face. "It is impossible. You know that better than I do."

"It is not forbidden. Once done, no one can undo it."

"You will be scorned by your own, and mocked for your choice of wife. Even the peasants will think you mad."

"Those who know you will not scorn me but envy me, and I do not care what is said or thought."

"I am serf-born, Addis. It might as well be forbidden."

"Aye, you lived as a serf, Moira, with all that means. But I lived as a slave. My degree was even lower than yours."

"That was an accident. A mistake."

"All of our births are accidents, and yours a mistake. I know we are taught it is ordained by God, but I do not believe it. Of all of the beliefs and customs that I have questioned since I returned, this one I know is wrong and I'll not be bound by it. It seems to me if an anointed king can be set aside, a serf-born woman can marry a baron's son. As rebellions against God's lawful order go, ours will be a small one."

She did not know how to answer him. The offer at the church door had been a rash impulse, but this had been contemplated and planned. The idea was too preposterous. Surely he saw that.

He frowned. "Are you thinking that you could not bear it, Moira? If we are mocked, or there is disapproval? Women can be hard on each other, I know, and it may be worse for you than for me. If you do not think you can live in my life, I can always live in yours. I can give Barrowburgh back to the king and become an innkeeper with you."

Dear God, he was serious. "Nay. Oh, Addis, you are speaking more madness. Think. Your sons will have serfs for a mother and grandmother. What of them?"

"They will have a mother whom they will cherish as I do, and want to protect. A woman loved by her husband, and a grandmother who was beloved by her lord."

His insistence was exhausting her spirit and making her lose hold of the solid truths of her own argument. Her emotions scrambled, and his accepting, loving gaze undid her. She shook her head with a final, vague denial before sinking into his arms.

He held her against his chest with her head tucked under his chin, gently caressing her back. "You will come back with me and bring life to those shadows and warmth to my heart as you always have, Moira. And I will learn to give to you as you have always given to me."

"I would only bring you trouble and shame. You are just too stubborn and willful to see it. There are some things that the Lord of Barrowburgh cannot order to his liking," she muttered, hiding her brimming eyes in his cotte. He could not know how much he tortured her with this hopeless dream. He made it sound so possible, so real, but the blood that coursed in her body had been taught by centuries that it could never be so. He would see that soon enough, and be grateful she had not agreed. But, oh, the thought of it, hanging there right out of reach, tempting her to a ridiculous excitement that truth and good sense could barely suppress. . . .

He tilted her face to his, and thumbed a tear off her cheek. "Are you refusing me, Moira?"

Her throat burned and her lips trembled. He looked so sad as he read the decision in her eyes.

"Then I ask a final gift before we part. I want you to sing for me. One of the love songs, as you did at the dinner. I would have the song be about you and me, so that I think of you whenever I hear it again."

"Nay, Addis. Please . . ."

"Would you refuse me this too? This final memory? It is a small thing."

It wasn't a small thing. It would shred her to pieces and she might never be whole again.

She sniffed and licked her lips and rested her cheek against his chest. Only his heartbeat would accompany her. She found a spot of tenuous composure and clung to it and somehow, miraculously, the melody and words whispered forth.

Her voice could fill a hall, but now it only traveled the short distance to his ears. His lips pressed the top of her head and stayed there. The song both anguished and exalted her, and his embrace supported a body that knew no strength. Images flew behind her blurring eyes as old memories loomed sharply in the heavy mood of the song. A youth mourning in her arms. A knight screaming in pain. A fiery-eyed man stripped of illusions and will.

Her voice faltered several times before the end. The final words were lost in a sob that she buried in his chest. He held her to his breast while she cried out her heart, and rubbed his cheek against her hair as a father might comfort a child.

His own voice came low and rough with emotion. "Do you wonder why I will not live without you? Your love and loyalty sustained and comforted me in ways I did not even know. Even in slavery, I think it was you my spirit sought when I looked up into the stars. You have been my best ally for years, aiding me even in death when you cared for the boy, protecting me that dark night when I lost the will to protect myself."

She huddled in the soothing sanctuary of his arms, and struggled to contain the flood that the song had unleashed. "When did you remember?"

"My heart knew as soon as I saw you again. The memories came slowly, in bits and pieces. They began taking form once I had Barrowburgh again. But I had begun to understand where I had to look for them before that."

She felt so close to him that she thought her very essence had merged into his. She found a blissful serenity there, and a loving warmth that stroked her churning emotions like a reassuring caress.

"Look at me, Moira."

She pulled back until she could see the scarred face, and the perfect other half.

"We belong together. You will come back with me and we will wed and the rest of the world can go to hell if they do not like it. And when our children come I will tell them the story of the bondwoman who loved from the shadows and expected nothing in return."

He was not really asking her to agree. It is how it must be, his expression said. And he was right. Rejecting what they shared would be a type of sin.

A streak of sorrow split the euphoria spilling through her. Her gaze drifted to the far wall that abutted the abbey. He turned her face back and kissed her. "Brian will come with us. It will not be Simon's blood that forms the man he becomes, but your love. He is not my son and I will not have him displace our own children though. He must be told the truth of it, but I will accept him like my own blood. He may decide later that he is suited to the abbey and choose to return here, but if not I will give him the Baltic manor that is mine."

She almost wept again. "That is not easy generosity, Addis. And I love you all the more for it."

"He is an innocent, and I cannot remain cold to anyone you love." He rose. "We will go and get him now, if you want. But I hope there is a spare pallet in this house for him. I do not want to have him in our bed tonight."

"I think we can find a spot in another chamber for him." She would make sure that they did. A very special loving awaited them when night fell.

He looked down at her with such naked love that she thought she might fly to the heavens.

"Then let us speak with the friars. But first we will stop at the church door." He held out his hand to her. "Come and say the words with me, Moira. Be mine forever."

She looked at that gesture beckoning her to their impossible future. Only the greatest love and loyalty would survive what awaited them. Her serf's soul knew that even if none of his souls did.

She placed her hand completely in his.

Be sure to look for Madeline Hunter's other enchanting romances. . . .

BY ARRANGEMENT
now on sale

and

BY DESIGN
on sale in January 2001

Read on for previews of these spectacular novels.

BY

ARRANGEMENT

now on sale

"Master David, I have come to ask you to withdraw your offer of marriage."

He glanced to the fire, then his gaze returned to her. One lean, muscular leg crossed the other, and he settled comfortably back in his chair. An unreadable expression appeared in his eyes, and the faint smile formed again.

"Why would I want to do that, my lady?"

He didn't seem the least bit surprised or angry. Perhaps this meeting would go as planned after all.

"Master David, I am sure that you are the good and honorable man that the King assumes. But this offer was accepted without my consent."

He looked at her impassively. "And?"

"And?" she repeated, a little stunned.

"My lady, that is an excellent reason for you to withdraw, but not me. Express your will to the King or the bishop and it is over. But your consent or lack of it is not my affair."

"It is not so simple. Perhaps amongst you people it is, but I am a ward of the King. He has spoken for me. To defy him on this . . ."

"The church will not marry an unwilling woman, even if a King has made the match. I, on the other hand, have given my consent and cannot withdraw it. There is no reason to, as I have said."

His calm lack of reaction irked her. "Well, then, let me explain my position more clearly and perhaps you will have your reason. I do not give my consent because I am in love with another man."

Absolutely nothing changed in his face or eyes. She might have told him that she was flawed by a wart on her leg.

"No doubt an excellent reason to refuse your consent in your view, Christiana. But again, it is not my affair."

She couldn't believe his bland acceptance of this. Had he no pride? No heart? "You cannot want to marry a woman who loves another," she blurted out.

"I expect it happens all the time. England is full of marriages made under these circumstances. In the long run, it is not such a serious matter."

Oh, dear saints, she thought. A man who believed in practical marriages. Just her luck. But then, he was a merchant.

"It may not be a serious matter amongst you people," she tried explaining, "but marriages based on love have become desired—"

"That is the second time that you have said that, my lady. Do not say it again." His voice was still quiet, his face still impassive, but a note of command echoed nonetheless.

"Said what?"

" 'You people.' You have used the phrase twice now."

"I meant nothing by it."

"You meant everything by it. But we will discuss that another day."

He had flustered and distracted her with this second scolding. She sought the strand of her argument. He found it for her.

"My lady, I am sure a young girl thinks that she needs to marry the man whom she thinks that she loves. But your emotions are a short-term problem. You will get over this. Marriage is a long-term investment. All will work out in the end."

He spoke to her as if she were a child, and as dispassionately as if they discussed a shipment of wool. It had been a mistake to think that she could appeal to his sympathy. He was a tradesman, after all, and to him life was probably just one big ledger sheet of expenses and profits.

Well, maybe he would understand things better if he saw the potential cost to his pride.

"This is not just a short-term infatuation on my part, Master David. I am not some little girl," she said. "I pledged myself to this man."

"You both privately pledged your troth?"

It could be done that way. She could lie. She desperately wanted to, and felt sorely tempted, but such a lie could have dire consequences, and very public ones, and she wasn't that brave. "Not formally," she said, hoping to leave a bit of ambiguity there.

He at least seemed moderately interested now. "Has this man offered for you?"

"His family sent him home from court before he could settle it."

"He is some boy whom his family controls?"

She had to remember with whom she spoke. "A family's will may seem a minor issue for a man such as you, but he is part of a powerful family up north. One does not defy kinship so easily. Still, when he hears of this betrothal, I am sure that he will come back."

"So, Christiana, you are saying that this man said that he wanted to marry you but left without settling for you."

That seemed a rather bald way to put it.

"Aye."

He smiled again. "Ah."

She really resented that "Ah." Her annoyance made

her bold. She leaned toward him, feeling her jaw harden with repressed anger. "Master David, let me be blunt. I have given myself to this man."

Finally a reaction besides that impassive indifference. His head went back a fraction and he studied her from beneath lowered lids.

"Then be blunt, my lady. Exactly what do you mean by that?"

She threw up her hands in exasperation. "We made love together. Is that blunt enough for you? We went to bed together. In fact, we were found in bed together. Your offer was only accepted so that the Queen could hush up any scandal and keep my brother from forcing a marriage that my lover's family does not want."

She thought that she saw a flash of anger beneath those lids.

"You were discovered thus and this man left you to face it alone? Your devotion to this paragon of chivalry is impressive."

His assessment of Stephen was like a slap in her face. "How dare such as you criticize—"

"You are doing it again."

"Doing what?" she snapped.

" 'Such as you.' Twice now. Another phrase that you might avoid. For prudence's sake." He paused. "Who is this man?"

"I have sworn not to tell," she said stiffly. "My brother . . . Besides, as you have said, it is none of your affair."

He rose, uncoiling himself with an elegant movement, and went to stand by the hearth. The lines beneath the pourpoint suggested a lean, hard body. He was quite tall. Not quite as tall as Morvan, but taller than most. She found his presence unsettling. Merchants were supposed to be skinny or portly men in fur hats.

He gazed at the flames. "Are you with child?" he asked.

The notion astounded her. She hadn't thought of that. But perhaps the Queen had. She looked at him vacantly. He turned and saw the expression.

"Do you know the signs?" he said softly.

She shook her head.

"Have you had your flux since you were last with him?"

She blushed and nodded. In fact, it had come today.

He turned back to the fire.

She wondered what he thought about as he studied those tongues of heat. She stayed silent, letting him weigh however he valued these things, praying that she had succeeded, hoping that he indeed had a merchant's soul and would be repelled by accepting used goods.

Finally she couldn't wait any longer.

"So, you will go to the King and withdraw this offer?" she asked hopefully.

He glanced over his shoulder at her. "I think not."

Her heart sank.

"Young girls make mistakes," he added.

"This was no mistake," she said forcefully. "If you do not withdraw, you will end up looking a fool. He will come for me, if not before the betrothal, then after. When he comes, I will go with him."

He did not look at her, but his quiet, beautiful voice drifted over the space between them. "What makes you think that I will let you?"

"You will not be able to stop me. He is a knight, and skilled at arms . . ."

"There are more effective weapons in this world than steel, Christiana." He turned. "As I said earlier, you are always free to go to the bishop and declare your lack of consent to this marriage. But I will not withdraw now."

"An honorable man would not expect me to face the King's wrath," she said bitterly.

"An honorable man would not ruin a girl at her request. If I withdraw, it will displease the King, whom I have no wish to anger. At the least I will need a good reason. Should I use the one that you have given me? Should I repudiate you because you are not a virgin? It is the only way."

She dropped her eyes. The panicked desolation of the last day returned to engulf her.

She sensed a movement and then David de Abyndon stood in front of her. A strong, gentle hand lifted her chin until she looked up into his handsome face. It seemed to her that those blue eyes read her soul and her mind and saw right into her. Even Lady Idonia's hawklike inspections had not been so thorough and successful. Nor so oddly mesmerizing.

That intensity that flowed from him surrounded her. She became very aware of his rough fingers on her chin. His thumb stretched and brushed her jaw, and something tingled in her neck.

"If he comes for you before the wedding, I will step aside," he said. "I will not contest an annulment of the betrothal. But I must tell you, girl, that I know men and I do not think that he will come, although you are well worth what it would cost him."

"You do not know *him*."

"Nay, I do not. And I am not so old that I can't be surprised." He smiled down at her. A real smile, she realized. The first one of the evening. A wonderful smile, actually. His hand fell away. Her skin felt warm where he had touched her.

She stood up. "I must go. My escort will grow impatient."

He walked with her to the door. "I will come and see you in a few days."

She felt sick at heart. He was making her go through with the farce of this betrothal, and it would complicate things horribly. She had no desire to play this role any more than necessary.

"Please do not. There is no point."

He turned and looked at her as he opened the door and led her to the steps. "As you wish, Christiana."

She saw Thomas's shadowy form in the courtyard, and flew to him as soon as they exited the hall. She glanced back to the doorway where David stood watching.

Thomas began guiding her to the portal. "Did you accomplish what you needed?"

"Aye," she lied. Thomas did not know about the betrothal. I had not been announced yet, and she had hoped that it never would be. Master David's stubbornness meant that now things were going to become very difficult. She would have to find some other way to stop this betrothal, or at least this marriage.

David watched her cross the courtyard, her nobility obvious in her posture and graceful walk. A very odd stillness began claiming him, and her movements slowed as if time grew sluggish. An eerie internal silence spread until it blocked out all sound. In an isolated world connected to the one in the yard but separate from it by invisible degrees, he began observing her in an abstract way.

He had felt this before several times in his life, and was stunned to find himself having the experience now. All the same, he did nothing to stop the sensation and did not question the importance of what was happening.

He recognized the silence that permeated him as the inaudible sound of Fortune turning her capricious wheel and changing his life in ways that he could only dimly foresee. Unlike most men, he did not fear the unpredictable coincidences that revealed Fortune's willfulness, for he had thus far been one of her favorite children.

Christiana Fitzwaryn of Harclow. The caves of Harclow. There was an elegant balance in this particular coincidence.

The gate closed behind her and time abruptly righted itself. He contemplated the implications of this girl's visit.

He had understood King Edward's desire to hide the payment for the exclusive trading license that he was buying. If word got out about it, other merchants would be jealous. He had himself suggested several other ways to conceal the arrangement, but they involved staggered payments, and the King, desperate for coin to finance his French war, wanted the entire sum now. Edward's solution of giving him a noble wife and disguising the payment as a bride price had created a host of problems, though, not the least of which was the possibility that the girl would not suit him.

His vision turned inward and he saw Christiana's black hair and pale skin and lovely face. Her dark eyes sparkled like black diamonds. She was not especially small, but her elegance gave the impression of delicacy, even frailty. The first sight of her in the fire glow had made his breath catch the way it always did when he came upon an object or view of distinctive beauty.

Her visit had announced unanticipated complications, but it had resolved one question most clearly. Christiana Fitzwaryn would suit him very well indeed.

BY

DESIGN

on sale 2001

She looked like a statue of calm dignity placed in a sea of vulgar chaos.

The market roared and splashed all around her motionless body. Peddlers of skins and barrels, of pigs and fish, crowded the small space that she had claimed for her wares. Her ragged gown, of a pale silver hue and displaying remnants of elegant needlework, contrasted starkly with the practical browns and flamboyant colors filling the square. Along with her blond crown and braid, it created a column of light tones in a very mottled world. She was all gentle fairness, except for her skin. Bronzed from the sun, it possessed a golden sheen that brightened her blue eyes.

It was the respite of pale serenity that first caught Rhys's attention as he walked through the market in front of the Cathedral. Then the unveiled hair. And the eyes. He had already slowed to see her face more clearly before he noticed her wares.

She did not hawk them. She stood silently behind the crude, upturned wooden box that showed what she sold. Her delicate face remained impassive, as if she did not notice the bodies jostling by. Sometimes pressing her. Sometimes deliberately. He was not the only man to notice that this tattered dove was very pretty.

He did not recognize her. Most of the vendors were old faces, seen here regularly. She was an alien most likely, and not from the city. She had come for the day to make a few coins.

He felt a little sorry for her. Despite her rigid poise, she struck him as vulnerable, in danger of being broken. He doubted that she was doing well. The box was low, no higher than her knees, and the wares were almost invisible. He had to stroll very near in order to inspect the items set out on it.

Crockery. He had no interest in such things, but he did have an interest in her. He casually lifted the closest cup and a spark of hope lit her cool gaze.

The cup was simple but well made. Surprisingly, it was not ordinary sun-baked terra cotta. It had been fired, and its shine indicated that it had been glazed.

"The walls are very thin. Do you have a potter's wheel?" he asked while he examined it. And her. She really was very pretty, but up close he could read fatigue in her lax expression, and discouragement in her blue eyes.

"Nay. I just used coils."

"With great care, though. The shape is very regular."

His interest attracted others, as was the way with markets. A stout woman, a wealthy merchant's wife from her dress, paused and peered down critically. Something caught her eye. Poking her chubby hand amidst the cups, she lifted a small figure.

He had been so distracted by the potter that he had not noticed the little statues. The merchants wife held a standing Virgin, maybe a handspan tall. It had been carefully modeled with swelling drapes, and painstakingly painted with blue and yellow glazes.

The woman examined the little figure, running her fingers along the face and back, holding it upright to judge its look. Rhys made his own inspection alongside.

"How much?" the woman asked, sharp eyed and ready to bargain hard.

"Eight pence."

"Eight pence!"

"Five, then."

The woman groaned and sighed and dawdled and debated. Finally the five pence emerged from her purse.

The potter seemed well pleased.

Rhys dipped into the wares, moving some aside. Two other statues were there. A Saint Agnes with her lamb, and a Saint Catherine with her wheel. She might have just repeated the figure and changed the attribute, but she had not done so. Each was unique in pose, and very realistic.

"Do you seek to buy something?"

Her voice had a little edge to it. Her blue eyes regarded him skeptically.

He knew what that look revealed. He had not been the first man to loiter around, pretending to be interested in crockery.

"You craft the statues too?"

"When I have the time, and the clay."

"They are all fired."

"I know a tiler who lets me use his kiln."

He lifted the Saint Agnes. "What are they for?"

That flustered her. "They are statues."

"Aye, but what is their purpose? The cups and bowls have a purpose. Everyone needs them. What is this saint for?"

"Devotion."

"There are churches for that, with much larger statues."

"Some people like to have one in their homes," she said defensively.

"Have you sold many?"

She grimaced, conceding the point. "At most one a day when I come to market."

"Then you should charge more than five pence."

She rolled her eyes. "If I only sell one at five pence, I will sell none higher."

"You will sell just as many, but receive what they are worth, and they will be more valued by those who buy them. These are not practical things. Most will give you nothing, but those who will pay five pence will pay a shilling." To prove it, he fingered a shilling out of his purse and placed it on the box.

She eyed the coin hungrily, then glanced at him, suspicious again.

Her caution did not insult him. A pretty thing like her, alone in the marketplace, probably received a lot of propositions. "For the statue only. But I must warn you. I am a freemason, and I may steal the pose for a stone saint someday."

Her gaze raked him with a quick assessment. He knew what she thought. He did not look like a mason today. His dress was too fine for work. A man did not wield a chisel and hammer in a long tunic and tall boots.

He drifted away, carrying Saint Agnes. He looked down at the little figure and laughed at himself. A man who could make stone statues hardly needed to purchase clay ones.

He supposed he had bought it as a form of praise, from one craftsman to another. And as a type of flattery, from a man to a woman. There had been a bit of pity to it too. He liked the idea that he had made the day a success for her.

He laughed again. A shilling for ten minutes with a pretty woman. Still, even without the statue, he would not have felt cheated.

But Joan's encounter with her mysterious customer is far from over. Later in the day, her brother Mark becomes involved in a savage street brawl, and it is thanks to Rhys's intervention that matters do not turn tragic. Afterwards, Joan is uncomfortably indebted to him . . .

✦ ✦ ✦

She knelt and began wrapping the crockery so it would not break on the walk home. To her shock the mason dropped to one knee and began to help. There was something disconcerting about his strength next to her. The warmth of his nearness flustered her in a foolish way.

His hands lifted a cup gently and rolled it in an ancient cloth. She almost stopped him. She did not want him to see and touch those pitiful bits of dirty rag. He might recognize them for what they were, the remnants of a life that had been shredded and despoiled. Suddenly, unaccountably, she knew that she would want to die if he pitied her.

"You sold the last statue," he said while he took a bowl from her hands and carefully packed it in the box.

She nodded while she quickly wrapped the last cup. "I asked for a shilling like you advised. You were right. He paid it."

He smiled over at her. She felt herself blushing under his subtle, meandering gaze. She grew more flustered yet. Her hands became clumsy, and the cup rolled out of its rag, down her lap, and onto the ground.

He took the rag and made quick work with the cup. Rising, he offered his hand to help her up.

She looked at that hand, and something sad swelled her heart and burned her throat. It was just a simple gesture, but it had been years since any man had freely given her even this small courtesy.

She accepted and got up quickly. Her palm felt the dry warmth of his, and the calloused skin. He did not dress like a mason, but he owned the firm hands of one. And the broad shoulders. He was not a bulky man, but a tight strength was evident in his tall, lean lines.

Mark lifted the box and they headed across the square. Once again the mason walked beside her.

She did not want him following her. His help touched vulnerable memories that she could not afford to acknowledge. He reminded her of old times when someone always protected her, and no one expected her to be strong, and no man ever dared to leer. He weakened something in her core, and made her wobbly and nostalgic. She could not afford the luxury of his kindness any longer.

"My brother will stay with me. Again I thank you, Master. . . ." she realized that she did not know his name.

"Rhys."

"I thank you, Master Rhys."

She said it with a note of farewell, but he did not leave. He continued to accompany them through the lanes.

"You need not walk with us. We have delayed you too much as it is."

"I will see you out of the city. Those squires may have decided to regain their pride with an easy revenge."

Her mind saw again the danger Mark had faced, and Rhys's brave help.

The memory halted abruptly at some details ignored in the fear of the moment.

"That squire acted as if he knew you," she said.

"I have seen him about Westminster."

"You live there?"

"I live in London, but my work takes me to the palace most days."

Her heart began a slow thudding of caution. "You said that you would report him to his lord. Was that an idle threat?"

"I pass Mortimer most days. If I wanted to speak with him, I expect that I could." He did not say it boastfully. She had asked a question, and he simply answered it.

"You practice your craft for him?" She heard the bitter accusation in her tone. It gave voice to the sudden heat in her head. He had helped her and she should be grateful no matter who he was and whom he served, but terrible emotions much older than this day started churning her heart.

He angled his head to see her face. A bit of that steely glint had returned to his eyes. "Aye."

"Have you worked on his castles? His fortifications? Do you repair the walls of the keeps that he destroys while he rapes the realm?"

"Rarely. Castle walls do not require tracery and statues."

"But you serve him nonetheless, as surely as his knights and his archers."

"I serve the crown."

"The crown is under his foot."

"The squire was right, woman. You speak too freely."

"It is the only benefit of poverty. Freedom to speak since my opinion is meaningless. At least I am not a lackey to a butcher, like that squire." *And you.*

He heard the last words even though she did not say them. His face hardened at the insult, but he did not respond to it.

His presence no longer felt comforting and protective. Rather the opposite. If he moved among the court he was dangerous. If he served Mortimer, even as a craftsman, his honor and character could not be trusted.

That saddened her. It had been nice to believe in him for a while. It had been beautiful to think that he was generous.

"Do you live outside the city?" he asked.

"Aye."

"In Southwark?"

"Aye." She did not hesitate with the lie. He had asked if they were alone and now he asked where they lived. Those were the kinds of queries she got from men who soon offered a bad bargain. He might be smoother than most, but he was no different.

She castigated herself for her foolish trust in his kindness. One could know a man by whom he served, and he served the worst. He no doubt expected her to repay him, and not with crockery. He liked her in that way. It was in the warm looks he gave her.

That worried her. She did not want the interest of a man who passed Mortimer every day. She did not want him remembering anything about her, least of all where she could be found.

At the gate she stopped and faced him.

"I thank you," she said, trying to make it friendly but dismissive.

"Are those the only words that you know? Besides sharp talk that is both dangerous and insulting?"

"What other words do you want?"

"Not the offer of your favors like you fear. However, since I risked a fight with a dagger, learning your name would be nice."

"Forgive me. It is just . . ."

"I know how it is, pretty dove. You are wise to be careful."

"Joan. My name is Joan." There was no danger in giving it. There were thousands of Joans in London.

Mark called impatiently from the gate. Rhys backed away and made a vague bow. "Until we meet again, Joan. And try to stay out of street brawls."

She watched with relief as he strolled back into the city. She also experienced a little stab of wistful regret. There had been a few delicious minutes there when he made her feel like the girl she had once been.

They would never meet again, if she could help it.